HOUR OF NEED

THE LAWS OF MAGIC SERIES

MICHAEL PRYOR

RANDOM HOUSE AUSTRALIA

A Random House book
Published by Random House Australia Pty Ltd
Level 3, 100 Pacific Highway, North Sydney NSW 2060
www.randomhouse.com.au

First published by Random House Australia in 2011

Addresses for companies within the Random House Group can be found at www.randomhouse.com.au/offices.

National Library of Australia
Cataloguing-in-Publication Entry

Author: Pryor, Michael
Title: Hour of need / Michael Pryor
ISBN: 978 1 74166 310 5 (pbk.)
Series: Pryor, Michael. Laws of magic; 6
Target audience: For secondary school age
Dewey number: A823.3

Cover illustration by Jeremy Reston
Cover design by www.blacksheep-uk.com
Internal design by Mathematics
Typeset in Bembo by Midland Typesetters, Australia
Printed in Australia by Griffin Press, an accredited ISO AS/NZS 14001:2004
Environmental Management System printer

10 9 8 7 6 5 4 3 2

For Zoe Walton, ace editor, who has been with The Laws of Magic from the start. She's made it a better story.

One

'YOU'RE THE ONE WHO BETRAYED US! I ALWAYS KNEW it was you!'

Aubrey Fitzwilliam flinched as the accusation echoed on the rock walls of the cave that had been their home for almost a month. Slowly, he put aside the spellcraft notebook and climbed to his feet, trying not to startle the wild-eyed Holmlander. A restraining spell was on his lips but he was unwilling to use magic unless he had to, not with the magic detectors around Dr Tremaine's estate below.

'Traitor!' von Stralick snarled at him. 'You, and the rest of them! Everywhere!'

Softly: 'I'm not a traitor, Hugo.'

'Liar.' Fists clenched, Hugo von Stralick, the ex-Holmland spy, advanced. 'We have photographs.'

'Put the stone down, Hugo. You're sick.'

'Hah! Sick, am I?'

A grunt, then the stone thumped into the wall not far from Aubrey's head. He sighed. Von Stralick may have been sick, but enough was enough. Aubrey lunged and caught him around the waist. A feeble blow or two landed on Aubrey's back, then von Stralick faltered, groaning. His knees buckled and Aubrey had to move quickly to avoid falling on top of him.

'Traitor,' von Stralick murmured as he lay stretched out on the rocky floor. His eyes fluttered, then closed. His face was a disturbing chalky-white. He was shivering, too, and when Aubrey touched his forehead he was dismayed at how hot it was.

Alarmed, he dragged von Stralick back to the pile of tree branches that was his bed and arranged him as comfortably as he could. Von Stralick's lips moved, a meaningless stream of half-words and names, as if he were alternately reading from a street directory and a poorly compiled dictionary. What had begun as a simple cold, a few days after they'd found the cave in the crag, had worsened gradually until the Holmlander had collapsed while working on their sketch maps of Tremaine's estate. In the days since then, Aubrey had been dividing his time between tending him, finding food and water, and working on the spells that could win the war, all in isolation.

Aubrey had thought von Stralick had been getting better, but it had obviously been wishful thinking. The fever and the delirium hadn't broken. Aubrey was now worried that the ex-Holmland spy was going to die.

Aubrey lifted von Stralick's head and held up the canteen. Water dribbled out of his mouth, but Aubrey thought he swallowed a little. He sighed at the prospect of the water wasted, knowing he'd have to collect more, spending hours holding the canteen to the rock crevices to catch the remnants of the frequent rain that swept across the heights. When he was so close to finalising the construction of his spells, he hated losing time like that.

The weather had been trying. In this northern part of Holmland, summer had hurried off the stage and autumn had well and truly taken its place. The nights had become decidedly chilly, the rain more frequent, the days noticeably shorter. None of this had helped von Stralick's condition.

Aubrey studied von Stralick's face. The spy's teeth were bared as he shivered, and Aubrey decided he had no choice but to risk a gentle heat spell.

He'd been avoiding magic. With Dr Tremaine so close, Aubrey hadn't wanted to do anything that could alert the rogue sorcerer to their presence, not before he was ready to implement the spells he'd spent so much time over. With von Stralick this ill, however, he had little choice.

He composed himself and reworked a basic Thermal Magic spell, adjusting the parameters for location and dimension to encompass von Stralick's wasted frame. Aubrey tugged his filthy jacket around him as he took care with the intensity variable, to provide a gentle warmth rather than a roasting heat.

Von Stralick's shivering faded as the spell began to work.

Aubrey nodded and ran a hand through his hair – hair that had long forgotten its military cut and was starting to resemble the pelt of one of the more disreputable forest animals, the sort that skulk about around the roots of trees waiting for something to die and fall from the branches. He was glad that the only human being in close proximity was insensible, for he was sure he smelled dreadful. If he looked anything like von Stralick's red-eyed, grimy, dishevelled appearance, he was ready to apply for a position as understudy to the Wild Man of Borneo.

Aubrey monitored the heat spell, and was relieved. Von Stralick had settled. Aubrey chewed his lip for a moment, then touched the Holmlander's forehead. It was much cooler, and he allowed himself to hope that some sort of crisis had passed.

He picked up his spellcraft notebook from where it had accidentally been kicked during the struggle. His pencil was worn to a stub, but the break from his magic preparation had been useful in refreshing his perspective. When he studied the intricate spell formulation he'd been working on, he realised that it was nearly finished.

What had begun as a mission to find Dr Tremaine's estate and to confront the rogue sorcerer had suffered a major setback with von Stralick's illness. After the Holmlander collapsed with fever, Aubrey had no choice but to nurse his companion. As his condition worsened, Aubrey had much time on his hands – but using this rare gift, he had formulated a daring move that could end the war with a single stroke.

THE CRAG THAT OVERLOOKED DR TREMAINE'S RETREAT was high in the Alemmani Mountains. It caught the wind, no matter from what direction it came, and it constantly reminded Aubrey that this part of Holmland was the natural home of ice and snow – and probably bears and wolves. 'Forbidding' was the kindest thing that could be said about it, but its dramatic outlook probably appealed to the rogue sorcerer. That, and the relative isolation.

After leaving Stalsfrieden, their three-hundred-mile cross-country scramble had taken Aubrey and von Stralick more than a fortnight. They'd become expert in avoiding Holmland troops, but Aubrey had come to understand that 'living off the land' sounded altogether grander than the reality, which was actually a constant scrounging for food and water. Occasionally, while pawing at the leaf mould in the darkness of woods, he'd wished he'd studied mycology instead of magic, just so he could have known the difference between the edible mushrooms and the attractive ones that end up driving people mad. Unwilling to court such a fate, he had to forgo mushrooms as a possible dietary addition.

On their journey, four days after leaving the ruins of Baron von Grolman's golem-making factory, it had been von Stralick who had insisted on finding some news. While Aubrey hid in what proved to be a mosquito-infested bog, von Stralick, after doing his best to improve his bedraggled appearance, strolled into the reasonably sized town of Pagen and bought a newspaper.

Aubrey had been sickened by the triumphant headlines that crowed over his father's disgrace. More correctly, of course, it was Aubrey's disgrace: 'the traitor son of Albion'. He took some solace in that it confirmed that Caroline and George had arrived home safely, because Sir Darius had implemented Aubrey's plan: he had denounced his own son before the Holmlanders could publish their photographs. Aubrey was now, officially, the blackest of black villains in Albion. He was the son of privilege who had turned his back on everything the nation had done for him.

When Aubrey stared at the headlines, he could almost hear the cries for his blood, the press running riot; he only hoped that his father's pre-emptive action meant that he could stand firm, positioning himself as the wronged father of an ungrateful son, and that the public would feel sorry for him.

Aubrey wasn't confident, however, that this would mean that he would be treated as a hero in Holmland. Traitors rarely were. If he dared to make himself public, a cell was no doubt waiting for him somewhere secret and unofficial, and a messy, undignified fate would soon be his.

Or something even more dire, he thought, judging from what he'd glimpsed of the activities of Dr Tremaine's retreat in the weeks since they'd arrived at their destination.

Dr Tremaine's stronghold was a local landmark. From its position right on the edge of an impressive granite cliff, it had a view over the mountains and the woods that surrounded it, then the open expanses of farmland. The city of Bardenford was perhaps twenty miles away, clearly seen by day or by night. The retreat wasn't cut off, however. A tarmac road had been rammed through the forest, switching backward and forward up the face of the mountain until it arrived at the gatehouse. The road was wide enough for supply lorries and comfortable enough for town cars.

Over the time of Aubrey's enforced vigil, Dr Tremaine had come and gone, sometimes several times in one day, mostly driving himself in a bright red, open-topped roadster. Aubrey had come to recognise the scream of the motor as it hurtled along the road in a way no other driver dared.

When Dr Tremaine was present, prominent Holmlanders often visited. As well as the Chancellor, many uniformed figures were brought to the door, the amount of brass and the number of medals on their chests signalling that these men were important and probably bullet-proof, thanks to the amount of metal they wore.

After several of these meetings, Dr Tremaine had leaped into his motorcar and shot down the road, and Aubrey had been wracked with frustration. Had Dr Tremaine some afterthought that couldn't wait? Was he going somewhere else with news of what he'd just learned? Or was he looking for a rendezvous with one or more of the Holmlanders, a roadside meeting that they might not welcome?

Aubrey wondered if the man slept at all. He was a whirlwind, a force of nature in his machinations to turn the formidable estate into a base and a site for magical operations of an as-yet-unspecified nature. The tell-tale wafts of magic that prickled Aubrey's magical senses had been alternately tantalising, puzzling and extremely, extremely worrying.

Within the walls of the estate were a number of buildings. From the thick cables and the unceasing whine, one clearly housed an electrical generator. Another sported a tall chimney and could be a foundry or furnace of some kind.

The purpose of the scattering of other structures – clearly newer than the main house, and perhaps temporary – was uncertain, but Aubrey wouldn't have minded wagering that at least one was a laboratory. The others? Living quarters, perhaps? Workshops? Prisons?

Cut off as they were, the lack of information frustrated Aubrey. He was desperate to know what was going on. What about the siege of Divodorum? What about the progress of the wider war? And what about his friends?

He worried about Caroline and the way she'd farewelled him after the Stalsfrieden mission. He examined the incident from a dozen different points of view, a *hundred* different points of view. He probed it, dissected it, weighed and analysed it. Then he abandoned any effort at a scientific approach and he began to alternate between wild optimism and unutterable pessimism, both states being totally resistant to evidence. With little effort, he was able to construe Caroline's action as pity, as irritation, even as forgetfulness, before he veered around and started thinking it might have been a sign of actual affection. This being the conclusion he hoped for most, it was naturally the one he was quickest to discount.

Long ago he'd accepted that his mission – his personal mission to win Caroline – had gone by the board. Matters of the heart were out of his hands, overtaken by matters military and political. *Out of my hands?* He nearly laughed. As if matters of the heart had *ever* been in his hands.

He had to derive satisfaction from properly undertaking his intelligence gathering task, and he took some grim pleasure when he saw something that indicated the level of success of his sabotage at Baron von Grolman's factory.

This noteworthy observation had occurred a week ago, when a lorry had made a canvas-shrouded delivery. When it unloaded, Aubrey had been instantly on his feet.

Three Holmland soldiers were needed to manhandle the ominous metal shape from the back of the lorry. When they stood it upright on a trolley, it towered over them. It took all their effort, but the monstrous golem-machine hybrid was eventually wheeled into one of the temporary buildings to the north of the main house.

Aubrey had hoped that his efforts to destroy the hideous creations back in Stalsfrieden had been successful. The contagion spell embedded in the enhanced coal that was the vital, energising element in the creatures would infect golem after golem. Besides, if the spell hadn't been successful, Dr Tremaine would have had hundreds of ghastly mechanised soldiers ready to storm through Allied lines and lead a Holmland assault on Gallia, and he was sure that they would have heard of such a triumph while crossing Holmland.

But why had a single mechanised golem been brought to Dr Tremaine's retreat?

Movement below had caught Aubrey's eye and when he had the binoculars focused again, Dr Tremaine was entering the building where the mechanised golem had been taken.

A tense hour later, Dr Tremaine burst out of the back doors of the building, his arms full of metalwork. He shouldered through one of the gates at the rear of the estate. He strode to the edge of the cliff and, with one disgusted motion, flung the metal wide. The pieces fell in a glittering arc, but Aubrey had time to see a boxlike head and what was unmistakably a compact chimney.

Since leaving Caroline and George, Aubrey had had few moments of pleasure, but he smiled as he noted Tremaine's actions in a notebook – adding to the pages and pages of observations, all in fine, approved Directorate form.

The most alarming development he'd seen, however, had been the magicians who had been brought to the stronghold. Aubrey had found it hard to believe the number of well-known experts who'd been bundled into the outbuildings, though it did explain the disappearances of prominent magical people over the previous few months. He'd recognised Maud Connolly, Parvo Ahonen, Charles Beecher and a score or more prominent theoreticians and scholars. None of them showed any delight at being there, unless manacles and gags had suddenly become signs of honour rather than devices of restraint.

This influx of magical practitioners and theoreticians was disturbing, especially when Aubrey added Professor Mansfield and Lanka Ravi to their numbers. At Baron von Grolman's factory, Dr Tremaine had mentioned that he had these two luminaries in his keeping, which suggested that he was assembling a formidable array of magical talent, but to what end?

One of the first magical theoreticians to arrive at the complex had been Professor Bromhead, Trismegistus chair of magic at the University of Greythorn for twenty years. A few days after he'd been dragged from a motorcar, the aged savant had appeared in a walled garden to the west of the main house. He'd wandered about, attended by an armed guard. Aubrey hadn't recognised him at first and he had focused on the lonely figure simply because of a strange device attached to his face. It was a cross between a muzzle, a helmet and a clamp, a metal and wire contraption enveloping the man's head, but particularly strong around his mouth and jaw. After some careful focusing of the binoculars, Aubrey was finally able to make out who it was and, grimly, he understood that at least part of the function of the device was to stop Professor Bromhead from speaking – and to stop him from casting a spell.

Each of the savants who arrived – some in the middle

of the night – appeared later in the walled garden, guarded and wearing the same cage, confirming their identity as magicians, even the ones who Aubrey didn't know by sight. They were allowed this exercise time for an hour every second day, but otherwise they were hidden away in the clutch of outbuildings to the north of the sprawling two-storey hunting lodge that was the main house.

Nothing good could come from Dr Tremaine's assembling such a battery of magical knowledge. Aubrey could continue to observe, hoping to communicate this intelligence with the Directorate and then wait for orders – or he could contrive a way to stop the most dangerous man in the world taking the next step in his bloody plan.

With only a few rocks and his wits at his disposal – and with a deathly ill companion to care for – the latter was an unlikely choice, but Aubrey had never resiled from a challenge. He was in a position to intervene, and so he would.

Late the next morning, lying on his stomach at the entrance of the cave and barely breathing, Aubrey held Dr Tremaine in the sights of the rusty Oberndorf rifle that von Stralick had stolen from a farmhouse on their cross-Holmland scramble. The rogue sorcerer was perfectly positioned, standing on the road outside the gates of his cliff-top retreat. Aubrey swallowed, acutely conscious that all his spellwork and preparation had led to this: he had one chance to remove Dr Tremaine and put an end to his warmongering. A careful, steady squeeze of the trigger and it would all be over.

A sound came from behind him. Aubrey tensed, then forced himself to relax. Von Stralick was sleeping comfortably since his fever had broken.

Aubrey waited a moment, but when all was quiet he wiped sweat from his forehead with a finger and looked to re-centre his sights.

In the long nights tending to von Stralick and thinking about how to end the war, Aubrey had come to understand, with more than a little reluctance and with a great deal of conscience-searching, that he had to put aside the misgivings he had about firearms. It was the best method he had – the *only* method he had – to do what was needed.

It was time to shoot Dr Tremaine with a very special projectile.

A standard bullet wasn't going to stop the rogue sorcerer; Aubrey had seen him walk away after being shot at close range. Something extraordinary was called for and Aubrey had devoted himself to it.

Trapped in the cave and tending to the dangerously ill von Stralick, Aubrey had brought together all his thinking about magic, all of the reading, experimenting and theorising, to construct the complex array of spells which had replaced the bullet in the sole cartridge they had. This magic was some of the most intricate that he'd ever attempted, merging elements from a number of wildly different spells he'd worked with in the past. Hour after hour, in between tending von Stralick, he'd taken apart compression spells, intensification spells, amplification spells, spells that juggled aspects of Familiarity, Entanglement, Attraction, combining them and recombining them, splicing, reworking until he was able to construct a spell-ridden object smaller than his fingernail, but as deadly as anything he'd ever created.

Much of the spell was based on his study of the transformed Beccaria Cage that was now armouring his body and soul against premature separation. He'd also incorporated characteristics of the ensorcelled pearl that had been both a refuge and prison for Dr Tremaine's sister, Sylvia. The result was a highly compressed binding spell, overlaid with homing spells to counter any misalignment in the old Oberndorf or in Aubrey's aiming.

When the spell struck its target, Dr Tremaine would be caged in a magical prison, a prison that combined the strengths of the Beccaria Cage and the Tremaine Pearl. The prison would be unleashed, capture its target, then it would compress itself and its contents until it was the size of a marble. The entanglement spell would activate, and the prison would be reeled in, landing back with Aubrey. Dr Tremaine would be imprisoned, neutralised, and he could be brought to Albion for trial.

All Aubrey had to do was to squeeze the trigger. One shot and he could go home and restore his name, knowing the Holmland war effort would collapse without Dr Tremaine's guiding hand. It would all be over.

Ignoring second thoughts, doubts and qualms, he settled himself in his prone position. He regripped the rifle, making sure it was stable on the flat rock he was using as a firing platform. He found Dr Tremaine with the sighting post and adjusted until it was aligned with the notch. He took a breath, let it out slowly, then drew in another and held it.

The war was about to end.

Two

AUBREY BLINKED. HIS HEAD HURT. THIS WAS ODD FOR, as far as he knew, a moment ago it hadn't.

A few other things had changed as well. For one, he thought he'd been staring at Dr Tremaine through the sights of a rifle, but now he was staring up at the shadowy ceiling of the cave.

'The rifle.' Von Stralick's voice came from nearby. 'It blew up.'

'Blew up?'

'You have blood on your cheek.'

'And egg on my face?' Aubrey sat up, which transformed his head into a paragon of pure, thundering pain. He stifled a groan and put both hands to his temples. His gaze stumbled across the cave entrance. The carefully constructed firing platform had fallen apart, and what had been the Oberndorf rifle lay in pieces on the stones.

'Here.' Von Stralick held out a mug of water. He was still pale, but the half-mocking smile that had been missing during his illness was back.

'What happened?' Aubrey asked.

'Most peculiar, it was.' With a grunt, the Holmlander sat on a rock next to Aubrey. 'I saw you squeeze the trigger, then the rifle burst apart without a sound. The barrel flew back and struck you on the forehead.'

'Ah.' Aubrey considered this. 'Remind me to use a brand new rifle if I ever try this again. One that is a little less rusty would be useful.'

Von Stralick shrugged. 'When I stole it from that farmhouse, I felt that beggars could not afford to be choosers, as you Albionish so delightfully say.' He brushed the knee of his trousers for a moment. 'You were trying to kill Dr Tremaine?'

It was Aubrey's turn to shrug. 'I wanted to bring him to trial.'

'By shooting him?'

'It was a magic spell.'

Von Stralick listened without interrupting until Aubrey finished explaining, then he rose, somewhat shakily, and went to the cave entrance. He stood in the shadows and gazed toward Dr Tremaine's estate. 'When I first met you, Fitzwilliam, I was sure you were of little account. You have, however, forced me to revise my opinion.'

'And this is a good thing, I take it?'

'You have surprising capabilities. Dr Tremaine would do well to be most wary of you.'

'I doubt he gives me much thought at all.'

'You should hope so. It could mean that you may be able to take him by surprise.'

FOR THREE FRUSTRATING DAYS, WHILE VON STRALICK gathered his strength under Aubrey's care and while Aubrey did his best to concoct a replacement plan, Dr Tremaine's estate was even more a hive of action than it had already been. Lorries arrived in convoys, backed up to the outbuildings and were loaded up before grinding their way down the mountain again. Aubrey made careful note of these deliveries; he estimated the volumes of the packing crates and made particular count of the coils of wire that were delivered – dozens of them, each the height of a man. He also was intrigued by dispatches – furniture and equipment were shipped out of the estate, but also personnel. Exasperated-looking civilians were herded into the backs of lorries, but also many of the muzzled magical theoreticians. Even while itemising each departure, Aubrey was intensely irritated by not knowing how many of these people were present when he arrived at the Tremaine estate. How could he determine how many were still there?

Dr Tremaine came and went twice before von Stralick announced he was fit for action. That, of course, was a matter of definition, for von Stralick's belt was two notches smaller, and his skin was greyish rather than radiating good health.

'We need a foray,' the Holmlander said as night fell. The customary chill was in the air as soon as the sun disappeared. 'It is most necessary.'

Aubrey was once again lying on his stomach at the cave entrance, using binoculars to monitor a late lorry departure. Filing cabinets had been loaded into it from the main house which, to Aubrey's mind, didn't bode well. 'I'm keen to find out exactly what's going on in those outbuildings, but only if you're fit enough.'

'I am recovered sufficiently, and if I don't set foot outside this cave I am likely to go mad.' Von Stralick did a few arm stretches. 'And I am not the only one.'

'I beg your pardon?'

'You have been like a lion in a cage, pacing up and down, finding it hard to sit still. Your frustration is most obvious, and I apologise for making you wait.'

'Sorry, Hugo. Something is going on down there, and being so close like this and not knowing what it is . . .'

'You do not like not knowing. I understand that. Therefore, let us go and find out.'

'Capital. Through the woods at the base of the cliff is the only way to go, obviously, but we need to choose the best place to cross the road.'

He brought the binoculars to his eyes to determine the best route but at that moment his field of vision was filled with blinding red light and he jerked back with an oath. Almost immediately, a cloud of dust and smoke rushed toward them, followed by a patter of debris, and he scrambled back into what he hoped was the safety of the cave. Blue-green spots danced in front of his eyes and he shook his head, trying to make them disappear.

The cave walls shook as another thumping concussion hit and dust rained down on them. Aubrey and von Stralick both lay on the rocky floor, arms over their heads as one more, then another explosion erupted, slashing through the narrow cave entrance with ragged orange brilliance.

Eventually, all was silent. Aubrey raised his head and crawled on all floors until he could peer through the dust and smoke.

Dr Tremaine's estate was a ruin, with only the main house still standing. It was virtually untouched, almost huffily facing away from the blackened wrecks that had once been the newer buildings. A row of poplars that had separated the main house from the outbuildings had been shredded, but in doing so had probably shielded the old hunting lodge from worse damage than the single broken window on the second floor.

'Someone didn't want anything left,' Aubrey said. The dust and smoke was quickly being driven away over the cliff by wind, but the nose-singeing, acrid smell of high explosives was enough to make him screw up his face.

Von Stralick rose and slapped dust from his sleeves. 'Overly dramatic, but effective. A fire would have done just as well.'

Aubrey shrugged. Dr Tremaine rarely did anything without three or four reasons lined up behind each other like divers on the high board, each waiting to show off her new trick. With the estate's clifftop position, the explosions would have been seen for miles. A signal, perhaps?

More noise rose from below. Shouting, then Dr Tremaine's familiar figure bounded from the main house. He gestured in the direction of the gates, which were hastily opened, then he disappeared around the corner. The roar of an engine became a scream and the sporty red motorcar skidded into view, then blasted around the circular driveway. Flames from the ruins of the out-buildings glinted on his goggles. He looked possessed, a demon driver with a long white scarf trailing from his neck. The guards at the gate cried out and jumped back as the motorcar slid sideways on its approach. Dr Tremaine grinned maniacally as he dragged on the wheel, turning into the skid, then the powerful engine snarled, the back wheels bit, and the car shot through and onto the road. For an instant, Aubrey was sure Dr Tremaine's scarf was going to get tangled in the gate, but the fringed ends twisted and untwined themselves with audacious, casual magic.

The car vanished into the dark avenue of trees that led down the mountainside. Aubrey grimaced. It appeared as if Dr Tremaine had cleared his plate before moving on to the next course.

The howl of the engine echoed from the stony face of the hills, growing fainter as it hurtled toward Bardenford. Aubrey made a fist and drummed on the stone in front of him. He had an appointment with Dr Tremaine, but it frustrated him that he didn't know when or where it was going to be.

Three

WITH THE CARE THEY'D LEARNED IN THEIR CROSS-country ordeal, Aubrey and von Stralick eased themselves out of the cave and down the rock face. As they approached the estate in the darkness, soft noises came from the multitudinous and unknowable doings of a forest at night time, overlaid with the settlings from the conflagration site – creaking timber and ashes hissing where dew was falling on coals. Occasionally a guard would call out to his comrades and once, as they neared, Aubrey could swear he heard a bottle clinking on glass. He decided that they must be confident that Dr Tremaine wasn't coming back for some time, which was vastly reassuring.

The wall of the estate was built of stone, deliberately rough cast to give it a rustic appearance. The barbed wire on top of the twelve-foot wall, however, was definitely a new addition, quite out of keeping. The barbs glinted in the lights of the main house.

'Someone has been busy.' Von Stralick pointed at several tree stumps close to the wall to their left.

'Clearing overhangs, I'd say.' Aubrey was disappointed. It would have been handy to find a tree near the wall. 'It suggests that whatever is going on inside is worth protecting.'

'Or *was* worth protecting, before it was blown up. Time for some of your magic?'

'Unless you have a very large stepladder hidden in your jacket. Ah.'

'Ah?'

'I'm rethinking, Hugo, as we speak, because I've just spotted the magic detectors on the wall.'

On the top of the wall, just beneath the lowest strand of barbed wire, was a series of featureless black boxes. Aubrey could see two between their position and the gates, the nearest only a few yards away. Turning to his left, he could make out another a stone's throw away. He imagined the field of detection was limited to the fenceline to avoid unnecessary alarms from stray magic inside the estate.

Von Stralick scratched his chin. 'This will make things more difficult, I assume.'

'Definitely. Any magic strong enough to spirit us over the wall will set off the alarms. Even these guards wouldn't ignore that sort of thing.'

'I'll go back to the cave and fetch my very large stepladder, will I?'

'If you could, it would be handy.' Aubrey stared at the nearest magic detector. Significantly, it didn't stare back. It simply sat there smugly, daring him to try something.

Apart from an overactive imagination, he thought, *perhaps I'm going about this the wrong way.*

Instead of trying to avoid detection, why couldn't he simply prevent the machines from alerting the dozy guards? After all, a magical alarm that couldn't do any actual alarming was, essentially, a box – and a box wasn't going to stop Aubrey Fitzwilliam from getting over a wall.

While von Stralick leaned against the wall with remarkable patience, Aubrey juggled the possibilities. Typically, magic detectors blared a warning, siren-like, when magic intruded into their area of scrutiny.

Sound travels through air. If I can remove the air from the vicinity of the detectors they'd be doing their best to alarm, but their efforts will be pointless.

Aubrey rubbed his hands together. Aware that he was letting a problem get slightly personal, he was looking forward to seeing how smug the magic detectors would be in a vacuum.

Aubrey had dabbled with air evacuation spells – an application of the Law of Transference – to render mis-creants unconscious, so he had a foundation to work with. The range of effect and the dimensions of the spell were the crucial elements. He wished he could run a tape measure over one of the detectors, but he had become reasonably good at estimating by eye. A dome-shaped coverage would be best, he decided, and he opted for a volume that was – naturally – half of a sphere. Calculating πr^3 in his head gave him a few forehead wrinkles, but in the end he had it. The spell would have to come into being and produce its effect with little time lag, so he concentrated on making it as condensed as possible. He added an operator that controlled copies of the spell, to account for the detectors either side of the stretch of wall they were going to breach, then he pronounced the spell crisply.

He tensed a little when he felt the domes pop into being – a tickle of saltiness on the skin of his face – and then nothing, and he grinned. He had rarely been so pleased to see nothing happening. Instead of announcing spell failure, in this particular case nothing happening meant success.

Von Stralick had fallen asleep. He was leaning against the wall, eyes closed, his chin sagging nearly to his chest. Aubrey shook him gently. 'We're ready.'

Von Stralick was alert immediately. He withdrew his revolver. Aubrey blinked, but it made sense – of a brutal kind. He could get them over the wall, but Hugo was going to make sure that they could deal with any unfriendly reception on the other side.

The levitation spell rolled off his tongue. He felt his feet leave the ground and reached out to steady von Stralick, whose eyes went wide as they rose. They drifted easily up the rough stone face of the wall but when they reached the barbed wire Aubrey felt horribly exposed. If one of the guards looked in their direction, they were in trouble, but he was trusting that the darkness of the night and the unexpectedness of this mode of entry would make it unlikely that they'd be noticed.

He increased their ascent and once they topped the last strand of barbed wire he reached down with a foot and gently pushed against the nearest of the metal poles embedded in the wall to hold the wire. It gave them some forward momentum, enough to send them drifting a few yards inside the perimeter.

Aubrey was telling himself not to feel satisfied when he looked over his shoulder at the wall. With a cunning sort of timing and from surfaces that were previously featureless, the two nearest detectors chose that moment to jet forth dozens of blinding white beams that rotated, sweeping back and forth like miniature searchlights, lighting up the sky, the rocky crag, the main house – and two floating intruders.

Von Stralick swore. Aubrey inverted the levitation spell and they dropped to the ground, fetching up behind a large rhododendron. Shouts came from the main house, and more from the darkened gardens.

Von Stralick grinned fiercely as they crouched in the darkness. 'Not quite the outcome you were hoping for?'

'I didn't think Holmland magical engineering would be that imaginative,' Aubrey said. 'Sound *and* light alarms? That's like wearing belt and braces at the same time.'

'What do we do? Back over the wall?'

Aubrey was tempted, but also reluctant to leave. They'd made it this far, after all. 'Can we deal with four guards?'

'Four would normally be no trouble, but they are armed.'

The lights from the magic detectors made shadows flit across the gardens, turning the vegetation, garden furniture and scattering of statues that had survived the blast into an eerie wonderland. Aubrey scanned the surroundings, his mouth dry, his heart thumping. A hundred things he'd learned in his Directorate training jostled for attention in his mind. The darkness would be an advantage, for one thing. Secondly, von Stralick and he knew how many guards were on patrol, while the guards wouldn't know how many intruders were in the vicinity, which had to be an advantage.

The sort of advantage that could become a weapon.

'Don't move,' he whispered to von Stralick.

Von Stralick nodded, then squinted, whipped out his pistol and snapped off three quick shots at guards who had appeared.

Aubrey groaned, but he hastily grabbed at aspects of the Law of Seeming, the Law of Amplification, the Law of Affinity and the Law of Patterns, holding their many constants and variables in his head. While trying to concentrate, he couldn't help hearing shouts, or half-glimpsing figures moving from shadow to shadow. The guards were making use of their familiarity with the estate, working their way around the still smoking ruins and the bulk of the main house.

Forget them, he told himself. *Focus!*

On all fours, Aubrey scrabbled until he found a patch of bare ground at the base of an oleander bush. With a twig, he sketched a rough stick figure and rushed through the first spell. Immediately, the stick figure popped out of the ground and stood upright. It was a tiny, shaky creation, only as tall as a wine bottle, two dimensional and barely tangible. While it shivered and swayed, it was joined by twenty identical, spindly shapes as Aubrey repeated the spell. Then he swung his arm wide, as if sowing seeds, and they vanished.

Immediately, he was gratified to hear a Holmlandish voice cry, 'What was that?'

Von Stralick scurried to his side. He held his revolver at the ready and peered into the night. 'Something dramatic would be useful, Fitzwilliam. Soon, too, by preference.'

'One moment.'

Aubrey ran through another spell, then cupped a hand over his mouth. He rehearsed his Holmlandish and whispered 'Over here' into his hand. Then, as if he were throwing a stone, he whipped his arm in a long arc. Instantly, his voice cried out from the far edge of the estate: 'Over here!'

'I have them,' he growled into his hand and after he flung it a shout boomed from the parterre, the formal geometric garden directly in front of the main house: 'I have them!' Quickly, he followed these outbursts with more, distributing them about the estate: near the cliff top, by the gates, past a dimly seen collection of outbuildings that were still standing near the fountain.

The Holmland guards were clearly startled by this assault. They shouted warnings, adding to the tumult as Aubrey continued to send his voice to all corners of the estate. Within minutes, the Holmlanders were convinced they were set upon by an army, outflanked, possibly surrounded.

The guards' level of jumpiness was heightened by the stick figures Aubrey had sent scurrying about the estate. They crept from bush to bush, darting between trees and rushing along paths before diving into garden beds. Their insubstantial nature made them hard to see, but the suggestion was enough to make the guards extremely panicky.

Of course, armed guards being armed guards, panic led to shooting. Aubrey and von Stralick flattened themselves against the ground as bullets whipped overhead, accompanied by more shouts from guards who warned their colleagues they were being shot at. The fact it was their colleagues who were doing the shooting was a possibility that none of them countenanced. They were more concerned, naturally, with the clear danger coming from the intruders, who they were sure numbered in the hundreds.

The stick figures continued to scamper about, man-sized now and taking on more substance as Aubrey exerted himself. They shook vegetation, crunched along the gravel of the driveway, rattled through the debris of the explosion. One managed to break a window on the glasshouse – which was immediately rendered an unglasshouse when two guards sent a volley of shots in that direction.

Aubrey kept the phantom sounds and movements working, not giving the guards time to regroup or confer. He threw a line of confusion around them, shouting and shaking, flitting and threatening, pushing them in the direction of their remaining lorry, which stood near the gatehouse.

Once they were backed up against it, peering into the dark and firing away while shouting at the others not to waste bullets, Aubrey summoned his strength and drew on the smouldering coals of the nearest ruin.

A dozen of the stick figures scampered to the heat and dived in, combining and instantly becoming a stick figure giant – insubstantial, but terrifying in its flaming presence, towering at the height of the treetops, alive with fire and wrath. In careful Holmlandish it boomed, 'WE HAVE THEM NOW!'

One of the guards screamed. The others began shooting at the gigantic fiery figure, which affected it not at all. Then, as Aubrey had hoped, fingers crossed so hard they hurt – one of the guards had the presence to leap into the lorry and start it.

Aubrey didn't blame the guards. Even *he* was impressed by the angry flaming giant, stick figure or not.

The sound of the engine was better than any order to embark. The other Holmlanders flung themselves into the lorry, still firing wildly at the stick giant – which hadn't moved – and then the lorry roared out of the gates.

Von Stralick stood and dusted himself off. He flipped the safety catch on his revolver. 'I could have managed all of them.'

Aubrey ran a hand across his brow and let out a long, slow breath. The flaming giant collapsed. 'I'm sure you could have, Hugo.'

Four

WHILE THE MAIN HOUSE WAS TANTALISING, AUBREY wanted to start their investigation in the ruins of the outbuildings. If, as he suspected, they'd been specially constructed for whatever project Dr Tremaine was pursuing – and destroyed now that this project was done – they might hold some important clues.

Von Stralick found a rake in a potting shed. Aubrey relit one of the lanterns discarded by the terrified guardsmen and held it steady while von Stralick sifted through the ashes of the building that had been nearest to the wall.

It didn't take long before Aubrey decided that the fire following the explosion, at least, had been deliberate. 'Do you smell that?' he asked von Stralick.

The Holmlander was using the rake to topple the remains of a long, metal bench. 'I smell many things. What do you smell?'

'Petrol.' Aubrey kicked at some wooden panelling, then crouched next to it. He ran his finger along an uncharred section then held it up to his nose. 'Can you think of any good reason for petrol to be splashed on walls?'

Von Stralick snorted, which was response enough to indicate that he, too, could only think that the application of petrol to the walls of buildings was unlikely to be an attempt to brighten up the place.

The use of a fire accelerant made Aubrey all the more curious as to what the buildings had formerly held. 'Formerly' was the key word here, for he would have expected to find more debris, more ordinary, everyday contents half-destroyed by the blast and blaze combination. The convoys of lorries had stripped the buildings quite effectively.

Except . . .

A glint caught Aubrey's eye. He tilted his head, the better to see it, and another mirror-bright streak flashed near the first. Carefully, he raised his lantern and picked his way through the debris until he crouched and inspected what he'd found.

It was a river of silver.

'Hugo, can you come and use your rake here? Let's see what we can uncover.'

A few minutes work with the rake, assisted by some judicious kicking and shuffling, and Aubrey and von Stralick were able to stand back. Amid the ash and charred timber, a fine silver tracery stood out, many branched like a white tree in winter.

'And what do we have here?' von Stralick said softly. 'Melted metal?'

'That's what it looks like.' Aubrey scuffed at it with his boot. It came away easily, breaking into pieces. Gingerly, he picked up a fragment and was glad it had cooled.

'How many metals are silver-coloured?' von Stralick asked.

'Most of them, apart from gold and copper.'

'That narrows it down somewhat.'

Aubrey dropped the fragment into a pocket, stepped over a pile of shattered window frames and made his way to the next hut. He scuffed about for a moment. 'Whatever it is, it's over here, too.' He shook ash from his boot. If it actually were silver, what did that mean?

He glanced up at the main house, which glowered back at him with flaming eyes, the windows reflecting the last of the fires.

'Come on, Hugo,' he said, holding up the lantern. 'Let's see if we can get into the main house.'

Von Stralick twisted the rake in his hands. 'Patience, Fitzwilliam, patience – an intelligence operative's first lesson.' He grunted. 'Now, what do we have here?'

Von Stralick pushed aside some ash, then he flipped the rake over and let the head drop. A hollow boom made him pause. 'There you have it.'

Aubrey directed the lantern light at the trapdoor von Stralick had found. 'I should have known.'

'That all is not as it meets the eye? That is an intelligence operative's second lesson. A hidden trapdoor suggests that we have something worthwhile beneath it.'

'How do we know it was hidden? It could have been prominent, in the middle of the floor.'

Von Stralick jabbed with his rake at an offensively smouldering object off to the side of the trapdoor. 'If you want something to be prominent, you do not put a big mat on top of it. If you *do* want something to be hidden, you put a big mat on top of it.'

'You make a good point, Hugo, if a little heavy-handedly.'

Aubrey reached for the latch, but the metal was still hot. Von Stralick deftly used the rake to tip the door back. When it fell, Aubrey slashed a hand in front of his face in a feeble effort to keep ash and dust from choking him. He screwed up his eyes and, when he opened them again, he was confronted with a set of metal stairs.

'You have the lantern,' von Stralick said. 'After you.'

'You have your revolver *and* a rake. You should go first.'

'This was Dr Tremaine's estate. I think that your magic could be more useful than a revolver. Besides, I know you have this perverse need to be heroic.'

'Hugo, you are too generous.'

Aubrey stood at the top of the stairs and extended his magical awareness, hoping that his hesitation would be seen as sensible preparation rather than nervousness. Immediately, he was struck by a wave of magic coming from magical residue in the basement below. His magical awareness meant that he saw rising and falling pitch and he tasted pressure, which was an unsettling grey-green colour. Dozens of other sensations assailed him. He gritted his teeth, refusing to let the assault unsettle him but still uncertain of what it meant. It was like standing in front of a fire hose and trying to determine the shape of a specific drop of water. He had to get closer if he were to divine anything specific.

Something that was a little more than apprehension and a little less than fear surfaced in his stomach. This was, as Hugo had pointed out, Dr Tremaine's estate – and they were intruders. While they had remained unscathed so far, it didn't mean that they were safe. All it meant was that they hadn't run into the serious dangers yet.

If cowardice were surrendering to fear and heroism prevailing over it, Aubrey wondered what trying to distract fear by whistling in an erratic manner was.

'Is that wise?' von Stralick said. 'Unless it's part of a magical ritual, I'd advise you stop it.'

Aubrey took a deep breath, and marched down the stairs with his lantern before him.

The stairs led to a heavy steel door, riveted and reminiscent of the doors Aubrey had seen in submersibles. With Hugo at his back, Aubrey unlatched it, stretched out his arm and shone the lantern inside.

The basement space was large, extending far beyond the range of the lantern. It was low-ceilinged, a barrier of earth separating it from the building above and from the effects of the explosion and fire.

Having learned a thing or two about entering places that were potentially magically hostile, Aubrey stood just outside the basement and studied it as carefully as he could without actually setting foot inside.

He was immediately taken by the cables that were slung along the walls. Thick bundles were wrapped at intervals with tarred rubber, looping around the perimeter of the room and criss-crossing the ceiling like gloomy Christmas decorations. He tried to estimate how much electrical power the basement would take.

A few tables and chairs, a desk or two and a single filing cabinet were the mundane features of the room and wouldn't be out of place in an office in Trinovant. The bays that were measured out along the walls, however, were anything but ordinary. For a moment, Aubrey searched for the plumbing fittings, for the bays looked like nothing as much as stalls for a row of shower baths. Each one was a yard or so in width, with a swinging louvred door that left plenty of room top and bottom. Many of the doors were ajar, to show that instead of brass plumbing fittings, these stalls had leather straps attached to the back wall.

Aubrey had never given much credence to the belief that buildings could absorb the influence of deeds conducted within their confines but, for a moment, he was prepared to dust off that conclusion and re-examine it. This basement made him extremely uneasy, had him flicking his gaze from side to side, into corners, at shadows. It wasn't just the magical residue, although the place was thick with it. He was certain that bad things had happened here.

He glanced over his shoulder. Von Stralick was looking as troubled as Aubrey felt. He was gripping the rake and holding it in front of him like a weapon.

'I'm going to have to step inside,' Aubrey said, 'if we're going to learn anything more.'

'Be my guest.'

As soon as Aubrey's foot touched the floor on the other side of the doorway, he plummeted through space.

Even the shock of finding himself outside, in the night air, falling at a great rate, didn't stop Aubrey – for a split second – being lost in admiration at the cleverness of the spell. He'd been immediately translated from the basement to a position off the edge of the cliff at the rear of the estate. For a normal burglar it would be a death plunge, but after a moment's panic – in which he let go of the lantern – Aubrey was able to bring his rapid descent to a halt, thanks to his refined levitation spell. As he steadied himself, bobbing with one hand outstretched and touching the cliff face, he watched the lantern continue its long fall to the rocks below, where it splashed in a burst of burning oil.

Aubrey bit his lip as his stomach lurched. Briefly, he wondered why an organ of digestion would react in such a way to narrowly escaping death like that, and then he consigned the question to the Unknowable Mysteries of the Universe file.

The night was still, clouds hiding the stars. In the distance the lights of Bardenford twinkled and made the town look like a fairy kingdom. Like thistledown, Aubrey bobbed alongside the sheer granite immensity of the cliff until he was calmer, then he spoke the syllables to take him up again.

He had the levitation spell so much to heart now that he only paid his ascent half a mind while the other half analysed what had just happened. Dr Tremaine must have left a compressed spell behind. With the right trigger, it would dispose of intruders without his having to worry about the efficiency of the guards.

All of which implied that the rogue sorcerer perhaps hadn't finished with this facility at all.

Aubrey drifted over the lip of the cliff, where a stretch of lawn ran toward the house and the outbuildings. The grass was longish, which Aubrey attributed to the difficulty of finding volunteers to mow so close to the edge of such a precipitous drop.

With solid ground underfoot and still pondering deeply, he hurried in the direction of the ruins, only to meet a wild-eyed von Stralick, who advanced on him, revolver at the ready.

'Fitzwilliam!' Von Stralick lowered the revolver. 'Where did you go? What happened?'

'Dr Tremaine left a nasty little spell behind. Clever, but nasty. I was shifted bodily off the edge of the cliff.'

Von Stralick's eyebrows shot up. 'I'm glad you went first then.'

The same thought had occurred to Aubrey. 'Your revolver wouldn't have been much use to you if you'd gone ahead.'

Von Stralick squinted at it and thrust it into his belt. 'Perhaps not.' He laughed. 'I am glad you yelled.'

'I did?'

'I heard you, so I ran out of the basement instead of following you into it.'

On the way back to the basement, von Stralick found another lantern, and then picked up the rake he'd abandoned. He lit the lantern and hung it from the rake that he carried over his shoulder.

'It is a light burden,' he said carefully.

Aubrey had to award him points for making a pun in a language that wasn't his own, and he promised himself that he'd share it with Prince Albert, that most avid collector of puns.

When Aubrey again found himself falling, wind whipping his hair, he was extremely impressed. Dr Tremaine had been careful in his warding, leaving *two* compressed spells to fling burglars off the cliff.

After the third time, however, Aubrey began to fume.

He found von Stralick sitting on the stairs leading to the basement. 'Again?' the Holmlander asked.

'Again. But this time . . .'

Aubrey held the doorframe and leaned inside while von Stralick poked the rake and lantern past him to provide illumination. What Aubrey saw made him rock back so quickly that von Stralick had to juggle the rake to avoid losing the lantern.

Just inside the door, in a neat row flush with the wall, was a line of a dozen or more metal cylinders, smaller cousins of ones that Aubrey had seen only too recently in Baron von Grolman's golem-making facility.

Aubrey's curiosity immediately ordered him to leap inside and inspect the cylinders, to pull them apart until their nature was ascertained to the last detail. Accustomed as it was to getting its own way, when Aubrey didn't immediately comply his curiosity went off and sulked, allowing him to proceed with more rational care.

'Don't set foot in there, Hugo, until I can work out what's going on.'

'Fitzwilliam, you will find me patience incarnate.'

Aubrey extended his magical awareness and hissed. Each one of the cylinders held an identical clutch of spells. Not just similar, as would normally be the case in casting the same spell a number of times, but absolutely, manifestly identical.

His curiosity roused from its sulking. It was as if this one datum, this one piece of information, was a particularly juicy-looking rabbit lobbed in front of a dog. This time, Aubrey couldn't help but let his curiosity loose to chase it and see where it led.

Could it be that Dr Tremaine had made great strides in efficient spell reproduction? Had he perfected a method of copying spells quickly and accurately? It fitted with other data Aubrey had been assembling – the machine-golem hybrids, the spells to control wounded soldiers, the enhanced coal that powered the golems. All of this was too much magic for one person, even Dr Tremaine – but Aubrey had difficulty thinking of Dr Tremaine recruiting and training other magicians to take over this burden of replicating spells.

Create a spell, then use a reproducing spell to make copies. Or was it the work of a magically constructed and potentialised engine, a spell-copying machine? With a supply of engineered canisters ready to be filled, identical spells could be churned out over and over again, as seemed to be the case here. The first three cylinders had melted and burst, evidence of the spells having been triggered. The metal looked like aluminium, or thin steel, strong enough to be packed and stored, light enough to carry, but not presenting any impediment to the operation of the spells.

Aubrey was left with one poser. How was he going to investigate the basement without setting off a dozen transference spells? He didn't fancy having to catch himself mid-plunge again and again. What if he tired and his concentration slipped?

He shuddered, then he hummed a little, deep at the back of his throat, before a smile spread across his face. He reached into his pocket and pulled out a penny. The profile of King William stared at him. Aubrey saluted, then flipped the coin into the air.

It bounced on the stone floor, rolled a little, then wobbled to a halt and lay there, unmoving.

'Non-living objects don't trigger the spells,' Aubrey said aloud and, for a moment, his brain hared off in a wayward direction, wondering if this spell could be turned into a very effective method of ridding a place of vermin.

Von Stralick pursed his lips. 'What if the spells are triggered according to weight rather than one's living status?'

'Good point, Hugo. Fortunately, I've already thought of a way to test this.'

They spent the next fifteen minutes hauling objects of increasing weight from the gardens, down the stairs and launching them into the basement, where they accumulated, stubbornly not being transported over the edge of the cliff: a garden gnome, a large flower pot complete with daphne, a birdbath and finally a sundial nearly as tall as von Stralick.

'So.' Aubrey dusted his hands together. 'I think we've proved that it's not entry into the basement that triggers the spell, but the entry of something *living* into the basement.'

'Not exactly.' Von Stralick thrust a hand through the doorway. He remained untranslated.

'Just so. Touching the floor is the crucial trigger.'

'And am I correct in surmising that you want to enter the basement without touching the floor?'

'That I am. Stand still.'

Aubrey ran through his levitation spell. Von Stralick flailed a little when he rose, and he whirled his arms in circles. 'This is most awkward.'

'Steady, Hugo. You should be perfectly stable if you don't move too quickly.'

Von Stralick looked sceptical, but he eased his frantic movements. 'And how do we move ourselves along if our feet can't touch the ground to propel us?'

'We use our hands.' Aubrey seized the doorframe. 'Keep close to the wall and push yourself along. And mind your head.'

Their progress was clumsy, but steady. Aubrey found that if he leaned toward the wall, he could shuffle both hands and move toward the part of the room that interested him the most: the strange stalls, especially since he could now see a connection ran from the cables into each stall.

'You are rather good at this, Fitzwilliam, this magic business.'

'Thanks, Hugo. I do my best.'

'Zelinka said you were an outstanding talent.'

'She did?' Aubrey was startled and pleased. Madame Zelinka was not effusive, but she had seen enough magic and operational magicians for Aubrey to value her judgement.

'And Dr Tremaine had a high opinion of your abilities, too.'

'I beg your pardon?'

Von Stralick eased his way around the corner of the room. 'It was in your file. Don't look so surprised. You should have known that the Holmland intelligence agencies have a dossier on you. One that I helped to compile.'

Aubrey remembered first encountering von Stralick when the Holmlander was a trusted part of the Holmland spying machinery. Naturally he would have reported his encounters with Aubrey. 'I suppose the son of the Albion Prime Minister deserves a dossier.'

'The foreign Prime Minister's son who just happens to be a remarkable magician, with a decidedly heroic bent. The last I saw it, your file was a rapidly growing one.'

'Nothing scurrilous, I hope,' Aubrey said faintly. It was all logical, but it was unsettling, nonetheless, to think of strangers dissecting his life.

'They tried, but couldn't find anything.'

'I'm glad,' Aubrey said, but he found himself perversely irritated by this. Did this mean there was nothing in his past that was scandalous, or that any incidents weren't worth reporting, or was it that he'd managed to keep his mishaps secret? He wasn't sure which was preferable.

Aubrey reached the nearest bay, while still trying to assimilate this latest information. He assumed von Stralick himself would have a dossier by now – his erstwhile employers would have begun one immediately he disappeared from their network. But would George have one? Caroline? His mother? Such considerations made him queasy.

Grappling with the metal uprights, Aubrey dragged himself around until he faced the open door of the first stall. The door had no lock, just a simple latch. Inside, it was barely more than shoulder wide. Aubrey sniffed. The magical residue was a dull orange aroma mixed with a salty sound, a melange of disquieting sensations, but cutting through it was a more ordinary sensation: a genuine smell. He wrinkled his nose at its unpleasant, slightly rotten, meaty odour.

He asked for the lantern. Von Stralick held it up while Aubrey pulled himself closer to inspect the straps, making sure not to touch the floor. The leather was new, still unsupple, and the buckles were bright brass, except where they were stained. Aubrey scratched at the crustiness on the straps, then rocked backward.

'Dried blood,' von Stralick said.

'I'd say so.' Not a lot of it, but enough to mean that someone had been strapped against the wall – one set of straps around the throat, one at chest height, one around the hips, and the last keeping the legs and feet together – and then suffered something that had made them bleed.

Numbly, Aubrey inspected the floor. It was scuffed and slightly dusty, but unstained. The bleeding hadn't been substantial.

The next bay showed no signs of blood, but the next did, and the one after that. After checking the thirty-six bays they found nearly half of them showed signs of blood – and one of them had something else.

Aubrey scooped up the wire mesh helmet. It was the same as he'd seen prisoners wearing when they were exercising in the gardens. It wasn't heavy, and the lantern light glinted from its surface. Inside, a swivel-bolted mechanism was clearly designed to hold the tongue and stop the wearer from talking, but what intrigued Aubrey most was what looked like an electrical socket, firmly welded to the back of the helmet.

'This is to keep magicians quiet?' von Stralick said. 'So they can't cast spells?'

'Apparently,' Aubrey said, but he had an inkling that its purpose was much more sinister than that. He peered at the socket at the rear of the helmet, deeply unhappy at the implications that were circling like carrion crows. Then he looked up and all the suspicions he'd been harbouring coalesced into a moment of profound horror.

Five

A SINGLE CABLE DANGLED FROM OVERHEAD. WHEN von Stralick moved the lantern to get a better view, Aubrey saw that the cable was tangled and would easily have extended into the stall if it were straightened.

It had a plug on the end of it.

Abruptly, the helmet felt unclean. He dropped it and wiped his hands on the seat of his trousers. Filthy though they were, it was good, clean dirt rather than the taint this device carried.

'All of the bays have cables, don't they?' Aubrey asked von Stralick.

The Holmlander held up the lantern. The next bay had a cable hanging into it, and so did the one after that. Propelling themselves by dragging on the uprights, they floated along the row of doors, opening and leaning in. Cables led into all of them.

'This is magic?' von Stralick asked.

'Of a kind. Blended with electrical engineering.'

'For what purpose?'

'I'm still thinking about that.' *And I don't like what I'm coming up with.*

Von Stralick sighed. 'Mysterious is all well and good, but I'd prefer the mystery were on our side rather than the other.'

'I'm sure there are people in Holmland saying the same. All Dr Tremaine's cards are unlikely to be on the table.'

It never hurt Aubrey to remind himself that Dr Tremaine's goal was to perform the Ritual of the Way to achieve immortality for himself and his sister. To that end, he was fostering bloodshed, which he needed on a huge scale to implement the spell. Bringing the world to war was the first step, but he needed a titanic battle, one that would unleash death on a hitherto unimaginable scale. Since the beginning of the war, forces had been massing on the eastern front with Muscovia and on two western fronts: one through the Low Countries and on the border with Gallia, and one on Gallia's north-east border near Stalsfrieden and Divodorum.

In the long, worrying days watching over a delirious von Stralick, Aubrey had time to wonder about the disposition of the Holmland armies. Having two fronts on the Gallian border a hundred miles apart puzzled him, but his brooding had thrown up an awful possibility. Could Dr Tremaine be planning to link the two fronts? It would make a battlefront of staggering proportions, just the thing he would need to achieve his ends.

The prospect was horrifying. Such a battlefront would commit huge quantities of war matériel, directing the entire output of whole nations to destruction. It would throw thousands, tens of thousands, of soldiers against each other. It was a possibility that any sane person would recoil from. No-one with any semblance of humanity would plan such a thing.

This, of course, meant it was entirely within Dr Tremaine's scope of imagining, which left Aubrey grappling not with *what* but with *how*.

Aubrey found that he had drifted up toward the ceiling. He reached up and steadied himself, then turned to his magical awareness. Immediately, he bared his teeth as the basement became a chaos of magical splatters, cast-off residue from the intense magic that had taken place. Through the pseudo-sight that came with being magically endowed, it was like being in the studio of an extremely careless and extremely prolific artist, one who specialised in subjects malignant, festering and brooding.

Aubrey didn't want to get close to the residue smears. They throbbed, which suggested that they still contained some magical power – the nature of which he couldn't divine. Something unhealthy, something to do with channelling and amplifying was the best guess he could make.

'Hugo.' Aubrey pushed against the ceiling, moving himself until he was directly over one of the desks in the middle of the basement. With a few syllables, he adjusted his elevation until he could nudge a pile of sodden papers with a toe. 'If you were in charge of the Holmland forces, how would you go about uniting the division that is currently bogged down in the Low Countries with the one that's dug in around Divodorum?'

Von Stralick was peering at where a thick electrical conduit entered the room, high up on the wall near the stairs. Hand over hand, he lowered himself, then cocked an eyebrow at Aubrey. 'Ah, the hypothetical! You Albionites love your games to fill in time. Charades, Donkey Tail Pinning, Hypotheticals.'

'It's not a game. You have some knowledge of the Holmland military mind. You should be able to put yourself in the shoes of the Supreme Army Command.'

'That is not so difficult. More difficult, of course, is to predict what Dr Tremaine will do.'

'Imagining yourself a Holmland general will be enough for now.'

'There is not much to guess at, then. I would transport many, many troops to Stalsfrieden. A division or two. Or three.'

'Forty, fifty thousand men? Why Stalsfrieden?'

'It has good rail connections to Fisherberg. From Stalsfrieden, they can march to the Divodorum battlelines – or march to the Low Countries.'

'Would it make good sense?'

'Good sense is a slippery concept in war time, Fitzwilliam. I'm sure a build-up like that would appeal to many of the generals, which is probably reason enough to do it. We have been fighting for a short time, really, and many of them are impatient for what they see as glory. Commanding a force that made such a bold move would be very good for a career.'

Another thought crept up on Aubrey and elbowed him uncomfortably. 'What if these new divisions simply aimed to capture Divodorum?'

'That would be even bolder, and therefore more praiseworthy. Any general who championed such a strategy could become a hero.'

'It's not just Divodorum that I'm thinking of. It's what lies on the other side of Divodorum.'

'Ah. A direct route via river, rail and road to Lutetia.'

'The Gallian capital would be laid bare.'

'So which is it? Opening a wide front across the north of Gallia? Or a lightning strike toward Lutetia?'

Both would require much bloody fighting. Either would do for Dr Tremaine's purposes. 'I'm starting to think that Dr Tremaine, as usual, has more than one iron in the fire.' Aubrey swept his gaze around the basement. 'I've seen enough.'

'I think I saw enough a long time ago,' the Holmlander said.

Once outside, Aubrey took a deep breath and spoke the syllables that lowered them to the ground. The smell of ash and smoke was clean compared to the air in the crypt below.

Helmets, cables, restraints and blood. Nothing good happened down there. He still didn't know exactly what it was, but he knew it was important. Dr Tremaine wouldn't have spent a month here if something important hadn't been going on.

'What time is it?' The clouds were breaking up to show that the stars were still there, bright and constant. He wondered if the soldiers at the front could see them.

'Just after four. We have an hour until dawn.'

Aubrey yawned. 'Enough time to investigate the house.'

Von Stralick went to reply, but stopped and put a hand to his ear.

Startled by von Stralick's concern, Aubrey turned in the direction the spy was facing.

A motor, approaching but still distant. As Aubrey strained to make it out, he heard the crunching of gears that announced the beginning of the mountainside ascent. It suggested a lorry rather than a motorcar.

'The guards are coming back?'

'With reinforcements, most likely.'

'I had hoped we'd have more time,' Aubrey said. 'We haven't learned much, not really.'

'Quickly then.' Von Stralick picked up the rake he'd dropped. 'Take the lantern.'

They ran through the gardens to the house, approaching from the west. Von Stralick didn't slow down as they sprinted up the broad stairs from the gardens and across the terrace. He used the rake as a jousting lance and crashed through the glass doors. 'No time for finesse!' he cried.

Together, they lurched through the debris into a sunroom that was lavishly laid out with wicker furniture and a grove or two of potted palms. Gingerly, von Stralick brushed splinters of glass from his jacket.

Aubrey remembered the Directorate training facility, another handsome estate that had been taken over by military. Some things would, of necessity, be the same. 'Somewhere on the ground floor should be an operations room. Near the front door?'

They found it off the entrance hall. Once, it had probably been the grand dining room, but instead of a long table and heraldic banners it was fully stocked with desks, each with typewriter and telephone, plus extensive pigeon holes on the walls for routing of documents.

While von Stralick hurried among the desks, glancing at documents that looked promising, Aubrey cast about in a circle, feeling for any trace of magic but being frustrated when all he could detect were mild touches in too many different places. Nothing outrageous, nothing promising at all.

To judge from the dowel hanging on the walls, and the traces of paper caught in them, maps had been torn down and disposed of. Smouldering remains in the huge fireplace showed that files and documents had also been eliminated. He stirred the ashes with a poker, hoping to find something that had only been half-burned, but whoever had had that job had been extremely thorough. The ashes were uniformly black and useless.

With a grunt, von Stralick used both hands to pick up a head-sized lump of stone from the mantelpiece. He rolled it over in his hands. 'Remarkable.'

'I beg your pardon?' Aubrey stared at the banded stone, dark green and blue, glittering in the lantern light.

'This is Green Johannes stone.'

'I'm pleased about that, but don't we have more important things to worry about?'

'I'm surprised to see it here. When I'm surprised, I become curious — and since I've seen how you respond to your curiosity I've decided to listen to mine.'

'Tell me then, Hugo — what's surprising about Green Johannes?'

'Johannes stone is only found in one tiny mine near Korsur, just on the Holmland side of the Gallian border. It comes in a number of varieties and Green Johannes is very, very rare.'

Aubrey looked up from the undeniably attractive striped stone. Something buried in his memory was struggling to make itself known, trying to rise above the snippets of information, the sawn-off ends of ideas and the half-formed conclusions that swirled about in the deepest recesses of his mind.

'Valuable, is it?'

'Greatly. It's worth a thousand times more than Brown Johannes, a hundred times more than Blue Johannes —'

'I see the pattern, Hugo. It's the most valuable Johannes stone there is.'

'Apart from Crystal Johannes, but the last of that was mined a hundred years ago.' Von Stralick hefted the shapeless stone. 'This is freshly extracted. See? It hasn't been worked or polished.'

'Which is all well and good, Hugo, but what's your point?'

'I'm not sure. Again, like you, where Dr Tremaine is concerned I take note of anything out of the ordinary.' Von Stralick carefully replaced the Green Johannes on the mantelpiece.

Aubrey's memory wasn't being cooperative. He shook his head. 'I wouldn't have known that lump of stone was out of the ordinary.'

'That is where you're fortunate to be associated with a Green Johannes collector.'

'To tell you the truth, Hugo, I have trouble thinking of you as a collector.'

'Fitzwilliam, you still have much to learn about the spying business. When I was a cultural attaché to various Holmland embassies, being a collector gave me good reason to be out and about, poking my nose into various emporia. I became quite an expert in Green Johannes ware, to my surprise.'

'Where's your collection now?'

'Probably in the home of one of the Chancellor's good

friends.' He glanced at Aubrey. 'I do not want you to think that my antipathy toward the Chancellor and his cronies is due to my collection's being stolen. I'm much less straightforward than that.'

'Hugo, I promise: I'll never think you're straightforward.'

Von Stralick looked wistfully at the lump of stone. 'It's a fine specimen.'

'Don't worry. Once we've sorted out all this mess, I'll help you start your collection again. I think we have a pair of candlesticks made out of the stuff, up in the attic somewhere. I'm sure Mother and Father wouldn't miss them.'

Especially since Mother called them ghastly and bundled them away as soon as she could.

'That is decent of you,' von Stralick said. 'And I use that word carefully, knowing what it means to you Albionites.'

'In a land of understatement, there is no higher praise than being called decent.'

Von Stralick put a finger to his lips. 'I have an idea.' He strode from the operations room.

Aubrey decided to continue investigating the operations room. He began rummaging through the nearest Out tray, looking for incriminating invoices or delivery dockets, something to give concrete evidence of the comings and goings, but all he found were internal documents. It was as if the outside world didn't exist.

This room had been the centre of Dr Tremaine's activities for over a month. It was inconceivable that he could leave no trace of what he'd been up to. If Aubrey had time he was sure he could find something, but admiring a piece of undeniably handsome stone had meant little time was left before the lorry would arrive.

'We have to go,' von Stralick snapped as he rushed back into the operations room.

'Did you find anything useful?'

'I found the switchboard. Three operators, it had, if each required a chair. No documents, but as I hoped, one of them had used a pencil on the counter to list frequently called exchanges. I have them. They may be of some use.'

He handed Aubrey a scrap of paper. 'Many of the numbers are in Fisherberg, but more are in Bardenford.'

'That's only natural. Bardenford is the nearest major city to the estate. The others?'

'Scattered around Holmland, the important cities and ports, Stalsfrieden on the border with Gallia.' Von Stralick tapped the list with a finger. 'The only oddity is the exchange listing for Korsur.'

Aubrey frowned. Why was a Holmland village, the home of Green Johannes, featuring in Dr Tremaine's schemes? 'I may have an idea.'

Von Stralick stopped. 'You have no shortage of ideas. Tell me, though: is it a good one?'

Aubrey answered a question with a question. 'What's your experience with interrogation, Hugo?'

'I've been on both sides. I prefer to be the one asking the questions.'

'You can do it humanely?'

'Ah, now there's a question.' Von Stralick took his time before answering. 'In my view, torture is a most unreliable way of obtaining information. People will tell you anything to make it stop, so how do you know what to believe?'

'You've done this?'

'I've seen it done by stupid people and by people who thought they were clever. It is distasteful.'

'But the other way. You can get information from people without using torture?'

'I have my methods.'

'Good. When these guards come back, what do you say to capturing them and getting information out of them?'

Von Stralick nodded sharply and, together, they ran from the operations room – but just before Aubrey left, he snatched a handful of rubber bands from one of the desks.

AUBREY AND VON STRALICK POSITIONED THEMSELVES IN the bushes on either side of the stairs that led from the doors of the main house. From there, they could see the gates; soon, the lorry, after complaining its way up the steepest part of the ascent, lumbered through the entrance to the estate.

Aubrey had one hand in the pocket of his jacket as the lorry crunched its way along the gravel of the driveway, white in the night-time. He was prepared. He'd put together a spell using the Law of Amplification, the Law of Action at a Distance and the Law of Propensity and he was confident. The guards would be in the one place at the one time and he was sure he could bind them with the ensorcelled rubber bands.

The headlights of the lorry flashed across the bushes as it followed the curve to the main entrance. Aubrey couldn't help but duck, even though he was well hidden.

With a screech of brakes, the lorry pulled up. One of the guards alighted, followed by the broad-shouldered driver. They stood inspecting the main house as if they'd never seen it before and Aubrey waited, frustrated, for the others to climb down from the rear of the lorry.

Aubrey ground his teeth. If he enacted his spell now he could lose the advantage of surprising the other guards, but if he waited, they'd separate and he could lose the chance.

Von Stralick nudged him and glared. Aubrey parted the bushes, squinted, then quickly stood and threw the rubber bands. He chanted the spell and then ducked again, joining von Stralick scuttling through the vegetation along the front of the house.

When they reached the corner of the house, they had a good line of sight. Aubrey's magical awareness allowed him to see the enspelled rubber bands, hooping through the air toward the unsuspecting guards. The bands were expanding as they went and moving with a single intent like a flock of birds. He clenched his fist and, silently, cheered them on.

At the last moment, the shorter of the guards looked up and cried out, but it was too late. The bands swooped, and in an instant they were looping and tangling in precisely the way Aubrey's spell had encouraged them.

Aubrey was on his feet and running as the oaths and cries came from the guards. Von Stralick overtook him. When the Holmlander reached the knot of swearing intruders on the gravel, he leaned against the lorry and yawned. He brandished his revolver. 'Do not move,' he said, in Holmlandish, 'if you value your life.'

Immediately, all struggling ceased. A throaty female

voice responded. 'Hugo, I hope you have a way out of this mess, for all our sakes.'

Von Stralick leaped as if the lorry had suddenly become red hot. 'Zelinka? What are you doing here?'

'Helping my friend George Doyle find you two, of course. Now, get me out of here.'

Six

THE DRAWING ROOM OF THE MAIN HOUSE HAD remained a drawing room, even while the rest of the place had been taken over by Dr Tremaine and his lackeys. It remained, however, a drawing room of a Holmland hunting lodge, which meant that it was full of furniture that was so heavy that each piece could be used to anchor a battleship. The walls were panelled with depressingly dark wood, but only a little of this could be seen in between the hunting trophies that made Aubrey think, as soon as he entered the room, that entire walls were looking at him.

The trophies were the stuffed and mounted heads of beasts that had proven they were slower, duller or unluckier than their comrades. Many of these were local animals – boar, a bear or two, even a few desperately unfortunate wolves – but some had obviously been brought in from far, far away. Unless, Aubrey reflected, a circus had become lost, crashed, and a horde of jungle animals had taken up residence in the woods of the Alemmani Mountains.

After von Stralick did his best to convince a sceptical Madame Zelinka that his gaunt appearance wasn't a true reflection of his state of health, she sat on a vast leather sofa and, with some distaste, set about combing through her hair with her fingers to get rid of the remnants of the ensorcelled rubber bands. Her dark green, no-nonsense skirt and jacket were also sporting the remains of the rubber and von Stralick stood behind her, picking it off her shoulders.

George sat in an armchair, ran a hand over his short military crop, shrugged, glanced at his nondescript black trousers and jacket, shrugged again, then jammed a beret back on his head. 'Lovely place. Have you had it long?'

Aubrey was delighted to see his old friend again, but his presence – and the presence of the mysterious Madame Zelinka – posed a thousand questions. Not the least of them concerned the whereabouts and health of Caroline Hepworth, and it had taken all of Aubrey's strength of character not to try to shake the answer out of George in the driveway.

Aubrey couldn't sit. He paced the room, back and forward in front of a dormant fireplace wide enough to roast an entire ox.

'What were you doing driving a Holmland lorry?' von Stralick asked.

'We were coming up the mountain as it was coming down,' Madame Zelinka said. 'My Enlightened Ones insisted that I would be more comfortable driving than walking, so they took it.'

Von Stralick chuckled, rounded the sofa and sat by her side. 'And the guards who were in this lorry?'

'They are out there, in the woods. Under the watch of my people.'

'What did you do to them, old man?' George asked Aubrey. 'They were terrified.'

'I threw a scare into them. A magical scare.'

'They panicked when they thought we were going to drag them back to this place. Quite happy, they were, to be tied up to trees.'

'No doubt.' Aubrey remembered their terror. 'Now, George, what on earth are you doing here?'

George surrendered. 'You win, Madame Z.'

'If you insist. One of these Albionish wagering games,' she said to a puzzled von Stralick. 'Doyle wagered that he knew what question Fitzwilliam would ask first, and I had to guess another.'

Von Stralick was perplexed. 'Your winnings?'

Madame Zelinka shrugged. Her face, usually grave, had a hint of a smile. 'He owes me a favour. I shall call on it some time.'

George blinked. 'Er . . . Not when it's too inconvenient, if you don't mind.'

'What is inconvenient for you may be convenient for me. We shall see.'

Aubrey could never resist a sidetrack. 'And what was the question you thought I'd ask first, George?'

'I thought you'd ask about Caroline, old man.' George grinned.

'Ah.'

'Remarkable strength of character, your forbearance. Before we get to her, though, you need to know that

Madame Z and her pals have come over to our side.'

Madame Zelinka made a face. 'We have not come over to your side, Doyle. How many times have I told you this?'

'Probably a few dozen,' George said. 'All the way from Trinovant to here, if I recall correctly.'

'We have ways and means to cross borders,' Madame Zelinka said, responding to Aubrey's naked curiosity. 'The Enlightened Ones always have.'

'Which is why the Directorate contacted them, apparently,' George said. 'Commander Craddock was hoping that they might be able to do something.'

'This is only the third time in our history that we have abandoned our neutrality,' Madame Zelinka said. 'It is not done lightly, but Dr Tremaine . . .'

Aubrey jumped in. 'Your people see the threat that Dr Tremaine is posing to the world?'

'It is greater than you imagine, perhaps.'

'Greater than destroying nations?' George said. 'Greater than killing hundreds of thousands of people?'

Madame Zelinka shook her head. 'The wisest magicians in our order think that he aims to control magic himself.' She looked at Aubrey. 'Have you heard that he has been abducting magicians from all over the world?'

'After seeing unwilling magicians being delivered here, I'd put two and two together.'

'They are here?'

'They're gone now.'

She hissed through her teeth for a moment. 'The magicians are part of his plan.'

'How? What?'

'We think that he has found a way to use their magical ability, whether they are willing or not.'

'As if we needed another reason to stop him,' George said gruffly.

'Tell me about Albion,' Aubrey said abruptly. 'What about Mother and Father?'

George crossed his arms. 'You'll be pleased to know that your father did exactly as you wanted. You've been declared a traitor and you've been vilified the length and breadth of the land.'

'Ah. That's good.'

'Well, I wouldn't say that it was good, but it was enough to save your father and the Progressive government, as you'd hoped. In fact, having been betrayed by a blackhearted villain of a son has actually gained Sir Darius a great deal of public sympathy.'

'Splendid,' Aubrey muttered.

George went on. 'An ungrateful son, one who shunned his father's example and spurned all that Albion had to offer.'

'I think I understand the picture, George.'

'Speaking of pictures, Holmland has supplied some of those photographs they took, with your being chummy with Baron von Grolman and the like.'

Aubrey sighed. 'It was inevitable.'

'While the newspapers aren't printing them just yet, they're all making reference to them. How you're breaking the heart of your mother, betraying your country to the enemy, the promising talent who became the Turn-coat Thaumaturge, the Wicked Wizard, the Malignant Magician, the Dreadful Young Man.'

'Dreadful Young Man?'

'That was the *Daily Post*. They always have unconvincing headlines.'

Madame Zelinka tapped the armrest of the sofa. 'I think that is enough, Doyle.'

'Just giving him the flavour of the press.' George fiddled with a cuff for a moment. 'When news of the photographs was made public, the uproar was astounding, but thanks to your warning, at least everyone was calling for *your* head, old man, rather than calling for your father's.'

Despite all this unfolding as planned, Aubrey was a little hollow inside. 'And how are Mother and Father? Really?'

'To the public, they're heartbroken and dismayed,' George said, 'but, really, they're proud, if a little concerned. They said to tell you that.'

'You've seen them?'

'Caroline wouldn't let us talk to anyone before we spoke to your parents – not even the Directorate. Once we left you in Stalsfrieden, she drove us like a Fury through Gallia, picking up Sophie's parents along the way, before she commandeered a sloop to get us to Trinovant. You would have loved to see the way she stood up to any official who tried to stop us.'

'Oh yes,' he said faintly.

'I have to tell you, old man, that your mother was shocked by your plan. She thought it was outrageous.'

'I agree with her,' Aubrey said. 'It was outrageous. It *needed* to be outrageous.'

'I think it took your father about half a minute to realise that. He said you were extremely clever.'

'He did?'

'Brave and clever, he said, while he dried your mother's tears with his coat sleeve. Then she said you were too noble for your own good.'

His mother had actually cried? Aubrey grimaced. He hadn't meant to distress his parents this much. His mother was usually extremely pragmatic and he'd been certain she'd see how necessary his plan was.

These are distressing times, he thought. *Maybe for mothers more than most.*

He became aware of the scrutiny from Hugo and Madame Zelinka. Steadfastly, he kept his gaze on a startled-looking ocelot on the wall just above George's head. 'You said that you were able to find Sophie's parents?'

'Friendly people, overjoyed to see her and her brother. And more than happy to leave Gallia for Albion.'

'Gallia is in a poor way,' Madame Zelinka said. 'Morale is low, the government is fighting within its own ranks.'

'Sophie's brother helped convince them that leaving Gallia would be sensible, at least in the short term,' George said. 'After he'd explained what a fool he'd been, of course.'

Aubrey had been wondering how the reconciliation would go between Théo Delroy and his parents. While Aubrey was only pretending to be a traitor, Théo had actually enlisted in the Holmland army.

'The Directorate was more than happy to see Professor Delroy,' George said. 'Apparently he has news about Holmland financial dealings that may be useful in our war effort.'

'Baron von Grolman's machinations, I hope,' Aubrey added.

'I'd say so. Somehow I don't think that the secret buying into Albion businesses that he's been doing over the last few years is going to come to much after Professor Delroy, the Directorate and the Exchequer finish their investigations.'

Aubrey's head was awhirl. So much information after being deprived of it for so long was like putting a rich meal in front of a starving man. 'What news of the war? Are we winning?'

'It's hard to tell,' George said. 'The Gallians have managed to halt the Holmland advance at Divodorum, and we've combined with their troops, troops from the Low Countries and some jolly welcome reinforcements from the colonies to hold them up on the north-west front.'

'A stalemate,' Madame Zelinka said.

'For the moment. A bloody stalemate. The weather, old man, has either been a godsend or a curse, depending on your point of view. Both sides have trenches and barbed wire stretching for miles now, but dust is driving everyone mad.'

Aubrey didn't think it was the best time to raise his nightmare scenario of a continuous battleline, joining the two fronts, but he had no doubt that Dr Tremaine was formulating some way to end the stalemate. 'And Muscovia?'

'Much fighting,' Madame Zelinka said. 'Nothing decisive. All dug in, like at Divodorum.'

'And any news from Holmland?'

'Ah, yes, Holmland.' George looked at Madame Zelinka, who looked straight back at him. 'Lots of interesting news from Holmland. For a start, Madame Z's people say there's a build-up near the border town of Korsur, south of Stalsfrieden. It's puzzling because Korsur is a small place, no strategic importance at all.'

Aubrey raised an eyebrow at von Stralick. 'We have an indication that Dr Tremaine might have some connection with Korsur. Does the Directorate have anything to confirm this?'

George looked thoughtful and went to answer, but Madame Zelinka cut him off: 'Korsur is not important. Tell him.'

George scowled and, suddenly uncomfortable, rubbed his hands together slowly before answering. 'From what Madame Z's correspondents have told us, and some bits and pieces that Commander Craddock mentioned, it looks as if there is considerable unrest in Holmland over the war. Some sign of an underground opposition, it seems like.'

'That sounds good.'

'Count Brandt's efforts didn't go to waste. His sister is rallying dissidents and objectors, and the opposition is gathering strength thanks to a few handy developments.'

Aubrey grimaced. Holmland wasn't Albion. While Albion wasn't perfect, the role of women was changing for the better. Holmland, by comparison, still had an appallingly old-fashioned attitude to women. Count Brandt's sister may find it difficult to organise support.

'The Directorate is doing what it can to help this movement?'

'Funny you should say that, because both Commander Craddock and Commander Tallis were more than eager to send a special team to help the few operatives we still have in Fisherberg. A special team with very special abilities.'

Aubrey had a growing sense of unease. 'Special abilities.'

'Caroline and Sophie, old man. They've been sent to Fisherberg to foment unrest.'

AUBREY COULDN'T HAVE BEEN MORE DUMBFOUNDED IF Dr Tremaine had suddenly appeared and told them that they would soon wake up and find it was all a dream.

Astonishment reduced him to politeness. 'I beg your pardon?'

'You can imagine that I'm not overjoyed about it, old man, but times are desperate, as Commander Craddock repeated more than once after he'd inducted Sophie into the Directorate. I don't think that he was happy about sending them, and he was even less happy about your mother's involvement.'

'What? Wait – this is too much. My mother?'

'Lady Rose and some of her friends spent time with Directorate people, then with Sophie and Caroline. Sophie was getting some magical training when I had to leave if I was to go with Madame Z.'

Aubrey's head was spinning. 'I'm glad Sophie was getting some more magical training.'

'A week of it,' George said. 'She was frightfully keen.'

'A week isn't enough, but it's something.' He stared at George. 'Fisherberg. They've gone to Fisherberg.' *Dangerous, enemy heartland Fisherberg.*

'Lutetia first, apparently, with a list of notable suffragists your mother gave them. After that, yes, they're set to infiltrate Fisherberg.'

'I don't believe it.'

'Look, old man, Commander Tallis said that since there's already some unrest in Fisherberg about the war this was actually one of the more sensible missions going on at the moment.'

'There are more preposterous schemes than sending two neophyte operatives into the heart of Holmland?'

What if Caroline were recognised? They'd all been trained in clandestine operations, but Aubrey could only guess at the measures that would have to be taken to avoid detection in Fisherberg.

'Apparently. Commander Tallis wouldn't tell me what they were, but he assured me that a hundred more lunatic schemes were currently under way, with another hundred on the drawing board.'

'I can't accept that.'

'That's what I said, but when Prince Albert said it was so, then I had no choice but to believe it.'

'You saw Bertie?'

'You don't think we've all been standing still while you've been gallivanting about, do you? It's been a busy few weeks, old man. The prince insisted on seeing us – Caroline, Sophie and me.'

'How is he?'

'Working as hard as ten people, but that's not unusual in Trinovant at the moment. He said he wanted a chat, to talk to those who'd been close to the front, but most of his questions were about you, to tell the truth.'

'Ah.'

'He was worried, but we told him that you'd be all right. Caroline was most forthright, and scolded him when he expressed some doubts.'

Aubrey would have liked to have seen that.

George continued. 'He ended up having a good laugh at the concrete elephant escapade, at least.' George paused, scratched his chin, then cocked an eye at Aubrey. 'Before we left, your father took us aside and asked us to give you a message, the next time any of us saw you.'

'And?'

'He said that he trusted that you'd do your duty.'

'That was all?' von Stralick said.

'It's enough,' Aubrey said. He sat back in his chair weary but strangely satisfied. No instructions, no list of things to take care of or keep an eye on, no admonitions.

He trusts me.

It was almost startling, to have such a clear declaration. Aubrey realised that with these few simple words he'd achieved something he'd been struggling for years to attain. Or had the trust been there for some time and only now was he able to recognise it?

He decided that he was on the verge of pondering the issue too deeply, a sensation like reading a simple word over and over until it begins to lose all meaning. He backed away and told himself to accept his father's words at face value.

'George, you've told me about what the Directorate had planned for Caroline and Sophie – but what about you?'

George leaned back and crossed his arms behind his head, so perfectly smug that his photograph could be used instead of a dictionary definition of the word. 'Special Assignment, old man. Very Special Assignment.'

'I see.'

'Craddock and Tallis emphasised to me exactly how special this assignment is.'

'It sounds as if you've fully understood the degree of specialness.'

'I have a knack for that sort of understanding, apparently.'

'And what is it?'

'The assignment? I'm to make sure you don't get shot, old man, by anyone who recognises the Traitor of Albion.'

'I see.'

'The Directorate has sent out the word to trusted operatives, explaining your real status, but I've been given credentials that will allow us access to Gallian authorities and the like, as long as you hang back and don't make yourself conspicuous.'

It made sense. The Directorate couldn't simply announce that Aubrey was innocent, not with the photographs still in circulation. Something more than a denial was needed.

'I'll do my best, George, to look shabby and uncouth. No-one will suspect that I'm me.'

'I don't think that will be much of a problem, not with the way you look at the moment.'

Aubrey straightened his jacket. 'How's that?'

'Splendid. It's made me overlook the dirt, the creases, the general tattiness. Now,' said George, 'we couldn't help noticing, as we drove up, that most of this place has been blown up. I'm assuming you were responsible for that, old man?'

'Sorry to disappoint you, George, but Dr Tremaine destroyed his own estate.'

Madame Zelinka frowned. 'Why would he do that?'

Why indeed? 'I'd say that he's either finished all he came here to do, or something significant has happened to make him revise his plans.'

'Rather drastic revision, that.' George adopted a listening posture, with his elbow on the arm of the chair and his chin in his hand. 'Now, why don't you tell us what you've been up to?'

Going back to the beginning, Aubrey couldn't avoid mentioning von Stralick's illness, for it explained their relative inactivity, but he tried to glide over the details. His efforts weren't enough, however, to stop Madame Zelinka from pulling von Stralick's face close so she could examine him.

'You need a bath,' she said.

Von Stralick brushed off his filthy lapels. 'An excellent idea. It would be a shame to waste the facilities here. And afterwards? A tour of the hunting trophies? I thought I saw a notably fierce iguana back there.'

Before Madame Zelinka could reply, George stood up, suddenly alert. 'What's that?'

Immediately, any slight semblance the group may have had to a polite drawing room gathering disappeared. Mostly, the indications were subtle – a sudden tension in postures, a cocking of the head, a half-rising to feet – but von Stralick's hand went to his pistol before he shook his head and chuckled. 'Some sort of night bird, Doyle. Do not alarm yourself.'

'If that's a night bird, I'll eat this extremely grubby Holmland cap.'

'He is correct.' Madame Zelinka was rising from her chair. 'It was Katya, signalling from the woods. Someone is coming.'

'There,' George said with some satisfaction. 'Don't let anyone tell you that George Doyle doesn't know his way around the outdoors.'

Seven

AS THEY DOUSED LANTERNS AND HURRIED ALONG the darkened hall, Madame Zelinka explained about her troop of Enlightened Ones. A neat two dozen, many of the members were drawn from those who had helped in the delicate work around Baron von Grolman's factory in Stalsfrieden, but a few had been drawn from Albion and elsewhere after consultation with Commander Craddock – a point that Aubrey found almost unbearably intriguing.

'Katya is my second in command now,' Madame Zelinka said. 'And some Gallians have joined us expressly because we're helping you.'

'Gallians?'

'They said that they are friends of Maurice. Does the name mean anything to you?'

'A friend,' Aubrey said, remembering the caretaker of the dilapidated Faculty of Magic at the University of

Lutetia – someone else who monitored Aubrey's progress from afar.

'Quickly now,' von Stralick said as he led the way towards the terrace.

George let out an oath. 'What clod left a rake lying here? I nearly stepped on it.'

'Never mind,' Aubrey said. 'Through these doors.'

They burst onto the terrace to find a shadowy figure loping toward them, her blonde hair partly covered by a knitted cap. She had a rifle slung over her back. 'Katya!' called Madame Zelinka. 'What is it?'

'Nine lorries, full of troops.'

Katya had been the most helpful of the supposedly neutral Enlightened Ones, most likely due to her unpleasant history with Holmlanders in Veltrania, her state of origin. Aubrey had no doubt that she would have been in favour of a more active role for the ancient order.

'Where are they coming from?' Von Stralick already had his pistol in his hand.

'No idea. We have the four guards who fled this place bound and gagged.'

'Four guards?' Aubrey said. 'Six left here, not four.'

'Ah! Two must have made their way down to Bardenford and raised the alarm.'

The stuttering sound of small arms fire echoed from the mountains around them. It was answered by the more authoritarian chatter of a light machine gun.

'We are trying to hold them off,' Madame Zelinka said after listening intently, 'but we are not equipped for a full-scale battle. We must help them.' She took a step toward the gate, then paused and looked back.

Aubrey went to follow, but von Stralick put out his

arm to block him. 'We will take care of this, Fitzwilliam. You and Doyle should go.'

'Where? I can't go back to Albion, not yet.'

'Fisherberg,' George said. 'Where else would Dr Tremaine go after abandoning this place?'

'You're not thinking of a rendezvous with Caroline and Sophie, are you?'

'Two birds with one stone, old man. They might be grateful for some help, and we could track down Tremaine while we're at it.'

It was an attractive suggestion, but Aubrey examined it from all sides just to make sure his personal desires weren't influencing his decision – and he had an idea.

'Very well, but I want to make a detour along the way. To Korsur.'

Von Stralick raised an eyebrow. Madame Zelinka looked interested. George was puzzled. 'Korsur, old man? Because of Madame Z's report of troop activity?'

'Hugo and I found a telephone register in the switchboard room. Korsur was the only unimportant place to receive multiple calls.'

'What if it's just because someone's mother lives there?'

'A single anomaly can be important. If you add Madame Zelinka's already mentioned Holmland troop build-up in the area it begins to look suspicious.'

'Two anomalies, then.'

'But when we have a third, then we move from "interesting" to "likely to be significant". Hugo?'

'Wait here,' von Stralick said.

In a minute, von Stralick was back. He shone his lantern on the lump of stone he held in the crook of one arm. 'Green Johannes.'

George stared. 'And Green Johannes to you, von Stralick. Whatever that means.'

'This is a very expensive piece of Green Johannes stone. It comes from Korsur, and it's freshly extracted. Someone here has been there recently.'

Aubrey reached out with a finger. The stone was warmer than he would have expected. 'I tend to believe that, where Dr Tremaine is concerned, coincidences don't exist. If he has an interest in Korsur, then we should be interested too.'

'The journey should be easier than the one we had, Fitzwilliam,' von Stralick said. 'Make your way to Bardenford and you should be able to catch a train to Hollenbruck. Many miners move about the area from all over Holmland. Many accents, some who only speak Holmlandish as their second language. You shouldn't stand out.'

'I'll leave the talking to you, old man,' George said to Aubrey.

'You'll have to walk from Hollenbruck to Korsur,' von Stralick said. 'We shall meet you in Fisherberg.'

'Sooner or later,' Madame Zelinka added, and when she glanced at von Stralick Aubrey saw another player in this drama, one with motives all of her own.

CONFIDENT AFTER HIS RECENT IMPLEMENTATION OF HIS revised levitation spell, Aubrey took George through the garden and to the very edge of the cliff at the rear of the estate. The darkened forest was hundreds of feet below, but the increased gunfire coming from the woods on the other side of the estate was enough to convince

George that this was a reasonable, if precipitous, direction to go.

Aubrey managed the spell with alacrity, and was somewhat put out by George's refusing to open his eyes on the entire downward journey, even when the muffled thumps of twin grenade explosions came from the estate overhead.

Once on the ground, they followed the river until they found a crossing, a shallow ford a mile downstream, one that – from the hoof prints – was a favourite of stock. They pushed on for an hour. George embellished his account of the crossing of Gallia, the finding of Sophie's parents, spiriting them out of the country, reporting to the Directorate and the aftermath. Even though he minimised his own part, Aubrey could see that time and time again the journey would have foundered if not for George's perseverance and ability to find a middle approach between disparate ways of thinking.

In turn, Aubrey shared with George the hardships of crossing Holmland, a far more dangerous task than journeying across friendly Gallia. Despite some past antipathy with the ex-Holmland spy, George showed some sympathy for von Stralick's illness and the difficulties it had caused.

While they trudged through the night, keeping as much as possible to the forested paths and avoiding roads, Aubrey told of the horror they had found in the basement of Dr Tremaine's estate. He was still trying to grasp the full implications of the ghastly apparatus and a hundred details that he hadn't realised he'd taken in began to emerge through George's gentle probing.

Every detail he remembered, every small item that he'd

filed away for later consideration, pointed to the fact that Dr Tremaine was working in ways that were not only mysterious, but were interlocking in a manner that was extremely ominous. Aubrey felt as if he were managing to catch sight of the smallest corner, the barest hint, of a huge and vastly complicated map made by a master cartographer.

KORSUR WAS ONE POINT OF AN UNEVEN TRIANGLE THAT ran over the Gallia–Holmland border. Stalsfrieden was about twenty miles away to the north-east of the tiny village, while Divodorum – over the border – was about thirty miles away, roughly north-west. Korsur itself wasn't far from the Mosa River, the actual border between the two countries.

Two days after leaving Dr Tremaine's retreat, Aubrey and George heard the sound of artillery from the north grow louder as they approached the tiny town, walking the five miles from Hollenbruck, the town with the closest station. They paralleled a road through heavily wooded country that was a series of low hills and shallow valleys.

Avoiding the road itself proved to be a wise decision. It allowed them to see the road block without being seen themselves and, when they found a well-concealed position amid a stand of alders, it enabled them to survey the village before they approached.

It was professional caution that prompted this, and Aubrey was glad that George and he had taken the time to stretch out on their stomachs and use their binoculars. It didn't stop George, however, from muttering a low oath, nor from Aubrey checking his binoculars to see if they were working properly.

'George,' he said, 'they aren't Albionite troops, are they?'

'They're wearing Albionite uniforms.'

The armed soldiers that were patrolling the entire perimeter of the village, two hundred or more of them, were indeed wearing the distinctive khaki tunic and trousers of the Albionite infantry. Aubrey couldn't make out a regimental badge at the shoulder, and none of the troops had the customary rifle patches above the breast pocket either. He picked one of the nearer soldiers – a private who was hauling sandbags for a machine gun emplacement that was blocking the main road into Korsur – and scrutinised him carefully, starting at the peaked cap and working downward.

When Aubrey reached the man's boots, he echoed George's oath. 'They're not Albionites,' he confirmed. 'No puttees, and I've never seen any Albionite wearing black, knee-length boots like that.'

'You're right. No Albionite mudgrubber would be seen dead in footwear like that.'

'I have an idea who might, though. Do you remember when we were in Fisherberg? The Imperial Household Guard?'

'Those beggars? The ones who thought they were a cut above everyone else, strutting about as if they owned the place?'

'They may have been arrogant, but they did have a preference for a distinctive type of black, knee-length boot.'

'So, we have Holmland troops, masquerading as Albion troops, blockading a tiny, out-of-the-way Holmland village. What *is* going on?'

'I don't know yet, but if we add this to Dr Tremaine's interest in this place, I'm more than keen to find out.' Concealing the identity of troops was a highly dubious undertaking and Aubrey dreaded what it indicated – and he feared for the inhabitants of Korsur.

He moved the binoculars over what once would have been an idyllic outlook. Korsur was a handful of buildings, all whitewashed, neatly arranged around a minute village green, complete with a bordering duck pond. Smoke came from chimneys, the steeple on the church stood proud against the blue sky. The perfection of the scene was marred, however, by the activity of the Albion-uniformed soldiers.

A score of them were working on a road barricade, intent on making it a substantial emplacement, with a heavy machine gun guarding the main road into the town. The rest were standing around the perimeter of the village, almost shoulder to shoulder, unsmiling, weapons at hand. They were facing inward, toward the village.

The commander – a colonel? – inspected the perimeter guards and once he was satisfied took up position in front of the sandbags, standing with his hands behind his back in the middle of the road, looking back toward Hollenbruck and occasionally checking his pocket watch.

Aubrey sketched the lie of the land in his notebook: a handful of neat houses, one road through the centre, a smaller joining it where the church marked the centre of the place. He followed this secondary road past the barricade being erected, and it wound into the forest and the hills, where a plume of dark smoke rose. 'The Johannes mine,' he said, and pointed.

George grunted. 'Even if this Green Johannes is a

national treasure, as von Stralick claims, I don't think the Holmland bosses would commit troops to guard it.'

'Not dressed in enemy uniforms, no.'

'Nor to guard the villagers.'

'They're not guarding the villagers, George. They're stopping them from running away. Tell me what you see.'

George picked up his binoculars. After a moment, his jaw tightened. 'Children. Old people. Being menaced by their own soldiers pretending to be our soldiers.'

A young mother, with a babe in arms and a toddler hanging onto her skirt, came out of the inn. Weeping, she tried to ask one of the officers what was going on but the soldiers who were only a few yards away from the inn prevented her from approaching. The officer ignored her entreaties. Even though she was only a few yards away, he turned his back on her.

It was as if she didn't exist.

All day, Aubrey and George observed as the troops patrolled the tiny town. The distraught villagers kept pleading with the soldiers and begging the officers. One of the soldiers became irritated and rammed the butt of his rifle into the stomach of a particularly loud old-timer. In the uproar this caused, a well-built greybeard took the opportunity and burst through the line, roaring and heading for the woods. Aubrey silently cheered this act of defiance, but the greybeard was quickly caught and clubbed to the ground. After that, the villagers moved away from the perimeter and clustered on the village green next to the pond. Some were crying, others were fearful. The village and its surrounds became a place of ugly, tense anticipation.

The afternoon wore on. Eventually, defeated and dispirited, the villagers returned to their homes. Light came from windows, the soft, yellow light of oil lamps rather than the bolder light of electricity or town gas. Aubrey could smell food cooking. Life went on, even with a few hundred ominously beweaponed soldiers only a few feet away, black silhouettes against the white-washed buildings.

From their observation post in the alders, Aubrey used binoculars to study the soldiers. None of them was a baby-faced, fresh recruit. These were hard-eyed, lean men with the air of those who'd seen action before. All day, Aubrey had heard barely a handful of words passing between them. They moved with precision and efficiency, guided by gesture and a terse, limited set of hand signals.

Aubrey scowled. He scrambled back into the stand of alders to find George cleaning his Symons pistol and munching on some food he'd been given by the Enlightened Ones. 'One good thing about Holmland sausage,' George said. 'You can't tell whether it's gone off or not, so it sort of lasts forever. Like a bite?'

'We have people in trouble here, George.'

'What? Holmlanders being guarded by Holmlanders? Isn't it their problem?'

'Even if we forget Dr Tremaine's interest in this place, which I haven't, I'm not happy about civilians being threatened by soldiers, no matter from what country.'

George thought this over. 'They do appear to be in a pickle.'

'More or less. And I do hate to see people in a pickle.'

'I know that, old man. So what are we going to do about it?'

Aubrey cocked his head and listened for a moment. The faint, distant sound of a motor gave him an idea for infiltrating the village. 'Help them, of course.'

Eight

'JUST GETTING RID OF THESE SOLDIERS WON'T BE enough,' Aubrey said as they jogged south toward Hollenbruck, the direction from which he'd heard noise. The sun was setting behind the hills. 'Something more must be done.'

'You say that as if getting rid of the soldiers is a simple thing.' George was munching on an apple even as they ran. 'I counted two hundred of them, with nine officers including that colonel. I don't think two fellows with pistols and brave hearts are going to worry them much.'

Aubrey vaulted over a rotting stump. 'True. So what we lack in numbers, we have to make up for with magic and outright trickery.'

'I love trickery.' Then George sighed. 'I wish Sophie were here. She'd be helpful in the magic department.'

'I'd be glad of any help.'

'She's been learning magic at a great rate, old man.

She's like a sponge, and she's come on in leaps and bounds.' He caught himself. 'Not that I think of her as a leaping and bounding sponge, mind you.'

'I suggest you keep that one to yourself, George.'

'I shall.'

The distant rumbling Aubrey had been keeping track of was noticeably nearer. He picked up the pace as they moved through the trees. He was careful to keep the road in sight at all times, even though this was difficult as the light faded. When they were a mile from the village, he stopped where the road curved around a large boulder so they were hidden from the road.

'I'm afraid of reprisals,' Aubrey said as they caught their breath. The warmth of the sun was still leaching from the stone and it felt good as he leaned against it. 'If we remove the troops, what's to stop the Holmland command sending more?'

'I could answer that question better if I knew what the troops were doing there in the first place.'

'True, but let's put that aside for the moment.' Aubrey lifted his head. The lorries he'd heard were definitely closer. 'What if we take this in two stages? Firstly, we remove the troops. You can call me squeamish, but I'd rather not kill any of them if we can help it.'

'You'll get no argument from me on that score.'

'Secondly, we hide the village.'

'That sounds perfect. How are you going to do it?'

'I'm not quite sure yet. That's why it's the second step rather than the first.'

George slapped him on the shoulder. 'I have confidence in you, old man. Put that brain box to work.'

'Don't worry – it's going full bore.'

'What about the first part of the plan? Removing the soldiers?'

'For that, we need to get close, which is why I've been waiting for this lorry. Quickly, take off your jacket.'

George didn't argue, simply unbuttoning the garment and handing it to Aubrey. 'Is that all? Are you sure you don't want my trousers as well?'

To George's palpable horror, Aubrey paused a moment before shaking his head. 'Jacket is enough, George, but if you can spare that cap I'd be grateful.'

George handed it over without a word.

Aubrey scurried out into the middle of the road with the jacket and cap. He arranged them hastily and then dived back behind the boulder.

'That won't trick anybody, old man.'

'I'm not done yet.' Aubrey had the spell ready, a variation of one he'd used an age ago, when trapped in the late Professor Hepworth's workshop with its murderous magical guardian. He spoke quickly, conscious of the approaching lights, and was relieved when the clothing began to fill out as if being inflated. Within seconds, in the gloom, it was easy to see a large man lying face down in the middle of the road.

George snapped off the safety of his pistol, reminding Aubrey to do the same, just as the lorry came into view, heaving itself up over a shallow crest before setting out on the long slope that would bring it near the boulder behind which Aubrey and George were hiding.

Aubrey grew tense. Crouched as he was, his leg muscles were threatening to cramp at the most inconvenient moment. He wiped his brow with the back of his hand and was conscious that he hadn't sweated as much during the day when it had been much hotter.

As the lorry neared, its headlights caught the prone shape. The lorry slowed, approached, slowed again, then stopped with brakes that noisily indicated their lack of maintenance.

'Wait until they get out,' Aubrey whispered to George.

The driver's door was flung back, groaning with the same complaint as the brakes, but instead of booted feet touching the macadamised road, a fierce electrical light stabbed out. Before Aubrey could move it swept across the road and pinned him against the boulder. He heard the unmistakeable sound of five, then six, rifle bolts, then he lost count, which didn't really matter because half a dozen was probably enough.

'Ah, Fitzwilliam! We thought we'd find you hereabouts! Care for a lift?'

Aubrey's jelly legs almost betrayed him as he rose, with George at his side. He plucked at a remark he'd prepared earlier, one that he felt useful whenever surprised and wanting to appear unfazed. 'What kept you, Hugo?'

'What kept me, Fitzwilliam? Your Miss Hepworth and your Miss Delroy, that's what kept me. They're in the back of the lorry.'

IT TOOK A FEW SECONDS OF COMPLETE FLABBERGASTEDNESS before Aubrey and George regained enough control of their bodies to sprint to the rear of the vehicle. Caroline and Sophie – in anonymous Holmland garments – looked down at them, smiling and sceptical.

George roared with laughter and seized Sophie by the waist. He lifted her bodily over the backboard, then whirled her away. She laughed with him as they spun up the middle of the road.

Aubrey was caught open-mouthed. He knew that by now he should have held out his hand, bending at the knee, to help Caroline down. Then he should have gazed into her eyes and said something that was witty, disarming and thoroughly heartfelt. After that, he would have batted away her half-formed thanks and endeared himself to her in every possible way.

He mentally rehearsed the swoop and stoop, but then became aware that Caroline was regarding him coolly. 'Aubrey,' she said. 'I'm glad to see you.'

He found a grin dragging his mouth upward. It was an acceptable start. After her unexpectedly emotional departure the last time he'd seen her, he wouldn't have been surprised to hear her say: 'Please forget what happened. It was an unfortunate lapse. I've come to my senses now, so never speak of it again.'

'Hello, Caroline,' he said and he flailed for something to add. 'I didn't expect to see you here.'

He closed his eyes for an instant, then he went to apologise for a greeting entirely devoid of panache – and George and Sophie nearly crashed into him on their final madcap swing.

Sophie laughed again. 'Aubrey,' she said, still making the first syllable of his name sound like 'Ow'. 'Madame Zelinka and Hugo found us in Fisherberg and brought us here.'

Von Stralick strolled along the side of the lorry, Madame Zelinka at his side. They were both smiling: him broadly, her less so, as was her way. 'Perhaps we should discuss this somewhere else?' the Holmlander said.

'We can't go far,' Aubrey said, 'not unless we want to run into a Holmland special unit disguised as Albionite infantry.'

Von Stralick raised an eyebrow. 'You have much to share with us.'

Caroline leaped down from the back of the lorry, landing lightly. Aubrey broke out in a very different sort of sweat when she steadied herself by taking hold of his shoulder. He enjoyed the sensation while part of his brain – a needlessly analytical part – insisted that he'd never seen Caroline need to steady herself before.

'Hugo, shouldn't we back the lorry in beside this boulder?' she asked and then her fingers brushed away something from the nape of Aubrey's neck. He nearly fainted on the spot.

In minutes, it was done. Even better, the lorry was disguised with branches torn from nearby trees, which allowed them all to sit under the canvas in the rear. A shaded lantern helped them share provisions. They sat facing each other on the benches with the food spread out on an ammunition box between them: smoked salmon, bread, pastries and milk that von Stralick had thoughtfully packed in Fisherberg. George and Sophie were next to each other, as were Madame Zelinka and von Stralick. Aubrey couldn't help but notice that Caroline sat next to Madame Zelinka, on the opposite side of the lorry from where he was. He ran through a thousand possible explanations for that, until he was quite giddy, then gave up and just enjoyed the fact that she was there.

After Aubrey and George explained the situation in Korsur and were greeted with expressions of puzzlement and concern, von Stralick recounted what had happened after the separation at Dr Tremaine's retreat.

'When we left you on the cliff top,' he said, 'we were fortunate that the Holmland troops were most foolish. Zelinka's people created havoc in the dark. Once the soldiers were lured from their transports, it was an easy thing to slip through the convoy and steal the rearmost lorry.'

'After disabling the others, of course,' Madame Zelinka added. She was holding von Stralick's hand. 'They faced a long walk down the mountainside.'

'I wanted to come straight to Korsur, to find you,' von Stralick said, 'but Zelinka insisted on going to Fisherberg.'

Her face was unreadable. 'I had business there.'

Von Stralick studied her for a moment with a mixture of exasperation and tenderness. 'She took all of her people and told me to wait at a house in Castermine, just outside the middle of the city.' He shook a finger at her. 'I thought it was one of your Enlightened houses, whatever you call them, but it belonged to the Albion Security Directorate.'

'We were there,' Caroline said. All through the narrative of von Stralick and Madame Zelinka, she had been disconcerting Aubrey even more than usual by managing to make a Holmland farm worker's ensemble look attractive, despite the way the jacket was scrunched up by a sharply pulled-in belt. Or – he swallowed when he contemplated this – perhaps because of this arrangement.

He was snapped out of his ponderings about intelligence operative couture by Caroline's amused expression.

'Aubrey? Did you hear anything we've just said?'

'All of it. Every single word. Something about a house.'

'We'd completed our Fisherberg mission. Or, at least, as much as we could for the present. We were waiting to slip out of the city.'

'Which is the opportunity I provided,' von Stralick said. 'Although they hesitated when I told them I was going to Korsur to try to find you.'

'Hesitated?' George said.

'A fraction of a second, I think it was. Possibly less.'

'Do not tease, Hugo,' Madame Zelinka growled.

'I cannot help it, my dear. It amuses me so.'

'Since it amuses you so, then I think we need to go and inspect the motor of this vehicle. I think it was developing a problem.'

'A problem?' Von Stralick lifted an eyebrow. 'Ah, a problem. I understand, my dear. After you.'

Madame Zelinka led a chuckling von Stralick into the darkness.

George coughed into his hand. 'This might be a good time to show Sophie the lie of the land. I thought I spotted a ridge not far away that could provide a useful outlook over Korsur.'

Sophie had her hands together in her lap as she sat on the bench. Her hair was bright under a black bonnet. 'Taking note of surroundings is an important function of the field operative.'

'You're a quick learner, my gem,' George said. 'A few days of Directorate training and you're reminding me of things I've already forgotten.'

Hand in hand, they slipped into the night, leaving Aubrey and Caroline alone.

She tugged at a loose bit of hair. 'A neat spell, the illusory body on the road.'

'A variation on something I'd been fiddling with for ages.'

'Clever, and useful. You need to perfect it.'

'I'll add it to the list. I think that makes item number eighty-four.'

Aubrey leaned forward. He put his elbows on his knees and rubbed his hands together. The last few weeks had been difficult. Imagining what was happening in Albion and having to deal with the very real prospect of von Stralick's dying, while suffering considerable deprivation himself, had almost used up his resources. 'Thank you for coming,' he said softly.

Caroline adjusted her hat, a loose, practical item, perfectly suited to general farm work. 'It's good that von Stralick came along when he did. It saved a great deal of trouble.'

'Getting out of Fisherberg?'

She fixed him with an inscrutable look, one that he'd be quite happy to spend hours unscruting. 'Aubrey, if he hadn't have come along I would have had to find you by myself, and I had no idea where you were.'

Aubrey repeated Caroline's words in his mind and finally accepted that she'd said what he thought she'd said. No matter how he tried to doubt or misunderstand them, he couldn't. 'Thank you,' he said eventually, smiling a little. 'I'm over… over…'

'Overjoyed? Overcome? Overthrown?'

'Overwhelmed. Quite, quite overwhelmed. I hadn't dared to hope.'

'Hope what?'

'Hope all sorts of things.'

Caroline's lips twitched at this. Then she shuffled across and sat next to him for a moment, looking at him closely. Aubrey's heart forgot how to beat for a moment and when it started it lurched along in fits and starts, mostly at the gallop. The air in the back of the lorry seemed thinner. Or thicker. Or something. And had time started playing up as well?

Caroline rose. She studied him for a moment before sitting on his knee.

He wasn't quite sure exactly how it happened. If pressed, he would have asked for three or four hundred pages to write a description of the series of impossibly graceful bendings and movements that ended up with her perched there with one hand on his shoulder. He didn't understand – and he was sure that it defied physics – how Caroline could be so light on that tiny patch of his leg, and yet so weighty in the way her presence affected him. Her gaze, for instance, probably clocked in at about fifty or sixty tons, to judge from the effect it was having on him.

He never wanted to move. Never, ever, ever. Let the heat death of the universe come along and he'd be quite happy to still have Caroline Hepworth sitting just like that, on his knee, looking at him without speaking. The tiny light of the shaded lantern was irrelevant. He saw everything, every infinitesimal detail, as if it were the brightest of bright middays.

It was so perfect, so hoped for, that Aubrey knew that it couldn't last. He glanced around.

'What are you doing?' Caroline asked very, very softly.

'Looking for whoever is going to interrupt us.'

'That's a pessimistic outlook.'

'Wars, especially, have a habit of ignoring the lives of people.'

'If you follow that through, it suggests living for the moment is best.'

'Live without planning? Without dreams? That sounds rather limited.'

'And that sounds rather like Aubrey.'

A light touch on the back of his hand and strong fingers intertwined with his. He swallowed as a ball of heat ignited in his chest.

I do believe things might work out well.

'I have a plan,' he croaked.

'I'm sure you do. But let me tell you about what Sophie and I have been up to, first.'

Nine

AUBREY HEARD THE WHOLE EXPLANATION. IN FACT, he'd never heard anything so well. Afterwards, he could have recounted it word for word, backward, so intently did he listen. He could have described every detail of the interior of the rear of the lorry. He could have itemised every night-time sound that came from the woods outside. He could have listed scents, sensations, impressions, every one of them apprehended with all his being, for at the time he knew that he'd remember it forever.

Caroline wasn't sure how much of the idea of the mission came from Lady Rose, but after Caroline and Sophie were briefed by Craddock and Tallis, they were handed over to her. She introduced them to the leaders of the Albion Suffragist Movement, women who Lady Rose knew well. These formidable women provided names and addresses of suffragist women in Holmland for Caroline and Sophie to memorise.

Aubrey made a valiant stab at keeping his incredulity under control, but he had fears it may have shown on his face. 'You were sent to promote a suffragist uprising in Holmland?'

She shrugged and the effect was so delightful that Aubrey spent some time thinking of a way to get her to do it again before he realised she'd answered. 'I beg your pardon?'

No-one could make a moue like Caroline, and she made an exquisite one that stunned Aubrey into immobility before she continued. 'It may have begun like that, in the office of whoever plans ridiculous schemes, but Lady Rose, Sophie and I had our own way of looking at it.'

'A far more sensible way than a female insurrection, one would hope.'

'Indeed. We decided that limiting ourselves to Holmland showed singular lack of imagination.'

Aubrey adjusted the arm he had around Caroline's waist – the luckiest arm in the world. 'I think I see where this is heading. You thought that the middle of a continental war would be a good time to advance the cause of votes for women across the world?'

'Aubrey, enfranchising women has been far too long coming.'

'Granted, but is this the time?'

'That's the argument that's always used to keep people in their place. I'm sure that before the abolition of slavery there were many well-meaning people shaking their heads and asking the same thing. There's never a perfect time for massive social upheaval, so we may as well do it now.'

Aubrey had to agree. 'It would send a good message.'

'We've been exhorted to help our country, but we

haven't been trusted with the vote. It was time to put an end to that, so we negotiated with your father.'

'He's an advocate of votes for women. He's had the devil of trouble getting his party on side, though.'

'Which is why he was very interested when we put this to him. He used it in a party meeting, insisting that tabling a bill for female enfranchisement was actually a vital part of Albion's war strategy.'

'No-one would come out and argue against a vital war strategy.'

'Of course not.' Caroline touched him on the chest, just over the spot where the Beccaria Cage had left its mark. 'Aubrey, at last! Votes for women!'

'Splendid. There's just a little matter of a war to get out of the way first.'

'Quite right. Once the Albion Suffragist Movement was assured of your father's commitment, all sorts of possibilities opened up. Our mission was revised to include a visit to Lutetia to encourage the Gallian Women's Rights Association to follow our route, before Sophie and I went to Fisherberg to find Count Brandt's sister.'

'No doubt you were authorised to give certain undertakings? Money? Access to intelligence?'

'Aubrey, we didn't have to promise anything. Ilse Brandt was already organising her own resistance to Chancellor Neumann's regime, and since most Holmlandish men were connected with the war in one way or another, she'd been using her female friends and acquaintances. Our assistance will make her organisation stronger, but it was on the way before we arrived.'

'A remarkable woman, just as her brother was a remark-able man.'

'She's nearly twenty years younger than he was. She told me how Count Brandt had left home before she really came to know him.'

'That's sad.'

'When she was older, in her teens, he'd visit and tell of his studies and his travels. When he came, he always brought her a present from wherever he'd been lately. He spoke to her, she said, very formally, in a way that she found both hilarious and endearing. That was when she came to love him in a way that she couldn't before.'

'Now, in his memory, she's continuing his work to bring Holmland back to its people.'

'It's her work too, Aubrey. She's not just filling in for him.'

'I didn't mean that.'

'I'm glad.' She paused. 'I know you didn't. Forgive me.'

'Of course.'

'I can be a little prickly when people make assumptions about women.'

'Really?'

This time, the squeeze on the shoulder was more of a pinch. 'Don't affect innocence, Aubrey. You know me very well.'

'Let's say I do. Is that a bad thing?'

'That you know how I feel about the way women have been treated? No. I'd say it suggests a certain familiarity.'

'And you're uncomfortable with that?'

'Would I be sitting on your knee if I were?'

'No. Probably not. Certainly not.'

'There you are, then.'

A SUBLIME TIME LATER, DURING WHICH THEY DIDN'T TALK at all, George and Sophie came back. Aubrey was disappointed when Caroline detached herself from his embrace, but understood that a time and place for everything was a useful, if unsatisfying, motto.

'I say.' George wore a huge grin and he leaned over the backboard of the lorry. 'You should hear all the magical stuff that Sophie's been getting up to, old man. Sounds as if she could be useful for whatever you're planning here.'

Sophie playfully tweaked him on the shoulder. 'George, Aubrey is an expert. I am a learner.'

'Sophie had some special instruction from Commander Craddock's people,' George said.

'Not enough,' she said, 'but they said that my talents are mostly in the magic of seeming and illusion.'

'Which is how you were able to slip into Baron von Grolman's factory,' George pointed out, 'even though your magical talents were as rusty as an iron anchor.'

Aubrey blinked. 'All anchors are iron, George.'

'Are they? That's a lot of rust, then, which is my point.'

'A point that we'll allow to slide gracefully by. Sophie, I have two items that you'll be most helpful with.'

AUBREY ENCOURAGED SOPHIE TO CREATE A SMALL LIGHT for them to work by, and he was pleased to see how readily she managed the spell. As basic as it was, doing spellcraft like this was a way to refine one's talents and keep them at one's fingertips. He ignored the occasional flickering of the little floating ball of light as Sophie maintained it while they scratched away at spells in notebooks.

Caroline, George, von Stralick and Madame Zelinka left the spell workers alone in the rear of the lorry, but Aubrey heard them outside, discussing supplies, ammunition and communication.

'Aubrey,' Sophie said, holding out her notebook, 'what do you think?'

The first thing that struck Aubrey was her bold handwriting, and how few crossings-out she'd made, even though she'd covered page after page with spell elements. He felt his hand moving to cover his own notebook, suddenly aware of his customary mess of workings, made worse by handwriting that his masters at Stonelea had despaired over, resigning themselves to the fact that 'scratchy' was the best it was going to get.

Crosses, substitutions, arrows to second thoughts written vertically in margins, letters and numbers getting closer together as the ideas came faster and faster . . . His pages were typical Aubrey work, not really fit for public consumption, not unless he actively wanted to inspire a headache in the reader.

Conscious of her anxious gaze, he worked his way through Sophie's spells and was impressed by her approach. It wasn't the way he would have done it, but that was the point. He'd asked her to help, so he had to support her way of going about it. It was good — clever, efficient, smooth in its application of the Law of Seeming — but it simply wasn't his way.

He was aware enough to realise that this was a leadership lesson, coming at a time he hadn't been expecting it. The point of delegation wasn't giving someone a job and then doing it for them. That defeated the whole purpose.

He could see a few places where the interlocking spells could be refined, and he knew that the co-efficient for parameter in the spell that would help people lose their bearings wasn't in the right place, but these were small problems, things he could help with.

As he assisted her with these improvements, he realised that, soon, Sophie was going to face a major choice in her life. Her avowed career was journalism, but she also had an eye on politics, much as Caroline and Aubrey had. She was also proving to be a capable member of a special missions team, so that career would no doubt be open to her if she chose. On top of that, Aubrey could see that she had an aptitude for magic.

Choices, he thought, and was immediately glum. Such choices, such thinking about the future was currently pointless. The immediate future was war, and it was so all-encompassing that it was impossible to see anything on the other side of it. 'After the war' had already become a wistful, longed-for time, somewhere in the never-never.

A figure emerged from the shadows. Caroline. 'We have a few hours before dawn. I suggest we all get some sleep.'

Even though Aubrey felt startlingly alert and alive, he understood the need for rest. 'Excellent idea,' he said to a world that, in this immediate vicinity at least, was remarkable.

Ten

'YOU ARE RIGHT, FITZWILLIAM.' VON STRALICK TOOK the binoculars from Aubrey and focused them carefully. 'This is no ordinary unit.'

The next morning, Aubrey and von Stralick were lying, prone, looking over the village of Korsur. The troops were still in place and still uncomplaining as they made breakfast. Extremely businesslike was the best description he could come up with, and he recorded that thought.

'I'm not heartened by that,' he said.

'You shouldn't be. The commander is the extremely well-connected Colonel Kirchoff, once head of the Imperial Household Guard. In a trade where brutality is tolerated, he has a fearsome reputation.'

'Which makes me wonder why he and his troops aren't at the front instead of guarding a village full of old people.'

'A point that may be of some interest to you. I heard

that after Kirchoff left the Imperial Household Guard he formed an elite unit under the direct control of your Dr Tremaine.'

'You haven't mentioned this before.'

'If I tried to tell you everything I've heard of Dr Tremaine doing, we'd be here until doomsday.'

The awkwardness of that figure of speech struck both of them at the same time. Von Stralick shrugged in apology before going on. 'Kirchoff's unit has undertaken a number of tasks for Dr Tremaine. Unpleasant tasks. Unsavoury tasks.'

'It must be useful, having a special unit you can order around when you need it.'

'Exactly. Where a spot of violence was needed, or someone needed to disappear, Kirchoff and his boys were the ones to do it.' Von Stralick grimaced. 'I suspect something dire is going to happen here.'

'When?'

'Soon, to judge from the way Kirchoff is checking his watch.'

'He was doing that yesterday.'

'He is a patient man, from all accounts. Not a lot of imagination, which is a blessing considering some of the things he's reputed to have done, but patient.'

Aubrey scratched at a patch of dirt on his cheek. 'Is he disciplined?'

'He is the model of Holmland military discipline. There are no distasteful orders, as far as Kirchoff is concerned.'

'So he won't argue when you and I go down there and tell him to take his troops and leave?'

Von Stralick didn't reply. For some time, he didn't even move. He kept the binoculars trained on the spare figure of Colonel Kirchoff, standing with his hands behind his back in the middle of the road, in exactly the same place Aubrey had seen him the previous day.

'Fitzwilliam, this is a bad plan.' Von Stralick put down the binoculars. 'Kirchoff won't take orders from a traitorous ex-Holmland spy and the traitorous son of the Albion Prime Minister.'

'True, but will he take orders from Dr Mordecai Tremaine?'

AUBREY HAD LEFT CAROLINE, GEORGE AND SOPHIE WITH instructions on what to do if his plan failed. They were vague instructions, because he didn't like to think too much about what a failed plan would mean for him. They mostly suggested asking Madame Zelinka for help in getting away alive.

'Look, Hugo,' Aubrey said as their lorry approached the roadblock. Von Stralick battled the large steering wheel as if he were trying to propel an elderly and well-fed aunt around a dance floor. 'Kirchoff is waiting for someone or something. If Dr Tremaine arrives with orders, I'm sure the good colonel will be receptive.'

Von Stralick spared a glance at Aubrey. 'You've managed to impress me, Fitzwilliam, as well as make me extremely nervous. You look and sound just like him.'

Aubrey hoped so. It was the only way he could see of avoiding a messy end, and while an end came to everyone, he wasn't happy about the prospect of a messy one.

He had taken on Dr Tremaine's appearance before, in order to deceive a guardian spell the rogue magician had left on the Banford Park research facility. That spell had only required a physical resemblance, not a vocal one, and still it had strained his abilities. Thus he was grateful to have Sophie's assistance with the illusion spell. Her natural talent and her recent instruction helped enormously, and he was able to add some solidity to her spellwork in a neat piece of magical collaboration.

'I won't speak,' Aubrey said to von Stralick. 'Not at first, anyway.'

'Just like Dr Tremaine.'

'Exactly. I can't just look and sound like him – I must *act* like him.'

Which means swagger, he thought, *and arrogance, and absolute certainty about everything.*

This was the challenge, of course. Appearance was one thing, but behaving like the rogue sorcerer, the man who moved whole countries about to achieve his ends, that was another.

He wiped his sweaty palms on trousers that were now black and immaculately pressed and then stared at the glistening perspiration that immediately sprang back. Impossible. Dr Tremaine didn't sweat nervously.

He spoke a few soft words and his hands were encased in gloves that were, to all appearances, soft and expensive black leather. He pushed his cape back on his shoulders and settled, just as von Stralick brought the lorry to a halt.

Colonel Kirchoff signalled to the machine gun emplacement. He was taller than Aubrey had realised, a thin man with a gaunt, almost mournful, face. He had his hand on the pistol at his belt as he approached.

'Turn around,' he said when he reached von Stralick's

window, unimpressed by von Stralick's grubby jacket and cap. 'Go back. This is a military –'

He broke off. His eyebrows shot up. He snapped to attention and saluted. 'Dr Tremaine, sir!'

Aubrey glanced at Kirchoff, then looked away.

Von Stralick leaned out of the window. 'Everything is in place?' he asked in Albionish.

Kirchoff dropped his salute, and looked puzzled. 'Of course, as you see,' he replied in the same language.

'Excellent.'

Without moving his head, Aubrey could just see Kirchoff leaning to one side to peer into the cabin of the lorry. Was the man suspicious? The yawning gulf of nervousness behind Aubrey's rib cage widened and threatened to swallow a few more major organs.

'Dr Tremaine, sir,' Kirchoff said, 'are you here to give us the orders to carry out the next phase of our assignment?'

Von Stralick cut in, every inch the officious assistant: 'Are you sure you have fully completed the first phase?'

Kirchoff gave von Stralick a look that suggested there was no difference between the ex-spy and a bucket of rotten fish. 'Of course. The crystal has been shipped out from the mine. None of the inhabitants have left since we surrounded the village. We have the Albion uniforms ready, we have the weapons in place, we have chosen the three lucky survivors and sequestered them. This was all completed yesterday, on schedule.'

Aubrey became aware that he had been gripping the door handle of the lorry harder and harder during Kirchoff's careful itemising of his unit's duties. They were going to massacre the villagers? For what purpose?

And was the man actually referring to the mysterious Crystal Johannes? Was this the great secret of Korsur that Dr Tremaine was so interested in? It didn't make sense – the rogue sorcerer wasn't interested in wealth. His ambitions were far more lofty than mere riches.

Crystal Johannes. He was sure one of his lecturers had mentioned it in passing. Or had he come across it in a footnote somewhere? The memory nibbled at him, then darted away, like a shy trout approaching a fly.

Aubrey made what he hoped was a Tremainely sound of disgust and flung open the door of the lorry. 'Enough!' he barked and was glad to hear the timbre of his voice was utterly different from his norm. He strode around to join the wide-eyed Kirchoff. With every ounce of force he could muster, he slapped the colonel on the shoulder and was pleased to see the man stagger a little. 'I'm sure you've done a fine job here, Kirchoff,' he said. 'I'm glad you've been so conscientious, but my plans have changed.'

'Changed, sir?'

'I want you to pack up your men and take them back to Fisherberg.'

'I'm sorry, sir? You're calling off the massacre?'

Aubrey swung on Kirchoff. 'Are you questioning me?' he said, casually.

Kirchoff actually went pale. Aubrey wondered what had happened in the past between the two men. 'No, sir. Not at all.'

'Good, but I thought I'd point out that it would be hard to conduct a massacre when the colonel in command doesn't have a sidearm.'

Kirchoff's hand went automatically to his belt. Aubrey

pointed a finger and Kirchoff's firearm leapt out of its holster and flew straight into Aubrey's very Tremaine-like hand. Aubrey glanced at it and removed the safety. 'Fine weapon.'

'Yes, sir,' Kirchoff whispered. His gaze was fixed on the revolver.

Aubrey snapped the safety back on, then tossed the revolver back to Kirchoff, who nearly dropped it. 'Show me your men.'

Aubrey was relieved that his little reminder of Dr Tremaine's abilities had worked as well as he'd planned. Some work with George's pistol, a pencil and piece of paper, and the Laws of Familiarity, Sympathy and Attraction, and he'd had his little demonstration ready, a way of reinforcing that Kirchoff was dealing with a master magician.

Aubrey closed his fist, crumpling the enspelled drawing of a pistol, and slipped it in his pocket. With von Stralick at his side, he strode along next to the chastened colonel, wanting to get rid of the troops quickly, but also needing to first find out as much information as he could about what had been happening in the village.

'We came in yesterday morning, as instructed,' Kirchoff said in a low voice. Two old men were standing on the green a stone's throw away. One of them was glaring, the other was bewildered. A young woman was with them. She wore a white cap and cried as she held a baby in her arms. 'We were all in Albion uniforms, and only speaking Albionish.'

'How did the men handle that?' von Stralick asked. Aubrey had to admire him. He smiled as he walked, and he asked exactly the sort of questions an eager assistant might ask.

'Most of them chose not to speak at all, once I'd explained what would happen if they spoke Holmlandish.'

'I see.'

Aubrey stopped. Smoke was still rising from the mine. 'The crystal,' he snapped. 'How did you transport it?'

Kirchoff rubbed his chin nervously. 'With none of the miners left, we had to find someone among the old men, someone who knew what he was doing.'

Aubrey stood with his hands behind his back, doing his best to adopt a Tremaine pose of deep and private thought. Carefully, he caught von Stralick's eye.

The Holmlander nodded. 'Wasn't it premature, dispensing with the miners like that?' he asked Kirchoff.

'They were my orders,' Kirchoff said stiffly. 'No word of the Crystal Johannes find was to leave the village.'

'Your actions in dispensing with the miners is a rather free interpretation of that order,' von Stralick said.

'Free, but effective.'

Aubrey whirled and fixed Kirchoff with what he hoped was a Tremaine glare. 'I hope this old man knew what he was talking about. If that crystal was damaged . . .'

Kirchoff began to sweat, a thin sheen just above his eyebrows. 'We had to bring in our largest lorry, and special timber to crate the slab for its trip to Stalsfrieden. The old man supervised.'

Largest lorry? Slab? Aubrey couldn't ask the direct question – he was Dr Tremaine, he was supposed to know – but he was bursting to know how big this piece of Crystal Johannes was.

And to know why Dr Tremaine desired it so much that he was prepared to butcher a whole village to keep its existence a secret.

Despite Kirchoff's penchant for following orders, he was still reluctant to leave what he obviously considered a job half-done. After inspecting the soldiers – a more incurious bunch Aubrey had never seen, none of them showing any interest in their colonel's visitors – he offered to 'take care of matters', as he put it.

Aubrey found it hard to keep the disgust from both Tremaine's face and voice. 'I have other plans, Colonel, and I need you and your men to be at a safe distance.'

Kirchoff wasn't a fool, Aubrey decided, and he knew that arguing with Dr Tremaine wasn't a pastime that led to a long and productive career. He saluted. 'How far is a safe distance, sir?'

'Hollenbruck should be unaffected. I'll give you an hour.'

KIRCHOFF'S UNIT BROKE FORMATION AND LEFT WITH THE same cold efficiency they had taken the village. Not a word was spoken after Kirchoff's orders were given to his officers. The entire stowing of kit and disassembling of emplacements was done silently.

Aubrey and von Stralick were on the side of the road, watching the departure. Kirchoff was in the leading lorry and saluted as it rolled out.

When the last lorry disappeared around the bend, von Stralick slipped into the woods. Aubrey stood where he was, retaining his Dr Tremaine appearance in case Kirchoff returned. He saw the villagers congregating once again on the green, amazed at the turn of events but unwilling to approach him, for which Aubrey was grateful, for it gave him some time to contemplate what it was like to be Dr Tremaine.

So this is what it's like to be feared, he thought. Once Aubrey – as Dr Tremaine – had confronted Kirchoff, every action of the colonel had been dictated by fear. He was fearful of having done the wrong thing, of not having followed orders properly, of making a mistake. There was a kind of respect in Kirchoff's eyes, too, but it was the sort of respect a beaten dog gives a capricious master. *Keep on his right side!* it said. *He's dangerous!*

The rain George had been predicting finally began to fall. Gloomily, Aubrey ignored it. He didn't like the way fear was used to move people. It fostered negativity and distrust. It crushed hope, denied joy.

But it was effective.

Von Stralick, Madame Zelinka, George, Caroline and Sophie came out of the woods. They were all armed, apart from von Stralick. 'I told them all was safe, but they preferred to believe otherwise.'

'Just being careful,' George said. 'Something I've learned, of late.'

Caroline stood directly in front of Aubrey, pistol in one hand, the other on her hip. 'I don't like your looks, Aubrey. Can you do something about them?'

'A pleasure.' Aubrey dispensed with the Dr Tremaine aspect, casting it aside like a soiled garment. 'Better?'

'Much.'

As Aubrey and his friends approached the green, avoiding puddles where they could, the villagers, one by one, came out of their dwellings in hats and heavy coats.

Finally an old gaffer – the one who had spent most of his time glaring at Kirchoff's troops – confronted them.

'And who would you be?'

Aubrey hesitated. What could he tell them? 'Friends,' he said in his best Holmlandish.

The gaffer shuffled forward. He removed his cap and held it in both hands in front of him while rain pelted on his bald head. 'What have we done?' he demanded. 'To be treated like this?'

Aubrey did his best. 'It's the war.'

'Those Albionites.' The old man spat on the ground. 'They were going to kill us, weren't they?'

'I –'

'They killed the miners. The last ten young men in the village and they killed them.'

'They wanted to join up,' a woman called, 'but they weren't allowed!'

'They were needed in the mine?' Aubrey asked. 'To find the crystal?'

The gaffer eyed Aubrey. 'You heard of that? Never seen the likes of it, any of us. As big as the church door, it was.'

'Unbelievable,' von Stralick breathed. 'Nothing like that has been found for centuries.'

And Dr Tremaine has happened to fall on the place just after it was uncovered, Aubrey thought.

'What happens now?' the gaffer said.

That's an extremely good question. His deception had undone Kirchoff's deception, but for how long?

He put up a hand. 'Kirchoff talked about choosing survivors. He said they were taken away.'

The old man scratched his chin. 'Survivors? Trudy and her children were tied up and put in the church.' He pointed at the young woman who had called out.

Survivors. Aubrey gnawed at this. Why would Kirchoff want survivors? Why would he organise survivors *before* the massacre started?

Aubrey nearly slapped himself on the forehead as the answer came to him. 'Thank you,' he said to the old man. 'You'll be safe now.'

'We will? How do you know?'

'I guarantee it.'

'YOU TOLD US THAT THERE WERE REPORTS OF UNREST from Fisherberg, about the war,' Aubrey said to George after they had all withdrawn to the edge of the village. The rain was still heavy as the Enlightened Ones made camp, but Aubrey hardly noticed. Pieces were falling into place.

'That's right, old man.'

'The stalemate has made people unhappy with the war,' Sophie said. 'Caroline and I did what we could to make them more unhappy with it.'

'I thought as much. So imagine the response in Fisherberg if this massacre had gone ahead.'

'Opposition to the war would disappear,' von Stralick said. 'A helpless village destroyed by perfidious Albionites? No patriotic Holmlander would fail to respond to that.'

'Keeping aside a few survivors would guarantee that the outrage would be known. It was well planned.' Ghastly, horrible, but well planned – so it had all the hallmarks of a Dr Tremaine plot.

Except that his plots usually had other plots hidden inside them, Aubrey thought. *So what's the plot within the plot here?*

'This Crystal Johannes,' Aubrey said to von Stralick. 'A slab that size. How much would it be worth?'

'It's incalculable. Priceless.'

That couldn't be it. What good would a lot of money do for Dr Tremaine now? He had all of Holmland at his beck and call.

Aubrey scowled and wiped rain from his brow. *Think!* he ordered himself. What would someone like Dr Tremaine want Crystal Johannes for?

As soon as he thought it, he knew it was the wrong question. Not 'What would someone like Dr Tremaine want Crystal Johannes for?' but 'What would *a magician* like Dr Tremaine want Crystal Johannes for?'

Any answer to that was likely to be very dangerous indeed.

Caroline's pistol was suddenly in her hand again. 'Lorries approaching.'

Madame Zelinka gave a short laugh. 'We do not have to worry.'

'No?'

'These are friends. These are the rest of my Enlightened Ones.'

Eleven

After some hours of sleep in the rear of their lorry, Aubrey emerged into an afternoon where the rain had stopped. The clouds were breaking up and going their own ways, like old school friends after a reunion, and blue sky was beginning take possession of the sky. His neck and back ached. He found his friends around a fire near what had been the machine gun emplacement on the main road into Korsur.

He dragged up a log and sat on it, stifling a groan. Von Stralick and Madame Zelinka were sharing a cup of coffee, while George and Sophie huddled, trying to ignore the dripping that came from the overhanging oak. 'The appearance spell,' he explained after noting the questioning looks from Caroline and Sophie. 'It was more draining than I expected.'

'Ravi's Second Principle of Magic,' Sophie murmured. 'The spell was complex, working on a number of levels.

It must have had an effect.'

Aubrey shrugged, then winced at the muscles thus abused. 'I've had worse.'

George had a suspiciously fresh-looking slice of bread in his hand. Aubrey assumed the Enlightened Ones must have brought some supplies from Fisherberg. 'Where are we off to?'

'We have some work still to do here,' Aubrey said. 'Remember the second step in our plan?'

'We've removed the troops, which is a good start.' George looked about, vaguely, then turned to Sophie. 'What was Step Two?'

'We have to hide the village.'

'That's right. Fear of reprisals.'

Each of them glanced at the village. Wholesome smoke and the smell of cooking was coming from chimneys again. Children were jumping in puddles, laughing as if they were the first ever to engage in such an outlandish activity.

'Kirchoff isn't an idiot,' von Stralick said. 'Our ruse will be discovered, eventually. He will hurry back to complete his task and hope that Dr Tremaine doesn't find out.'

'Which is why Sophie and I were working on Step Two last night,' Aubrey said. 'Sophie?'

Sophie reached into her pack and took out her spellcraft notebook. 'Misdirection. It could save the village.'

Von Stralick wrinkled his brown. 'Misdirection?'

Sophie gripped her notebook in both hands, suddenly uncertain. 'If they cannot find the village, they cannot destroy it, true?'

George beamed. 'Sophie, my gem, that sounds like a splendid Step Two.'

Sophie nudged him with her elbow. 'Whoever is coming will be using maps and compasses –'

'And roads,' George said, 'following signposts.'

'We do not have to move the village off the map,' Sophie continued. 'We simply have to make it easy for those looking for the village to get lost.'

'Confusion,' Aubrey said. 'Bafflement.'

'Making a thing appear to be what it is not,' Sophie said. 'If the road to Korsur looks like the road to somewhere else, it will be ignored. If north looks like north-east, or south-west, it will do them no good.'

'We've had many variables to take into account,' Aubrey said, but he felt excitement rising, the excitement that came from a magical challenge.

'The Law of Familiarity,' Sophie said. 'It was most important.'

'And the Law of Patterns, and the Law of Action at a Distance and an important application of the Law of Seeming.' Aubrey's voice trailed off when he saw Caroline's tolerant smile. 'Sorry. Boring magic talk?'

'I'm sure it's interesting to both of you,' Caroline said. 'I think I'm speaking for the rest of us when I say that we'd much rather see your work in action than hear it discussed.'

With that, they set about making a village vanish.

'IF I DIDN'T KNOW BETTER,' GEORGE ANNOUNCED IN THE darkness, 'I'd think I'd eaten some bad oysters.'

'I doubt the Holmland army will be sampling seafood on its way to destroy Korsur,' Aubrey said, but he knew what George was talking about. Almost as an afterthought, he'd woven a spell that would cause a faint level of nausea when facing the direction of the village. He hoped it was subtle enough to encourage anyone approaching to look in other directions, where Sophie had done her best to make more attractive options appear.

Night had fallen by the time that Sophie and he had completed the hiding of Korsur. Aubrey began the project assuring himself that he would simply coordinate and help Sophie along with her spell definitions. Soon, however, the discussions involved him to an extent that he was seeing places to concatenate spells, joining them together to enhance their effects and their efficiency. Naturally, he cast the spells that enabled this concatenation and one thing led to another ...

The result was a dizzying locality, a hidden village and a thundering headache that tested the limits of his skull. He did his best to hide his discomfort as Sophie was looking wan after her efforts and he didn't want to make her feel worse.

Midnight was nearing by the time all was done. Aubrey was yearning for a soft place to stretch out – rock, stone, slab of concrete – but von Stralick chose this time to stroll over from the fire where he'd been conferring with Madame Zelinka. He brought a lantern and squatted next to where Aubrey was sitting, his back against a lorry, a groundsheet spread out beneath him.

'Fitzwilliam, I need to tell you something I neglected to mention earlier.'

Aubrey yawned, which made his headache move around abominably. 'Neglected? I can't imagine you neglecting anything, Hugo.'

'Perhaps neglected is not the right word.'

'What about "held back"? I'll wager that's more accurate.'

Von Stralick still hadn't regained all the weight he'd lost in his illness, but he was definitely looking more robust. Aubrey decided that Madame Zelinka must have been taking good care of him. 'Before we left Fisherberg, I had time to meet an old colleague of mine.'

'From your spying days?'

'Indeed. She confirmed much of what the Enlightened Ones reported about the useful opposition to the Chancellor. She also gave me a file before she had to flee Fisherberg.'

'Had to flee? Why?'

'For the same reason I'm not welcome there. The faction of the intelligence service that is now in the ascendant is not the faction to which we once belonged.'

'Where?'

'Where what?'

'Where did she go?'

'Really, Fitzwilliam, does it matter?'

'It does if you're suspicious. Which I am.'

'Do not be. I trust her with my life.'

'I hope it doesn't come to that. The file?'

'Copies of memoranda from the Holmland Supreme Army Command, among other things. They contain details of what they're calling the next phase of the war.'

Von Stralick gave him a battered folder, bulging with documents. Aubrey leafed through them and grew increasingly wide-eyed. Troop dispersals, matériel requisitions, supply invoices – and maps. Many, many maps.

'The Directorate would give anything for this.'

'I'm sure they would.'

Aubrey closed the file and rested his hands on top of it. Von Stralick's face was shrouded, silhouetted as he was against the campfire. 'Why are you doing this, Hugo?'

Von Stralick picked at some mud on the knee of his trousers. 'Because I am a loyal Holmlander.'

'Passing secret documents to the enemy is an action of a loyal Holmlander?'

'Loyalty is a complex thing, Fitzwilliam, as I'm sure you've found.'

Aubrey recalled his discussion with George about rational patriotism. Blindly following anything was not good. Rationally following something, aware of the issues, the strengths and shortcomings, was better.

'You think that this information will help Albion bring the war to a swift conclusion.'

'I do. A long, drawn-out war would be bad for everyone. Decisive action is needed.'

'Then why have you waited until now to give it to me?'

Von Stralick was silent for a moment, nodding. 'It's you, Fitzwilliam. You are the problem.'

'Me?'

'It is difficult to understand you, Fitzwilliam. You are an Albionite, but you do not always act in the interests of Albion. Not obviously.'

'I beg your pardon. I always act in the interests of Albion.'

'It is hard to see that nursing a Holmland spy back to health is in the interests of Albion, for instance.'

'Ex-Holmland spy,' Aubrey mumbled, his thoughts elsewhere. *Had* he been acting against Albion?

'And what about in Stalsfrieden? You had a herd of giant concrete animals at your disposal. You could have killed all the Holmland soldiers stationed there.'

'It mightn't have been as easy as you think. I barely had those beasts under control,' Aubrey said, but he remembered the chaotic events as they escaped the clutches of Baron von Grolman. Did he overlook a chance to wreak even more havoc?

'Don't forget what you've done here,' von Stralick continued. 'You've saved the population of an entire Holmland village from being killed. Is that in the interests of Albion?'

'I made sure Albion wasn't blamed for a massacre, that's all. Now Dr Tremaine doesn't have an outrage to rally ordinary Holmlanders behind.'

'Then you went on and saved the village from any reprisals.'

'More of the same. It makes good strategic sense, protecting Albion's interests.'

'And that is all?'

It was Aubrey's turn for silence. Behind them, his friends and the Enlightened Ones were outlined against the glow of the fire, talking in low, casual murmurs. 'I don't like to see innocent people being hurt,' he said eventually. 'Sorry.'

'Tcha! Don't be afraid of compassion, Fitzwilliam. It is one reason that I am giving you this file.'

'What?' Aubrey blinked and ran a hand over the dossier. 'Er, any other reasons?'

'You think about your actions instead of blindly going ahead. That reassures me that I'm doing the right thing.'

Aubrey cleared his throat. *Was it getting cold?* 'I appreciate it, Hugo.' He opened the file and raised an eyebrow at the assorted photographs of Holmland generals and political leaders. Good portrait quality photographs. 'And what exactly is the Supreme Army Command planning next?'

'It's all in there,' von Stralick said. 'Feints, withdrawals, build-ups. I spent most of the journey here piecing it together, and I'm not sure that I have it all straight, but it looks as if the generals want to push into Gallia via Divodorum rather than through the north-west.'

'I had fears that this could be the case.'

'Troops have been falling back and digging in on the western front to hold the line.' Von Stralick leaned forward and sifted through papers. 'All other capacities will be directed to the Divodorum region. A massive effort will be made to break through into Gallia and crush its resistance. Soon.'

Aubrey had a moment of insight. This could be a pivotal moment on which the entire outcome of the war depended. Like a boulder balanced on the peak of a hill, a push and it would roll one way, a different push and it would roll the other.

If this Holmland plan were successful, the world that this would create wouldn't be one that Aubrey would be happy living in. A battle to break through at Divodorum could be big enough to present the world with an immortal Dr Tremaine.

Reasons aplenty to stop this from happening, but Aubrey also spared a thought for the men on the ground. He'd had a glimpse of the developing war front when they'd skirted the trenches outside Divodorum and what he had seen was the dusty, benighted plight of the infantry, dug in amid the blood and terror, holding their positions or trying to advance inch by inch. He remembered the lads who were joining up when George and he had attempted to do the same. Had they met their fate in the squalor that was the trenches?

If Aubrey could do something to prevent these ordinary men from being ground away, stone against stone, that was reason enough to risk his own life – and the life of his friends, loath though he was to contemplate this.

'Note how the generals talk about strategic aims,' von Stralick said, 'and tactical movements and battleground outcomes. From their vantage point, well behind the lines, it all makes sense.'

'I'm sure it does. To them.' Aubrey hummed a little, thinking. 'Thank you, Hugo. You've given me something else to worry about.'

'My pleasure, Fitzwilliam. In the time I have known you, I've come to think that I'd rather have you worrying about a problem than most other people.'

Von Stralick flipped an ironic salute then slipped off, taking his lantern with him. Aubrey watched the night, the moving figures that were the Enlightened Ones, the shapes of the humble buildings of Korsur, and he reluctantly made an effort to take this new ball of worries and roll it to the corner of his mind.

Twelve

THE THREE LORRIES WERE A RAGTAG ASSORTMENT, but they were efficient and reliable. They made short work of any grade but the steepest, and laughed when two shallow streams needed fording where bridges had been blown up – but Aubrey found them to be the most uncomfortable mode of transport since their wild escape in the belly of a concrete elephant. The seats in the rear were hard wooden slats, dust was sucked into the passenger area with an efficiency household appliances could only dream of, and the suspension had the almost magical ability to amplify every jolt, bump and judder straight through the chassis into the spine of the unfortunate passengers.

During the journey, sitting in the rear of one lorry with his friends, Aubrey questioned von Stralick, trying to find out more information about the Holmland deployment.

'Who's in charge of this?' he shouted to von Stralick sitting next to him. The back of the lorry was only covered by canvas, so the noise was appalling. Caroline was opposite, doing her best to talk to Sophie and Madame Zelinka, while George was frowning over a Holmlandish newspaper one of the Enlightened Ones had given him. Despite his extraordinary lack of ability with languages, George couldn't ignore the prospect of a good newspaper.

'This new push? Since it's the army alone, the Supreme Army Command is rubbing its hands together at the prospect of glory and stealing a march over the navy. But inside that august body is the Central Staff.'

'Central Staff? Sounds harmless enough.'

'The Central Staff is the six most senior generals. It is responsible for the conduct of the war.'

'Along with the Chancellor.'

'The Chancellor takes care of the politics, but is cunning enough to realise that running a battle is a specialised task. He leaves the details to the Central Staff.'

Aubrey sat back. Canvas flapped at his back, and he barely noticed the concerned look Caroline flashed him.

'You're humming again,' von Stralick said.

'Just thinking. How far is it to Divodorum?'

Aubrey desperately wanted to contact the Directorate. He was acutely aware that they were in highly dangerous territory and that they had intelligence that could be crucial to the outcome of the war. It was his duty to let the Albion intelligence services know what was going on.

After discussing it with his friends, the decision was to get to their secret base in Divodorum and use the wireless installation there. The problem was that Divodorum was on the other side of the border. When Caroline, George, Sophie and Aubrey had made the dangerous crossing from Divodorum to Stalsfrieden soon after the Holmlanders attacked, it had been chaos. Avoiding patrols and supply lines had been a heady, perilous business. Trying to get three lorries across would have been impossible if not for the Enlightened Ones.

Madame Zelinka reminded them that, over the centuries, the Enlightened Ones had perfected the art of crossing borders unseen and unmolested. She'd put the matter in the hands of Katya, who had conferred with the passage specialists among the Enlightened Ones. The result was this circuitous journey, which was paralleling the Mosa River and taking them through wilderness that looked as if it had remained undisturbed for years.

'How far? I have no idea,' von Stralick said, 'but I have a feeling that it might be an interesting journey.'

MANY TWISTINGS AND TURNINGS LATER, ALL SLOPING downward and bringing them closer to the river through woods that looked impenetrable until one of the Enlightened Ones hanging out of the window of the lead lorry directed the way, they found what Katya assured them was a well-used crossing place – or had been, when the Romans had built the bridge. Now, the bridge was a crumbling ruin, to Aubrey's eye, pilings well spaced and disguised by creepers and other tenacious vegetation. The Mosa was broad here, a hundred yards or more of deep, swift water, but Katya and half a dozen of her comrades darted off into the undergrowth while Aubrey and his friends wondered how they were going to get across, let alone the lorries.

The ropes and timbers that the Enlightened Ones returned with looked sturdy enough, but Aubrey wasn't convinced, even when Madame Zelinka assured him that such materials were kept in caves on either side of such crossings, all over the Continent. Katya explained that it was a matter of bridging the approach with the materials, then, after a lorry had driven as far as it could, the next span was bridged while the span already crossed was disassembled to provide the material for the subsequent span. Once the lorry was safely on the other side, the materials were gathered and the process was to be repeated for the others.

Aubrey was glad to step back and let the Enlightened Ones take charge. The speed of their construction spoke of many years' experience, and the way the lorry was driven over the narrow beams made Aubrey stare. When he came to walk across the same narrow beams, he appreciated the skill involved even more.

It took most of the morning, but the crossing was managed with only a few moments of terror from the more height-averse of the small band.

Material packed and stowed in a cave nearby, they were on their way to Divodorum. Caroline kept a space in the back of one of the lorries for Aubrey and, snatching happiness where he could, he was comfortable by her side. So much so, he fell asleep on her shoulder.

He was woken when the movement of the lorries became smoother. Divodorum was in sight and the town was almost unrecognisable.

The devastation shocked Aubrey and emphasised, more

than anything else that had happened, how removed he had been from the realities of the war. Absorbed as he'd been by the need for survival, he had no grasp of what had been happening on a larger scale – but he'd been aware he'd been unaware, and it had grated on him.

With the lorries pulled off the road, screened by some quickly cut branches, they surveyed the city. 'Divodorum itself has been under attack?'

'Sorry, old man,' George said, 'I forgot you've been out of things.'

'The Holmlanders used railway guns, pulled up near Stalsfrieden,' Sophie explained, 'and airship attacks, too.'

Mention of Stalsfrieden reminded Aubrey that the slab of mysterious Crystal Johannes had been taken there, and he wondered if a cross-border expedition mightn't be in order, once they'd reported to the Directorate.

'An aerial battle took place last week,' Caroline said. 'After days of Holmland airships dropping bombs on Divodorum, Gallia managed to scrape together a dozen dirigibles and two score ornithopters. They met a Holmland force and repelled them thanks to Major Saltin, but they suffered horrible losses.'

'Major Saltin? He's alive?' While they were in Divodorum on their previous mission, news had come to them that Major Saltin had perished in an accident.

'He survived his crash, but had to walk twenty miles, avoiding Holmland patrols, to get back to Divodorum. Since then, he's been in the thick of things, of course. According to reports, he's still in the city, rallying troops at the fortress, helping to handle reinforcements as they come in via train and sending them off to the front.'

'The townspeople?'

'Mostly fled. With the railway bridge down, a temporary depot has been set up on the other side of the river. Despite Holmland efforts, it's still open. People are using the road bridge, but crossing the river and joining the train is the quickest way out.'

The more Aubrey studied the cityscape through his field glasses, the more signs of destruction he could see. Not just the obvious artillery and bomb strikes, but fire had raged through parts of the city too. He saw few signs of occupation apart from a lone figure hurrying along the embankment near the Divodorum docks. The way he kept looking upward, over his shoulder, was an indication that he fully expected death to rain from above at any minute.

'We'll just have to hope that our base is still intact,' Aubrey said. He cleaned the lenses of the field glasses before he put them away.

Aubrey had a great deal of affection for the facility he and his friends had set up in Divodorum. Left on their own with repeated instructions to hold the location, together they had worked to make the dilapidated factory secure and comfortable. George's considerable handyman skills, plenty of building materials, and lots of time on their hands had transformed the place into a communications centre and base for forays into Holmland.

But it was more than that, Aubrey recalled fondly as the lorries set off again. The four of them had made it a snug refuge. With war pressing close, with the streets alert and nervous, twitching at the thought of Holmland spies, they had laid in supplies enough to keep their spirits up. With Sophie and George's cooking, with friends close by, and despite living in what had been a factory, Aubrey had enjoyed their time there.

He hoped it hadn't been bombed.

When the lorries reached the outskirts of the city, they encountered streets that weren't deserted, but neither did they have to battle their way along. Aubrey counted three cafés that were still open, despite the hard times, and two of them had tables on the street where a handful of patrons was enjoying the sun. The sight of two lorries in convoy and not heading toward the fortress did cause some curiosity, but Aubrey imagined that enough unusual events had occurred in Divodorum for the phenomenon to be shrugged off.

When the lorries pulled up at the gates of their base, in the industrial quarter near the river, Aubrey held up a hand, listening, stopping anyone from alighting, but the only sound he could hear was the distant pounding of artillery and the sound of a siren that came from the direction of the airfield.

'Still looks secure,' George said when he joined Aubrey outside the gate. He held up the large padlock and inspected it. 'It's the same one I left on it.'

Aubrey chinned himself up and was relieved to see, undisturbed, the dominoes he'd distributed about the perimeter, all magically entangled and ready to sound an alarm if intruders crossed the boundary. 'All looks well,' he said, dusting his hands together. 'Now, who has the keys?'

George peered at the lock, then at Aubrey, while making a great show of patting all his pockets. Sophie looked quizzical. Caroline gave a sigh of impatience, then took the lock in hand while extracting two curious wire shapes from her belt. In seconds, the lock fell apart.

Once the main doors had been hauled back, the interior of the factory beckoned. Aubrey stepped inside and took in the smell of glue and leather, and was satisfied with their work. They'd gone to great pains to make this floor of the factory look like the bookbindery it was meant to be. He ran his hand over a bench strewn with leatherworking tools and was confident that the only visitor had been the dust fairy, and she'd brought friends.

With evening drawing in, Von Stralick and Madame Zelinka supervised the Enlightened Ones as they backed the lorries into the yard and began unloading the supplies. George and Sophie disappeared, carrying some of the boxes of provisions the Enlightened Ones had brought with them. Soon, the smell of frying onions wafted from the kitchen and Aubrey's stomach was rumbling.

Caroline waved to him from the other side of the factory. 'I want to check the antenna,' she called, pointing up the stairs.

Aubrey considered whether that was an invitation. It was possible, but assuming such would be most gauche, and asking if he could come would sound even more gauche. Since he had no desire to head a list of Great Moments in Gaucherie, he stayed mum.

Caroline gazed at him for a moment from the far side of the factory floor, past the dozen or so Enlightened Ones who were carefully balancing large crates between them on their way downstairs, past the bookbinding paraphernalia, past the dust and neglect, and he saw her face as clearly as if he were standing next to her. She smiled. 'Will you come with me?'

ON THEIR PREVIOUS VISIT TO DIVODORUM, THEY HAD LAID out the antenna by stretching it in an array from parapet to parapet, criss-crossing the roof. It couldn't be seen from the yard below, let alone the street, but it made the roof a difficult place to traverse.

'All is in order,' Caroline murmured as she walked along the first stretch of wire, trailing a delicate hand near, but not touching, the wire.

'You do fine work,' Aubrey said as he followed her. The tarred roof of the quondam factory was flat, at least in theory, and it provided a fine outlook over Divodorum, where the familiar sights of the university and the fortress were obvious, even in the gathering darkness.

He stopped and put a hand to his eyes, the better to see. That tower near the fortress was new. Higher than the guard towers, it looked spindly and makeshift – and was it actually within the walls of the fortress itself?

'It's important work.' Caroline reached the end of the roof. She ducked under the next wire with one supple movement, then began to track back the other way. 'We must get your information back to the Directorate.'

'Of course.' Aubrey took a last look at the mysterious tower and joined her. Caroline was a slim shadow in the darkness ahead of him, but unmistakable nonetheless. In fact, he was sure he could pick her form out in any 'Spot the Silhouette' competition. The thought made his collar hot and tight and he nearly missed Caroline reaching the end, ducking and making her way back to where he stood.

A roar came from the north-west, a heavy pounding that brought them up short and held them unmoving for a minute or two. When it stopped, he could make out Caroline's eyes in the darkness. They were solemn.

'Gallian or Holmlandish?' she asked.

'Holmlandish, I'd say. They're the only ones with those twelve-inch guns.'

Caroline glanced back at the source of the barrage.

'Nine-hundred-pound shells,' Aubrey added. 'Nasty.'

'You can tell that from the sound?'

'Not exactly. Hugo had some documents about what the Holmlanders are hauling up to break the lines. I think they're sending the Gallians a few goodnight wishes.'

Caroline paused for a moment, then turned her head toward the north-west. 'You're sure they'll come in this direction?'

'If they do, they'll punch right into the heart of Gallia.'

Caroline didn't say anything for a while. A breeze stole through the night and ruffled the hair at the back of her neck. In a movement so artless and unconscious that Aubrey nearly wept, she caught an errant lock and twisted it to and fro for a moment.

'We don't want that,' she said finally, briskly. 'What are you going to do about it?'

'Get some advice from those who should know best,' he said. 'Is the antenna in good shape?'

'It's acceptable.' She sighed and stretched. 'From the sounds of it, I may be in for a long night.'

Thirteen

CAROLINE HEPWORTH WITH DARK CIRCLES UNDER her eyes, Aubrey decided as he watched her slowly mount the stairs from the basement in the pre-dawn light, was still a delight. He fumbled with the coffee pot, eager to make sure that her mug was full and hot. 'Here.'

'Just what I need – my ninth coffee for the night.'

Aubrey bit his tongue. It was her tenth and it wasn't actually night any more. He could make out the stacks of timber and discarded ironwork in the yard, if dimly, but he was starting to understand that correcting such things wasn't important. 'Did a response come through at all?'

Caroline sat at the table and inhaled from her coffee, closing her eyes for a moment. 'Interference.' She made a face. Lovely though it was, Aubrey accepted that it was her version of a grimace of disapproval. 'The Holmlanders have found a way to distort messages. We had to change frequencies often, randomly, but we finally managed to communicate.'

'We have orders?'

'We do.'

Aubrey couldn't help himself. 'Was there anything about me?'

'I wouldn't know, would I? You're the decoder.'

'Really? You know how to use the machine as well as I do.'

'I left *most* of the work to you. I only ran the first few, to make sure they were coming through properly.'

'And was I mentioned?'

'Only inasmuch as you were named in the orders. It was as if you hadn't done anything unusual, haring off the way you did.'

Aubrey's estimation of the wiles of Commanders Craddock and Tallis, already significant, rose again. He wondered what it would take to faze them.

'They prize initiative,' he said and he went to pour himself a coffee. Before he could, however, the floor and walls of the factory shook, and dust trickled from overhead. In the distance, an explosion sounded – a deep, frightening thump quite unlike the artillery barrage of the night before.

He was on his feet in an instant, but he wasn't quick enough to beat Caroline to the front door. She clung to the frame with one hand and pointed to the north with the other. 'There!'

Near the fortress, a pillar of flame rose to the heavens. Overhead, banking away from the site of the explosion, was a single airship. It was a sleek model, smaller than the usual giant dirigibles, and it was moving fast. He braced himself for further explosions but either the craft was having trouble with its bomb delivery or it had discharged its payload.

The fiery pillar was subsiding, but Aubrey didn't like the look of it. The way the dense black smoke wrapped around it and the streaks of unsettling green amid the flames made it look unhealthy. He couldn't feel anything, not at this distance, but he was sure that if he was nearer he'd be able to taste the magic.

A sleepy-looking George joined them, his sandy hair in disarray. 'Good Lord,' he said. 'Is that what Divodorum has been putting up with since we left?'

'I don't think so,' Aubrey said. 'If this sort of thing had been regularly falling on the city, I'm not sure that we would have found anything when we came back.'

Madame Zelinka and von Stralick came down the stairs. Von Stralick looked well and remarkably spruce in the clean clothes he'd found in the basement store room. 'This is not good.' Madame Zelinka was grim. 'From the roof, we could see that the bomb landed near the river.'

'Not the fortress?' Aubrey said.

'Not far from it. They missed? Were aiming for something else? Who can tell?'

'The explosion had something uncanny about it,' Aubrey said. The combination of magic and aeronautical engineering was a worrying development.

'We should investigate,' von Stralick said.

'I agree.' Caroline put her coffee mug on the table and rose. 'Now would be best, I'd say.'

'It would,' Aubrey said, and he took his courage in his hands, 'but you need to stay here and get some sleep. You've been up all night.'

Caroline looked at him evenly. 'As have you.'

'I slept while you were busy. I even managed a bath and to find a new uniform. I'm more rested than you are.'

Caroline faced him squarely, obviously tired but equally obviously not willing to admit it. George and von Stralick looked uncomfortable. Madame Zelinka simply shrugged. 'I shall ready my people.'

Von Stralick, full of tact on this occasion, jumped to agree. 'Excellent idea. I shall assist you.'

'George?' Aubrey said. 'Have you something you should be doing?'

'That's right. Sophie needs some help in the workshop. She had plans for better concealing this place through some magical innovation or other.'

Aubrey waited for George to nab the coffee pot and two cups before hurrying off, but Caroline jumped in before he could start. 'Now, Aubrey, are you reassuming command of our unit, expanded as it is?'

Very carefully, Aubrey nodded. 'I suppose I am.'

'Which means that you're *ordering* me to stay behind, despite the fact we'd worked out that such a command structure ill-suited our special group?'

'When you say *order*,' Aubrey began, choosing his words with all the care of a bomb disposal expert deciding which wire to cut, 'I was actually using it in the sense of "a very sensible suggestion, one that is open to discussion".'

'Ah. I hoped so.'

'And?'

'Nothing. My staying behind and getting some sleep is probably a good idea. I was too tired to realise when you first suggested it.'

Aubrey turned this statement around and examined it from all sides before responding. 'So you'll stay here and rest?'

'Since it wasn't an order in that old-fashioned, inappropriate way, of course I shall.'

'Caroline, if I ever stop taking it for granted that I can't take you for granted, you'll disabuse me of that notion, won't you?'

She yawned, covering her mouth with an effort. 'Of course I shall, Aubrey. Of course I shall.'

WHILE VON STRALICK MARSHALLED THE LORRIES, AUBREY had an idea. He had a notion that being independent of the vehicles might be an advantage, so he went via the kitchen to the rear yard of the factory. He hoped that the bicycles they had purchased on their last sortie in Divodorum were still safely locked in the shed, and when he used the key he'd retrieved from a nail behind a dreadfully obsolete calendar, he was relieved to discover that some vigorous work with a pump was all that was needed to make the bicycles fit for use again.

George was finishing a slice of toast and butter as he approached with Sophie. 'Ah. Good thinking, old man. Should we drag out civilian clothes?'

Aubrey hesitated for a moment before answering. 'Let's stay in our field uniforms. I'm thinking that we might need to make an official visit to the fortress.'

'Capital. I'll take care of business while you hover at the rear.'

'I beg your pardon?'

'You're the Traitor of Albion, remember? I have the proper credentials to get us into the place. As long as you tag along as my batman, it shouldn't be a problem.'

'Wait – batman?'

'I've thought this through, old man, and I'm sure it's best if you pose as my military valet.'

'Your batman.'

'That's right. It gives you an excuse to be with me, and it gives the Gallians an excuse to ignore you. No-one looks too closely at a batman.'

Sophie poked George. 'You are enjoying this. Do not tease so.'

George spread his hands, a picture of innocence. 'I'm just doing what I can to keep this team operating at peak efficiency, my gem. Part of which are my orders to keep Aubrey from being shot, which is what I intend to do.'

As THEY MADE THEIR WAY ALONG THE DOCK ROAD THAT ran alongside the river, Aubrey had to grit his teeth and squint, as if facing a grit-laden gale. 'You can't feel anything?' he asked Sophie, who was riding next to him.

She shook her head. 'I'm not as practised as you. I had never heard of this confusion of senses that you speak of.'

Ahead, one of the last of the warehouses was ablaze – the source of Aubrey's magically induced discomfort. A small crowd had gathered and stood on the riverbank side of the road in front of the warehouse. The Enlightened Ones were standing next to their lorries, a distance away, with von Stralick and Madame Zelinka conferring with two or three of their comrades. Smoke swirled into the air, and it moved with a sluggishness that Aubrey didn't like at all.

'I wish I hadn't either.' Aubrey had drifts of purple light on his tastebuds; the effect was verging on painful. At the same time his skin crawled with what he could only liken to anchovy flavour; he longed to scratch, but knew it would do no good.

George and he had had some experience with magical bombs dropped from Holmland airships back in Trinovant, enough for him to feel the similarities. This one had fallen about half a mile from the fortress, which loomed on the other side of the river. Aubrey wondered if it was the result of poor aiming or faulty equipment, or whether the bomb had fallen exactly where it was meant to.

At that moment, they passed the last of a row of oaks and the fortress came into view. He stared at it in disbelief.

In the middle of the fortress, in what must have been the parade ground, rose an iron construction, nearly as tall as the guard towers themselves. It was a madcap construction of girders, struts and bracings, obviously makeshift despite its size. Four great arms projected from the top, and it reminded Aubrey of nothing as much as a windmill made of the contents of a scrap metal yard, but he doubted that the arms could rotate, so massive were they.

'It looks like a giant electrical fan,' Sophie said. 'So big. What is it for?'

'I think we may have to find out,' Aubrey said, 'but not before we do what we can about this fire.'

Fifty yards away from the blaze, Aubrey signalled his friends to stop. He didn't want to come close, not immed-iately, not now that he could see what was engulfing the warehouse.

While the fire was roaring away, doing its best to consume the building, anything made of metal had come alive. Beams writhed like tentacles in the flames. Roofing iron rippled, curling and uncurling like beckoning fingers, while fire roared through the gaps.

Aubrey gnawed at his lip. He tried to divine if this animation of non-living materials was the intended outcome or simply an accident, but the magic ebbed and flowed, powerful and erratic one instant, almost vanishing the next.

George tapped him on the shoulder. 'Look.'

On the other side of the river, soldiers were gathering on the walls of the fortress to watch the fire. 'You'd think they'd try to do something about it,' Aubrey said and he started sifting through possible magical assistance he could bring to the situation. Weather magic, though he was loath to try it? The Law of Transference, with the river so close at hand?

'I think they are waiting for help,' Sophie said. 'From the river.'

A whistle sounded as a vessel approached from upriver, steam coming from two smokestacks. The purpose of the craft's second chimney was revealed when the vessel tied up to a jetty opposite the blazing warehouse and a jet of water arced from the rear of the boat onto the flames.

'A steam pump.' Aubrey was impressed by the technology, but dismayed when the plume of water stuttered and cut out. Crewman scurried about, shouting and arguing. The water jet resumed, but the fire fighters had trouble keeping it constant.

Aubrey concentrated. 'Ah. The regulator valve is magically enhanced to maximise output.' He bit his lip. 'The spell is fluctuating.'

'Poor spellcrafting?' Sophie asked. 'An effect of the magical fire?'

'Perhaps.' Aubrey glanced at the fortress and the strange tower. 'Perhaps.'

Spray wafted to them on the breeze and the crowd retreated, away from the jet of water. Aubrey wiped his face. The fire fighters were making some headway – the flames were noticeably less vigorous, but girders were still writhing about on either side of the huge gap that had opened when part of the roof collapsed. Madame Zelinka was organising the Enlightened Ones into squads.

'Let's leave this to them for the moment,' Aubrey said. He eyed the peculiar tower in the fortress. 'We have other matters to investigate.'

They pedalled across the Market Bridge, half a mile downriver from the blaze, and looked to where the fortress stood.

The guards at the gatehouse were diligent, and prompt enough as they examined George's credentials, but Aubrey was concerned at how fatigued they looked, as if they hadn't slept for days. The younger of the two guards – and neither of them looked seventeen – yawned almost continuously while his comrade summoned Major Saltin on the telephone.

'Doyle!' the Gallian cried as soon as he came into view. He was wearing his navy blue air service uniform, but Aubrey noted that it had been patched at the shoulder, and one sleeve was singed.

Saltin saw Aubrey. He stopped, eyes wide, mouth moving silently. Aubrey was alarmed that he was about to cry out but George was alert. He took Saltin's arm. 'You don't know my batman, do you, Saltin? Private Taylor?'

Saltin gaped at George. 'Taylor? Batman?'

'My servant,' George said jovially. 'A dab hand at shining boots, aren't you, Taylor?'

Aubrey saluted with what he hoped was the right touch of servility. 'Sir.'

'Taylor,' Saltin repeated dubiously. 'What is going on?'

'War is a confusing time, Saltin,' George said, 'but I have some information that might help clear things up. D'you have anywhere we can speak in private?'

Saltin scowled, but then he brightened. 'Do not tell me that this is Mme Delroy I see here? M'mselle, why aren't you back in Lutetia? You are the only intelligent one writing for that newspaper of yours!'

Sophie extended her hand. 'High praise from the Chevalier of the Skies.'

'Chevalier of the Skies?' George repeated. 'Is that one yours, Sophie?'

'Her reports have been good for my career.' Saltin beamed. 'But now, come away, I have much confusion that needs removing.'

Fourteen

'So you are not a traitor, Fitzwilliam,' Saltin said, 'despite what the newspapers say.'

Major Saltin's office was on the ground floor of the administration wing of the fortress. Aubrey, George and Sophie were sitting in front of Saltin's desk in hard chairs. Behind Saltin a window looked over the parade grounds, and it was only with difficulty that Aubrey tore his gaze away from the unlikely structure that towered where the central flagpole had once stood. Before he could respond, George cut in.

'Traitor? Aubrey? I should think not, Saltin. If it weren't for Aubrey, Divodorum would be overrun with giant mechanical golems.'

'Mechanical golems?' Saltin fingered his moustache. 'This sounds as if you have a tale to tell me.'

The tale took some telling, enough for Major Saltin to interrupt it in the middle and summon coffee, apologising for the poor quality before the story resumed. Aubrey had to admit that Saltin was a fine audience. He listened attentively and seethed at the perfidy of the Holmlanders, shook his head at the outrageousness of Dr Tremaine's plans and groaned at Sophie's description of Lutetia in the grip of political infighting.

Aubrey finished by detailing his suspicions about the Holmland build-up in the area. 'What do you think, Saltin?'

Saltin sat back in his chair and laced his fingers on his chest. 'We saw preparations before our last airship was shot down. Pushing through Divodorum could be tempting.'

Saltin glanced to the north-east. Aubrey could imagine him seeing right through the walls, over the earthworks, past the forests to where the Gallian troops were dug in. 'We have been expecting reinforcements,' Saltin said, 'but we have been disappointed.'

'Can you hold the line if you don't get them?' George asked.

'Yes. For how long, though, I'm not sure.'

Aubrey frowned, thinking of Stalsfrieden and the Crystal Johannes. 'What if Dr Tremaine brings up something magical to throw against you?'

Saltin sat up in his seat. 'Magical? Such as?'

'I don't know,' Aubrey admitted, and he drummed the arm of his chair with frustration.

'We've been promised more magical neutralisers from your Directorate. They should help our defence.' Saltin waved a hand at the window. 'After all, our main protector is of Albionish design and it has been most helpful.'

'The tower. It's a magic neutraliser,' Aubrey said with

wonder. He could barely restrain himself from leaping out of his chair and racing out to examine it.

He had the rewarding feeling that came when a number of disparate data fell into place. The bizarre tower was a gigantic magic neutraliser. It explained the odd behaviour of the fireboat pumps, and probably explained the way the warehouse fire across the river ebbed and flowed. The warehouse must be on the edge of the neutraliser's area of effect.

'Grateful as we are,' Saltin said, dragging Aubrey from his thoughts, 'I wish your Albion thinkers had put more effort into the design. It is hideous.'

'Isn't that because it's built from scrap?' George asked.

'We used what we had. The plans that were sent to us were deliberately flexible when it came to materials. Except from the vital parts, which were shipped to us very carefully. First to Lutetia via airship, then by train, and finally by barge to our docks.'

'But how have you coped with no magic here, in the fortress?' Sophie asked. 'You'd have it embedded in a hundred little places.'

'We do. It's been a nightmare of plugging and patching, finding what no longer works.' He chuckled. 'The hot water boiler in the officer's quarters had a magically enhanced relief valve that burst when the neutraliser began to work.'

'Cold baths, eh, Saltin?' George said.

'It is a small price to pay,' Saltin said, 'to know that the fortress is safe from magical attack.'

'As long at the neutraliser can cope,' Aubrey said.

'Do you have any reason to think it cannot?'

'No. But I didn't think that magic neutralisers could be built on that scale, either.' A thought came to Aubrey.

'That dirigible, this morning. It was trying to bomb the neutraliser?'

'They have been trying for some time, but the tower interferes with their craft the same way as it interferes with our hot water. So far, they have missed.'

'And managed to hit a warehouse or two,' George pointed out.

'Divodorum is suffering,' Saltin agreed, 'but we remain strong.'

WHILE AUBREY INSPECTED THE NEUTRALISING TOWER under the supervision of Major Saltin, Sophie dragged George into the town on an expedition to find food. Aubrey found the construction fascinating. Four massive legs, made up of multiple steel girders bolted together, slanted up to a platform. Bracing these legs was an erratic web of timbers of all sizes, completely enclosing the interior of the area bounded by the legs. The array interlocked so completely that Aubrey suspected the whole thing had been organised by a corps of lacemakers who had grown tired of doilies and who had leaped at the chance to create something on a monumental scale.

High overhead, projecting from the lofty platform, was a metal cylinder. When Aubrey shaded his eyes, he could make out that it must be at least a foot in diameter and was solid, not a pipe, although Aubrey was prepared to wager that this was because both ends were capped and that the workings of the neutraliser were inside. He could feel the tell-tale emanations of magic that trickled from it – a passive but immensely powerful spell at work.

Both ends of the cylinder jutted out past the edges of the platform by a good three feet. Attached to each end of the cylinder was the most puzzling aspect of the entire construction: four slim metal rods, ten or fifteen feet in length, in the formation of a cross. By walking around and around the unlikely construction, Aubrey could see that the crosses were offset, not mimicking the angle of the other.

Aubrey spent some time trying to establish the extent of the magical protection afforded by the giant neutraliser. Under Major Saltin's amused eye, he backed away from the structure, trying a simple fire spell every few yards. Eventually, he had to exit through the gatehouse. Whoever had been in charge of enspelling the central core of the machine had done a fine job – or had been extremely lucky. The neutralising field was as nearly circular as Aubrey could make out, and it cloaked the fortress completely, ending some distance outside the walls.

Aubrey looked across the river to where the fire was still alive in the warehouse. Standing where he was, he felt the way the neutralising field fluctuated, pulsing almost like a living thing. He could imagine it rippling enough to touch the fireboat, or the warehouse – but if it extended as much that way, would it also shrink enough to put the fortress in jeopardy?

AUBREY ARRIVED BACK AT THEIR BASE JUST AS GEORGE and Sophie rode up, laughing, but Aubrey was immediately alert when he opened the front door to find the place was empty.

'Caroline!' He ran to the stairs. 'Caroline!'

'Aubrey,' Sophie said. George was propping their bicycles against the wall while she waited at the bench just inside the door. She lifted one of the many glue pots and extracted a sheet of paper. 'I think this note is for you.'

I am asleep, Aubrey read with the growing knowledge that he'd leaped before he'd looked. *Do not wake me. Aubrey: the orders are in the secure place.*

He swallowed. 'Was I too noisy?'

George shrugged. 'Unless she was cocooned in about a mile of sound-deadening material, I'd say so.'

The secure place had been organised before they'd left the base for their Stalsfrieden expedition. George had managed to construct a false ventilator cowling from sheet metal, and Sophie – with Aubrey's guidance – had used the Law of Similarity and the Law of Seeming to reinforce this camouflage. Inside were niches, shelves and boxes that were attuned via the Law of Affinity only to reveal themselves when Aubrey, George, Caroline or Sophie reached for them.

Aubrey quickly found the orders. Caroline had decoded all six pages. He hoped it hadn't taken too long, but he knew her pride wouldn't have let her rest until she'd completed the task.

He took the stairs to the roof and sat, cross-legged, in the late morning sun, his back to the brick-walled utilities shed, absorbed in the details of the orders, which were couched in roundabout military language but all the more startling for it.

The Directorate had been at an impasse in its plans for the Divodorum front, but now that Aubrey and his team were once again in place a vital delivery was on its way. A shipment of magic neutralisers would arrive in two days' time, and Aubrey's orders were to take them to the front before the Holmland assault began.

When he reached the end of the orders, he took to his feet and read them again while carefully pacing the length of the roof between the lines of antenna wire.

Some of his fears were confirmed. Magic neutralisers had no point unless magic was needing to be neutralised. The Directorate obviously was of the same mind as he was: when the Holmland assault came, it would be accompanied by magic.

Aubrey stopped, looked to the north-east from where the sound of artillery was a distant, constant punctuation, then scanned the orders again.

The Directorate's intelligence and analysis agreed with the information Aubrey had sent. The Holmland assault would begin within a week.

HE FOUND CAROLINE IN THE KITCHEN WITH GEORGE AND Sophie, who were preparing the midday meal in an easy partnership.

'Catch,' Caroline said and he managed not to disgrace himself.

'A potato?'

'One of many waiting to be peeled,' she said. 'Find a knife and lend a hand.'

'I shall, but I think you should all know that the Directorate is anticipating a Holmland attack within a week.'

'We know,' George said. 'Caroline told us.'

'Good, good. I suppose these potatoes need peeling, then?'

Soon, he was standing at a bench with Caroline, a large bowl of water between them. It was simple, homely work and, as such, Aubrey found it comforting to work with her on such a thing. Reaching for potatoes, dipping them in the water and fumbling about provided ample opportunities for them to touch hands, to apologise, to laugh and generally to put aside the war for a while. Even when great events were in motion, Aubrey decided, the ordinary things like food and friends needed attention.

Sophie banged a lid on the pot at the back of the stove. Her face was pink from the heat of the cooking and she wiped it with an apron she'd found. 'Aubrey, I have an idea.'

He didn't stop peeling. 'All ideas are welcome, Sophie. You know that.'

'Put it on the table, my gem,' George said, pausing in his carrot slicing. 'Share it with everybody.'

Sophie made a quick gesture, bringing her thumb and fingers together. 'Ah, I see. Table.' Aubrey knew that she had taken the phrase and remembered it. He wouldn't be surprised to hear it popping up in her conversation in the near future. 'I want to tell everyone what is happening here.'

'Everyone?' George said. 'That's ambitious.'

She threw him a smile. 'The people, I mean. News from the front, this front, has been sparse. When we hurried through Lutetia the newspapers were full of news of the war, but the news of the Divodorum front was laughable. Rumours, gossip, nothing more.'

'It must be hard to obtain reports from here,' Aubrey pointed out. 'Almost everyone has gone.'

'I want to send the real story of what is happening here.'

'I'm not sure about that,' Aubrey said. 'Military secrets, battle plans, things like that.'

Sophie threw her hands up in the air. 'Secrets! That is the way military people think. Do not the people deserve to know what is happening?'

'Well . . .'

'Do you think that Gallians are cowards, ready to collapse if they hear that things are bad? If the Gallian people know, it will only make them more determined to fight!'

George popped a disc of carrot into his mouth and chewed for a moment. 'If it's done properly, if a story is well written, it could rally the nation.'

'After all,' Caroline put in, 'the alternative hasn't worked. Keeping the people in the dark has made them more fearful rather than less.'

Sophie brandished a knife. Aubrey had never seen her so passionate. 'The government, the generals, they treat the people like children. In Gallia, where we had a revolution for the people!'

'We'd have to leave out anything that would be useful information for Holmland spies to relay back to Fisherberg,' Aubrey said and he realised that they now weren't talking about whether Sophie's idea was a good one or not – they were discussing the best way to implement it.

'That will be easy,' Sophie said.

'What about the censor?' George said. 'In Albion, all the newspapers have to submit war stories to the official censor for approval.'

Sophie laughed. 'Our government tried such a scheme, but it collapsed. None of the newspapers cooperated. All the cartoonists poked much fun at the idea.' She looked at George. 'Poked fun is correct?'

'You're perfect, my gem. Fun is poked, not prodded.'

'How would we get your story to your newspaper?' Aubrey asked, confident that with such a team, he would have at least one useful answer, if not two or three.

'George,' Sophie asked, 'do you have the time?'

George took out his pocket watch. 'It's just after noon.'

'Very good.' Sophie went to the door of the kitchen, opened it, and waved. 'This is Claude,' she said.

Claude was short and stocky, and when he took off his cloth cap he revealed a shock of thick, black hair that looked as if it would be an excellent defence against head injury. He bowed, nervously. 'Claude's father was the editor of the local newspaper,' Sophie continued. 'George and I found him on our way back from meeting Major Saltin.'

'I represent *The Divodorum Journal*,' Claude said in good Albionish. 'It is a dull name, but it has been with the people of Divodorum for fifty years. They are used to it.'

'Claude is the local correspondent for my newspaper, *The Sentinel*, but since the offices of the *Journal* were bombed, his job has been difficult.'

'I have photographs of the front,' Claude explained. 'I want to get them to Lutetia.'

'How did you get photographs?' Aubrey asked. 'Isn't the military sensitive about things like that?'

Claude beamed, showing a gap in his front teeth. 'I have friends at the fortress. They send provisions to the front in lorries. A lorry stops at a bridge just to the north. I jump on, spend time at the front, then jump back on the lorry to come home.'

'No-one objects? What about the officers?'

'I take photographs of them and promise I will send

them to their wives and sweethearts.'

Claude explained how he'd cross the river and catch a train to Lutetia with Sophie's stories and his photographs never leaving his grasp.

Sophie insisted that he had been a reliable contact in the past. 'I will have an account of the defence of Divodorum ready tomorrow,' she said.

Aubrey thought about the timing. The adage about two birds and one stone came to mind. 'Claude, if you can join us here at ten o'clock on Thursday, we have to hire a barge to fetch a delivery across the river. If you help us find a reliable bargemaster, we will pay and give you a lift.'

'A lift?' Claude raised an eyebrow at Sophie.

'We will take you across the river as our guest,' she said airily. 'It is an Albionish way of saying things.'

Fifteen

CLAUDE WAS LEAVING WHEN THE LORRIES WITH VON Stralick, Madame Zelinka and the Enlightened Ones drove in through the gates. The backboards banged down. A few of the Enlightened Ones had to be helped down by friends. Aubrey dragged open the front doors of the factory. 'What happened?'

'Nothing.' Madame Zelinka was grey-faced with exhaustion and something else – pain? 'And too much.'

'We have a major problem here in Divodorum,' von Stralick said. He eased Madame Zelinka to a chair, and Aubrey then saw that she was cradling one arm in the other.

'Only half the Enlightened Ones have come back,' Caroline said softly.

Von Stralick barked orders to Madame Zelinka's colleagues. The uninjured began unloading medical supplies from the lorries, while four sat on the floor, against the wall, roughly bandaged.

'What happened?' Aubrey repeated.

Von Stralick shook his head. 'Downstairs. Close the doors first.'

In the basement, the Enlightened Ones showed no trace of panic, just careful, methodical movements. The injured were helped down the stairs and onto the bedding that took up most of the floor space. Others distributed water.

Madame Zelinka refused to lie down. Von Stralick eased her into one of the ancient lounge chairs that George had bought when trying to make the place more comfortable. 'The fire, at the warehouse.' Madame Zelinka took a quick inhalation through her teeth, hissing as von Stralick eased her arm a little to arrange a sling around it. When he was done he kept a hand on her shoulder, gently. 'It has spawned something, a bad residue.'

Aubrey remembered the powerful spell remains that he'd found underneath Dr Tremaine's Fisherberg residence. 'It attacked you?'

'It is dangerous,' Madame Zelinka said. Her head bowed and she gestured weakly at von Stralick.

He took up the story. 'The fire was put out by the fireboat, but the animation remained and grew in strength. Zelinka was clubbed by a length of steel that was lying on the ground one minute, then hopping about the next. Soon the entire factory was alive. Our people were fighting for their lives.'

Aubrey shuddered. 'I might be of some assistance.'

'We can cope with animated building materials,' Madame Zelinka said through clenched teeth, 'but the situation is much worse than that.'

'The residue is draining into the river,' von Stralick

explained. 'It could contaminate the whole city. We left some of our people there to do what they could, but it could be very bad.'

'It will fester and grow if we don't stop it,' Madame Zelinka murmured. 'Divodorum, then downstream.'

Sophie, the native Gallian, was most horrified. She put both hands to her mouth before asking, 'The animation will spread?'

'It could.' Aubrey rubbed his forehead. 'Magical residue is unpredictable, but I'd say that every town downriver of Divodorum is in danger.'

'It is our duty to stop it,' Madame Zelinka said. 'We will rest, then go back.'

'I'd like to help,' Aubrey insisted. He was already running spells through in his mind.

'Help?' Madame Zelinka almost smiled. 'Do you remember the last time you tried to deal with magical residue?'

Aubrey had barely survived, and it was only the fortunate interference from the Beccaria Cage that had allowed him to escape. 'I'm willing.'

'I know, I know.' Madame Zelinka waved a tired hand. 'Stay here. Leave the residue to the experts.' She closed her eyes and leaned her head back. Her jaw was clenched against the pain.

Von Stralick caught Aubrey's eye and took him aside. While the Enlightened Ones moved about with quiet assurance, with Caroline, George and Sophie distributing food to the hungry, von Stralick spoke softly. 'She is in pain, Fitzwilliam. Surely you know some medical magic.'

'I don't. I have the greatest respect for those who do.'

'Respect?'

'It scares me.'

'I have trouble imagining you scared by such a thing.'

'It's . . .' Aubrey waved a hand, vaguely. 'It's so complicated, casting spells that work with all the bits and pieces inside you.'

'I am informed that you've rarely avoided complicated magic in the past.'

'This is different.' Aubrey ran his fingers through his hair. 'If I knew medical magic, I would have used it on you, Hugo, when you were sick. You know that.'

Caroline came over and passed them cups of tea. 'My training included basic first aid, Hugo. I'll do what I can.'

Aubrey hadn't liked letting Hugo down like that, but like most non-magicians, the Holmlander didn't have any idea about how complex magic was.

Feeling helpless as the Enlightened Ones regrouped, with Caroline's assistance, he went back upstairs to the kitchen. Sophie and George were busy ladling soup into mugs. George looked over his shoulder. 'Those potatoes won't peel themselves, you know.'

Aubrey looked at the pile on the bench and sighed. He picked up the knife and went to work, pondering the glamorous life of an international security operative.

LATER THAT AFTERNOON, AUBREY BICYCLED OUT TO where the Enlightened Ones were hard at work. Their skills were always of interest to him and he watched while the more actively magical of the corps stood at the perimeter of what he saw as a multi-chorused, multi-coloured stain that was spreading from the warehouse site, across the embankment and dripping into the river. Three or four of the Enlightened Ones were chanting spells, short and sharp, in a language unfamiliar to him. Two were waist deep in the river with their arms spread, heads down, as if they were herding fish.

Aubrey concentrated. He felt the pulsing of the residue as both cruel and threatening. He wasn't surprised, either, that it had the definite touch of Dr Tremaine. When he narrowed his focus, though, he became sure that even though Dr Tremaine's signature element was buried deep in the magic, his *presence* was missing. Aubrey was sure that this compression spell was another that Dr Tremaine had organised, but had allowed someone else to actually activate. It was more delegated magic, and Aubrey wondered how far Dr Tremaine had gone with this process.

Other Enlightened Ones were warily circling the smouldering remains of the warehouse. At intervals, one of them would crouch and use a small trowel to scrape away at the earth outside the crumbled walls. Aubrey had no idea what they were doing, but the malevolent animation that had seized the building was well under control.

AUBREY ARRIVED BACK AT THE FACTORY TO FIND THAT George and Sophie had procured a treasure trove of fresh vegetables, meat, fish and fruit. They'd even found milk and cream fresh that day.

After stowing his bicycle, Aubrey stood at the door from the yard and stared at the single long table that took up nearly half the length of the ground floor. It was covered with white linen, but Aubrey was sure that since the benches appeared to have vanished, the banquet table was actually several bookbinders' workplaces pushed together.

If the table settings were meagre, George and Sophie had made up for it with the bunches of fresh flowers in glass jars that were evenly spaced along the centre of the table, alternating with an assortment of candles. The dishes being handed around were cheered as they were brought out steaming – ragout, baked fish, a roast leg of pork, huge bowls of vegetables steamed, roasted and fried.

George saw Aubrey standing open-mouthed. He approached, wiping his hands on the brightly spotty apron he wore. 'You have a booking, sir?'

'For one,' Aubrey said faintly. 'In the name of Fitzwilliam.'

'I'm sorry, sir, but I've been instructed to usher you to a table for two in a corner away from the band, in the name of Hepworth.'

'Really?'

'Sorry, old man, just joking. It's find your own seat here tonight.' George rubbed his cheek with the back of his hand. 'It's funny, isn't it, how the little things can make a difference. Not a jolly lot, these Enlightened Ones, but feed them up and suddenly the jokes start pouring out.'

'Sometimes I think we're fighting for the little things as well as the big things.'

'Never a truer word was spoken. Would you like some dinner?'

'Yes please.' Aubrey stopped. 'I like your apron. The lace edge is a lovely touch.'

'It's quite fashionable. All the best people are wearing them in Lutetia, apparently.'

Aubrey actually found a seat next to Caroline and, for an hour or so, had fun eating, talking, passing platters of food right and left, and learning useful things like the best way to confuse a polar bear.

George and Sophie made sure the food kept rolling out of the kitchen for what was obviously a continuous dinner rather than something with discrete courses. The Enlightened Ones came and went as their shift at the warehouse ended, or started. The weariness of the returnees dissipated with the hospitality, but the faces of those who were leaving were pitiful, and many lingered for a last bite or riposte, or a whispered conversation with a friend.

As midnight approached, the dinner began to crawl to a conclusion. Caroline excused herself to the hairy Enlightened One on her left, and leaned over to Aubrey. 'I'm going to see if the airwaves have anything for us.'

'Do you think the Directorate might be transmitting tonight?'

'It's coming up to optimum reception time. It's best to make sure.'

'I'll come with you.'

'You get some sleep. I hardly have enough room in that booth for me and my equipment as it is.'

'We could try,' Aubrey said. His self-consciousness had obviously been lulled into a soporific state by the dinner, for the words were out of his mouth before he knew it. 'Sorry,' he said, but he was delighted when Caroline tapped him on the shoulder.

'Not tonight. It's too important.'

She left him staring into the air.

Sixteen

At first, when Aubrey woke, he was sure someone was standing by the bed. The tiny cubicle was pitch black but he had that half-awake certainty of another presence. He sat up and lit a match, ready to apply it to the candle on the floor, but the flare of light showed that he was alone.

He scratched at his forearm and that was when he realised that magic was in the vicinity. His skin was alive with the sensation of acidity, a sour lemon tang setting his teeth on edge. Odd crawling sensations muddled his vision for a moment and he realised that he was seeing a high-pitched whine.

He tilted his head, listening: in the distance, the thumping *pom-pom-pom* of artillery, while a barge was chugging up the nearby canal.

Aubrey climbed out from under the blankets and tugged on a pair of trousers, slipping his braces over his bare shoulders. He lit the candle this time, then pulled aside the curtain that separated the sleeping cubicles from the rest of the basement. He held the candle high as he tried to work out where the magic was coming from.

On the opposite side of the basement, the door to Caroline's telegraph cubicle was ajar.

He hurried across the floor, stepping lightly, weaving his way through the maze of mattresses that the Enlightened Ones had thrown down, but when he reached halfway across the basement, he stopped and looked upward.

The source of the magic was directly above. He spun, paused, then – in an agony of indecision – actually rocked from one foot to the other, unsure which way to go. He wanted to check the telegraph cubicle, but the magical emanations from above were growing stronger.

With a glance at the stairs, Aubrey vaulted over the sleeping Enlightened Ones and pushed the door of the telegraph cubicle open.

The station was empty. Aubrey froze, taking in the scene. Caroline's headphones were sprawled untidily on the bench next to her transmitter key. A writing tablet was nearby, next to the coding machine, and a pencil lay on the floor. Aside from the desk lamp being extinguished, nothing showed the precision that was Caroline's mode of operation. It was plain that she'd left hastily.

He picked up the headphones and nearly dropped them again as magic leaped from the earpieces. His fingers prickled and he placed the headphones carefully on the bench before he wiped his hands on the rear of his trousers.

Then he bolted for the stairs, taking them two at a time.

He flung open the hatch that led to the flat roof, and poked his head out. For an instant, he had the strangest feeling: he was like a camera, taking a series of quick snapshots, one after the other.

First impression: the flat roof extended before him. The hatch was at one end of the roof, with the far end some seventy or eighty feet away. The antenna array Caroline had so carefully constructed took up most of that space, eight wires stretched fifty feet from one side of the roof to the other, each separated by ten feet of space.

Second impression: the night was overcast, with the clouds adding a thin pallor to the sky.

Third impression: artillery fire away to the north-east, drumbeats of doom.

Fourth and overwhelming impression: the roof was ablaze with magic and electrical discharges.

Aubrey went to drag himself onto the roof and was nearly driven back by one of the dozens of huge electrical eruptions that were fizzing along the antenna wires. The sparks were enormous, leaping feet into the air, hissing with malignant glee as they slid backward and forward, crashing together at speed and showering the roof with a rain of smaller sparklets.

Cursing, Aubrey squinted, momentarily dazzled. These weren't just electrical discharges – serious though that would be. These had magic about them, and it was the sort of magic that made him very, very wary.

Carefully, he climbed out of the hatch, holding a hand up in front of his face and keeping his back to the utilities shed. 'Caroline!' he shouted, then he reeled back as one of the giant sparks skated in his direction.

Are they arms?

Then Caroline threw a chair at him.

He ducked, already believing that Caroline had, at last, seen through him and was expressing her opinion by hurling convenient furniture at him.

'Aubrey!' she cried. 'Look out!'

His heart surged at her warning. He abandoned his misgivings as the chair flashed through the giant spark and smashed on the brick wall behind him. Aubrey ducked, then took a step toward where Caroline was backing away, scrambling under antenna wire in her haste.

Aubrey drew close to one of the wires, close enough for him to reach out and touch. He was about to call out to Caroline when, from the corner of his eye, he saw a giant spark humming toward him, arms extended.

He didn't have time to worry about how bizarre that notion was. He let out a yelp and threw himself away from its reach. Landing on a shoulder and rolling to his feet, he had to shield his eyes and back away as the magically imbued electrical phenomenon reached for him.

Aubrey's mind worked in two separate and distinct modes. One part was on the verge of gibbering as the spark grew in size, rapidly towering ten feet from the wire on which it balanced. The other part coolly noted how small sparklets were racing along the wire and merging with it to make a roughly human shape. It pawed unsuccessfully at him, then swayed and stretched. Half a dozen smaller sparklets skated along to join it, flowing right up its fingerless hand and making the entire creature swell, growing another foot or two in height, an electrical demon that leered with antic glee.

Aubrey swallowed and took another step away. He looked to Caroline, but she was trapped on the other side of the roof, with eight antenna wires between her and Aubrey – eight wires populated by a growing horde of demonic sparks that sped up and down, crashing into each other and growing in size, electrical demon shapes that capered and lunged at her.

Aubrey ducked as a chair leg slammed into the brick wall to his left.

'Sorry!' Caroline called.

The largest of the sparks, the one that had been menacing Aubrey, swivelled at the sound of Caroline's voice. As fast as thought, it skimmed along the wire until it reached the edge of the roof, then it extended a limb until it touched the next wire in the array, one wire closer to Caroline. Once it had grasped this wire, it performed a complicated manoeuvre, stretching and vaulting across, then reshaping itself until it once again had its four-limbed, demonic form. Joined by a rabble of smaller sparklets, it sped to the opposite end of the second wire and then repeated the process, vaulting across to the third – and again coming closer to Caroline.

Caroline hurdled a wire, keeping her distance, moving toward the far end of the roof, but Aubrey could see that she didn't have far to go before she'd be trapped.

Caroline had realised the danger she was in. Not wanting to come up against the parapet, she'd moved to her right until she reached the end of the wire – but was once more trapped by the edge of the roof on that side. Calmly, she faced the electrical demon that was fizzing toward her.

Aubrey wanted to call out to Caroline, offer suggestions, but he didn't want to break her concentration. She was balanced on her toes, alert, watching the creature and waiting for her opportunity.

The demon stretched out to touch its next wire. As soon as it did, Caroline threw herself under the wire she was standing against, then continued rolling under the next before coming to her feet. She glanced around and then seized a length of pipe from a stack of disused building material they'd used in renovating the factory.

'No!' Aubrey shouted. He started running toward her, then scrambled frantically on his hands and knees under the first wire.

Caroline held the pipe vertically, in both hands, perfectly balanced. The electrical demon paused for a moment as it assimilated a handful of attendant sparklets, then flashed along the wire toward her. When it came close enough, Caroline swung so hard she was lifted off her feet.

The electrical demon was unaffected. The pipe passed straight through and caught the wire, rebounding wildly before Caroline could bring it under control, but by then the creature had reached out and grasped it. Instantly, it flowed into the metal, its form melting like butter in sunshine. It dissolved from the antenna wire, crackled along the length of the pipe and Caroline was enveloped in a spitting, hissing radiance, an electrical cloak that made her jerk wildly before her eyes rolled back in her head. The pipe fell from her grasp and she slid to the tarred roof. A malevolent nimbus spluttered around her as she lay still.

Aubrey was running before he knew it. Without slowing, he plucked his penknife from his pocket and slashed at the wire ahead of him. Naturally, since it was under tension, it sprang apart and whipped past his face. He raced after it, caught the end and coiled the wire until he reached the edge of the roof where he slashed again, tucking fifty feet of wire under one arm.

Spells came to his lips — affinity spells, amplification spells. Coldly, he merged them together, opting for expediency and power over elegance.

The electrical glow had left Caroline's inert body and it had leaped back to the antenna wire, where it was reassembling itself into a demon. It swayed for a moment, then it hummed along the wire.

Aubrey swivelled in time to see it vault to the next wire, speed along to the other end, then leap across to the next, coming one step closer. He was clearly its new target.

Tiny imps of sparklets were gathered up and incorporated as it hummed from one wire to the next, careering from end to end then crossing, growing larger as it crackled its way toward him. Waiting for it, Aubrey's mouth was dry but his mind was clear. He cast the coil of antenna wire over the parapet while he held the loose end in his right hand. When the coil hit the ground, he ran through the spell that made sure it buried itself in the soil, and he paid out enough wire so that he had three or four yards at his feet, all the while refusing to notice the way his heart was thumping. Fear was knocking at the door, but he declined to answer.

The electrical demon crossed to the wire that Aubrey was standing next to. It didn't hesitate. In a shower of sparks, it screamed along the antenna, sizzling toward him with its arms outstretched.

Aubrey spat out a spell. He swung the wire in a flat plane above his head, slowly at first, then faster and faster, whirling until it whistled. When the electrical demon was barely ten feet away, he let go. Thanks to the spell, the wire hurtled at the creature, struck, then wrapped itself around its torso, tightening like a maddened python and sending a cascade of sparks into the air.

Balanced on the wire only a few feet away, the electrical demon started to squeeze free, but Aubrey was ready for it. He delivered the other half of the spell with venom.

The demon stopped its frenzied wriggling. For an instant, it propped on the wire and tilted its head to the heavens. In defeat? Resignation? Before Aubrey could ponder this moment of terminal cognisance, the demon elongated, then compressed − as if a giant had placed hands top and bottom and were using it as an accordion. With a thud and a whistle, the demon vanished, leaving the antenna wire vibrating. The entrapping wire came alight, crackling with blue fire, a glowing serpent in the night, then it fell to the roof, inert.

The demonic creature had been earthed. Grounded. Defeated.

Aubrey raced to where Caroline lay, slashing antenna wires with his knife to allow his passage. He paused to check that she was breathing, then he scooped her up and fairly danced across the mangled antenna array, not putting a foot wrong. Without a thought he held her over his shoulder and entered the hatch, descending the stairs with the surefootedness of an alpine creature much given to spending its life on near-vertical cliffs.

He hurried to the oval table, at war with himself. Part of him wanted to despair, but he was Caroline's hope and he couldn't afford the dramatics.

Her eyes were still closed. Her breathing was shallow and ragged. He touched her throat to find that her pulse was thready, erratic, and he felt the insidious brush of panic. He glanced at her dear hands to see them reddened and burned.

Concentrate! he told himself. *Time for namby-pambiness later!*

He extended his magical awareness. The creature had been electrical in its nature, but it had also had something magnetic as well, all bound together with magic. The residue was familiar — it had the taint he had detected in Caroline's headphones, and he knew, then, that this creature was responsible for the interference in the ether.

It had left its touch on Caroline. Many of her normal functions were being overwhelmed. Soon, she would be lost — unless he could perform some delicate medical magic.

Aubrey had a tendency to throw himself into gaps, wherever they occurred. He had a desire to do the right thing, even at personal cost. But medical magic? He was only too aware of the hazards. No matter how robust Caroline's constitution was, the human body was a complex construction. He could do untold harm.

In a decision that took less than a heartbeat, he decided that inaction here was worse than action. A world without Caroline was unthinkable.

Restoration and strengthening. He'd start there. Dimly remembered lectures came to him, masters at Stonelea mumbling about medical magic and emphasising that it should be left to trained practitioners. Dons at Greythorn insisting that the human body had a remarkable system for repairing itself, but sometimes needed help.

He called on the Law of Origins and the Law of Constituent Parts. Medical magic didn't substantially derive from these, but Aubrey was groping in the dark. He used what he knew best. The Law of Completeness. The Law of Intensification. Soon, he had a conglomerate spell with elements threaded together and supporting each other, combining to create what he hoped would keep Caroline Hepworth from dying.

Kneeling at her side, he pronounced the spell slowly, despite the urgency. He wanted to get this right – he *needed* to get this right. If sincerity made spells more puissant, then Caroline would be up and walking in no time.

He finished, hesitating a little over his signature element. Then he anxiously studied the face of the person who mattered.

Many people mattered to him. George. His parents. Even his grandmother. He'd come to understand, however, that Caroline Hepworth mattered to him in a way unlike the others. Her existence affected him in a thousand different ways. Through all of his self-consciousness, through all his doubting and second-guessing, he knew that she made him happy.

Her eyelids moved a little, but remained closed. He chewed at his lip. When her breathing become more even, more regular, he was glad he was kneeling, for he was sure his legs would have given way if he'd been standing.

He bathed her hands and bound them with bandages, taking his time, waiting for her to open her eyes. When she lapsed into sleep, he covered her with a blanket, where she lay on the table, and he woke George and Sophie.

Seventeen

THROUGH THE SMALL HOURS OF THE NIGHT, AUBREY tended to Caroline.

After sharing what he knew with George and Sophie, they helped him move her downstairs to her own sleeping cubicle. After that, Aubrey remained seated on a three-legged stool by her side as she slept an uneasy sleep. Twice she called out, without opening her eyes, making him start, and once she made jerky, warding-off motions with her bandaged hands. Risking personal injury, he took her wrists and held them firmly. She resisted, but only for a moment, before subsiding, muttering words that were ill-formed and unintelligible.

After breakfast had been served to the Enlightened Ones, Sophie parted the curtain and slipped in with a mug of tea for him and quiet concern for Caroline. She left, after patting him on the shoulder. He closed his eyes and brought the mug to his lips to savour it before tasting.

Caroline spoke. 'If I ask politely, may I have some tea as well?'

It nearly precipitated a disaster. Aubrey's eyes sprang open, he gasped and he tried to leap to his feet, all at once, while holding a container of extremely hot liquid. He swayed, wobbled, righted himself, then stared at his patient.

Her face was wan, but her smile was reassuring. She held up a hand, studied it, then put both hands together. Aubrey had done his best, but the bandages had made her elegant hands into bulky, gauze-laden mittens. 'It appeared from nowhere,' she said softly.

'You were checking the antenna?'

'I received some communication, then the interference was worse. I thought I might need to realign something.'

'It was magic.'

'Dr Tremaine?'

'Or a magician underling. I can imagine it patrolling the ether and doing its best to ruin communications.'

'And tracking down the source.' Gingerly, she sat up. 'I feel bruised all over.'

'Your hands were burned. I did what I could.'

She held one out. 'Let me see.'

'I'm not sure that's a good idea.'

'I have more medical training than you, Aubrey. I have to assess what needs to be done.'

'Are they painful?'

'Somewhat. You didn't put butter on them or anything like that, did you?'

'George advised against it. He said it was folklore of a bad kind.'

'He was correct.'

As carefully as he could, Aubrey began unwinding the gauze. She winced. 'Sorry,' he said. 'I'm being as gentle as I can.'

She favoured him with an expression that was equal parts exasperation and the sort of tenderness that made him melt. 'You're doing a fine job.'

'There.'

Caroline brought her hand up close. She turned it over to complete her inspection. 'No blisters, which is a good thing. Red and sore, but no real damage.'

'I'm glad.'

'As long as I don't have to engage in a serious tug-of-war in the next day or so, I should be able to manage.'

She began to pick away at the other bandage. Aubrey leaned over to help and, naturally, this brought their heads close together. Intent on working on Aubrey's awkward bandage knot, she leaned so her forehead rested against his, which he thought an arrangement extremely close to perfection.

Some time later – hours? days? – she straightened and tossed the bandage to him. 'Now, what about that cup of tea?'

CAROLINE WAS A MODEL OF PATIENCE AS SHE EXPLAINED successively to Sophie, then George, then Hugo, who had darted back to the base to fetch a piece of equipment needed by the Enlightened Ones, that she was, indeed, well and that while she appreciated their concern she wasn't about to take to her bed and become a valetudinarian.

George and Sophie went off to work on another article they were writing together. After waiting for Aubrey to make repairs to the antenna array and after listening to his warning to keep the time on air brief, Caroline tested the wireless. Her scowling told Aubrey the situation before her words did. 'I still can't get through.'

Aubrey gazed upward, through the wooden floor of the factory, through the roof, and chewed his lip. 'I'd hoped that disposing of that creature might have freed the air.'

'If one was made, then more would have been.'

'Not necessarily true. If the spell was enormously complex, the cost could be too great. But Dr Tremaine has organised his spellcasting, systematising and delegating it. Distributed spellcasting?'

Caroline closed the wooden door of the telegraph cubicle. She linked her arm with his and led the way to the stairs. 'You always say that Dr Tremaine is the foremost magician of our age.'

'He wouldn't have been appointed Sorcerer Royal if he wasn't, not with his background.'

'It seems to me, however, that it's not just his spells that are revolutionary, if that's correct.'

'His spells are staggeringly innovative.'

Caroline let go of Aubrey's arm and sat at the oval table. She played with a brush, one of the props they were using to make the place look like a real bookbinder's workplace. At the other end of the large, open space, near a sunny window, Sophie was using a typing machine while George was scribbling with a pencil. 'I'm guessing that Dr Tremaine is doing more than inventing innovative spells,' Caroline said. 'He's also changing the *way* magic is done. He's like that motorcar manufacturer, the one who's broken the process into its individual parts and changed his whole factory to that end.'

'Rivers? Harold Rivers?'

'That's the one. His mass production has meant that motorcars are rolling out of his factories at an unheard of rate.'

'But we're talking about magic, not machines.'

'Aubrey, I may know nothing about magic, but I can see systems at work. I have the distinct impression that Dr Tremaine is working on that level as well as the coalface of spell casting.'

Aubrey had never felt that he was the sole repository of good ideas. 'I think you may be right, but the implications scare me.'

'They scare me as well, which is why we have to stop him.'

THE NEXT DAY, AFTER A MESSENGER ARRIVED AT THE BASE with news of the arrival of their special delivery, Sophie prepared her story for Claude to take – but she couldn't resist giving the earnest young newspaperman last-minute advice as they accompanied him. He was dressed in his best suit, no doubt hoping to make an impression when he reached Lutetia, but Sophie reassured him that the editors would be more interested in his news than in his fashion sense.

After they donned civilian clothes to minimise attention, and with Claude directing, George drove the wagon he'd bought to the riverfront a hundred yards from the collapsed railway bridge. The busyness on the docks had the vitality of old. The river was jammed with all manner of craft ferrying people and goods from one side to the other, where Aubrey could see the steam and smoke from a train that had just pulled up on the far bank. Claude ignored the touts who were offering to buy and sell anything he had and instead led them a distance upriver to where a barge was being loaded with crates of apples.

'Henri is my cousin's best friend,' Claude said, introducing them to the captain. He was nearly as venerable as the craft he was in charge of, but his back was straight and his eyes were bright. A stubby pipe was jammed in the corner of his mouth. 'He can be trusted.'

'Trusted?' Captain Henri said in heavily accented Albionish, made all the more obscure by his not removing his pipe. 'Of course I can be trusted. What have you been telling these young people? That I am a pirate?'

'We have a shipment waiting for us on the other side,' Aubrey said. 'A dozen large crates. You'll be able to manage them?'

Captain Henri took his pipe from his mouth and pointed it at the crate-loading. 'Lothar and Volker are made of muscle.'

The two deckhands were indeed mountains of men. One, blond haired, had stripped off his shirt in the sun, either because he was hot or because his mother had grown tired of sewing up the seams after he burst them. The other was the more muscular of the two.

'Lothar?' Aubrey said. 'Volker? Aren't they Holmlandish names?'

Captain Henri laughed. 'Of course. Holmlandish names for Holmlanders.'

George broke the uncomfortable silence that followed this announcement. 'Your deckhands are Holmlanders?'

'They are and have been all their life.'

'Even though we're at war with Holmland?'

Captain Henri scowled around his reinserted pipe. 'These fellows have been with me for years. I vouch for 'em.'

Claude cut in anxiously. 'We are close to the border here. We have always mixed, Gallians that way, Holmlanders this way. When the war was declared, most went home, but not all.'

'Those boys don't care about rich men in Fisherberg playing games with young men's lives,' Captain Henri said. 'Now, you want your shipment or not?'

Claude promised that he'd see the crates safely stowed before he departed on the train. Some last-minute instructions from Sophie and he was off, leaping from the dock to the barge as it pulled away.

While they waited, George and Sophie wandered along the riverbank and bought some very savoury goat's milk cheese, bread, a basket of pears and two bottles of fresh milk, thus pleasing the deckhands they bought from, who thereby had less to load, the barge captains, who grinned at the cash transaction, not to mention Aubrey and Caroline, who were the beneficiaries of this scavenged but delightful luncheon.

They sat under a pin oak that spread its branches wide, and they watched the commerce of the river and its banks while they passed Aubrey's penknife and the cheese to each other. Aubrey insisted on cutting Caroline's bread and cheese for her and remarkably – after a minor show of refusing – she accepted his help.

Aubrey was thinking of a dozen things at once, as was his wont, but he found time to notice how close Sophie and George were sitting to each other. Sophie had her legs folded up, with her striped skirt neatly draped around her. She wore a straw hat bravely perched on her head as she pointed out to George what he was missing in the bustle below.

Then he realised that Caroline and he were sitting just as close. He swallowed nervously and went to apologise but she hushed him with a twitch of one eyebrow.

'Just sit back,' she said. 'Enjoy the moment.'

He did and he wished it would go on forever.

WHEN THEY FINISHED THEIR LUNCH, GEORGE MANOEUVRED the wagon down from the road to the dockside with Sophie on the driver's seat beside him, wide-eyed but game.

The crates were large, as promised, each about nine feet long. Lothar and Volker, grunting, loaded them with the aid of some imaginative swearing, an amalgam of Gallian and Holmlandish, Aubrey guessed, and the way they brought the languages together gave Aubrey hope for the future.

When they returned to the base, Aubrey enlisted the assistance of Madame Zelinka's people to bring a crate inside – the one with a prominent '#1' stencilled on the end. He was confident no-one could simply walk past and carry the others off the back of the wagon, but he made sure the gate was locked.

While George unhitched the horses and tended to them

with Sophie, Aubrey studied the crate. The Enlightened Ones had rested it against the wall, next to the front doors, under the window. Nine feet long and narrow, it looked uncomfortably like a coffin for someone who was very tall and spindly.

Caroline appeared from the kitchen. She'd put on her fighting suit again, now that they were back in their base, and her feet were bare. In one hand she had a damp cloth. In the other, she had a pry bar. 'Here,' she said. 'I'm anticipating.'

'Anticipating?'

'You were about to start an argument about whether to open the crate or not.'

'Well, I wouldn't say argument —'

'Then you'd put forward the view that the orders didn't say anything about not opening the crate.'

'Didn't they? Let me have a look at them again.'

'Which you'd suggest was actually a way of telling us that the crates *should* be opened for good reasons.'

'Like inspecting them for damage during transit.'

'That's the sort of thing.'

'Or for sabotage.'

'We can't have sabotaged equipment going to the front.' She handed him the pry bar. 'In fact, you'd be derelict in your duty if you didn't open the crate.'

'I was just going to say that.'

She smiled. 'I know.'

Under Caroline's watchful eye, Aubrey took to the crate. He restrained an impulse to be indiscriminately destructive, something that pry bars seemed to inspire. He'd have to recrate the machine in order to transport it to the front so he eased off the lid instead of hacking at it. The nails groaned before giving way, only increasing the feeling that he was opening a coffin.

He straightened to find that on top of the packing material that was smothering the magic neutraliser was a large, buff envelope with his name on it.

'It's official, not personal,' Caroline pointed out. 'Last name only, no rank or initial. But it must be from someone who knows you well enough to assume you'd break into the crate.'

'Craddock,' Aubrey said after he tore open the envelope and scanned its contents. His eyebrows rose. 'He's aware of the wireless interference. The Department is doing its best to overcome it, but apparently every Directorate team near any of the fronts is having the same problem getting through. Tallis is furious.'

'Commander Craddock said that Commander Tallis is furious? Let me see.'

'I'm reading between the lines.'

'What else does it say?'

'The Holmland mobilisation in this region is continuing. Much rail traffic. Heavy armaments, troops, matériel, pointing to a concerted push. Albion and the colonies are sending reinforcements. Gallia too, but Holmland infiltrators have done a good job in blowing up railway bridges, apparently.' Aubrey read on quickly, noting that more magicians were disappearing, both in Albion and across the Continent – and reports were also arriving indicating that the disappearances weren't limited to magicians; magical artefacts were disappearing from museums and private collections.

His eyebrows rose. 'Dentists.'

'I beg your pardon?' Caroline said.

'Commander Craddock wants us to question any dentists we come across.'

'He's concerned about the state of the army's teeth?'

'He wants to know if any supplies have gone missing.'

'Dental supplies.'

Aubrey took a last look at the document and slipped it back into the envelope. He'd need to read it again, at least once more. 'Craddock is worried about something, but I'd wish he'd be a little less cryptic.'

'I think it goes with the job,' Caroline said. 'Any other changes to our orders?'

'No. We're to take the neutralisers to the front and then assist in any way.'

'We have a contact?'

'Lieutenant-Colonel Stanley, special magical advisor to General Apsley.' He smiled. 'They know about my non-traitor status!'

Eighteen

*W*ITH MIXED FEELINGS, AND FORTIFIED BY ANOTHER superb breakfast whipped up by George and Sophie, the next morning the four friends readied themselves to leave for the front.

Aubrey had told himself, over and over, not to make the base into a home. It was always meant as a staging post, one that could be abandoned at any time. Leaving distinguishing marks behind could be a very bad idea if the Holmlanders overran Divodorum. Being human, however, they had all accumulated bits and pieces, items taken from pockets and put on window sills and shelves – just for a moment, mind you, but eventually staying there for long enough to gather dust. Small accretions – coins, snippets of wire, stubs of pencil – had changed the factory much as barnacles change the hulls of ships.

Before leaving, Aubrey wanted to rush about with a sack and clear everything away, but the horses were waiting in their traces and snorting in the cool of the morning. He shrugged and contented himself with giving the keys to von Stralick. 'You'll clean up the place if you have to leave before we get back?'

'Of course, Fitzwilliam. I was moving from secret base to secret base before you were out of knee pants.'

'Infant fashion insights aside, you'll be moving on soon?'

'It is hard to say,' Madame Zelinka said. She had abandoned her sling, showing much the same sort of fortitude that Caroline had with her injuries. Aubrey decided that females must have a higher tolerance to pain than males. 'The situation is bad, but I think we're starting to bring it under our control.' In a startling show of affection, Madame Zelinka patted Aubrey on the cheek. 'Stay alive. All of you.'

Von Stralick looked fondly at her. 'Zelinka says that we may have to send a team downriver, to check on the spillage and whether it has got away from us, but most of us will be here for some time.'

'You have plans?' Sophie asked. 'If the Holmlanders break through, what will you do?'

Madame Zelinka laughed. 'We shall manage.'

Von Stralick pointed at Aubrey. 'Take good care of that file I gave you. Use it wisely.'

Under George's gentle guidance, the horses positively frisked along the quiet streets. Their hooves echoed from the cobbles, but the wagon was well enough sprung that the ride was smooth and comfortable. Sophie was sitting next to George in the driver's seat, while Caroline and Aubrey had their backs to them in the rear of the wagon.

Aubrey had made sure that they wore full Directorate field uniforms. Going closer to the front as they were, he thought it necessary. If, heaven forbid, they fell into enemy hands, they could be tried as spies if they were dressed in civilian clothes. On the battlefront, of course, there was only one sentence for such a crime and Aubrey had long ago decided to do everything he could to prevent his friends being shot.

Caroline and Sophie looked very much at ease in the black trousers and jackets, and Aubrey wondered if the Directorate had spent more time tailoring the female uniforms than the male. Their calf-length boots, too, looked suspiciously well fitting, while the berets had a definite stylish shape instead of the unformed blobs that George and he had to balance on their head through sheer willpower.

After reading the letter from Commander Craddock, Aubrey had examined the magic neutraliser before resealing the crate. He'd been impressed by the strides made since the early models. This model was about the dimensions of a long case clock, as tall as Aubrey was. It was made of metal overlaid with fine canvas stretched tight and painted black. Four balancing pegs were attached to the sides, ready to be hammered into earth.

Otherwise, the magic neutraliser was featureless, a bland oblong to be planted upright and activated by the spells already embedded in its workings. Aubrey longed to peek inside to see those workings, to establish how the machine tapped into the magical firmament to sense spells at large and then issue equal and opposite magic. He assumed the range of effect was greater than the models he'd first seen on the stage in Trinovant at the command of the double agent Manfred the Great, but obviously not as large as the titanic version in the Divodorum fortress.

These, though, had the virtue of being portable, and he was sure that Colonel Stanley would have the working parameters.

The fortress loomed ahead of them, on the left of the road that bent away to the earthworks that guarded the northern approaches of the city. The improbable construction of the massive magic neutraliser jutted up and Aubrey hoped it was doing its silent, important work with efficiency.

The wagon jerked, then jolted, then stopped. George clicked his tongue then said, gently, 'Steady on there.'

One of the horses whinnied while the other snorted. George tried to soothe them.

'What's wrong?' Aubrey asked George, trusting to his friend's farming background. Once again – for approximately the billionth time – he was glad he had George along. Aubrey rode reasonably well and knew his way around a horse, but he had little experience with wagons.

'Come now.' George clicked his tongue again, and took his hand from steadying Sophie's shoulder. 'Move along there.'

The horses set off again. Aubrey craned his neck, looking for anything unusual. A motorcar was making its way toward them, but it was moving very slowly, hardly a threatening sight.

He was curious. The horses hadn't seemed the skittish types. They had the placidity and even temper of most draught animals. 'George?'

'Just horses being horses, old man. They sniffed something that gave them a start, that's all.' He shook the reins, but the horses had already begun plodding along again. Aubrey peered at them for a moment, looking through the noticeably tiny gap between George and Sophie. If the horses had been people, he would have described them as sulking. They had their heads down and he could imagine them muttering to each other about the general unfairness of whatever situation had irked them.

He was about to interrupt Caroline's studying of a map to engage her in a discussion of animal behaviour and how natural it was to ascribe human characteristics to beasts when a huge explosion shook the earth.

The horses screamed and shied. Aubrey was on his feet, searching for the source of the noise, doing his best to stay upright while the wagon jerked like a boat in a storm. Caroline, too, stood but coped easily with the movement of the wagon as she looked toward the fortress.

George tossed the reins to Sophie and leaped from the driver's seat. She called out as George darted along the flanks of the frightened beasts until they could see him and he could grab their bridles. His movements were smooth and certain, and he kept up a stream of low, soothing words, doing his best to calm the horses as they stamped, eyes rolling.

'Aubrey.' Caroline took his arm and pointed toward the fortress.

The magic neutralising tower was gone.

IN THE CHAOS, IT TOOK SOME TIME AND SOME STERN talking to convince the guards at the gatehouse that Aubrey should be allowed to see Major Saltin. George stayed with the still-agitated horses just inside the gates, attended by an equally agitated guard who actually seemed glad at having a specific duty.

Inside the walls, the compound was thick with smoke and dust, and with Gallian servicemen running about, singly and in squads. Shouting echoed from the buildings and the guard towers. No-one knew where Major Saltin was, either, and resented being stopped and asked such a thing when there were more important matters at hand.

Aubrey did wonder how running about and shouting was more important, but he decided not to press the issue.

The friends rounded the fortress chapel and then stood, stunned, looking at what had been the parade ground before it had become the site for the magic neutralising tower. Now, it was the site of a ruin. The tower lay smashed across the gravel, crushing a flagpole that had been on one corner of the parade ground. Several vehicles were on fire at the edge, near the barracks, and the rear section of a lorry was in very small pieces near the stub of one leg of the tower. A large section of one of the arms had fallen awry and had caved in the roof of a service building. Flames flickered from it; soldiers were cursing and uncoiling hoses that had lain unused for years. The greasy smoke added to the hellish atmosphere.

Aubrey was pressing toward the infirmary as a possible location for Major Saltin when the man himself emerged from the officers' mess.

Aubrey waved. 'Saltin!'

The Gallian put up a hand and peered through the smoke. Before making his way in their direction, he grabbed a hurrying corporal by the collar and spoke sharply to him.

'It was sabotage,' Major Saltin announced when he'd marched close enough. His face was blackened with smoke or soot. He waved an arm at the wreckage. 'A baker's lorry parked near the base of the tower exploded. The driver has been identified as leaving the fortress on foot just before the explosion.'

'Casualties?' Aubrey asked.

'No-one killed, which is entirely fortuitous. Recruits were training at the far end of the field only half an hour ago.'

'Infiltrators,' Caroline suggested. 'Holmland has had time to send teams into Divodorum for something like this.'

'I know.' Saltin grimaced, then wiped his cheek with the back of his hand, which only smeared the soot, leaving a long black streak. 'We have had new people coming in every day, changing over, heading to the front . . . It has been difficult.'

'Heading to the front,' Aubrey said, 'that's what we're about to do. We have a delivery to make to the Albion forces.'

Sophie was suddenly the cadet journalist again, notepad in hand. 'Major Saltin, this leaves you open to magical attack. What are you going to do about it?'

Major Saltin straightened. 'Our best, m'mselle. Reinforcements are starting to get through now, and we have some magical personnel among them. You can tell your readers that Divodorum will never fall.'

He saluted, then marched toward the burning building.

Sophie smiled, a little bitterly. 'By the time my readers hear from me, they will know whether Divodorum has fallen or not. I ask because I hope to write about events after this war has finished.'

'You do? George said something about doing the same thing,' Aubrey said.

Caroline rolled her eyes. 'Aubrey, Sophie and George have a plan to work on this together, after the war.'

'So we gather what we can,' Sophie said, 'while we go about our duties.'

'Aubrey and I shall help,' Caroline said.

'As long as we're clear about what we don't mention.' Aubrey faltered at the stern looks from both young women. 'I'm sorry?'

'Secrets, Aubrey?' Sophie said. 'What reason can there be for keeping secrets after the war?'

'Why, I'm sure there must be . . . Military knowledge . . . Intelligence . . .'

'Be careful,' Caroline said. 'Just because we're working for them, we don't want to end up like them.'

'Who?'

'The hoarders of secrets. Those who know best. The ones who feel that they're entitled to know things that the rest of us can't be trusted with.'

'You've just described most of the intelligence community. And most politicians.'

'Exactly.'

Nineteen

THE ROAD FROM DIVODORUM TO THE FRONT WAS choked. The lack of recent rain may have had benefits – Aubrey would have hated battling through churned-up mud – but it meant they ate, breathed and bathed in dust every inch of the twenty miles.

Complaining, however, would have been churlish. A stream of marching soldiers on the other side of the road, wounded and exhausted from fighting at the front, was a reminder of the dangers ahead.

Their way forward was determined by the stop-start progress of the column they had joined. Reinforcements to replace those fortunate enough to trudge back to the fortress, mostly, but also supply wagons and lorries, and a few private transports driven by those brave enough – or greedy enough – to risk being caught up in fighting in order to make a profit.

Commerce went on, Aubrey decided as he waved a

hand in front of his face for the umpteenth time, an exercise in futility as it simply replaced dust-laden air with more dust-laden air. He wouldn't have been surprised if that nervous-looking fellow with the wagon load of melons would be as happy to sell them to a Holmland unit as a Gallian or Albion one. The crisis–opportunity nexus was never more clearly demonstrated, and Aubrey couldn't blame him.

Determining when they actually reached the front was a difficult matter. The battle zone wasn't clearly marked with 'Welcome To . . .' signs. While the fighting was some distance away, the area that the military had colonised extended for miles back from the actual trenches and barbed wire. What had been farmland and woods was now dotted with tents and abuzz with activity as a khaki-coloured city had been thrown up.

What looked chaotic did have some sense about it, as evidenced as soon as they followed the melon vendor's wagon off the road and onto a freshly made track into the woods. Military police appeared and asked for papers. The melon vendor's credentials were obvious and he was waved through with instructions on how to reach the quartermaster, but the Gallian Military Police officers took some time to assess the papers George handed over. Eventually, after some consultation with officers summoned via a makeshift field telephone, they were directed to a farmhouse a few miles to the west, which was – according to last reports – the headquarters of the Albion military in the region.

The farmhouse would have been pretty, Aubrey thought, in normal circumstances. Without the soldiers camped out the front. Without the lorries lined up near the barn. Without the pall of war hanging over the place.

The house itself was two storeys, built of local stone. The entrance sported a climbing rose that was gamely throwing out small white flowers. A small apple orchard ran away down the slope on one side, while the barn, pig sty and sundry other farming outbuildings that Aubrey was sure would give George a jab of nostalgia were on the other.

After more guards and more checking of papers, Aubrey and Caroline were led inside to see General Apsley while George and Sophie waited outside.

A huge desk had replaced the kitchen table in the largest room of the house. General Apsley stood behind it, facing away, hands behind his back and staring out of the mullioned window, over the yard, past the duck pond into the distance, where an artillery barrage marked the front proper. When Aubrey and Caroline were announced by the guard, he turned.

Aubrey had some trepidation when the general advanced and was hugely relieved when he extended his hand. 'Ah, Fitzwilliam. Timely, very timely.'

'Sir.' Aubrey shook, glad not to be denounced as the Traitor of Albion, and introduced Caroline.

Though General Apsley was a big man, he wasn't tall. His trunk was extraordinarily long, from his broad shoulders to his hips, but it was supported by legs that belonged to a much smaller person. Aubrey imagined that, sitting down, Apsley would tower over everyone.

Apsley studied both of them for a moment, keenly, then he said what Aubrey had been expecting: 'I knew your father, Fitzwilliam, when he was in the service.'

Apsley must have been a good twenty years older than Sir Darius. 'Did he serve under you, sir?'

'He did, indeed.' General Apsley indulged in a little moustache puffing. 'Had trouble following orders, but he was a brilliant leader. Brilliant.' He turned his attention to Caroline. 'I have one of your mother's paintings at home, young lady. It's the most startling thing I own.'

'I'm glad to hear it,' Caroline said carefully.

'We have a delivery for you, sir,' Aubrey said. 'I understand you're expecting it.'

'We are indeed, and Stanley can't wait to get his hands on it.'

'One other thing.' Aubrey reached for his satchel, intending to hand over von Stralick's file, but was interrupted by a knock at the door.

A small neat man hurried into the room. 'Ah, Stanley,' General Apsley said. 'I was just talking about you.'

Lieutenant-Colonel Stanley wore the Directorate field uniform of discreet black with minimum trappings. He was balding, with small round glasses, more like an accountant than a very senior intelligence officer. 'Fitzwilliam! You're here!'

'We came as soon as we could, sir. One dozen magic neutralisers ready for your disposal.'

Colonel Stanley beamed. 'Splendid! We're getting some indication of a magical build-up at the front, so these will come in handy.'

'We have some bad news, however,' Caroline said. 'The magic neutraliser in Divodorum has been destroyed.'

'That was the explosion earlier today?' General Apsley asked sharply.

'It was sabotage, sir,' Aubrey said.

'Any hope of repairing the machine?' Stanley said.

'No chance at all, sir,' Aubrey said. 'But they have

some magical agents on site. They're hoping they can do something, defence-wise.'

'I hope so.' Stanley took off his glasses, stared at them for a moment, then put them back on. 'Something is in the air, Fitzwilliam. I fear we are about to come under the hammer.'

'And that hammer promises to be a mighty one,' General Apsley said. 'Any sign of reinforcements while you were in Divodorum? We've been promised some colonials. I wouldn't mind a battalion or two of those Antipodeans. Plucky fighters, the lot of 'em.'

'Nothing while we were there, sir. Major Saltin, at the fortress, was expecting some at any time.'

'Excellent, excellent,' General Apsley said. 'Why don't you two go and treat yourselves to a cup of tea while we sort out the best place to deploy these machines?'

'Sir.' Aubrey saluted, then his hand went to his satchel – but seeing the map Colonel Stanley spread on the desk, he hesitated, especially when he saw Caroline's interest.

'Sir? Do you have a copy of that map we could take?'

'Of course. Can't say it's entirely accurate, but we revise it as quickly as news comes in.'

General Apsley pointed out the triple parallel lines of trenches that marked the front line of the Allied forces, with communications trenches running between them. The rearmost was the trench where reserves gathered, to replace the troops closer to the Holmland lines – or to ready themselves for an attack. The second trench was almost five hundred yards away, and the front line trench a further hundred yards nearer the Holmlanders. The long lines were marked by other, partially constructed trenches. Some were dead ends, some pushed into no-man's-land, some were simply false starts.

The landscape had been entirely changed. The narrow valley had been turned into a theatre of war.

Aubrey and Caroline left the two officers poring over the map and deciding where they'd place the magic neutralisers to the greatest advantage, and went to find George and Sophie.

They found them in the large mess tent that had been pitched on the other side of the barn. 'Care for a late lunch?' George asked. An empty plate sat on the table in front of him. 'It's simple, but filling, sausages mostly. Guaranteed to keep a soldier alive for a while, anyway.'

'The soldiers took the wagon away,' Sophie explained. She was using her fork to poke at what had once been an egg before army cooks had their way with it. 'They said we could eat here.'

'I wouldn't let them take it until we'd made arrangements for the horses,' George added. 'I didn't like to think of them abandoned or anything like that.'

'I'm sure they'll be looked on as valuable recruits.' Aubrey sat on the bench across from George and Sophie.

'They have handlers and farriers and people dedicated to taking care of horses. I'm happy with that,' George said.

'And what are we to do now?' Sophie had her notebook out and it was full of jottings about her Divodorum observations, from what Aubrey could judge reading upside down.

'We make ourselves useful to the Directorate,' Caroline said. 'Isn't that right, Aubrey?'

'It's right, but not terribly helpful. It's one of the drawbacks of being special operatives.' Aubrey drummed his fingers on the table. 'I'd like to see how the magic neutralisers are deployed. It's just the sort of information that might be useful, back at the Directorate.'

'I suppose that would mean going to the front,' George said. 'The front front, I mean, not this back front. If that's clear.'

'As the mud I'm glad isn't around,' Aubrey said. 'Do you have that map, Caroline?'

George moved his plate and cutlery. Caroline spread the map on the table and Aubrey frowned at it.

'One thing I should ask,' Caroline said to him.

'Just one?'

'For now.'

'Go ahead.'

'You're not thinking of leaving us behind and slipping up there by yourself, are you?'

Aubrey touched his forehead. For an awful moment he was certain that his thoughts were written across it in big, bold letters. He couldn't answer the accusation by denying it, because it *was* exactly what he'd been thinking, or by confirming it, because that would start an argument he'd never win, so he decided to lunge for a tactic he'd seen some of his father's politician colleagues use: he didn't answer the question that had been asked – he answered a completely different one.

'I never said that war isn't a filthy business. I condemn it utterly.'

Caroline crossed her arms. 'You're not answering the question.'

He had to smile. 'I long to see you in Parliament. I have some people I wouldn't mind seeing you skewer.'

'Aubrey.' Sophie pointed at him with her pencil. 'We will tie you up with ropes if you don't agree to take us.'

'George,' Aubrey appealed. 'There's no point my risking you three when I can nip up and back before you know it.'

George spread his hands. 'I know you're concerned for us, old man, but we're concerned for you. We're all nipping, or none of us nip.'

WHEN THEY FOUND COLONEL STANLEY IN THE BARN, HE was more than happy for them to accompany him. 'I understand that you're something of an expert on these magic neutralisers, Fitzwilliam,' he said, after instructing one of his agents to nail down the packing case again.

'I wouldn't say expert, sir. I've had some experience with them, that's all.'

'Well, that's better than any of us here. I'm more your transference magic sort of man, myself.'

'Really? Do you mind if I pick your brains on that, sir?'

Which is how Aubrey sat up the front of the lorry with Stanley and the driver, while the others were relegated to the canvas-covered back. It was slow going through the maze of tracks cutting through the woods and negotiating the ridges and the rocky creeks. As well, they were constantly being blocked by slow-moving supply wagons and lorries, twice having to back off the road to allow traffic in the other direction. A depressing number of ambulances, both official and makeshift, nosed their way through the marching soldiers, a reminder, if any needed it, of what could lie ahead.

Finally they debouched into a wide open area sheltered by a rocky outcrop. The large tents of a field hospital were the site of most activity, but the easternmost side of the glade had become a transport station with lorries unloading boxes of ammunition and foodstuffs.

'This is as close as we can get by motor,' Stanley said. He bounded out of the cabin and peered about. Lorries, carts, ambulances, and many, many soldiers were packed into an area the size of a football pitch. A few troopers, more phlegmatic than the others, had started campfires and were making tea or coffee.

Aubrey had never seen so many slumped shoulders in one place at one time. The men had the weariness about them that came from extreme privation. Some twitched at unexpected noises; others didn't move even when their name was called. War was grinding them to pieces.

Stanley hurried about with papers in hand, looking more like an accountant than ever, until he found the officer he was looking for. The officer disappeared toward a neat line of tents and came back with a squad of infantrymen. The sun was drifting below the tops of the hills by the time the squad had unloaded the magic neutralisers, strung the crates in intricate rope cradles, and begun shuffling in the direction of the trenches.

Aubrey and his friends were on their feet instantly, and followed.

The certainty that they were heading in the right direction came not from sight – although the trees became sparser and more shredded as they picked their way over ground that was broken by large holes thrown up by artillery shells – but through hearing. The sounds coming to them were faint, growing stronger and oddly punctuated, but unmistakably that of war. Aubrey's uneasiness grew as machine guns chattered insanely for minutes at a time before falling silent. He heard shouts in Gallian and Albionish and, more chilling, Holmlandish.

The enemy was that close.

Stanley led them through a defile where a creek had once run and then motioned for them to crouch. Spread out before them was the battlefield.

The place where Gallia and Holmland had fought to a standstill in the early days of the confrontation had once been a narrow valley, a gap between ridges of the rather grandly named Grentellier Mountains that separated Divodorum from Stalsfrieden.

The Grentellier Mountains were really more a series of low hills and ridges, lines of them running roughly north-west to south-east. One main road crossed this region, somewhat to the south of where Aubrey and his friends now found themselves; it was the route between the Gallian city and the Holmland one.

The valley snaked along, widening and narrowing as it went, varying somewhere between one and two miles across. The hills on either side were studded with artillery emplacements, wherever engineers could drag them. The valley floor itself had been transformed from a narrow wooded corner of the countryside into a maze of trenches, bunkers and barbed wire.

Aubrey felt small in the face of this theatre of war, but he knew that this was but a small part of the battlelines that stretched for miles in either direction.

'This is a crucial chokepoint,' Stanley said. He was crouching on one knee, sweeping his binoculars across the eerie scene. 'We must hold here. If we don't, the Holmlanders will pour through, double back, and chew into the rear of our lines.'

Aubrey's imagination, only too willing, provided a vision of the world looking down on this tiny patch. The attention of the powerful, the eager, the invested was, for a time, turned here.

'What's this place called?' he asked.

The officer lowered his field glasses and indicated to his right. A hundred yards away, a mound of rubble stood near the remains of a pond. 'We call it Fremont, after that farmhouse over there.'

'That's not a farmhouse,' George said. 'That's a ruin.'

Stanley shrugged. 'It was a farmhouse. Fremont was the name of the family who lived there, apparently.'

'Family?' Aubrey asked. 'Where are they now?'

Stanley had the good grace to look guilty. 'I'm afraid I don't know. Safe in Divodorum, I hope.'

Aubrey wondered if, one day, the Battle of Fremont would rate a paragraph in a history book, or if it would be a chapter of its own.

Sophie tapped Aubrey on the shoulder and pointed. 'Look.'

Against the setting sun, it was hard to make out but the tiny spot resolved itself gradually. 'An ornithopter.'

'Holmlander,' Stanley said after using his field glasses. 'I thought we'd shot down most of their observers.'

The ornithopter was travelling toward them. Caroline shaded her eyes. 'He's having trouble controlling the side slipping in the wind.'

Aubrey took Caroline's word for it. 'Do we have any aircraft in the area, sir?'

'Not many,' Stanley said. 'The last I heard was that we were anticipating a squadron or two.' He made a sour face. '"Expect them at any time" was the official phrasing.'

The ornithopter was flying very high. Aubrey assumed that it was the better to observe the entire battlefront. The guns of the Albionites and the Gallians were silent for the moment. Such a tiny target was impossible, they all seemed to agree, not worth wasting ammunition.

It was a sensible, rational military decision, but an optimistic rifleman obviously had other ideas: a shot rang out.

Immediately, the ornithopter lurched sideways, as if skidding on the surface of a frozen pond. Then it dropped, spewing a trail of smoke and flame.

'Remarkable,' Stanley breathed.

'He's doomed,' Caroline said. 'His tail control is gone. Fuel tank too. He might be able to glide it in, if he's very, very good.'

Good, or determined, that's just what the pilot was attempting. Aubrey found himself twitching and wincing with every jerky movement of the aircraft. The wings beat frantically as the pilot tried to kill his airspeed while retaining some control. The propensity of the machine to plummet like a stone while he was attempting this was a significant handicap, but he wasn't giving up.

Aubrey realised he didn't care if the pilot was Holm-landish, Gallian or from another planet entirely. Silently, he cheered him on. His hands curled into fists as the ornithopter stuttered and attempted to roll, which would be certain death for the operator – as opposed to the most probable death that awaited if he could glide the machine into a landing.

'You can do it,' George muttered and Aubrey knew he wasn't alone. He glanced at all of his friends and saw they were united in urging the pilot to success. Even the infantrymen of Stanley's squad were watching intently, clearly hoping the pilot would succeed.

The ornithopter twisted, then tilted to one side. Suddenly, in his attempt to right the craft, the pilot sent it hurtling across the lines.

It was heading straight toward them.

Aubrey couldn't help it. Even though he was crouching, he ducked as it flashed overhead at tree-top level, a black shadow against the sky. Caroline cried out and the machine, larger than life, stalled and slipped sideways before the nose lifted a little. It was no good. The ornithopter laboured and banked slowly in the direction of Divodorum, then it clipped the tallest trees skirting the road. The sound of the impact could be heard even at this distance.

Smoke rose from the site of the crash and Aubrey sank until he was sitting, aghast at what he had just seen, on the hard dirt.

Aubrey's father rarely spoke about his war experiences, but since, at the time, his deeds had been highlighted in the popular press, they had gained a currency that meant Aubrey had read about them from an early age. 'Adventures' was how they were inevitably described. Daring raids, perilous escapes, heart-stopping rescues, the stories of Darius Fitzwilliam's exploits had added to the reputation of the young man who was already a public figure before he went to war. Of course, the stories were later immensely helpful in garnering public support for his political career.

Even as a lad, Aubrey was aware enough to understand that the stories he read were coloured, so to speak. He knew his father, and Sir Darius would have laughed at some of the platitudes the man in the books regularly bandied about. Aubrey trusted the accounts of his father's service friends more. People like George's father, who was with Sir Darius when his military service was at its most dangerous. George's father was also reticent to discuss war stories, but the few fragments he let slip told of a man he would follow anywhere – brave and steadfast. He also hinted at the horrors of war and of those who didn't come back.

Aubrey glanced again in the direction of the ornithopter crash, then looked toward the barbed wire and smoke of the front. This was war: a vast machine that chewed up people.

Twenty

THE WEEKS SINCE THE HOLMLAND ADVANCE HAD BEEN halted had been well spent, Aubrey decided as they moved through the trenches. He knew that foot soldiers had been notorious scroungers ever since they'd discovered that waiting for the gates of Troy to open meant that they had a long camping holiday ahead of them. Those who were dug in at Fremont were no exception. In military parlance, they had entrenched themselves well, shoring up the sides of the diggings with rocks, timber and – if Aubrey was any judge – the remains of any shot-down ornithopters. Neatly fashioned walkways had been laid across marshy ground that would be a nightmare in rainy weather.

Dugouts had been scooped into the side of trenches at intervals; wary-eyed infantrymen watched as the squad passed with their magic neutralisers. In the manner of soldiers everywhere, the infantrymen were mostly sleeping or eating, making the most of a lull in the artillery barrage. Some were in disarray, missing parts of their uniforms, but Colonel Stanley had developed the selective blindness of the good officer and ignored such paltry matters. Aubrey noticed, however, that no matter how ragged the uniform, no soldier was without his soup-plate helmet. Aubrey touched his beret, which he was sure now looked more like a dust-ridden tea cosy, and felt vulnerable.

Lanterns appeared at intervals as the sun continued to set and the homely smells of cooking wafted through the trenches. For a time, these smells overcame the unfortunate stench of too many men living in such confined circumstances, circumstances that included a lack of running water and, in particular, sewerage. Aubrey was sure the commanders were following the manual in hygiene procedures, but he held his breath as he hurried past the most noisome pits.

When they reached the front line of trenches, Colonel Stanley consulted area commanders, explaining his job and asking for assistance in positioning the magic neutralisers. One by one they were erected and dug into the walls of trenches, to make them as stable as possible while keeping them out of the way of the troops who would be hurrying along the narrowness of the trenches. Stanley consulted Aubrey on every deployment, and fretted over the coverage that they were hoping to achieve. The range of effect of each neutraliser was meant to overlap – but that was the desired outcome and was based on laboratory trials. On the ground, things had a way of working out differently. From the schematics, Aubrey saw how the range of effect was designed to be linear, to keep the actual trench area safe. The intention was for the effect to extend twenty yards or so front and back, projecting out into no-man's-land, while reaching further to either side along the length of the trenches.

This, of course, was based on straight lines. With the best intention in the world, the trenches were not straight. They curved pragmatically, following contours, dodging around large boulders, winding their way across the battered landscape. The result of their deploying the neutralisers was inevitably going to be less than the optimum designed by the masterminds back at Darnleigh House.

But distinctly better than nothing, Aubrey thought, wiping grime from his face as they settled the last magic neutraliser into place in a position on the north-west extremity of the Allied position, about two miles from where they first reached the trenches. Colonel Stanley gestured at the sandbagged dugout that was nearby, where lantern light pushed away the night. 'Major Davidson is waiting for us with some supper.'

George tamped down some loose earth with his foot. 'Excellent. After you, Sophie.'

Aubrey hesitated and glanced at the sentry who was standing on a firing step and using field glasses to peer across to the Holmland lines. 'I'll be there in a moment.'

Caroline gave him a curious look, but she said nothing as she filed past with the others. Aubrey tapped the sentry on the leg, only to have him jerk and try to whirl around while grappling for the rifle that was standing by his side. Only Aubrey's steadying prevented him from falling off the firing step. 'May I take a look?' he asked.

The sentry was a narrow-faced fellow with a beaky nose, somewhere in his early twenties, with narrow shoulders and skinny frame. The helmet on his head made him look like a table lamp. When he gave Aubrey the field glasses, his hands shook. 'They're all yours, sir.' He swallowed and took off his helmet. 'You'll need this.'

The sentry ducked as Aubrey mounted the firing step, but Aubrey hardly noticed. He was too busy taking in the scene.

Glimmers came from the hills some miles behind the lines, where troops must be encamped with their cooking fires and lanterns, but closer at hand tiny splinters of light escaped from where the Holmland trenches lay. It was hard to judge, but Aubrey guessed they were roughly two hundred yards away across broken ground. A volley of shots sounded to his right and Aubrey instinctively flinched, crouching low, even though he couldn't tell if the rounds came from this side or that. No-man's-land was a place of shadows that collected in gullies or shell holes and were strained by barbed wire.

A flare went up, bathing the warscape in bright, pitiless light, banishing the shadows, making the ruined land suddenly sharp and hard-edged. A half-hearted stone's throw away from where Aubrey stood was a battered wooden frame with blades hammered in at angles, the ghastly medieval siege defence made modern. It was only one of countless hazards Aubrey could see, obstacles to breaching what looked like a sea of barbed wire.

On the other side of the wooden frame, draped over a ragged shell hole, was a body. Mercifully, it had slid halfway into the crater. Aubrey wondered if the soldier had thought he was safe, for a tiny moment, safe at the bottom of a hole made by a massive explosion, or whether he'd been shot earlier and had crawled, scrabbling at the hard earth, searching for a place of refuge before expiring.

Aubrey couldn't make out the uniform. It could have been Albionite, Gallian or Holmlander, or one of the colonials, nationality coming to nothing in the end.

The flare spluttered in its arc, winked, then disappeared after having done its job of providing a few seconds of light, enough for an observer to sketch details for tomorrow's troop movements. Aubrey stood silently in the dark for a moment, knowing that he'd been granted a glimpse into the dark heart of war.

A soft voice interrupted his thoughts. 'You see anyone?'

It took Aubrey a moment to realise that it was the sentry who was talking. The man was sitting on the firing step at Aubrey's feet, smoking and staring at the opposite wall of the trench.

'I'm sorry?' Aubrey asked.

'You see anyone out there?' The sentry added as an afterthought: 'Sir?'

'Not at the moment.'

'Ah. You're lucky, then. I always see 'em, flitting about out there.' A short, dry laugh. 'Imagination. Puts the wind up, though.'

'I'm sure it would.' Aubrey wasn't about to criticise anyone for that, now he'd gazed over the nightmare landscape.

'Sometimes they're real, though. Holmlanders sussing us out, looking for the best ways across. Raiding teams.'

'Raiders?'

'They send 'em over, every now and then. When they think we're not looking. Nasty work, if they get into our trenches.' Another dry laugh. 'Can't complain, not really. We do the same when we can.'

'You've been across there?'

'Twice. Both times I never thought I'd make it over there. Then I thought I'd never make it back. Three times? No thanks.'

'What's it like out there?'

Silence. Aubrey wondered if he'd offended the man, and then he thought the sentry must have nodded off. When he finally spoke, Aubrey started. 'It smells,' the sentry said. 'Something horrible.'

Aubrey handed back the helmet and the field glasses.

Supper was brutally sparse: bread and cheese, followed by bread and jam, served with tin mugs of tea. The dugout was well floored with boards that looked as if they had come from a farm building. Aubrey noted how Colonel Stanley and Major Davidson both ate exactly what the small squad of infantrymen outside the dugout ate. The lantern light was low, the conversation muted.

Major Davidson had been at the front for weeks and it showed. His uniform and his moustache were trim and neat, but every movement, every gesture was jittery. His eyes kept straying to the field telephone sitting on an empty ammunition box by his side, and to the entrance of the dugout with its screen made from jute bags. He was a man waiting for something, Aubrey realised. It was going to be dreadful, whatever it was: the call to advance, news of a Holmland breakthrough – the exact nature was uncertain. Uncertainty bred imagining, imagining bred fear, and fear bred more fear. As Commanding Officer, Davidson couldn't show his feelings, and this only made it worse.

The bread was stale and the cheese past its best but it was an awkward meal. Stanley tried to be positive, but Major Davidson had developed an armour plating against cheerfulness. He was polite, but restrained, as if any show of emotion could open the floodgates – and who would know what would pour out then?

He farewelled them, giving thanks for the extra protection of the magic neutralisers before vanishing back into the dugout, and to another sleepless night, if Aubrey was any judge.

Stanley took a deep breath, and then coughed to cover the fact that this was a bad idea. 'He's not unusual,' he said as he led them back toward the rear. 'All of the commanders are showing signs like that.'

'And the troops?' Sophie asked. 'What about them?'

Aubrey had seen Sophie and George talking to the infantrymen in spare moments, asking for their impressions, their stories. Their honest approaches had been rewarded, again and again, with even the most taciturn soldier offering a thought or two.

'They're finding it hard as well,' Stanley admitted. 'They hate the inaction, but they fear the prospect of action. It's an awful situation to be in.'

Another flare cast its light across the top of the trench. Dull hammering not far away made the ground shake and Aubrey raised an eyebrow. 'Tunnelling?'

'It could be,' Stanley said. 'It could be more trenching or shelling in the distance.'

Aubrey scratched his chin and he noticed that Caroline was also studying the ground in the light cast by Stanley's lantern.

Before anyone could react, it was George who tried to settle the matter. He used a pair of stakes that had been hammered in at chest height to lever himself up the side of the trench. He peeked over the edge and then dropped, shouting, 'Cavalry!'

Stanley goggled at George as Sophie helped him to his feet. 'Are you mad? Cavalry at night?'

Aubrey knew better than to doubt George. 'Use your whistle, Stanley, quickly.'

Stanley hesitated and that was enough for Caroline. She produced her pistol, pointed it at the sky and loosed three quick rounds.

Major Davidson bolted out of the dugout, his eyes bulging, brandishing his sidearm. 'What's going on here?'

'You're being attacked,' Aubrey said as calmly as he could. 'Rouse your men.'

'Attacked? How? What?' He spied the lone sentry. 'What's going on out there?'

'Horses, sir,' the sentry snapped. 'Lots of horses.'

Davidson swore and bounded up onto the firing step, pushing the sentry aside. He swore again. 'Get me a flare gun, damn you!'

The sentry darted into the dugout and staggered back with the bulky shape of a flare gun in his hand. With a show of initiative, he didn't wait to give it to Major Davidson. Instead, he fired it.

Aubrey leaped onto the firing step just as the flare bloomed overhead. The ghastly white light revealed that they were under an unlikely attack. Scores of horsemen were charging toward them across the war-torn landscape. Stunned, Aubrey took in the improbable sight of a massed cavalry charge, their brass-spangled, white-belted navy jackets, their plumed shakos, their raised sabres. They flowed across no-man's-land, weaving between obstacles without missing a step, holding the line as they leaped magnificently over the barbed wire as if it were hedgerows. A bugler was giving wind, urging his comrades forward.

Davidson blew his whistle, nearly deafening Aubrey, then he started shouting. Stanley assisted, running along the trench and rousing sleeping men, kicking their rifles at them.

Caroline leaped up onto the firing step. She took one look and then began reloading her pistol.

'It doesn't make sense,' Aubrey said. 'In this day and age? Here? A cavalry charge?'

George helped Sophie onto the step next to Aubrey, then joined her. 'Plenty of cavalry regiments around, old man. Probably some old general convinced someone that it was a good idea.'

A wicked chatter came from their left and the cheers went up from the Albionite infantrymen. Volleys of rifle fire sounded one after the other as the officers bullied the men into ranks.

'Against machine guns? Who'd ever think a cavalry charge against machine guns would be a good idea?'

Sophie tugged on his sleeve. She was wearing a helmet. It didn't fit and made her look even more petite than she was. 'Aubrey, it's not real. It's an illusion.'

Aubrey gaped. 'Everything? The horses? The noise?'

The cry went up to fix bayonets.

'It is very good magic. Many spells together.'

The charge was only fifty yards away, a line of warrior-laden horseflesh that was unfazed by any obstacle in its path.

Cries of horror went up from the Albionites as the charge came nearer and nearer. A grenade, hastily flung, exploded but didn't make a dent in the wall of galloping death. Aubrey could see the eyes of the horses, the whites large and panicked.

His pistol was in his hand. He didn't remember un-holstering it. 'Illusion?' he said to Sophie.

'Yes.'

He glared as the charge came to within forty yards – more panic from the Albionites – then thirty. The rifle fire was growing ragged, the Albionite ranks losing formation despite the oaths from the officers – then, when the horses reached the twenty-yard line, rising over the last of the barbed wire, they simply melted away like smoke on the wind.

'Magic neutralisers,' Aubrey said, and he tried to tell himself that the hammering of his heart at such a rate was entirely normal, given the circumstances. He sagged against the parapet. 'At least we now know that they work.'

THE NIGHT BECAME A LONG ONE. DESPITE THE DEBRIEFING, Major Davidson remained sceptical. Even Colonel Stanley's backing didn't convince him that the cavalry charge had been an illusion. After the second phantom infantry advance of the night, however, he began to understand.

Aubrey hoped that intelligence would help. With Major Davidson's aid, he commandeered some of the messengers who were racing along trenches, bringing reports from up and down the line of similar phantom attacks. He wanted them to spread the word that the attacks were illusory, and that the entire Allied line was firing at thin air and wasting ammunition.

Knowledge was one thing. The sudden appearance of what looked like an enemy attack was another. An hour later, a squadron of low-flying ornithopters swooped toward their position. This caused panic in the troops and, despite their officers telling them to stand easy, a fusillade of rifle fire sprang up from the trenches until the flying machines evaporated in the early morning light.

A red-eyed Major Davidson confronted Aubrey as he and his friends were going about the practical duty of rebagging the front of his dugout where it had toppled in the mad scramble caused by the cavalry charge. 'So what are we going to do about this, then? None of my men have had a wink of sleep all night. They were jumpy enough before this nonsense, but now . . .'

His voice trailed off and Aubrey knew that his men weren't the only ones who were being pushed to the edge. 'Miss Delroy here has pointed out some characteristics of the illusions. A competent magician should be able to detect them in plenty of time to warn your troops.'

'Magician, eh?' Davidson turned to Stanley. 'And exactly how many of your spell boys do you have at the front, Stanley? Is it three or four?'

'We've been asking for more frontline operatives for some time now,' Stanley said. He was both apologetic and unutterably weary. 'We're promised that they'll be here any time now.'

They were interrupted by a band of soldiers limping toward them. The leading sergeant gave Davidson and Stanley an exhausted salute. 'Major Long's compliments, sir, but could you spare some men? We've been doing it hard up the line a bit.'

The sergeant went on to report about the disaster a little further down the line.

The 4th Foot Regiment had been under siege all

night from phantom attacks without the help of magic neutralisers, getting no rest until they realised the attacks never reached them. Time and again, the horses would veer away and retreat just as they came close to the trenches, testing nerves and discipline until a suspicious corporal finally saw them passing right through solid barbed wire. After that they had successfully ignored lines of marching infantry, skirmishers and even a wave of dog attacks.

Then a real attack nearly succeeded in capturing their position.

It was a key location, the intersection of a number of important trenches and supply lines, a slightly elevated knob of land, perfect for machine gun emplacements. Having understood the news that the attacks were illusions, when a company of Holmlanders advanced on the position the order was given to ignore them, especially since they were wearing outmoded uniforms in brilliant scarlet, more suited to a hundred years ago than today.

When the scarlet-clad Holmlanders launched them-selves into the trenches and set about with bayonets that were deadly evidence of their non-illusory nature, the Albionites panicked and ran. It was only the efforts of a callow lieutenant in rallying a squad of men and firing by rank back along the trench that drove them off.

It had been a close thing, and a bloody one. After that skirmish, the inability to tell phantom attack from real one started to drive the men mad. Holmland snipers added to the despair, slipping into place during the phantom advances and having great success in picking off any confused Albionites showing themselves.

Davidson took this in calmly, despatching a squad to help, and Aubrey revised his opinion of the man again.

He was coping in circumstances for which no military training would have been adequate.

After that, things continued to fall apart. Aubrey found himself assisting Caroline with first aid, with Sophie and George as the other assistants in a makeshift infirmary where three important trenches intersected, half a mile from Major Davidson's dugout. Caroline had calmly assured the only qualified medic in the area that he was needed elsewhere, leaving the four friends to deal with less urgent cases.

Less urgent cases they may have been, but Aubrey hadn't known that so much blood existed in the entire world.

Hours stretched out. Amid the noise and confusion, Aubrey and his friends took turns in snatching sleep, curled up wherever they could find a space. It wasn't comfortable, and was barely restful, but it was better than falling over from exhaustion.

The men were generally stoic, putting up with basic cleaning and bandaging of wounds so they could hobble back to their companies, but occasionally a screamer was brought in. Not necessarily the most badly wounded, screamers kept up a hair-raising cry that could be heard up and down the trenches and did nothing to lift spirits.

Caroline was magnificent. Her orders were calm and never ambiguous. She saw events unfolding before they happened and was able to direct her efforts – and the fumblings of Aubrey, George and Sophie – to the correct patients as they needed it. Soldiers moved in and out of their first aid emplacement like morning commuters at an underground station, coming and going, coming and going, but never slackening until …

Aubrey straightened from knotting a bandage around the leg of a gritted-teeth veteran. 'Where are the rest of them?' he said and winced at the pain in his back.

'We're done,' Caroline said. She was washing her hands in a bucket of crimson water. 'For now.'

Sophie scanned the trenches in each direction. 'I cannot see anyone coming.'

'We're in a lull,' George said. He peered upward at a sky that was no longer night. 'And I'm about to say something I never thought I would.'

'And what's that?' Aubrey asked.

George looked glum. 'It's morning and I don't feel much like breakfast.'

Twenty-one

*I*N A WAR, BEARING STRETCHERS WAS AS VITAL AS FIRING rifles. Aubrey knew that, but he'd had enough. Not enough of carrying the poor soldier who could bleed to death if George and he couldn't get him to the field hospital in time, but enough of the appallingness that put young men on stretchers to bleed to death.

The sun, still low in the sky, flashed in Aubrey's eyes as George and he jogged as smoothly as they could. He couldn't spare a hand to shade himself, but this was a minor discomfort compared to the patient on the stretcher. On either side, Caroline and Sophie steadied the lad – and that's all he was – while the red stain spread on his chest. He'd lost consciousness as soon as they set out, which was a blessing, but Aubrey had an idea that jolting was the last thing he needed.

This isn't good, he thought. The breath laboured in his lungs. His muscles burned and his hands were aching from gripping the handles of the stretcher. *This isn't the way to solve anything.*

Seeing the battlefield and observing its furtive, haunted inhabitants, Aubrey had realised that the war had sprung a life of its own. It was a sprawling, greedy monster that was devouring soldiers and machinery and leaving wrecks behind. The allies were doing what they could, but battles couldn't be won on promises. Any time now, reinforcements were coming. Any time now, the special-ised magical help would arrive.

Dr Tremaine didn't work on an 'any time now' schedule. He moved heaven and earth to suit his ends, and he did it when he needed to.

A squad of wide-eyed youngsters hurried past headed for the front, rifles slung on their backs. Each of them had a pack so heavy that it made them run almost doubled over.

Once they delivered the wounded soldier to the field hospital, Aubrey and his friends could continue, making their way back to Divodorum and then across Gallia back home to Albion. They'd be able to give first-hand reports of the front, the deficiencies and snags and where best to help. If nothing happened quickly enough, he was sure that they could use Sophie's friends in the newspapers to create the sort of scandal that would have politicians scurrying to do something about it – or, at least, to be *seen* to do something about it. It was a reasonable, clever plan.

He glanced at the almost bloodless face of the boy they were rescuing. His freckles were now standing out starkly against his pallor.

It jabbed at him. While they were safe in Albion, boys like this would be dying. Aubrey would be fleeing danger, but leaving others to take his place.

As fond as he was of his own skin, there was something indecent about such a prospect.

They reached the chaos that was the field hospital just as the Holmland artillery opened up on the trenches they'd left behind. The Holmland Supreme Army Command wasn't giving the Allies any rest.

'This is what they must call softening up,' George said after they'd handed over their burden to real doctors, bloodied and harassed, but with knowledge that none of them had.

'It would seem so,' Aubrey said. They found some shade, an obstinate laurel tree next to one of the smaller medical tents. The smell of disinfectant was strong and Aubrey shuddered. 'They'll aim to make us exhausted, frightened, on edge, and then launch a major attack. It's from the manual.'

'I'm sure the magical feints are not,' Sophie said. 'Generals are suspicious of magic, I hear.'

'They used to be,' Caroline said. She was stretching, pushing her hands up over her head in a display that drew glances from those hurrying past, officers and troops alike. 'Now they're happy to entertain any possibility that could help them win. Isn't that right, Aubrey?'

'Certainly. That's why Dr Tremaine has had no trouble convincing the Holmland Supreme Army Command about his tactics. They love success.'

George snorted. 'Supreme Army Command. They wouldn't be so chuffed if they could swap with some of their front-line infantry.'

Aubrey sometimes imagined his mind as a long line of dominos, with bits and pieces of information – observations, readings, overheard conversations – as tiles, standing independently until one is given a tiny shove.

This time, George Doyle was that shove.

Aubrey jumped to his feet. 'Does anyone know where Colonel Stanley is?'

'Before we left, he said he was going to check the other neutralisers,' Sophie said. 'Then he was coming back to headquarters.'

'What is it, Aubrey?' Caroline said. 'You have that look again.'

'What? This look?'

'Not that one. Another one. The one that says you have a hare-brained, dangerous idea that could save the day.'

'Day-saving is one of his specialities,' George pointed out to Sophie. 'And if ever I saw a day that needed saving, it was this one.'

They found Colonel Stanley halfway from the front. He was making hard work of it, pushing against a mass of troops heading to bolster numbers against the expected attack. He cheered up remarkably when they greeted him.

'Transference Magic?' he shouted over the tramp of marching feet and boom of artillery, the allies beginning to return fire. 'It's been a while, to tell the truth. The last few years I've been in admin, mostly. Not much chance for practical magic.'

'You're the best we have,' Aubrey shouted back. 'If you can help, I might be able to buy us some time.'

'For our reinforcements to arrive?'

'That's it,' Aubrey shouted, loudly enough to attract stares. He lowered his voice. 'But I need to know if I'm attempting something incredibly stupid or not.'

MIDDAY WAS NEAR BY THE TIME THEY FOUND A DUGOUT IN the secondary line of trenches, one that showed signs of being temporarily unused. Wooden packing boxes were scattered about, and a wit had used one of the uprights that supported the ceiling to begin a list of fine restaurants in Trinovant.

While troops hurried past in both directions and the crackle of rifle fire sounded near and far, George and Sophie organised the packing boxes into instant seats while Aubrey wandered vaguely to the far end of the dugout and lit a lantern to illuminate the map that was spread on the wall, an old Gallian map of the region. He rocked back and forward, toe to heel, humming softly at the back of his throat while he studied it. He was aware that his friends were busying themselves, but if pressed, he probably couldn't have nominated exactly what they were up to.

Aubrey took the map from the wall and spread it on a few packing boxes that George and Sophie had just dragged together. He sat and began tracing the various tracks that had been pencilled in.

Colonel Stanley approached, and Aubrey looked up. 'Sir, I need your help in constructing a transference spell. Several transference spells.'

'What sort of transference spells? Moving material? It's easier and more reliable to do it the conventional way.'

'I want to shift people.'

Stanley raised an eyebrow. 'Snipers, eh? We tried shifting snipers about, early on, but you know the disorientation such a thing causes, even if you can find a magician who's capable of such high-level magic. They wouldn't be much use for anything after moving a single sniper any distance at all, either. Too costly.'

'I'm aware of the Principle of Cost.' He held up a hand, anticipating Stanley's next objection. 'Sir, I also understand the implications of the Law of Transference, where the further a magician proposes to move an object by magical means, the more complex the spell.' Aubrey rested his elbows on his knees and leaned forward. 'I'm not afraid of a little complexity.'

'I'm glad of that, Fitzwilliam, but I understand that you're not a transference specialist.'

'I'm more of a magic generalist, I suppose.'

'Quite. My experience *is* in this particular field and I can assure you that we've canvassed all the possibilities and costs of such magical action and we've ruled them all out.' Stanley crossed his arms on his chest and glanced at Caroline, who was seated nearby, stripping down and cleaning one of her firearms. George and Sophie were also doing their best to appear as if they weren't eavesdropping while they compared stories from their notebooks. 'I must say that I'm disappointed. I'd been expecting something rather more innovative, if I can put it that way.'

Aubrey contemplated the rough boards that made up the floor. 'I wasn't thinking of snipers,' he said softly.

'Good.'

'I'm thinking of transporting all the members of the Holmland War Cabinet and the generals of the Central Staff from their comfortable positions in Fisherberg to the middle of no-man's-land.'

Again, Aubrey was immensely proud of his friends. They barely reacted, accustomed as they were to the outlandish. Caroline merely caught his eye and nodded, while George rubbed his hands together in anticipation.

Sophie looked startled for an instant, but when George took her hand she bit her lower lip and looked determined.

Colonel Stanley, however, made up for their lack of surprise by a superabundance of his own. He half rose, then his knees gave way and he sagged onto his wooden box. His mouth opened and closed several times before anything emerged. He flapped a hand, once, then pointed at Aubrey before faltering. When a sentence finally made its way from his lips, it was broken, the essence of disbelief: 'You . . . No . . . It's impossible . . . That's the most . . .' He settled for shaking his head. 'No. No. No.'

Before Aubrey could respond, Caroline cleared her throat and raised a finger, drawing Stanley's attention. 'Colonel? He's quite capable of it.'

Slowly, his head swivelled, turret-like, until he was gazing at Aubrey. He swallowed, a mighty Adam's apple moving up and down his throat. 'How do you propose to do this?' he croaked.

Aubrey sighed. 'Well, it's not easy . . .'

The limitations of long-distance transference were immense. Many recent experiments suggested that some sort of uncertainty was built into such shifting, with potentially disastrous results. The relative locations and determining them were crucial in hoping to achieve any satisfactory result. Such a thing was fiendishly difficult.

On top of that, Aubrey knew about costs to a spell caster. The more complex a spell, the more sapping the effect on the magic user. Transference spells were staggeringly complex, and the reaction was potentially enormous.

Approaching such a scheme in a conventional manner was fraught with danger and, most likely, doomed to failure. Which is why Aubrey was banking on another line of attack.

'Colonel, bear with me, if you would. The source of magic is human consciousness, correct?'

'That is the current accepted theory.' Stanley hesitated. 'You understand that I'm being cautious here. I have no reason to believe otherwise. Human consciousness intersecting with the universe itself spawns the magic field, for want of a better description. A talented and skilled magic user can shape this to their will through constraining and channelling the medium of language.'

'I couldn't have put it any better myself,' Aubrey said. 'It's the shaping and wielding that cost the magic user. The more shaping, the more wielding, the higher the cost.'

'So transference magic has traditionally been small scale and with less-than-bulky objects. Very rarely over distances and rarely on living objects.' Stanley addressed the others, who had given up on their transparent pretence of not listening. 'Living objects being more complex than inert ones, you see.'

'I'm confident I can construct a spell that will take account of all the required elements – parameters, variables, constants – and bring these important Holmlanders to the front. What I want to build into the spell is a mechanism that will deflect reactive flow – the cost, if you will – back onto the collective humanity in this region.'

'Good grief!' Stanley straightened. 'I've never heard of such a thing.'

George snorted. 'Welcome to working with Aubrey Fitzwilliam, sir.'

'Is such a thing possible?' Stanley asked, and he stroked his chin. 'I mean, I can imagine it –'

'"If it can be imagined, a magician can do it,"' Aubrey quoted. 'Baron Verulam.'

'Of course, of course.' Stanley's voice shook with excitement. 'With so many people in this area, the shared cost would be negligible. No-one would notice it.'

'That's what I was hoping.'

Stanley stood. He smacked a fist into a palm. 'But this is remarkable. Extraordinary.'

'Innovative?' Sophie offered.

'Well, naturally it's innovative . . .' The colonel trailed off. 'This could change the course of magic studies for decades.'

Aubrey shrugged and added the codicil that was hanging unspoken in the dugout. 'If it works.' He shuffled in his satchel and pulled out the papers that von Stralick had supplied. He spread them on the map. 'The Central Staff. The Cabinet.'

'Ah.' Colonel Stanley's face fell. He sat, heavily. 'For a spell like this to work, you'd have to know exactly where they are. Not to mention their height and weight, necessities like that. I don't suppose you do.'

'Not exactly,' Aubrey said. 'I was thinking of splicing some other sorts of spells into the usual transference spells.'

Stanley wrinkled his forehead. 'Splicing?'

'I've had some success in bringing spells together, to make the best of each. I know it's not exactly the traditional way of going about things . . .'

Stanley literally chewed this over, working his jaw while he examined the photographs. Aubrey had to give the man his due – he was taking Aubrey's wild suggestions seriously instead of dismissing them out of hand.

Or dismissing them any other way, Aubrey thought, *dismissing being rather final, whether done manually or by some sort of mechanical device.*

'Exactly what are you suggesting?' Stanley said finally.

Exactly? Aubrey thought. *Good question.* 'I want to use aspects of an application derived from the Law of Seeming, the Law of Completeness and the Law of Intensification.'

Stanley's jaw sagged again. 'What? But you can't just mix and mash like that. It's magic we're creating here, not some sort of goulash.'

'I think we can take these photographs and use them, thanks to the Law of Seeming, as our locative element of the transference spell. We can use them to pinpoint our subjects, as it were.'

'You can't do that,' Stanley said. 'I mean, one wouldn't ordinarily consider using that sort of magic in this application. Transference needs coordinates, densities, figured as precisely as possible.'

'It has, true, but has this sort of thinking actually *limited* applications of transference magic? The failure of specialising, perhaps? If I can wrangle something out of the Law of Similarity, it will make the newspaper pictures more real, more like their subjects, and that's what I'll splice the aspect of the Completeness principle into so that the spell will be urgently seeking the original based on the Law of Familiarity –'

'Wait. Stop. Please.' Stanley put his hand to his forehead and actually swayed. 'You want to juggle all of these spell elements on top of the mind-cracking difficulty that is a standard transference spell?'

'In a nutshell, sir, that's about it.' Aubrey rubbed his hands together. 'I wouldn't be attempting this for a lark, sir, but in this situation I think something out of the ordinary is called for.'

'Quite, quite,' Stanley muttered, his head down. He looked up, sharply. 'Off hand, I can think of a hundred different reasons why such a lunatic approach wouldn't work, but you've also made me think of a few improbable ways in which it could.'

'You'll help me, sir?'

'Help you? I'll do what I can but you're already well beyond my magical help. What do you need on a more mundane level?'

'A lot of paper, some pencils, erasers, plenty of food, coffee, tea, water and some camp beds.'

'Camp beds?'

'For my friends here. They need it.'

'Excellent, old man,' George said from where Caroline, Sophie and he were sitting, watching the discussion. 'I was beginning to think you'd forgotten about us.'

'Never, George. Never.'

Twenty-two

AUBREY GAVE UP MEASURING THE HOURS IN ANY conventional way. Instead, as the night drew out, he understood that his working was marked by the number of times that Caroline or George put a cup of tea into his hands while he pored over maps, photographs and screeds of paper. Colonel Stanley and Sophie worked by his side, elbow to elbow. Early in the process, their contributions were important and saved him from knocking his head against the innumerable brick walls that constructing a revolutionary spell entailed, but gradually their suggestions grew less and less frequent until they mutely watched as he built magic of dizzying complexity.

Stanley, at first, was horrified at Aubrey's decision to use a number of ancient languages in the one spell, and argued against it with impeccable precedents on his side. Aubrey calmly presented his alternatives, with examples, and gradually won the colonel's grudging acquiescence.

Aubrey covered page after page in a large ledger, scrawling elements and operators, bringing together disparate variables that, at times, seemed to be surprised at finding themselves in the company they did. Dimly, he became aware that more lantern light was required in order to see his workings properly but, before he asked, George attended to the situation. Equally dimly, he knew that the dugout was a still centre in the middle of turmoil, with much hurrying and shouting just outside, and the more ominous noises of war – firearms, small and heavy, whistles and artillery – not far away.

Aubrey sweated, particularly, over the elements meant to control location and time. He wanted the entire War Cabinet and the Central Staff to arrive together, and they'd be coming from vastly different starting points. Trying to restrain these factors into a single manageable area was like trying to catch a cloud with a colander. His head ached but he ploughed on with no thought of giving up.

Enhancing the images of the men he wanted to transport was also the stuff of headaches, and once he had a solution to this he was then faced with the difficulty of splicing what was essentially a complete spell into the body of another. In what order should the components unfold? Was there one answer for this, or was it a matter of sorting through possible solutions for the one that was best?

False starts came more and more often. Sophie and Colonel Stanley began to murmur encouragement until even that fell away. Stanley became more of an office boy, handing Aubrey paper and sharp pencils, brushing away the debris from furious erasing. Sophie took on a proofing role, gently correcting any basic errors of expression that were creeping in more and more often as Aubrey feverishly scribbled down the elements that captured the vista of his conception.

His body became a distant thing, its discomfort shallow. Knots in his neck, pain in his fingers from gripping the pencil, twinges in the small of his back from bending over the table, trying to keep the spread of papers organised, but he ignored them all. They were insignificant.

In the middle of these demands, Aubrey found himself in an odd frame of mind. Mired in the pressure of finding a solution to a formidable problem, he was enjoying himself. The density of brain work was exhilarating. He felt alive and invigorated. He was anticipating potential obstacles long before they emerged and so was able to sidestep them, or even turn them around so they became strengths instead of weaknesses. As this mood continued he began to look forward to difficulties, for he was sure that he would be able to resolve them, and each resolution was a moment of extra joy, a spike of satisfaction that made him glow all the more fiercely.

Until he hit an obstacle that stopped him dead.

At first, he smiled and tried recatenating some elements, then he substituted operators in the spell to approach his desired effect in a different way, but he still found the obstacle in his way. He went back a few steps and completely recast a significant section of the spell. He was pleased with this as it actually tightened up some aspects of the duration of the actual transference, but after he'd completed this recasting, the spell still wouldn't gel.

He took a step away from the table and rubbed his face with both hands. His vision blurred for a moment when he tried to focus on the entrance to the dugout, but he hardly noticed, so hard was he thinking.

It's the simple things that resist our efforts to manipulate them, he thought as he turned back to the offending section. Nearby, Caroline murmured something to Sophie. They may have been words in Albionish, but Aubrey was currently juggling Akkadian, Demotic and Phrygian so he couldn't understand a word they were saying.

The sticking point was the location point for the arrival of the Holmland warmongers. Aubrey had a neat area picked out. A hundred yards into no-man's-land, almost directly in front of their current position, was a large double shell hole formed where two shells had exploded close together. From there, the Holmland trenches could be reached via a rough scramble through one of the rare muddy sections of no-man's-land, then past the usual barbed wire emplacements, a shattered fence line, and the grotesque pock-marked landscape that had once been woods and farmland.

Aubrey had chosen this location because he wanted the Holmlanders to arrive there and suffer the horror they had been insulated from. He wanted them to experience what they had sent so many others into – but he wanted them then to escape and, once they'd understood what they'd created, he hoped they might reconsider everything. He'd come to appreciate that reality had a bracing effect on plans and he was hoping that the shock the Holmlanders were about to receive might make them think again about the course of action they had chosen.

A few hours in no-man's-land should suffice, he'd decided, enough to make them think they were going to die. Perhaps he could organise an Allied military advance, or a raiding team or two, or even an artillery bombardment in the area. Surely this would inspire them to seek their own lines, no matter how difficult they might think the passage would be?

After that, a renewed artillery bombardment of Holmland trenches would hammer home the point. Aubrey could imagine the politicians and the generals arguing about their lives versus military objectives. At best, Aubrey was hoping for a retreat. At worst, a halt in the planned Holmland advance. Whatever the outcome, time would be gained, precious time to bring up Allied reinforcements.

So the location for the arrival of the Holmlanders was a key part of his plan – and here it was, proving more difficult than Aubrey had imagined. He wasn't sure if was the necessary effect of bringing together a dozen people from widely spread origins, or if it was the difficulty alluded to by Colonel Stanley, the need for precise location elements in any transference spell, but nothing he tried addressed the issue of exasperating vagueness when it came to fixing the location point. When he ran through the most recent draft of the spell it had potential outcomes that included spreading all twelve men over a hundred miles or so, or having them arrive at daily intervals for nearly a fortnight. One hastily abandoned option would have had the Chancellor's cronies appearing at different heights ranging from a few miles above the surface of no-man's-land to a mile or so underneath it.

Vagueness, uncertainty. He couldn't excise it from the spell, no matter what he tried. He gnawed at the elements for location and tried to constrain them, elucidate them, enhance them and define them, but nothing worked.

'Aubrey.'

It took him a moment to recognise his own name. 'Caroline?'

She stood, neat and sublime in her uniform, managing to convey both concern and utter confidence in his work.

'George, Sophie and I agree. You need to walk away for a moment.'

Aubrey worked his mouth a little before answering. It felt as if he'd been chewing on ashes. 'I do?'

'It's obvious you've come up against something you can't sort out. You need a break to refresh yourself.'

'But how did you know?'

'You've been clenching your teeth. You only do that when you run into a problem that you can't solve straight away.'

'Ah.' His jaw was aching, now that she'd pointed it out. He rubbed it and reflected on the observational powers of his friends. 'How long have I been at it?'

'It's just gone past 2200 hours.'

'Seven hours.' His eyes were smarting. 'I think I'll step outside for a breath of air.'

George was immediately at his side. 'Capital idea, old man. I'll join you.'

Sophie smiled bravely at him from the other side of a steaming mug of tea. On the way out of the dugout, Aubrey saw Colonel Stanley slumped in a corner, snoring, his head propped on some excess sandbags.

George held out an arm and prevented him from leaving while a squad of sappers jogged past, shovels in hand and carrying slit lanterns, then he signalled for Aubrey that the way was clear.

Aubrey stretched more than his legs as he wandered along the trench. He rolled his shoulders and swung his arms and felt as if his whole body was uncoiling.

A flare bloomed in the sky, turning night into a ghastly sort of day. Aubrey found a step and carefully levered himself to the parapet. Finding a loophole in the sandbags, he surveyed the scene, reminding himself of exactly what he was doing.

George joined him. 'A scrap of land,' he said softly. 'Hardly worth fighting over.'

'We're not fighting for that scrap of land. We're fighting for what it represents. Not fighting for it would mean we were giving in.'

'I wouldn't be happy with that,' George said, 'but I wish we didn't have to. I suppose it's stand up or be knocked down.'

'Something like that.' Aubrey sought for his location point and found it, unmistakable in the broken landscape. He thought it a perfect place to see how stupid war was. He could even worm his way out there himself, if he followed that chain of pot holes, and then worked his way under that forest of barbed wire someone had risked himself to set up. Aubrey traced the route with his eye, then the flare faded and left him thinking.

Three closely spaced explosions erupted on the ridge behind the Holmland lines. 'We're shelling the hills, now?' Aubrey asked.

'Communications have been spotty, up and down the line, but we've been told that artillery commanders have been ordered to use their initiative. If they see a target up there, they can have a dash.'

'Have a dash. Sounds jolly.' Aubrey peered into the night for a moment, its blackness hiding the magnitude of his task.

An idea jumped out of the darkness and hit him between the eyes. He stared, unseeing for a while, examining the idea from all sides, to see if its lunacy was simply ridiculous or if it was the special sort of outrageousness that he had come to value. 'I have to get back to it, George.'

'See? It did you good, getting away for a while.'

'It did that,' Aubrey said vaguely, his mind working elsewhere at a rate hitherto thought impossible. 'Which way is the dugout?'

When they entered, Stanley was at the makeshift table, yawning and doing his best to focus on the scattered papers in front of him. Aubrey noticed that his eyes were bloodshot. 'Impressive stuff, Fitzwilliam. Damned impressive.'

'Sir.'

Sophie stretched out on a bench under a map of Stalsfrieden. George went to rouse her, but Aubrey shook his head. 'Let her sleep.'

'Are you sure?'

'I might need her later. Let her sleep now.'

George nodded and found a blanket for her.

Caroline was sitting on a packing case, tinkering with wireless equipment. 'You should get some rest, too,' he said to her.

'I slept earlier.'

Aubrey had no idea whether she had or not, but immediately understood that arguing the point would be futile. 'Nice capacitor.'

She held up the thumb-sized component she'd been polishing. 'It's a valve, Aubrey, but thank you for trying.'

He smiled, vaguely, and addressed his workings. He straightened some of the loose sheets of paper he'd torn from the ledger, and then reordered them. He screwed one up and discarded it.

Then he took a deep breath. Re-engaging with a spell of this difficulty was like standing on a high diving tower, readying for the plunge.

Only if the water was aflame with burning oil, he thought, *and full of crocodiles. Flameproof crocodiles, with long snorkels.*

He realised his mind was spinning off in peculiar directions and he admonished himself. He needed to use every possible brain function in the pursuit of an answer to his problem. Spinning was not to be tolerated.

The obstacle that had brought him to such an abrupt halt needed a very special solution and he now thought he had one. The trouble was, it required his casting the spell from the middle of no-man's-land.

Since the reunification of his body and soul he had been acutely conscious of his whereabouts in a more than physical sense. Wherever he was, he was *present* in a very real and concrete way. Knowing this, he thought he could use his own location as a homing beacon. He could act as a human set of coordinates.

Drawbacks aplenty presented themselves, but as he looked for other ways around the impasse, he kept coming back to this one. It had the advantage of simplicity – and the disadvantage of acute personal danger. While he didn't shy away from acute personal danger, he didn't go out of his way to seek it, either. He was willing to entertain alternatives. In fact, he was willing to offer champagne, dancing and a night on the town to any useful alternative, but none presented itself, even with such entertainment on offer.

He also had an inkling that some people around about might want to have a say about whether it was a good idea or not.

The trench raiders managed it in their midnight excursions, he told himself. The barbed wire teams managed it when they crept out to stretch out more of the cursed stuff. No-man's-land wasn't an impossible place to be. It was simply extremely dangerous.

'I have it, Colonel,' he announced.

Stanley looked up from where he was working through a pile of papers. He took off his glasses and rubbed the bridge of his nose before replacing them. 'Fitzwilliam, I only understand half of what you've done here – less than half – but from what I've seen, I think you do too.' He narrowed his eyes. 'And if it's true, I'm wondering if you've really thought this thing through.'

'Sir?'

'If you can bring the Chancellor and his friends to the middle of no-man's-land to throw a scare into them, why not simply bring them here and we'll shoot the lot of them?'

It was the colonel's tone that shook Aubrey most. It said 'I'm a reasonable man' and 'All things considered', decidedly rational things like that. It was the tone used in lecture theatres and board rooms all over Albion.

In military terms, it *was* a sensible suggestion. Lieutenant-Colonel Stanley wasn't a monster. He was a hard-working man, doing the best he could. He probably had a wife and family and a dog waiting for him at home in Albion.

Yet he was calmly suggesting a massacre.

In some ways, it made sense. Lop off the head and Holmland would be in trouble. It might run around for a while, squawking, but eventually it would realise the state of affairs and it would fall over.

Shoot a dozen to save thousands. Hundreds of thousands. Millions.

As arithmetic, it made perfect sense, but Aubrey had

never thought that humanity could be reduced to a matter of counting. What sort of a world would it be if that sort of thing was considered a good plan? What sort of country would it be that endorsed such action?

He was sure it wasn't the sort of world that he was trying to save – or to make. He was also sure that Caroline would agree, and George and Sophie.

So what if a superior officer ordered him to do it?

'Sir, that would be extremely efficient,' he said, carefully not agreeing with the suggestion. 'We need to put some arrangements into place, however. What's the time?'

Caroline had been following the exchange between Aubrey and Stanley carefully. 'It's just after eleven.'

'I need some rest before I cast a spell like this. What if we aim for 0100 hours?'

'The wee small hours,' Stanley said, with a wisp of a smile.

'And we follow it with an artillery barrage at 0200 hours, directly opposite our position here.'

'Eh?'

'A show of strength. Can you arrange it?'

Colonel Stanley frowned. 'I'll have to find a communications post.'

'If we arrange it now, sir, I think it would be best.'

As soon as Colonel Stanley left, Caroline put aside her wireless equipment and buttonholed Aubrey. 'And what exactly are you planning?'

Don't lie. Tell the truth, he thought. *Part of it, at least.* 'I can't do this if it means shooting people in cold blood like that.'

'Good. Although it's always puzzled me why the temperature of the blood is important. Hot or cold, I don't like it.'

'You shot Dr Tremaine.'

'A special case, but if you make me think too long about it I'll be very annoyed because I'll start to feel inconsistent.'

'Can't have that.'

'No.'

A Gallian-accented voice broke in. 'So you're being sneaky again?'

Aubrey turned to see George and Sophie looking at him. Between them were notebooks they'd been sharing, working on another writing project. Sophie was sleepy-eyed but alert.

'I prefer "clandestine",' he said.

'We approve,' George said, 'however you want to describe yourself. So if you're not going to slaughter the Chancellor and his friends, how's all this going to play out?'

Aubrey outlined the plan, simply leaving out the necessity for him to be the locus of the spell. 'And the artillery bombardment is icing on the cake,' he concluded. 'The Chancellor and his friends will see what it's truly like out here. Being the people they are, they're bound to try to take command once they're safely in their trenches. I'm wagering that this will create all sorts of chaos.'

'Should win some time for reinforcements to get here,' George said.

'Neat and precise,' Caroline said. 'And it has the virtue of not turning us into murderers. And I fully understand the irony of saying such a thing in the middle of a battle zone, but there you have it.'

'"War is confusion" according to the Scholar Tan,' Aubrey murmured. 'I used to think that he meant in tactics and battle plans, but I'm starting to understand just how wise he was.'

'To more practical things,' Caroline said, 'what about resting, as you suggested?'

'I'd love to, but the best thing to do is to get this under way before the colonel comes back. I'd like to spare him any repercussions.'

'You're assuming there will be repercussions,' George said.

'Oh, I'm sure we'll have plenty of repercussions to go around,' Aubrey said.

'Don't worry, Aubrey,' Caroline said. 'We'll take care of that.'

'But before I start, I'll need a large clear area in here. I have to work on the floor. And I need some powdered chalk for a restraining diagram.'

George was already starting to move boxes. 'Good luck with finding chalk, old man. It's not exactly High Street around here, if you haven't noticed.'

'Would flour do, Aubrey?' Sophie said. 'I saw a store dump just along the way.'

'Perfect. I was going to stretch my legs a little anyway.' He reached out and shuffled the papers together that held the final version of his spell workings. He stowed them in a satchel.

Caroline had a large box in her arms. She paused. 'What do you need those papers for?'

Aubrey was so smooth, he picked up a few beats rather than missing one. 'I thought I'd sit outside while you ready the dugout. I still have some memorising to do.'

It was only the slightest of prevarications. The spell was well and truly seared into his brain after all the work he'd done on it. What he'd actually be memorising was the best route to his selected shell hole.

He left his friends discussing the neatest arrangement of boxes and that gave him some hope. He simply couldn't countenance the idea that his last memories of his friends would be of them arguing over the placement of makeshift furniture, so it suggested he *must* be coming back alive. If he had to have last memories of his friends, he wanted them to be heartfelt protestations about love, friendship and what a difference he'd made to their lives. Some tears would be acceptable, but he was afraid they would be more likely to come from George than Sophie or Caroline, so he scratched that from his imaginings. The phrase 'life won't be the same without you' had a comforting ring and he contemplated that as he wandered along the duck-boards until he found the store.

The corporal in charge was suspicious until Aubrey showed his Directorate identification and after that he couldn't be helpful enough. Aubrey settled for two pounds of flour in a brown paper bag. In the dim light of the store he made out a stamp that said it had come all the way from Antipodea. He was unaccountably pleased that as well as sending their strapping soldiers, the colonies were also sending foodstuffs. Loyalty indeed.

Aubrey found a nearby firing bay and had a quiet conversation with the captain of the Lancefield Fusiliers who was on duty. Captain Robinson was young enough to be impressed with Aubrey's credentials and intrigued by the possibility of a magical trench raid, as Aubrey put it. He offered some suggestions to make the way easier, as well as some burnt cork for his face. He also gave Aubrey a password, at which Aubrey blinked, felt a cold wind on the back of his neck, and realised that he'd just avoided a horrible fate. If all went unaccountably well and he was able to crawl back toward the Albion trenches, he would have been in dire trouble without a password. Anyone approaching in the middle of the night was assumed, sensibly, to be a Holmlander up to no good.

A handshake, a slap on the back, a helmet thrust into his hands and Aubrey was up over the top and into no-man's-land.

Twenty-three

*A*UBREY HAD NEVER FELT SO EXPOSED. HIS IMAGINATION, never needing much prompting, immediately told him that dozens of snipers with supernaturally good night vision were all taking bets on which of them would be the first to bring him down.

Which would be an achievement, he thought, as he was as down as it was humanly possible to be. If he were any downer, he'd be moving in a subterranean mode. Wriggling along on his stomach, he'd positioned the sack of flour directly in front of his head, following the theory that a bullet would be better off hitting anything, foodstuff or not, before it hit him.

The next hour was a mixture of terror, panic and loss of skin. Periodic phantom attacks swept across the ruined landscape. Cavalry charges, waves of infantry, and even an elephant brigade at one stage. With each one Aubrey experienced the gut-wrenching trepidation that the phantoms had been designed to inspire. Every time a wave of attackers appeared from nowhere he huddled in shell holes or rolled up as close as he could to barbed wire barriers until he was sure that the shadowy figures weren't real. Then he crawled on, pushing his bag of flour in front of him, and dragging the satchel with his precious notes behind him.

At one stage, Aubrey froze when, some distance away, a figure approaching his level of furtiveness made its way between two shattered trees. Aubrey watched as the stranger progressed in inches, swarming along on his belly. Since every movement was taking him close to the Allied lines, Aubrey decided that he was a Holmlander raider.

Aubrey's heart, which had been running at a steady gallop ever since he left the Albionite trench, showed it was fully capable of a lift in tempo. Aubrey was tempted to blame the trembling in his hands on the sheer amount of blood being pumped about his body by the overactive organ, and not on fear – but he wasn't that foolish. He was right to be afraid in a place where evidence of certain death was only too plain and too commonplace. Once again, though, all his rational thinking and appraisal had little effect on his body and its reactions. Accepting that being afraid was sensible was one thing. Trying to slow his heart was another.

Aubrey lay beside a mound of earth thrown up by an explosion and his hand moved almost of its own volition toward his sidearm. The range was extreme, so there was no point in his having it in his hand, but nevertheless something in him wanted to be armed in such a situation. Shaking, he made a fist of the traitor hand so that it couldn't open his holster, and he peered toward the enemy raider.

A slight 'clink' came from the raider. In his hands, he held a cylinder a few feet long, blackened but showing a tiny gleam of metal. He pushed it ahead of him as he crawled.

After making the noise, the raider didn't move for some time. Aubrey applauded his discretion. At night, sentries on both sides used hearing as much as sight.

The raider was moving again, but he wasn't getting any closer to the Allied lines. Aubrey risked taking out his field glasses and saw that the raider was unscrewing the cylinder, working with both hands.

Another 'clink' and the end of the cylinder popped off, but before anyone from either trench could commence firing, a torrent of ghostly figures poured from the cylinder as if it were a Roman Candle. In an instant, the figures had assumed solidity, colour and shape, milling about uncertainly until the last had emerged, then they arranged themselves in a line. A cavalry charge, complete with regimental colours and a bugler, thundered toward the Albion trenches.

The raider quickly reversed and began scrambling back to Holmland territory. A wild fusillade of shots rang out from the Albionite lines where someone wasn't willing to bet that the cavalry charge was another illusion. Aubrey pulled his head in, aiming to make himself the smallest target possible.

By the way the shots died out quickly, Albion officers had summed up the situation and declared the cavalry as unreal. He lost sight of the horses as they crested a barbed wire barrier and plunged in the direction of the trenches, and he'd also lost interest in them because of something much more urgent.

Someone was nearby.

He cursed himself, internally. He'd taken his eye off the Holmland raider, lost him in the shadows – and someone else had crept up on him.

He caught his breath. That fall of earth over there couldn't be natural, especially since it had followed a scraping sound; the two together were enough to make his gaze dart about, trying to sort harmless shadow from Holmland raider. The difficulty was, in this frame of mind everything looked like a Holmland raider – and a battle-hardened one at that. That broken wagon, for instance. That tangle of barbed wire. And that smashed ammunition box could be *two* Holmland raiders at least.

He sought for some magic, something silent but disabling, but his mind was too full of the transference spell to accommodate anything else. Fragments eluded his grasp as he clutched for them.

He felt the tip of the blade touch him just behind the ear, just before he heard the voice – very soft, very deadly. 'It would be a very bad idea to move, except to take your hand away from your pistol. Turn slowly.'

For once, Aubrey followed orders, to the letter, to see Caroline on the ground next to him. He could have kissed her, so he did.

THEY HAD TO NESTLE VERY CLOSE TO EACH OTHER TO FIT into the tiny shell hole Aubrey had found. It had a bank thrown up toward the Holmland direction, which was useful, but it was open to the Albion side, so they had to – perforce – come even closer to whisper in each other's ear. To communicate, share intelligence, status reports, that sort of thing.

'You were appalling,' Caroline said and her breath on his ear nearly made him swoon. She, too, had used the burnt cork on her face and looked exotically adorable. 'You may as well have worn a sandwich board saying, "I'm about to sneak off and risk my life to try to save you all."'

He was moderately crestfallen; he found it hard to be entirely crestfallen with Caroline in his arms. 'It was that obvious?'

'Not to someone who doesn't know you. Colonel Stanley probably assumes you're following the orders he thinks he gave you.'

'You noticed that too?'

'Between the three of us, we have most things covered.'

'I feel like I'm up on stage for you all to laugh at.'

'No you don't. You feel surrounded by loyal and concerned friends.'

'One of whom followed me out here.'

'Captain Robinson was kind enough to tell me where you'd gone. He's a lovely man.'

'I'm sure he is. And I'm sure he fell over himself to help you.'

'Something like that. Or it may have been Sophie. We both questioned him.'

Aubrey spared a moment to feel sorry for the captain. The poor man hadn't stood a chance. 'But that doesn't explain what you're doing out here. This is magic. I know what I'm doing.'

'That's as may be, but the three of us agreed that someone had to be with you to take care of what you'd forgotten.'

'Forgotten? What have I forgotten?'

She looked sternly at him. 'We're just taking it on past experience that you've forgotten something.'

Aubrey should have been offended, but couldn't be. He was surrounded by faithful and concerned friends. 'You know, this is the strangest conversation I've ever had in the middle of a battlefield.'

'I want you to remember it, Aubrey. For a long time.'

'I shall.' Realising he was taking his life into his hands in a way he hadn't been anticipating, he gazed into Caroline's eyes and said: 'I want you to go back.'

'Go back? To our trenches?'

'That's right. I can't take you into danger like this.'

Through a tilting of a shoulder and an abrupt shift of her hips, they were suddenly as far apart as they could be in a shell hole a few feet across. She crossed her arms and fixed on him. 'And what makes you think that you have any say in my actions?'

Aubrey instantly decided it was a poor time to bring up small things like his being her commanding officer. 'Now, I understand that you're angry, having come all this way . . .'

'Angry? If you think this is angry –'

'Irritated, then. Annoyed. Miffed.'

'Miffed? *Miffed?*'

'I didn't mean miffed. What's that word that sounds like miffed but describes exactly how you're feeling right now?'

Aubrey could hear the slow breath Caroline took as she tried to control herself. 'Aubrey, my being here is my decision to make, not yours. You simply have to overcome this desire to move people about to suit your own ends.'

'It's not that.' For an instant, Aubrey felt as if he were balanced at the top of the world's highest skiing slope, then he plunged. 'It's just that I couldn't bear it if anything happened to you.'

Caroline was silent for a moment. She touched her cheek with a hand, then went on: 'If I got in the way of whatever it is you're planning, you mean.'

Aubrey realised that matters were well and truly running away from him, but in this unlikeliest of places he had a moment of insight, a moment of apprehension where he understood something that had been frustrating him for ages. 'It's your decision to make,' he said slowly, 'not mine.'

She speared him with a look. 'What did you say?'

He grinned. 'This is why some people back in Albion are so afraid of women's suffrage, you know. They don't realise that we all have the right to self-determination.'

'Aubrey, you're going off at a tangent.'

'Not really. Thousands of men, oldsters mostly, take it for granted that they can tell women what to do. The idea that women should be in charge of their own lives is completely alien to them. It may as well be a foreign language.'

'Ah. You've seen our problem.'

'Independence. Freedom. Liberty.'

'Well worth fighting for, I would think.'

He took her hand. He was pleased – and relieved – when she didn't resist. 'I'm sorry, Caroline. I shouldn't order you about like that. I accept your decision, whatever it may be, but –'

'I don't know if I like buts.'

'But please – can you accept that I feel protective toward you?'

She studied him. 'I can.' She paused and she touched her lips. 'Probably because I feel the same way about you.'

Aubrey had never been punched so hard that it made him smile, but he imagined it was something like the sensation he had now. 'You do?'

'All in all, Aubrey, I'd rather be near you when you're in danger than not. Especially since that might mean I could do something about it.'

It was difficult to talk, Aubrey found, when he was smiling as broadly as he was. 'I understand entirely.'

He wasn't exactly sure what happened next, but suddenly – without any apparent movement – he had an armful of Caroline.

They talked – in low, private voices – and waited for the right hour to come.

Aubrey reluctantly disengaged himself. 'We have to move.'

'Do we?'

'Only if we want to win the war.'

'Oh, very well then.'

Aubrey explained about the need to find the double shell crater he'd spied earlier. Then he had to detail his plan for Caroline. Carefully. Without leaving out anything, or covering up in obfuscation.

When he finished, she crossed her arms and studied him. 'That is one of the more fanciful, flamboyant, outrageous schemes you've come up with.'

'Ah ha.'

'And probably the most heroic.'

'It is?' Aubrey felt the warmth of a blush creeping up from under his collar.

'It's one of the things I love about you, Aubrey. The extent of your imagination is only matched by your willingness to put yourself in harm's way for the right cause.'

'I do?'

'That, and your penchant for two-word answers when you're dazed.'

Dazed was a fair description. Aubrey was still lagging behind, trying to come to terms with what Caroline had said. 'I don't!'

'And there you have it.'

Aubrey shook himself. 'And here's where you try to dissuade me from this course of action, correct? Where you try to tell me it's too dangerous, too risky, something like that?'

'I should say not. I wouldn't think an expedition with you would be complete without an extremely hazardous situation.' Caroline peeped over the lip of their shell hole. 'I can see the best way. Follow me.'

THE DOUBLE SHELL HOLE PROVED TO BE JUST AS AUBREY had hoped. Large, and close enough to the middle of no-man's-land to serve his purposes.

He began preparing the spell. Caroline divided her attention between him and the surroundings, keeping low but alert, pistol in hand.

Firstly, Aubrey had to organise a relatively flat area. To this end, he'd brought the wonderfully named entrenching tool, the neat folding spade favoured by raiding and expeditionary forces. He used it to level the bottom of the crater, working steadily, and eventually used his hands as much as the metal tool, sweeping the dry earth away until he had rough oval area formed from the intersection of the two shell impacts and, once again, he was grateful that the weather was clear. Rain would no doubt have filled the bottom of the crater and the earth was fine enough to make the sort of glutinous mud that would be a misery.

He crawled around the perimeter of the desired area with the flour, marking his restraining and focusing diagram with a substantial line. Making the required symbols was trickier, but they were necessary adjuncts in bringing the results of the spell to the correct location and to no other. The symbol was a combination Aubrey had invented after some consideration, bringing together the spiral of the Babylonian sigil for 'sun' and the Chaldean symbol for 'moon,' both powerful symbols in their day for renewal and return, handy in this context.

He knew that these symbols were relics, survivors from an earlier age of magic when it was less scientific, but at this stage he was willing to call on whatever help he could.

Aubrey rubbed his nose, which was suddenly itchy, then he sat back on his heels and looked at the sky. For an instant it shimmered, but not with any colour the normal eye could see.

'What is it?' Caroline whispered.

'Magic. Lots of it.'

'Where?'

'The Holmland lines. And it's getting nearer.'

'A good reason to move ahead with your spell?'

'With all haste.'

Originally, Aubrey had imagined himself standing, arms spread in dramatic magical mode, perfect for greeting the surprised Holmlanders. Discretion, however, told him that standing up in the middle of no-man's-land would be an unfortunate idea, akin to volunteering for target practice in the role of target rather than marksman. He opted for the rather less imposing position of sitting cross-legged, ensuring his head was well below the level of the lip of the crater.

Following Aubrey's instructions, Caroline took up a position at one end of the crater, outside the diagram. He shook the photographs from his satchel and spread them in front of him, anchoring them with earth – and he came to his first hiccup.

He couldn't see them well enough in the dark. He needed to see the faces, and see them well, in order to use the Law of Familiarity to draw the owners of the likenesses to this location.

Helplessly, he patted his chest in a forlorn longing for the marvellous appurtenances vest of George's invention. If he had it, it might have included the handy cat's eyes, neat devices that fitted over the eye to provide useful night sight.

While I'm at it, he thought, *I might as well wish for a cease-fire and a magic carpet to take us all home.*

He wasn't about to give up because of a minor problem like this. He could summon a glowing light but was reluctant to do so in an arena where a cigarette lit for too long could attract a sniper.

He gnawed his lip, aware of Caroline's calm scrutiny,

knowing that she'd soon realise that he'd hit a snag, but appreciating her silence. Of course, it meant he had to live up to that confidence, but that was a role he was willing to adopt.

Attempting another spell wasn't his preference. With the complex transference spell already packed into his memory, trying to wedge in another was fraught with danger – but he had a theory that casting a second spell in a language diametrically different from those used in the transference spell could prevent confusion.

He had a spell in mind. He'd read about some recent experiments in using the Law of Amplification on parts of the eye in an effort to remedy sight problems. The footnote that had lodged in Aubrey's memory mentioned one outcome where the function of the rods in the eye, the light receptors, was intensified, resulting in the experimental subjects being dazzled in ordinary light.

Naturally, after reading this Aubrey had turned the experiment around in his mind and considered that such an outcome could actually mean useful seeing in condition of low light.

Aubrey had a very healthy regard for his eyes. His imagination left him in no doubt that losing sight would be a dreadful blow – not being able to read, ever again? An awful fate. In normal circumstances, he would be quite happy for experiments on sight to be done by careful researchers in good laboratories. Since squatting in the middle of shell hole halfway between two armies dedicated to wiping each other out was about as far from normal circumstances as it was possible to be, he accepted the necessity to undertake such a spell on himself.

He understood it, but it didn't mean that he was entirely happy about it.

Keeping a brave face, and knowing that Caroline would see through that façade immediately, he constructed the spell in his mind using Vedic, the ancient language of the Indus people, a whole continent and a sea or two away from the languages he'd used for the transference spell.

The effect was immediate and profound, to the extent that he actually had to squint a little and shade his eyes, so bright were his surrounds. He could clearly make out every detail of the photographs, from the Chancellor's bald head to the extraordinary array of whiskers, sideburns and beards on the faces of the other Holmlanders. Each of the men was posing proudly for the camera, chest outthrust and doing his best to present himself as the epitome of a wartime leader.

Aubrey took the spell from his satchel and riffled through the pages. It was undoubtedly the most complex, the most convoluted and the longest spell he had ever attempted, but as he cast his eye over each element he was confident that he held it deeply in his mind ready for casting.

That he could cast it, he was confident, but he was apprehensive about the consequences. A thin, cold voice asked if he was really sure of the state of his reunified body and soul. Would it stand the sort of backlash that such a spell could produce? He touched his chest, briefly, and shuddered at the prospect of returning to the appalling half-dead state, balanced on the edge of slipping away forever. Even with his plan to deflect much of the recoil onto the world around him, he was sure he would suffer.

He looked up to see Caroline's gaze on him. Her eyes were bright and fierce in his enhanced sight, unblinking in their resolve, and she broke her silence: 'I believe you can do it.'

It was enough. In his hour of need, it was enough. He nodded, closed his eyes for a moment to compose himself, and began.

In a remarkably apt simile, somewhere in the middle of the lost time of spell casting, it came to him that it was like marching through an unknown city, late at night, with a thousand wrong turns available at any minute, the consequences of which were grim.

The strain was most apparent in his mind and his mouth as they worked together to produce the language that was doing the work of wrestling the magical field, raw and inchoate, into the methodical, patterned arrangement that was a spell. As was typical for a dense spell, it began to take on a quasi-life of its own, the syllables and elements actively resisting being shaped, making the job harder and harder as it went on.

Aubrey lost all sense of his surroundings, swept away as he was in the ordeal of spell casting that was unlike any other he'd endured. His focus was on each syllable, each word, each element of the spell as it came to be pronounced. They lined up unwillingly, testing his resolve as they waited, shifting uneasily, losing their shape and intent. It was the force of his will alone that kept them in line and maintained them in the way that he needed. Each one presented itself, was spoken clear and correct, then it was replaced by another, and another and another.

In the magic firmament, Aubrey Fitzwilliam was making a spell, most powerful, most sweeping. He didn't flag. He had the fate of nations and of individual people in his hands. When he saw, far away, his signature element at the end of the line of spell elements, he realised that he was nearly finished. He gritted his teeth, knowing it would be mad to waver now, so he took each element as it came and gave it its due. He spoke them and made them real.

Finally, only his signature element was left. He uttered it, proud to have completed what he'd done.

Then he doubled over as if kicked in the stomach. His magical senses flared. He felt as if he were caught in a vast current, one that was tearing him in all directions, dragging his limbs, his torso, his very essence. Then it surged and spread, and he had an apprehension of it moving away, a wave, a ripple spreading and being consumed by the hundreds, thousands of consciousnesses in the area.

Including Caroline. She gasped and her eyes widened, but before she could say anything Chancellor Neumann, the head of the Holmland government, was standing in front of them.

Aghast, Aubrey watched as Caroline levelled her pistol at the chancellor and fired.

Aubrey reached for her, but the magical wave chose that moment to roll back and smash him into oblivion.

Twenty-four

AUBREY OPENED HIS EYES. HE REGRETTED IT immediately because every square inch of him hurt. His eyelids hurt as he levered them upward. Even the act of regretting opening his eyes caused him pain.

He was propped against one wall of the shell hole. A surge of panic struck him until he checked with his magical senses and was relieved to find that his body and soul were still united.

The effects, then, of the massive spell were physical rather than spiritual. For a moment, he wallowed in knowing that he wasn't going to die – at least not straight away – but the battering he'd received from the magical backwash soon overwhelmed that small pleasure.

A measure of triumph filtered through the pain. The fact that he was alive meant that he'd been able to deflect the worst of the spell's reaction onto the collective consciousness around him. The fact that Chancellor

Neumann was here in front of him meant that the spell had worked, at least in part.

Numbly, with his enhanced sight still working, he looked past his outstretched self – every movement of his eyeballs a twitch of agony – to see a dozen angry men sitting like schoolboys on the floor of the crater. They glared at him, but the most furious, his bald head a beacon of anger, was Chancellor Neumann.

Chancellor Neumann was wearing extremely formal clothes – swallow-tail jacket, striped trousers, starched collar – and Aubrey wondered what he'd been doing when the spell plucked him away. At the opera? An audience with Elektor Leopold?

In a land where facial hair was a point of pride, the Chancellor was a leader in more ways than one. Currently it looked as if two extremely fluffy cats had clamped themselves to his cheeks, but they were having trouble clinging, so livid was the leader of Holmland.

The others were a mixture of middle-aged and older Holmlanders, conventionally well dressed or in uniforms that showed little sign of the wear that comes from being at the front lines. Some looked stunned while others were working themselves up to the level of self-righteous anger their leader was displaying. Aubrey recognised General Sterne and the aging Admiral Tolbeck, both of whom were composed. Gerhard Moln was near them, the industrialist who had been brought into Chancellor Neumann's inner circle and who had become the Minister for Armaments. He was eying the sides of the crater.

All of the Holmlanders, quite obviously, were not accustomed to sitting at the bottom of a shell hole. While Aubrey mastered his physical discomfort, they were bobbing their heads, jerking and hunching their shoulders as a hail of bullets criss-crossed just above them, humming and buzzing like angry insects.

Carefully moving as little of his body as he could, he inched an elbow aside – more pain, red rockets going off inside his skull – and touched someone he hoped was Caroline. 'Tell me you have a pistol trained on them.'

'I do, with another prominently in my lap.'

'It hurts.'

'What does?'

'Everything.'

'That might make things difficult.'

'Things?'

'Getting back to our lines, for instance.'

Aubrey wasn't thinking that far ahead. 'You didn't shoot him?'

'The Chancellor? I fired over his head. It was the quickest way to get him to sit down. I didn't want him shot by an alert Holmlander who saw someone standing in the middle of no-man's-land.'

'You will die for this,' Chancellor Neumann said in guttural but fluent Albionish. 'Both of you.'

Without changing her expression, Caroline raised her pistol and fired straight up into the air. Immediately, their position came under even heavier fire, machine gun as well as rifle. Caroline didn't flinch, but several of the Holmland generals and politicians pulled their necks in so far they looked like tortoises who'd decided that staying at home was better than going out.

'We'll die like all the young men you've sent here?' Caroline asked.

It didn't take Aubrey's enhanced sight to see realisation

at work. Eyebrows rose, eyes widened, heads shook uncertainly. Several of the Holmlanders evidently refused to believe the conclusion that was becoming more and more obvious, and looked offended at the state of affairs.

'Where are we?' one of the generals demanded. 'What is going on?'

'We are in the disputed stretch of land between the Holmland trenches and the Allied trenches,' Aubrey said. 'Right where your army is about to launch a major assault, if our intelligence is correct.'

'Fremont?' another general burst out. 'We will all be killed! We must leave this area immediately!'

With uneasy satisfaction, Aubrey noted the confirmation that the Holmland assault was about to fall on this area.

'It's acceptable for young Holmlanders to die, but not you?' Caroline said.

'We are important men! We do not belong here!'

'I'll leave you for a moment to consider the unintended irony of that statement,' Caroline said.

The Holmlanders huddled, muttering, casting evil glances at Caroline and mostly ignoring Aubrey. He was glad for this. It was about all he could handle.

'Now, Aubrey,' Caroline said without taking her eyes from the Holmlanders. Her face was faintly luminous, a sheen on her skin where the burnt cork didn't reach. Aubrey wondered if dawn were on its way, or if it was the effect of his enhanced eyesight. He was willing to contemplate that he might simply be delirious. 'What are we going to do with you?'

'That's what Matron used to say just before she dosed us with castor oil.' Speaking still hurt, but he felt as if he'd left agony behind and moved to a steady state, the relativity of pain being brought home in a new and interesting way.

'I don't doubt you deserved it, but that's neither here nor there. You've achieved your aim, bringing these men here. Now it's time for us to get back to the trenches before the artillery bombardment starts.'

'That's right. That was part of the plan, wasn't it?' Woozily, he groped for his watch, but he had trouble finding the end of his arm. 'What time is it?'

'Nearly 0130. Is there anything you want to say to these men before we leave?'

Aubrey nodded. Unwisely, as it proved, for it felt as if his teeth were about to fall out, with minor detonations accompanying each one. After a moment of intense wincing, he hunched himself until he was as upright as he could manage. Bullets continued to crack not far overhead, a reminder, if any was needed, of the peril of their situation.

'Fitzwilliam,' Chancellor Neumann snarled, 'for a boy, you are causing us considerable nuisance. Dr Tremaine was correct in saying we should be wary of you.'

'I'm flattered that Dr Tremaine thought I was that important.'

'Important?' The Chancellor laughed, a strange sound in the middle of no-man's-land. 'Tremaine drew up a list of potential problems. You were just below the silting up of the Auldberg Harbour and just above the shortage of rat poison in Tahlversen.'

Aubrey shrugged. He felt he could be philosophical about such slights. 'You've been brought here for a reason.'

'To kill us all!' one of the younger generals blustered. Aubrey thought he could be General Ebert, a hero of the same war in which Aubrey's father had distinguished himself. 'You are fiends!'

'You make interesting assumptions,' Aubrey said. 'They probably tell us more about your thinking than mine.'

'What is your purpose, then, in bringing us here if not to murder us?' the Chancellor said.

'No-one is murdered in war, Chancellor,' Caroline said. 'Many killings, no murders. Hasn't that ever struck you as strange?'

Chancellor Neumann glanced at Caroline, then dismissed her from his notice. Not a wise move, Aubrey felt. 'I repeat: what is your purpose?'

Aubrey sighed. 'I want to stop the war.'

Chancellor Neumann snorted and a laugh or two came from the more hardy of his cronies. 'That is an easy task, not requiring our presence. Simply convince your father to surrender. The war will end immediately.'

'I don't think you understand. I want Holmland to withdraw, to stop this warmongering. For you – all of you – to come to your senses.'

'Do you think we don't know about war?' General Sterne called. 'We are soldiers!'

'I'll warrant you haven't seen a war like this. It's a new century. War has changed.' Aubrey grimaced as the pain in his head reasserted itself. 'Besides, not all of you are soldiers. How are you liking this, sir?'

Aubrey directed this question to one of those not in uniform, a thin man with a drooping moustache. His grey striped trousers were rapidly losing their expensive look. He shook his head and turned away, flinching as a chatter of machine gun fire bit into the bank of the shell hole and sprayed them all with dirt.

Aubrey pressed on. 'I'm not so presumptuous as to think I could give you a lesson in politics, but in this new world the generals take orders from the politicians. End this horror, all of you.' He paused and glanced at the sky. 'Look around. This isn't a state for humanity. This is a hell you've created – but it's a hell you can put an end to.'

He took Caroline's hand. She squeezed it and refused to let go, so he pointed with the other. 'Gentlemen, your army is just over there, dug into trenches. If you keep your heads down and follow the line of wire, you should reach it. Dozens of your men have managed to. When you're safely in their midst, look at them. Talk to them. See if this is a fit and proper condition for them. See if you can be proud of this.'

'Be careful,' Caroline said to them. 'They are accustomed to our soldiers raiding their trenches. You don't want to be mistaken for Albionites, but convincing your men that you are who you say you are may be difficult.' She gestured with her pistol. 'Go now.'

Chancellor Neumann glared. 'You are not serious.'

'We're very serious,' Aubrey said. 'We're leaving. You can stay here, if you like, but an artillery bombardment is about to start at any minute.' *If Colonel Stanley made the right arrangements.* 'The only relatively safe place is in that direction. I'd wish you good luck, but I'm not sure how I feel about that so I'll wish you a soldier's luck instead.'

The Holmlanders conferred. In the end, General Ebert led the way. He scrambled to the lip of the crater and showed good sense by pausing and scanning the way ahead before crawling over and disappearing into the gloom. One by one they followed, cursing and muttering, until only Chancellor Neumann was left.

'This will not be forgotten, Fitzwilliam.'

'I hope not, sir. Lessons are best remembered, not forgotten.'

'Dr Tremaine won't be happy with your interference.'

'You can apologise for me next time you see him.'

'Hah! That may be sooner than you think, Fitzwilliam.' Neumann spat on the floor of the crater, then turned and crawled away.

'Are you ready?' Caroline asked.

'Ready for what? A spot of dancing?' It was a valiant stab at insouciance, but the jest fell flat. This wasn't a place that fostered humour. His mind drifted back to what Chancellor Neumann had said about Dr Tremaine and he wondered if the rogue sorcerer actually was in the vicinity.

'To be dragged back to the trenches, if that's what it takes.'

While being dragged by Caroline wasn't the worst prospect in the world, Aubrey thought their chances could be better if he propelled himself. Gently, he flexed his arms, then his legs. They burned, as if he'd been exercising to exhaustion point, but they were functional. He'd hurt, but he'd manage. 'Lead the way. I'll be right behind you.' He looked up at the dark grey that was the overcast sky. No stars looked down. 'What time is it?'

'Too close to bombardment time.'

Despite the maze of no-man's-land, they managed to find Captain Robinson's emplacement again, thanks to Caroline's impeccable sense of direction. Passwords accepted, they were greeted by the astonished officer and his machine gun crew. Once they'd scrambled into the duckboarded and reveted trench and were surrounded by sandbags Aubrey felt safe for the first time in hours.

He shaded his eyes at the faint lantern light, hoping the vision enhancement spell would wear off soon but adding it to his list of bodily woes in a congratulatory binge of self-pity. After all, if he ached, he was alive, and had survived the implementation of an audacious plan.

'Sleep,' he said to Caroline. He had his arm on her shoulders, supporting her. Or it may have been the other way around. He was sure that invisible gnomes were hitting each of his joints with hammers, but everything was still moderately wonderful. 'Which way to our dugout?'

A deep, disturbing 'whump' shook the ground. It was immediately followed by another, then another. It was as if Aubrey's knee-shattering gnomes had grown up and become giants, then taken it into their heads to pound away at the landscape with mountain-sized sledgehammers. He blinked, couldn't see, and realised the enhancement spell had worn off. The sky was full of the smoke caused by a massive explosion, then the process was repeated, with the addition of a patter of earth and assorted military items falling on top of them.

Caroline pulled him down, forcing him close to the reinforced front wall of the trench. There, they huddled in a universe entirely composed of noise – deafening, all-encompassing noise: gargantuan footsteps, thunder brought down to the ground, the heartbeat of an earth-quake. Aubrey ran out of metaphors as the pounding went on and he concentrated on seeing how close he could get to the rough timber at his cheek.

Amid the tumult, just when he thought no bodily sensation could make itself known in such pandemonium, a flicker made him wince, a nagging tug inside his chest. He rubbed it as he would an insect bite, but this brought no satisfaction. Then his jaw sagged. He lifted his hand, then he concentrated his magical awareness on the site of the irritating sensation.

He had confirmation that Dr Tremaine was nearby.

It was undeniable. Even though the magical connection they shared was erratic, when it evinced itself it was an unmistakeable sign that the rogue sorcerer was close at hand. Aubrey closed his eyes, did his best to ignore the concussions that continued to smash away at no-man's-land, and tried to concentrate.

The magical connection, at times, acted as a conduit. In their past encounters, Aubrey had been able to sense aspects of Dr Tremaine, vague impressions of memories and thoughts, but this time all he could feel was an apprehension that he could only interpret as excitement tinged with anticipation.

Captain Robinson came striding along the trench, all enthusiasm and brio, oblivious to the shelling around them. He was speaking, but pointlessly for his words had no chance of being heard. His gestures, however, made his unheard words clear: everyone was to get ready for an advance.

Aubrey couldn't believe it, but by the time this had registered Captain Robinson was yards away, continuing his job of rallying the troops.

It was easy to see how it had happened. The artillery barrage summoned by Colonel Stanley had clearly been interpreted as the prelude for an advance. Commendable initiative, in this time of erratic communications, but entirely misplaced in this instance.

'Wait here,' he said to Caroline, miming his request with both hands, but he was left foolishly gesturing because at that moment the artillery barrage stopped.

The result wasn't silence because the earth was still settling, protesting at the indignities inflicted upon it, dirt still falling like hail.

A commander's whistle sounded. Aubrey's abused ears took a moment to work out that it came from off to his right, in the direction that Captain Robinson had gone. He sprinted in that direction, lurching from one side of the trench as his body did its best to propel him forward with the objective of stopping the poorly timed advance. If Robinson's men pushed forward by themselves, it could be a disaster. Aubrey needed to warn them, to get the captain to fall back. He didn't want his plan to be the cause of needless deaths.

Men were scrambling up the sides of the trench, rifles in hand, shouting encouragement to each other and, more chillingly, wordless battle cries. Aubrey swarmed after them and stood for a moment on the other side of the parapet, trying to find Captain Robinson while simultaneously being stunned by how the landscape had been transformed.

It was as if the old no-man's-land had been stripped away and a totally new one dropped in its place – one that took the essence of the original no-man's-land and distilled it, creating a place that had all the horror of the old, but intensified a thousandfold. This new no-man's-land had been made by a madman, one who was entranced by smoking craters and desolation. Aubrey was sickened to think that might be a glimpse of where war was heading.

Robinson's men were charging. Their bayonets were fixed. In a ragged line, they advanced toward the Holmland trenches, thankfully meeting no resistance.

Aubrey tried to spy the officer, but at that moment a single shot came from the Holmland trenches. Aubrey pitched backward and felt himself falling slowly, dreamily. All his plans, thoughts and hopes ran away, no matter how he tried to clutch them, and then everything else did as well.

Twenty-five

MAGIC, AUBREY THOUGHT, IT MUST BE MAGIC.
One instant he'd been standing on the edge
of an Albion trench – rather foolishly, now he thought
about it – and the next he was lying in a very comfortable
bed in what looked like a Gallian chateau.

Extraordinary.

The bed was one of the old-fashioned four-poster
type, with heavy drapes and canopy of blue velvet. He'd
never liked the style, finding them dusty, but he was
willing to concede that it was considerably superior to
the frontline trenches. The lack of gunfire was a particular
improvement.

In a comfortable stupor, he allowed his gaze to roam
around a room that was the sort of gilt and plaster
confection that made him think of wedding cakes. Rather
too many cherubs cavorted about the cornices for his
liking, but it was clean and warm. The tall windows, with

more blue velvet drapes, showed him glimpses of trees that hadn't been shattered by shell fire.

So I'm definitely not in no-man's-land.

A formidable woman was sitting on a gilt chair not far from the bed. Aubrey decided that unless she had a penchant for wearing uniforms with red crosses all over, she was probably a nurse. She was studying him carefully and looked as if she were just dying for an opportunity to lunge at him and thrust a thermometer into his mouth.

She confounded this by shaking her head, then getting up and leaving the room. This was, Aubrey decided, very un-nurselike behaviour. His view of nursely behaviour – formed by close reading of *Nurse Lily's Adventures*, a romance book George had lent him – was that a real nurse would be tending him solicitously, gazing into his eyes while resting a comforting hand on his forehead. Either that or ramming a needle into his arm while lecturing him about the virtues of carbolic soap.

The door opened. Caroline entered, in uniform, and Aubrey felt as if he'd won a lottery. George and Sophie were close behind, and they were equally spruce.

Caroline stopped by the bedside. 'Nurse Lucas told us you were awake.'

Aubrey sat up and considered this. 'Nurse Lucas? I knew she was no Nurse Lily.' He shared a significant look with George.

'We don't have time for nonsense, Aubrey.' Caroline sat on the edge of the bed. She rested a comforting hand on his forehead and he was overjoyed. 'How do you feel?'

'Well enough, I suppose, for someone who's just been shot.'

'Shot?' George said. 'I'm afraid not, old man.'

Aubrey felt his head for a bandage and found only hair. 'I assumed . . .'

'You were standing on the parapet of the trench, doing your best to be a target,' Caroline said. 'A mine exploded. Part of the trench collapsed. You fell in and hit your head on a crate of tinned peaches.'

'Ah. Nothing heroic, then?'

'You stopped the Holmland advance, Aubrey,' Sophie said. 'That is very heroic, no?'

'They've pulled back?'

George cut in. 'The Holmland front line is still being held, but most of their forces at Fremont have been pulled back.'

'Wait.' Aubrey looked at the window. Gardens and blue sky remained serene. 'How long has it been?'

'Not quite two days,' Caroline said. Her reserve slipped a little. 'You were quite undone by your spell casting.'

'Holmland reports have been intercepted,' George said. 'They're trumpeting the fact that the Chancellor has been at the front. They're trying to make it into a propaganda coup.'

Caroline tapped him on the shoulder. 'The file in your satchel, Aubrey, the one Hugo gave you. We handed it to General Apsley and his staff. The photographs have helped confirm that the Chancellor and the members of the Central Staff were on the Holmland front lines.'

Aubrey was relieved. The file had been important in his spell making, but he was glad it was continuing to be useful.

'The best news is that the whole mobilisation at Fremont has stopped,' Sophie said.

'Forces were being devoted to keeping the Chancellor

safe, I suspect,' Aubrey said, relieved more than triumphant. 'Until he was able to leave without appearing cowardly.'

'Reinforcements have started arriving from Lutetia and Albion,' Sophie said. 'It doesn't matter if the Holmlanders regroup now, we are ready for them.'

'You bought time, Aubrey.' Caroline patted his pyjamaed shoulder and left her hand there. He covered it with one of his.

'And now it's time to get me out of here,' he said. 'Wherever here is.'

'We're on the outskirts of Divodorum,' Caroline said, 'well away from the front.'

'I venture that this isn't a military hospital. How did I get here?'

'That would be my doing,' came a voice from the doorway.

Aubrey stared. 'Bertie!'

Caroline, George and Sophie snapped to attention. Prince Albert made a face and closed the door behind him. 'Oh, please don't. Sit, all of you. I've had enough of that sort of thing this last week to last me a lifetime.'

Prince Albert was in the uniform of Colonel in Chief of the Crown Prince's Light Infantry Regiment, his own. Aubrey thought the green went well with Bertie's dark features, and his slimness set off the jacket very neatly.

The prince took off his cap and drew up a chair. He smiled at Sophie, after she and George had sat and Caroline had resumed her station on the bed. 'Miss Delroy, is it not?' he said in Gallian. 'I have been following your exploits with great interest. Your piece in the latest *Sentinel* was excellent. It's rallied Gallian spirits most splendidly.'

Sophie coloured delightfully and responded in the

same language. 'I do not know what to say, your highness.' She paused and looked at George, switching to Albionish. 'Your highness. Is that correct, George?'

The prince laughed. '"Bertie" is perfectly acceptable, Miss Delroy, at least in this room. I believe all four of you have earned the right to some familiarity, considering what you've achieved in the last few months.' He frowned at Aubrey. 'Now, Aubrey, malingering again?'

'Just practising, Bertie, in case I ever need to infiltrate a Holmland military hospital. I'll be up in a minute.'

'That's what I wanted to hear. I don't want to pin a medal to your pyjamas. Most undignified.'

'Medal?'

'Apparently I have one for each of you, but they'll probably have to wait, your mission's being top secret and all that. For now, I want to hear everything.'

Aubrey and his friends looked at each other. 'Where do we start?' he said.

'Start after the Stalsfrieden factory fire. I have reports of events after that, but they're so spotty I could use them as a leopard suit. Fill in the details, if you would.'

Telling the heir to the thrones of Albion and Gallia about their adventures became so much like old times that Aubrey almost forgot where they were. Caroline, Sophie and George all butted in, correcting his account, taking over, handing it from one to the other and laughing at the prince's astonishment. Sophie was hesitant to begin with but, heartened by the others, she even managed to groan at one of Prince Albert's execrable puns about firearms and finding people of the right calibre.

The tone of the recounting became more sombre as they came to describing the events at the front, and

Aubrey hoped that Bertie was taking this in. The front was no joking matter. The prince grew more and more angry when they described the hardships of the trenches, and Aubrey thought it was anger most well directed.

After Caroline narrated the last episode – sensibly, as Aubrey had no idea about how she'd dug him out of the collapsed trench, de-peached him and then organised a squad to carry him to medical aid – Bertie sat back, thinking.

'You've done a fine thing, all of you. A touch reckless, Aubrey, but effective.' He put his hands together. 'I like to think our generals are a little more aware of what they're sending our soldiers into than the Holmlanders, but am I deluding myself? Perhaps I should recommend that all members of our High Command must visit the front, and do so regularly. In fact, I've a mind to do so myself since I'm so close.'

'Begging your pardon, Bertie,' George said, 'I don't think you'd be let within ten miles of the front. You're too valuable.'

The prince grimaced. 'They do say that, don't they? I had enough trouble getting this far.'

'Which makes me ask,' Aubrey said, 'what exactly *are* you doing here, Bertie?'

'I'm doing my bit.' The prince hesitated and he turned his cap over in his hands a few times. 'I wanted to do something, you see. Even figureheads can, was my thinking.'

'You're far from a figurehead.' Aubrey knew how much work Bertie had done in the last few years. Ever since his father had grown incapable of fulfilling the role of king, Bertie had taken on many of his ceremonial roles as well as the tedious bureaucratic roles. Even though the public

knew the King was ill, Aubrey was sure they had no idea
how ill – thanks to Bertie's work.

'I appreciate that, Aubrey, but I decided a gesture or
two could be important. So I decided to leave Trinovant
and to rally the troops. And the alliance.' He nodded to
Sophie. 'You're aware that the alliance with Gallia has
been coming under some pressure?'

'It is true,' Sophie said. 'My father said that many people
are unhappy about the war. They think that Albion is using
Gallia as a wall to stop the Holmlanders. And there are
others who are unhappy with the way we are governed.
They want a king.'

'Gallian royalists, in this day and age. I can't believe it,'
Bertie said, without any hint of irony. He picked at the
braid on his cap. 'You forgot to mention the Gallians who
are horrified by such a possibility.'

'Gallia is used to political unrest,' Sophie said, 'but it is
a bad time for such things.'

'So you decided to shore up support with a goodwill
tour,' Aubrey said to Bertie.

'A little more than that, actually.' Prince Albert hesitated
a little and straightened his tie before going on. 'I took
the Gallian Crown Jewels with me to Lutetia and reunited
them with the Heart of Gold. After that I read an official
document to the Gallian assembly, declining our claim to
the vacant throne and promising that our family would
never pursue it.'

Aubrey had survived a few bombshells in recent times,
but he still hadn't grown used to them. Especially not
when dropped in his own bedroom.

Caroline recovered first. 'And how was this received
in Gallia?'

'Barely restrained relief is the best way I'd describe it. As Miss Delroy noted, it's a bad time to be arguing about such things. My quashing any possibility of an Albionite reclaiming the throne of Gallia was the best solution.' He chuckled. 'They held a banquet to commemorate this important occasion, but I think the unanticipated nature of my announcement caught them rather on the hop. They couldn't find the state silver to serve the dinner on and had to borrow some ancient gold plate from the sisters at the Cathedral of Our Lady.'

Aubrey's curiosity jabbed him. 'The Gallian state silver is missing?'

'Stolen, someone said, but the president told me that it had been sold. Silver prices have been going through the roof. He'd ordered that the state silver be sold and the proceeds put into the war effort, to show that the government was serious about sacrifice.'

'Of course,' Aubrey said, but another item was nagging at him. 'And His Majesty, the King? What does he think of these developments?'

'It was Father, of course, who thought this was the best course of action. He wanted to go with me, but the Privy Council advised against that in the strongest terms. When his doctors also spoke out, he subsided, reluctantly, and agreed when I said that I'd do it by myself. After he made up his mind, he was firm on it. Even when he took a turn for the worse, he insisted that I go.'

The state of King William's health was of great concern to every Albionite – and every Albionite with close knowledge of his illness was always concerned with how much to tell the public. The war was an additional complicating factor. A strong leader was an advantage in wartime; a gravely ill one a handicap.

'Prime Minister Giraud would have been happy at your announcement,' Sophie said carefully. 'He is a staunch republican.'

'Indeed he is, Miss Delroy. His glee at my announcement was palpable.'

'But what about the royalists who've been coming out of the woodwork?' George said. 'Sophie, you said your father was concerned about them.'

'He was,' she said. 'Some of them have made troubles.'

'As you say,' Prince Albert said, 'Gallia is accustomed to a level of unrest. I believe, and Prime Minister Giraud agrees, that the war against Holmland and its allies is far more important than a long-ago claim to a vanished throne. The royalists are patriots, after all. They will support the government in this time of crisis.'

'Wait,' Aubrey said. 'You said something about the Gallian Crown Jewels. I've never heard about Gallian Crown Jewels.'

'You're not the only one who does research, Aubrey. I've been busy ever since your discovery of that awkward document suggesting my claim to the Gallian throne. After Dr Tremaine's orchestrated announcement in Fisherberg, I've redoubled my efforts.'

'And given employment to many researchers, no doubt.'

'Hardly.' Prince Albert drew himself up, mock seriously. 'I rummaged about myself. Too sensitive, all this. I didn't want people talking. No matter how loyal they may have been, a horde of researchers would, simply by their presence, cause gossip.'

'Dusty work, researching,' George said.

'As I found, but I also found some interesting old books in libraries in various palaces about the country.'

'Bertie, you do understand that you're one of the few people in the world who can talk about more than one palace, don't you?'

'I'm aware of my position, Aubrey. It sometimes has benefits.' The prince shrugged. 'I'm sure that no-one has opened most of these books for years, centuries even, tucked away as they are.'

'You could donate them to a library,' Caroline suggested.

'Or build a new one,' George added.

'A new library?' Prince Albert considered this. 'A capital thought. I'll look into it, when this war is over.'

Aubrey wondered how many plans were now being appended with 'when this war is over'. Normal lives were suspended, human trajectories interrupted. He could see this conflict affecting a generation – *more* than a generation. It would be a marker for decades to come.

'I'm guessing,' he said, 'that one of these old tomes pointed you toward the possibility of the Gallian Crown Jewels.'

'Very mysteriously,' Prince Albert said. 'You would have loved these books, Aubrey. Full of magical stuff.'

'I was wondering about that.'

'It became a sort of leapfrogging that would have been vastly enjoyable if it weren't for the war. This book pointed to another book, which led to another document and so on. Eventually I found a chest right at the back of a shabby strongroom up north, in Reesdale Castle.'

'The Gallian Crown Jewels?'

'The Gallian Crown Jewels,' Prince Albert affirmed. 'Apparently they were whisked away during the Gallian

Revolution, for safety's sake, and ended up there.'

'Whisked away a bit more successfully than the Gallian king was,' George said.

'Quite.'

Aubrey had, of course, seen the Albion Crown Jewels many times and accepted that kings, by and large, were very serious about their treasures. A substantial collection was a concrete display of how great and powerful they were. Whenever it was hauled out, for one ceremony or other, it was a very deliberate reminder to the population that the holder of such whopping great lumps of gold and gemstones wasn't someone to be trifled with.

'The usual assortment, Bertie?' he asked. 'Crown, sceptre, that sort of thing?'

Prince Albert essayed a small laugh. 'The Gallian Crown Jewels indeed includes a crown. A modest one, compared to the great heavy thing that's in the Albionite collection, but the star sapphire it sports is quite immense. There's also an orb, a mace, a few rings and a rather ancient jewelled seal. The whole collection was in a bad way, but the crown confirmed what it was.' He glanced at Aubrey. 'I would have appreciated your being around, Aubrey, after I found it. Magical whatnot and all.'

'Ah.'

'I had to approach Commander Craddock, there being a marked shortage of experienced, trustworthy magicians at the moment. After some consultation with his research department, Craddock confirmed that the collection was imbued with magic that was slumbering.'

'Slumbering?'

'That's how he put it. When I mentioned the Gallian Heart of Gold, he became very excited.'

'I've never seen Commander Craddock excited,' Caroline said. 'How did he show this?'

'His nostrils flared.'

'Very excited,' Aubrey said. 'I'm surprised he didn't collapse after that.'

'He consulted some of his magical theoreticians again and confirmed my suspicions that reuniting the Crown Jewels with the Heart of Gold could be very useful for Gallia.'

'This reunification, Bertie,' Aubrey said urgently. 'It worked?'

'I have no idea. The sisters who take care of the Heart of Gold weren't surprised when I arrived with the jewels, which is really quite startling in itself. When they lay the items on a ledge in the back of the niche where they guard the heart, I'm sure it began to glow more brightly, but I could be imagining things.'

'I doubt it.' Aubrey looked around. 'Is that a wardrobe? And, if so, is my uniform in it?'

The cabinet he was indicating was decorated in high Gallian mode, pale blue, with gilt curlicues surrounding enough mirrors to make Aubrey fear for his life if the sun caught them directly. An elaborate panorama of a unicorn frolicking with a bevy of milkmaids stretched across the top. The unicorn looked decidedly nervous about whatever the milkmaids had in mind.

While Caroline was taking some time to distinguish the actual door knob from the countless silver buttons, handles and projections doubtless designed to suspend periwigs or recalcitrant servants from, Sophie turned to the prince. 'Do you think it will help, this magical bringing together?'

'Commander Craddock was anxious that it take place, which I take as a sign of its importance.'

Aubrey grimaced. 'I don't think, however, we should be looking for an army of spectral warriors to suddenly start charging across the sky, wiping the Holmlanders from the map. The Heart of Gold's magic is more of a preserving kind, building on what's already there. When it was stolen, Lutetia literally began falling apart.'

Sophie shook her head. 'I remember. Earthquakes, buildings falling down.'

'That sort of thing was the effect of its loss,' Aubrey said. 'I think that we can look to these artefacts to help once the war is over.' *There it goes again.* 'Some of the hurts may be healed. The nation might right itself more quickly, that sort of thing.'

A discreet, but insistent, knock sounded on the door. Aubrey was interested to see Bertie's reaction: it was both irritated and understanding, a blend that Aubrey didn't think was possible – but perhaps it came with being the heir to the throne. 'Enter,' Prince Albert said.

An aide in the same uniform as the prince hurried into the room. He tried to bow and salute at the same time and made a mess of the whole lot. His urgency made Aubrey uneasy. 'Your highness! Sir! It's . . .' He worked his mouth for a moment, then snatched a leather satchel from under his arm and thrust it at the prince. 'Sir!'

Prince Albert studied the satchel for some time before opening it and Aubrey's unease grew. A muffled commotion came from the open doorway, where wagonloads of brass glinted from the shoulders of officers who were gathering at the door the aide had neglected to close behind him. The officers were muttering ominously.

In the distance Aubrey was sure he could hear shouting.

He glanced at his friends to see that they, too, were alarmed. Caroline, holding his jacket on a coat hanger, looked out of the window then turned, open-mouthed, toward him.

I really don't want to be lounging around right now, Aubrey thought, but decided that it would be poor timing to fling back his bedclothes while Bertie was reading a letter that made him frown so deeply.

The prince folded the letter and replaced it in its envelope. For a moment, he looked into the middle distance, then he glanced at the envelope again before slipping it into the satchel, which he gave back to the aide, who was quivering at attention.

The prince stood. Carefully, he shook out the creases in his trousers and straightened his jacket. He placed his cap on his head and spent a moment making sure that it was neatly settled. He cleared his throat. 'I regret to have to tell you, but His Majesty passed away this morning.'

Inevitably, one of the generals at the door said it: 'The King is dead!'

The response came loud and clear from the others. 'Long live the King!'

They took this as permission to pour into the room, a horde of brass-laden officers, all wanting to get close to the new monarch.

The prince took this calmly. He nodded, then saluted. A score of arms snapped back a salute. 'Gentlemen,' he said. 'We have much to do. Albion has lost a great king.'

Aubrey saw it all. It was an impressive display of self-control from someone who had been taught, ever since he was old enough to understand, about the importance of duty. Bertie had known that this day would come, the day where an ancient tradition would swing into action and sweep him away, turning him from what he was into something else. The prince was thoughtful, grave, but very much in command. A young man, but one who was ready for this moment.

Despite this, Aubrey wanted to reach out to his friend, to acknowledge that there was something personal in this moment, something that was being lost in the overwhelmingly public ritual.

We may have lost a king, Aubrey thought, *but you've lost a father.*

Twenty-six

AUBREY DARTED BEHIND A SCREEN TO CHANGE AS the prince was whisked away by the generals, colonels and other nabobs who had congregated, aware of the significance of the moment.

Aubrey's head popped up and down as he grappled with trousers and boots, providing a series of glimpses of the hullaballoo as he bent and straightened, so that Bertie's progress stuttered along, shuffling across the room only to become bogged at the door by a crowd that was managing the difficult task of cheering solemnly.

A familiar figure detached himself from the flotilla around the ex-prince and strode toward them, moustache a-bristle. 'Fitzwilliam?' General Apsley said. 'You're up and about? Good. Planning meeting in the conference room on the ground floor. Five minutes.'

THE CONFERENCE ROOM HAD PROBABLY BEEN A DINING room when the chateau was new. It overlooked the remains of gardens that, on this side of the estate, now seemed to be growing sandbags and tents as the chateau continued its transformation into a regional headquarters. An extensive hospital had been set up with a summer house as its central building and Aubrey wondered how this new location signalled a shift in the ebb and flow of the war. It was certainly a move up from the farmhouse that General Apsley had been using, but Aubrey wasn't sure if that was a good thing or a bad thing.

With lunchtime approaching, George volunteered to reconnoitre the chateau, taking Sophie to help in case he ran into anyone who didn't speak Albionish. Aubrey was about to suggest that Caroline go with them, but her stern expression hinted that she wasn't about to be left out of what promised to be a top-level planning meeting.

Bertie was at the head of the table, looking – understandably to Aubrey's way of thinking – somewhat distracted. General Apsley was at the new King's right hand. He conducted the meeting while aides scurried about adjusting charts and maps on the easels that stood on the dais at the end of the room.

'The Holmland build-up is in disarray,' General Apsley announced to the assembly of field commanders, intelligence operatives, Directorate agents, deputy quartermasters-general and one young King. 'Their army is holding the line at Fremont, but their recent reinforcements have been pulled back instead of pressing forward.'

Ex-Prince Albert looked over his hands, steepled in front of his chin. 'I think you'll find that this is the result of Fitzwilliam's work.'

As every gaze around the table swivelled around and locked on him, Aubrey felt as he imagined a small patch of ground in no-man's-land would, the patch of ground that happened to be the centre of the coordinates of a massed artillery bombardment.

'Fitzwilliam?' General Apsley said. 'Your friends declined to say much about your doings until you were with us again. Best if you report now, I'd say.'

Aubrey took a deep breath. 'Yes, sir,' he said and outlined the events at Fremont before finishing with: 'and I'm hoping that's why the troops have pulled back. To escort the Chancellor and the others away from the front.'

General Apsley stared at him, mouth half-open, and he wasn't the only one in the room to adopt such a pose. 'My sainted aunt,' the general said eventually. 'You magicked the Chancellor and all of his crew into the middle of a battleground? Astonishing.'

'Fitzwilliam here is regularly astonishing,' Bertie said. 'We're lucky to have him on our side.'

Aubrey blushed. 'Just doing my duty, your highness. Your majesty.'

'At any rate, Fitzwilliam, you've struck a fine blow. Good show.' General Apsley glanced at a map of the battlelines behind him and beamed. 'The Chancellor and the others are bound to fall back to Stalsfrieden, where they can join the train. You've bought us some time, but I'm afraid they're not giving up. We have reports that more reinforcements are coming from the Central European Empire and from the eastern front. The Holmland generals aren't going to leave anything to chance, this time.' He glowered at the map before brightening. 'But we have some news of our own, let me tell you. Our reinforcements have arrived.'

Spontaneous cheering greeted this, most emphatic from the weariest, least well groomed of those present, the ones who Aubrey assumed had been spending time at the front.

General Apsley patted down this applause. 'We should have the last of ten thousand fresh men here by nightfall, including regiments from Antipodea and the sub-continent.'

This was greeted with murmurs of approval. The reputation of the Antipodeans had preceded them, while the sub-continental regiments were experienced and deadly.

The talk soon veered around to matters of supply and deployment. Aubrey's attention began to wander, but he snapped to alertness when two black-uniformed operatives slipped into the room. One took a satchel straight to General Apsley. The other, after looking about for a moment, made a bee-line for Aubrey.

'Fitzwilliam?' he whispered once he'd made his way close enough.

Aubrey indicated that he was, indeed, of that name, and in return received a message satchel.

'I've come straight from Darnleigh House,' the operative said. 'Orders were to get this to you post-haste.'

Aubrey looked for, and found, the tell-tale callus on the inside of the man's left forefinger, and confirmed his guess by the marks on either side of the man's chin where the straps of his flying helmet rested. 'What model ornithopter were you flying?'

The man blinked. 'A new model. The 780 Gannet. Special long-range capability.'

Some stern looks from nearby hushed Aubrey. He signed his thanks to the operative, who withdrew.

While a lieutenant-colonel delivered a paper about the possibility of a temporary rail bridge to replace the one lost at Divodorum, General Apsley was scanning the documents in the satchel he'd been delivered. Aubrey thought it best that he do the same.

One document confirmed Aubrey's speculation about the magnitude of the disappearance of magicians in Albion. It also summarised findings from their Gallian intelligence colleagues, who also noted that magicians had been vanishing.

Another document was a report from the remote sensing department. While Aubrey had had some contact with the field operatives who had the rare skill of being able to sense magic at vast distances, the bulk of these operatives worked from the basement of Darnleigh House. Commander Craddock's note, appended to the report, suggested that Aubrey might be interested in the activity report compiled by the sensers.

He was. A map provided with the report showed what the sensing department nominated as 'hot spots', areas of concentrated magic. The map had been matched and overlaid with a map of the Divodorum front, and then of the supply and transport lines back into Holmland.

In the days prior to Aubrey's great spell, objects of magical power were being transported toward the Divodorum front. Most were coming from the direction of Fisherberg by train, but calculated guesses indicated that some were coming by airship, others by river barge. Twenty-seven separate objects impinged themselves on the map, shining brightly like beacons, tracking day by day toward the battlefront – only to halt and then change direction after Aubrey's great spell.

These observations matched up with the sensations Aubrey had had in the trenches. Vast magic had been in the area. Had it been assembling to generate an attack, or was it merely giving strength to the illusory charges sent toward the Albion lines?

Now, according to the findings of the remote sensers, Stalsfrieden was ablaze with magical power. The only thing the commander of the remote sensing unit could compare it to was the emanation of the Heart of Gold in the middle of Lutetia. Aubrey immediately concluded that the magical artefacts had withdrawn with the Chancellor. Was this Dr Tremaine's doing? Was he withdrawing as well? What did it signify?

He rubbed his forehead. Intelligence was gathered to make sense of the confusion of war, but sometimes it was like striking a light in the middle of a midnight forest – the nearby trees could be seen a little better, but everything else remained decidedly ominous.

Once he read each paper, Aubrey passed it on to Caroline on his left. When Aubrey finished with the last document – a repetition of the puzzling request for information about any missing dental supplies – he sat back just as the lieutenant-colonel finished and General Apsley jumped to his feet.

'Excellent, Phillips, excellent.' He beamed. 'Now, I have some news directly from our High Command. The PM himself –' he paused to nod at Aubrey '– has signed these orders, which apply to each and every one of you here. We have the task, the most urgent task, of ensuring that our new King be returned to Albion immediately. This is the highest priority for all units, and we are to provide any assistance necessary to expedite this goal.'

Bertie frowned slightly, then nodded, and Aubrey knew that his friend had immediately understood the necessity for him to be removed from all possibility of danger. Having an heir to the throne near the front like this was barely acceptable, even given the rallying effect it had on the morale of the troops, but hosting the actual King? Preposterous.

Aubrey had also seen the thoughtful looks many around the table had been giving the new King. He guessed they were the more ambitious among them, deciding how best to commend themselves to the new monarch. Ambition never slept.

General Apsley went on to canvass the safest way to transport King Albert back to Albion, but Aubrey had other more important matters at hand. After taking in the information from the Directorate, he tried drawing diagrams to determine how Dr Tremaine fitted in.

His cogitations were interrupted when George appeared at his elbow. It didn't create any great interest as the room was abuzz with comings and goings; the brass at the table constantly had aides whispering into their ears with news, information and dinner menus, for all Aubrey knew, so one more was hardly noticed.

'You need to come with me,' George said softly, but urgently. 'Professor Mansfield has escaped from Dr Tremaine and wants to talk to you.'

Twenty-seven

*T*HE FIELD HOSPITAL ON THE EAST SIDE OF THE CHATEAU was a large and well-ordered, if sombre, place. George hurried Aubrey and Caroline through the rows of tents full of beds with men who weren't critically wounded, but who were definitely not capable of fighting in the near future. At the centre of the medical facility was a large tent in uproar. 'She's refusing to go into the operating theatre until she sees you,' George explained to Aubrey and Caroline.

'She's hurt?'

'She was on that ornithopter we saw crash, but it's more than that.'

George explained that Sophie had been co-opted into acting as an interpreter for the hurt Gallians who had ended up at the facility. George had done what he could, and when on an errand to find a particular chest surgeon he'd been recognised by the seriously injured

Professor Mansfield. She had implored him to bring Aubrey to her.

Having delivered Aubrey and Caroline, George hurried off to find Sophie.

Wounded men and stretcher bearers were clustered at the opening of the tent, which smelled of carbolic soap, ether and blood. From inside came shouting and the sound of breaking glass.

With Caroline at his side, Aubrey eased his way through the crush at the entrance to find a large space, well lit by electric light, a preparation area for those about to enter the operating area behind the two wooden doors at the far end of the tent. Screened-off beds were being shielded by nurses, while near the doors white-coated doctors struggled around a trolley. One – round glasses and an impressive pointed beard – staggered back and cursed in a most unprofessional manner. When he saw Aubrey, he barked in aggrieved Albionite tones: 'Are you Fitzwilliam? She keeps calling for you.'

'Professor Mansfield?'

'Calm her down, quickly. She needs surgery, but we have others just as needy who are waiting.'

With a word from him, the other doctors backed away from the narrow trolley. Aubrey approached to find his one-time lecturer in Ancient Languages draped in a blood-stained sheet, her eyes wild, her movements frantic. 'Aubrey? Is that you?'

Aubrey's heart went out to her. She had been the most energetic and most vivid of his Greythorn lecturers, and not only because she was the only woman among them, and nor was it the fact that she was by far the youngest. It was her animation and her vivacity that had appealed to him, but here it was transformed. Her eyes rolled, her small frame shivered, her face was blackened by soot, her hair hung in sweaty ringlets as she was sitting, gaze darting about as if she expected to be attacked from all sides at once.

He came to her side. 'Professor Mansfield.'

Her gaze locked on him. She gasped — a wrenching, tormented sound — and clutched at his arm with bony fingers. She buried her face in his chest. Awkwardly, he took her in his arms. 'Dr Tremaine,' she sobbed hoarsely, 'he's on his way to attack Trinovant.'

Trinovant? But Tremaine needs to be near a battlefront for the Ritual of the Way!

Aubrey felt as if he'd been standing on carefully constructed scaffolding made from his observations, speculations and deductions about Dr Tremaine and as he was about to reach out to grasp the final, clear understanding of the rogue sorcerer's plans the scaffolding dissolved beneath him.

Why is he abandoning everything?

Aubrey glanced at Caroline to find that she was staring with horror at the back of Professor Mansfield's head.

He looked down and nearly cried out. In a shaved patch, just above where her neck swelled out into the skull proper, was a socket.

The ghastly thing was an inch or so in diameter and had the appearance of hard, white ceramic. Scar tissue surrounded it, reddened and weeping in places, and Aubrey shuddered at the thought of the operation needed to insert such an abomination.

Professor Mansfield pushed away from Aubrey. Before he could ask what had happened to her, she chided herself. 'No, no, no! I promised Kurt I wouldn't cry. Not a tear, not at all.'

Aubrey took Professor Mansfield's shoulders, but at that moment he saw the bearded doctor hovering behind her. He pointed at his watch then at his leg in an awkward pantomime. Aubrey looked down and saw fresh blood on the sheet.

'They said I might lose my leg,' Professor Mansfield said softly.

'Don't worry.' The words came automatically to Aubrey's lips. 'You'll have the best of care.'

She grimaced, then gripped his arm again, hard. 'I won't, but it doesn't matter. Kurt risked his life to save us from that madman. He made a much larger sacrifice when we crashed, and I'm not going to dishonour his memory.'

'But how is Dr Tremaine going to attack Trinovant?'

'He has the Rashid Stone,' she said and Aubrey wondered at her state of mind, skating about like that. How badly shaken had she been by her experiences, let alone the crash?

'It's important?'

'Listen!' She glared at him and her fingers dug into his arm. 'He's collected magical artefacts from all over to enhance his magic, including the Rashid Stone. He's gathered magicians and savants from all over –' She broke off and coughed, her face contorting with pain. 'He's harvested their knowledge and harnessed their magical talent.'

'He wired you together.' Aubrey remembered the booths under Dr Tremaine's clifftop estate. Revulsion made the words stick in his throat. 'He treated you like a row of batteries.'

A flutter of a smile. 'You were always quick, Aubrey. As you should be with such parents.'

Aubrey did his best to be reassuring, but he found it difficult as he tried to fit this new data into his thinking. 'He did this to you and the others to achieve his goal.'

'You know what that is?'

'I do.' The Ritual of the Way. A blood sacrifice and then immortality for his sister and himself.

A thousand thoughts were rampaging in Aubrey's mind, calling for attention, insisting that he bring them all together to form a coherent, comprehensive theory. One of these thoughts rose above all the others and thumped the inside of his skull until he turned to it.

Dr Tremaine wouldn't abandon his preparations unless he had something more suited to his ends. 'He could have something better than the Ritual of the Way,' he said softly. The horror of anything that would surpass a magical rite needing the blood of thousands struck him like a blow. Only with an effort did he prevent himself from folding in the middle and falling to the floor.

'Aubrey.' Professor Mansfield brought her face close to his. She was shivering. 'Whatever he's doing, he must be stopped. He's going now!'

THE DOCTOR, HAVING SEEN THAT PROFESSOR MANSFIELD had collapsed, bustled in and, with the assistance of a horde of nurses, whisked the trolley through the wooden doors.

'She'll get the care she needs,' Caroline said. She took Aubrey by the arm and shepherded him out of the preparation area, which had exploded into action as soon as the impasse with Professor Mansfield had been resolved. Screens were dragged aside, trolleys and equipment rushed to bedsides, bandaged soldiers in wheelchairs hurried away.

Aubrey was deep in thought as they hurried back to the chateau. Through adroit nudging and steering, Caroline kept him from colliding with apple trees, water pumps and the many hurrying service people who had turned the estate into a headquarters. She even had to stop his progress with an outflung arm to prevent his running into a maintenance crew that was rushing to one of the new Gannet model ornithopters that had just landed in the large flat area to the west of the chateau.

General Apsley would need to be informed, Aubrey decided, plucking a single decision from the furore in his mind. News of this development needed to get to the Directorate immediately, so Trinovant could prepare for Dr Tremaine's assault. Not knowing the exact nature of the attack was going to make things difficult, but this warning would give a chance to ready the forces.

Aubrey was jerked out of his planning by the abrupt thumping of thirteen-pounder guns. He looked east, shading his eyes, looking past the line of poles that brought the telegraph line to the chateau. 'Anti-aircraft artillery?'

Caroline pointed. 'On the edge of the estate, near the road, the other side of the avenue of trees.'

Before Aubrey could make out the emplacements, he was stunned in two vastly different ways. With astonishment, he saw the target for the anti-aircraft guns while simultaneously feeling as if someone had implanted a hook below his sternum and yanked it skywards.

'Aubrey!' Caroline cried as he doubled over, then staggered a few steps. Around them, soldiers began running and shouting, which was never a good thing in Aubrey's experience. The sudden appearance of helmets did little to reassure him, and the looming presence on the horizon fully justified such preparations.

A skyfleet was steaming towards them.

Twenty-eight

ASSES OF OMINOUS DARK–GREY THUNDERHEADS
were heaped up, towering toward the heavens.
Advancing from the middle of this storm was a horribly
familiar line of cloud-forged warcraft led by a massive
battleship – a dreadnought large enough to make other
dreadnoughts think about doing some quiet dreading.

The sun vanished. Lightning flickered above the thunderheads and the day was suddenly cold. As the storm
surged toward them, wind sprang up, whipped at tent
flaps and sent leaves scurrying across the ground.

The anti-aircraft guns continued their determined
barrage, firing faster and faster as the skyfleet steamed
closer. The shells burst all about the cloud ships but did
nothing to stop their progress.

Dr Tremaine was up there. The jolt Aubrey had felt
was a tug on the link he shared with the rogue sorcerer.
It was a whiplash moment, then it was gone, but in that

instant he had Dr Tremaine's location as surely as if the sorcerer were standing on top of a lighthouse with a flag on his head.

Caroline was quick. Her eyes narrowed. 'Dr Tremaine? Is that how he's going to attack Trinovant?'

Aubrey went to agree, then another option presented itself with enough force to make him wince. He looked at the chateau, then he looked at the approaching skyfleet, then he looked at the chateau again. Was Dr Tremaine the master of multiple strategies? Of course he was. 'Yes. Probably. Maybe.'

Caroline followed his gaze. 'You think he knows Bertie is here.'

'Why not create some mayhem along the way to Trinovant? The disarray it would create would be useful, just in case his Trinovant mission fails.'

The wind picked up. Aubrey had to shield his eyes from dust. Sergeants strode about, shouting, bringing order to the chaos the skyfleet had caused. A large black dog ran about, barking at the soldiers, the flapping tents, the whipping wireless aerials on top of the chateau, and the flailing trees. On the other side of the chateau, horses whinnied and stamped.

Aubrey was still drained from his efforts on the battlefield, but he ransacked his brains for a spell, something to counteract the attack that was coming. He didn't spare any time wondering how Dr Tremaine knew the location of the new King of Albion. Magical means or ordinary spying, Dr Tremaine's methods were thorough.

Aubrey remembered the havoc created by a similar aerial fleet attack on Greythorn. Much damage was done by weather magic concentrated by the skyfleet, but it had also dropped at least one bomb Aubrey knew about. He wondered if he could manage some sort of deflection; not stopping any bombs, but simply sloughing them to one side of the estate. If he couldn't protect the whole estate, then maybe the chateau itself? What about the hospital, though? Could he shield it as well?

They ran, bent nearly double against the wind, weaving through the companies of soldiers who were being dispersed to dugouts and trenches about the estate. Aubrey was relieved to see that one private was dragging the black dog by a length of rope, while it continued to do its job of giving the wind a good barking at.

When Aubrey reached the side door of the chateau, he looked back. The skyfleet couldn't have been a mile away. Its passage was flattening trees and crushing cottages, creating a swathe of destruction across the countryside. A herd of cows took one look and scattered; each cow was grimly doing its best to achieve this 'galloping' it had heard of but never personally experienced. The madcap sound of cowbells added to the cacophony of shots, shouting, artillery fire and the overwhelming, all-encompassing scream of the wind.

'Get Bertie into the basement!' Aubrey shouted to Caroline. 'Tell him that Tremaine is here!'

Caroline glanced at the sky, then nodded sharply. The door was wrenched from her hand as soon as she turned the handle. It slammed back, almost ripping from its hinges. While guards struggled to heave it closed again, Caroline slipped inside.

Dimly, Aubrey heard the sound of breaking glass. He flattened himself against the stuccoed wall of the chateau. He had to shield his eyes from flying grit as he wrestled with the possibility of a spell.

At this distance, half a mile or so, the connection he had with Dr Tremaine was faint, almost ghostly. It tickled his awareness without giving much more impression than an itch that couldn't be ignored. It was swamped by the magical presence that was the skyfleet itself, wrought by magic from cloudstuff – and by a furnace-bright burning that came from the heart of the flagship itself. It had the texture of the magic Aubrey had sensed coming from the Holmland trenches at Fremont, the magic that coincided with the twenty-seven points of light in the Directorate's remote sensing.

Dr Tremaine wasn't leaving anything to chance in his attack on the new King. He was bringing his collection of magical artefacts to add power to his magic.

Aubrey anticipated the stormfleet behaviour he'd witnessed in Greythorn. There, the skyfleet had swept in and circled a single position, creating mayhem through weather magic, trapping those inside its whirling perimeter with a wall of cyclonic wind. If Dr Tremaine achieved this formation he could pound the chateau and the new King of Albion to pieces. Basement or no, anyone inside would be doomed.

He was rapidly spinning an idea into the beginnings of a spell. The buffeting of the wind made him wonder if he couldn't do something similar, some sort of displacement that could shift bombs. It would take a combination of the Law of Action at a Distance and the Law of Transference, but he might be able to shift a large enough volume of air to create a deflecting vacuum, or a vortex to spin a bomb aside . . . Of course, in order to cast these spells accurately, he'd have to spot the bombs as they fell, which would be a challenge in such conditions as the storm-brought darkness made the entire sky murky.

Aubrey's beret was ripped from his head. It spun away and was caught in a nearby rhododendron. Aubrey ignored it as the storm rolled toward them, a juggernaut of lightning and cloud. The skyfleet itself pushed from the middle of it, a formidable battleline of giant warships, ignoring the anti-aircraft fire that fell far short of its lofty elevation.

An untried spell, put together in difficult circumstances? Aubrey was ready but, before he could even articulate the first syllables that he was still arranging in his mind, the heavens were torn apart in a blinding flash. The thunder that followed made the anti-aircraft fire sound puny.

Aubrey blinked at the purple after-vision. He shook his head to clear it but his ears were still ringing as he scanned the sky. Lightning lanced across the black wall of cloud, ragged rips in the heavens, leaking brightness that made his eyes water.

How was he going to spy a bomb dropped in such conditions?

Wedged between the stairs and the side of the chateau, Aubrey extended his magical awareness, hoping to detect any magical emanations from falling bombs. It was a forlorn hope but desperation often gave birth to such unexpected offspring.

Even with his senses – mundane and magical – so attuned, Aubrey nearly missed the particular lightning bolt amid the garish display the heavens had become. In the split-second he had, he realised it was because of foreshortening – he didn't see it because it was coming directly toward him.

The next thing Aubrey knew he was lying in the rhododendron bushes near where his beret was lodged. The noises about him were muffled and dim. When he stood, on shaky legs, he realised he'd been deafened by the blast that had flung him sideways. Numbly, he contemplated the diamonds scattered on the ground at his feet for a few seconds, before he realised that they were actually fragments of glass. A soldier grabbed his arm, shouted something and pointed up, then ran toward the stairs of the chateau.

Pull yourself together, Aubrey admonished himself. He untangled his beret and held it in his trembling fingers. He smelled burning and looked up.

All the windows on the top floor of the chateau – the third – were gone. He couldn't see flames, but what he saw on the roof of the building finally stirred his feet into action.

Giant electrical figures were capering about, swinging from antenna masts, skating along wires, dancing on chimneys, a horde in a manic, sparking frenzy.

Aubrey ran for the stairs, bent double, for the skyfleet was rolling directly overhead. It was a vast, oppressive presence, bringing a howling wind that came from all directions. The storm cannoned into Aubrey and sent him reeling. Only by throwing out a hand and catching the newel post of the stairs was he able to prevent himself from being hurled away from the entrance.

Inside, the chateau was pandemonium as military personnel from privates to generals either tried to flee the assault on the chateau or assist the injured who were staggering down the stairs.

Aubrey sprinted in that direction and swam against the

current, mounting the stairs as fast as he could, while hoping that Caroline had managed to find safety with Bertie.

He was alone when he burst out onto the flat area between the turrets, the erstwhile site of the antenna array, just in time to see the last of the electrical fiends cavort on top of the flagpole, which had – until a few minutes ago – flown the Gallian flag. Its rough human shape and its magic left Aubrey in no doubt that it was a cousin to the creature he'd defeated on the roof of the Divodorum base, but before he could do anything the flagpole exploded in a hail of splinters that sent him sprawling to protect his face.

When Aubrey rolled to his feet, the malicious sprite had vanished. The flagpole was a blackened stub amid the slag and shreds of wire that had once been a carefully aligned antenna array.

Aubrey rubbed his aching head, realised that his beret had gone missing again, found it in a tangle of nearby metal and lodged it on his head while he stepped gingerly across the melted and charred remains that had been, briefly, a playground for Dr Tremaine's malign magic. When he reached the western parapet, he saw that the skyfleet was sailing away and taking the storm with it. Lightning jabbed down at the earth, making it look as if the ships were walking on giant, electrical legs, stalking across countryside with impunity. A telegraph pole exploded in a shower of sparks, then another, before the skyfleet crossed a ridge and Aubrey lost sight of its sparky spideriness.

A cry made him whirl to find Caroline joining him on the roof. 'Aubrey!'

While Aubrey had the highest estimation of Caroline's abilities, he nevertheless was relieved to see that she was unharmed. He veritably skipped across the roof, vaulting over a gaping skylight and dancing around a metal pole that jutted at an angle right through a dislodged downpipe.

She took his outstretched hand. A host of expressions flitted across her dear face before she settled on careful professionalism. 'Bertie is safe. The telegraph room exploded and is burnt out, but that's the only real damage.'

'You're unhurt?'

She tilted her head, but didn't let go of his hand. 'One must put first things first, Aubrey.'

'I did.'

The service door banged back. George and Sophie emerged. 'A right mess,' George said after surveying the damage. 'They won't be putting this back together in a hurry.'

Click, click, click. Aubrey had it. He ran for the stairs. 'Exactly, which means we need to be on our way.'

Banging down the stairs, Aubrey told Caroline what he'd seen on the roof – and he shared what Professor Mansfield had said with George and Sophie. 'We need to let the Directorate know,' he said over his shoulder, 'but it looks as if . . . Ah! General Apsley!'

At the bottom of the stairs, the general was standing like a rock in the middle of a stream. While others rushed about, carrying boxes and valuables, the general had his hands behind his back, taking account of proceedings with some approval. 'Fitzwilliam! Very good! This way!'

He broached the flood and ushered them into a drawing room to one side of the main entrance. The room was mostly gilt, mirrors and vases, a tiny showpiece designed to impress. It looked over the hospital area, which was, to Aubrey's relief, untouched apart from some flailing canvas and a few minor collapses.

Bertie stood as they entered. 'Relief seems to be the order of the day,' he said. 'I'm glad to see you, Aubrey.'

'Bertie. Sir. Your majesty.'

A quick smile. 'Enough of that. The general was eager to find you after I told him you'd know what just hit us.'

Aubrey addressed himself to the general. 'It was Dr Tremaine, sir, and I've just learned he's on his way to Trinovant. I don't think I need to tell you that he needs to be stopped.'

'Tremaine, eh? That was his magic?'

'It was. I've seen his skyfleet magic before, and the electrical attack was undoubtedly his.'

'Trinovant?' General Aspley said. 'Whatever for? I'd been led to believe that he was determined to organise a battle here, in Gallia.'

Aubrey screwed up his face in frustration. 'He was, but he's abandoned that plan. Whatever he has in mind now is unlikely to be less dangerous.'

'So he wasn't after our new King?'

'I doubt it. If he had been, we wouldn't be standing around and chatting like this.' Aubrey felt some more pieces clicking into place. 'He's stopped us letting the Directorate know that he's coming.'

'All the communication equipment is unsalvageable,' Caroline said. 'It would take weeks to repair the damage.'

Aubrey jabbed a finger into the air, at nothing in particular. 'As the skyfleet headed west, it was destroying the telegraph lines to make sure. He knew Professor Mansfield had escaped.'

'He's on the way to Trinovant?' Bertie's face was grave.

'We must get word to them.'

Caroline seized Aubrey's arm. 'And so we shall.'

THE ORNITHOPTER STOOD NEXT TO WHAT HAD ONCE been stables but was now being used as a mechanical workshop. The Gannet gleamed in the low light of the receding storm. Its wings were folded back in the resting position, reaching almost back to the massive extra fuel tanks that were responsible for its range.

In the wake of the storm, the chateau complex was subdued. The damage was remarkably minor, with flying debris having caused most of the destruction. Aubrey was pleased to see the black dog strutting about as if it had been solely responsible for seeing off the invaders.

Their departure wasn't so precipitous that some preparations hadn't been undertaken. General Apsley wasn't prepared to rely on a single ornithopter to get the news to Albion, so he had organised the dispatching of motorcycle riders to relay the news to the Directorate and the Prime Minister.

In the meantime, while the ornithopter was readied, Aubrey found a satchel of maps to which he added the notes he'd been accumulating. He also scrambled together some magical items he hoped would be useful. George and Sophie busied themselves in readying for their flight as Caroline was briefed on the new flying machine.

George hefted his rucksack. 'You can fly this, Caroline?'

Her eyes were bright. 'Oh yes, I'm sure I can.'

Sophie peered through goggles. 'I have never flown in an ornithopter before.'

'You're in for an experience.' George flung open the door and together they leaped into the back seat, where, to Aubrey's mind, they spent an inordinate amount of time becoming untangled.

Caroline vaulted into the pilot's seat, slammed the door and tied back her hair while she studied the controls. They looked familiar enough to Aubrey, but he noticed that the wing tilt indicator and oil pressure gauge had swapped position. He swallowed and peered at the dials, switches and knobs. What else was different?

'We're fully fuelled,' he announced, having found the appropriate indicator.

'Excellent,' Caroline murmured. Without taking her eyes from the panel in front of her, she snapped her seat-belt around her waist. Aubrey didn't have to be told; he quickly did the same and he heard two similar metallic catches from behind him.

Aubrey could fly an ornithopter, and fly it very well if his instructors could be believed. He knew, however, that he wasn't a patch on Caroline. He enjoyed the flying experience; she loved it, and her love translated into a sublime ability to pilot the notoriously cranky machine as easily as if it were a kite.

She leaned forward, and a tiny tip of her tongue pro-truded from a corner of her mouth. She paused for an instant, then flipped a switch. The engine coughed twice, then decided it was well enough to lurch into action. It roared and the noise of the storm was drowned out. Caroline's hands ran across the panel, engaging and testing components of the fiendishly complicated machine she was about to shepherd into the sky. Tiny lights winked on and off, and Aubrey felt flares of magic awaken from the various enhanced aspects of the ornithopter.

Caroline grasped the controls and used a thumb to open the switch on the right-hand panel. Instantly, the earth was left behind.

George cheered, but the launch was always Aubrey's least favourite part of any ornithopter flight. In any take-off, it felt as if his stomach were left well behind on the ground and then had to spend some time clawing its way back to reunite itself with the rest of his body. He swallowed to equalise the pressure in his ears. The thrashing of the great metal wings managed the impressive task of drowning out the roar of the engine, where all the pistons were labouring with the effort of hurling the bulk of the machine skywards.

The ornithopter spiralled, seeking its best flying altitude. Aubrey consulted a map.

'A heading, Aubrey?' Caroline glanced at him, her lip quirked upward.

'Two hundred and sixty degrees,' he said, surprising himself with such lucidity in the face of a Caroline lip quirk.

'Let's see if we can beat that skyfleet to Trinovant.' She adjusted the wing attack angle and the metal bird lurched, canted, then set off in pursuit of Dr Tremaine.

Twenty-nine

WITH THE AFTERNOON SUN MOVING WESTWARD, the glare made seeing difficult, but Aubrey thought he could make out a far-off line of dark cloud. As it was directly between the Albion capital and them, this tended to confirm Professor Mansfield's claim that Trinovant was Dr Tremaine's target – especially as Aubrey had felt the rogue sorcerer's presence as the skyfleet passed overhead.

George tapped him on the shoulder. 'Since we missed lunch, I thought some making up might be in order.'

'Rations?'

'Superior rations,' George said. 'After all, the chateau has been hosting Bertie. We've got good ham, cheese, proper white bread, smoked chicken. And I'm not quite sure how this chocolate cake made its way into my sack, but I'm only glad that I managed to slip it into a tin before it did.'

Sophie offered Aubrey a bottle. 'Ginger beer?'

Aubrey carefully opened it. 'What was ginger beer doing in a Gallian chateau?'

George considered this. 'In some ways – the ginger beer department, for example – that place was a little bit of Albion in the middle of Gallia.'

'The best of both worlds,' Sophie said and she passed a rough slice of bread to Aubrey. It was wrapped around some ham and cheese and he realised he was ravenous.

'Er . . . do you have a glass?'

'Drink from the bottle, Aubrey,' Caroline said without turning her head. All her attention was on the windscreen and the control panel; she was constantly trying to coax a little more speed out of the ornithopter, trimming the wings, levelling the flight. 'Then hold it up to my lips, would you? I'm parched.'

The next hour was spent on a precarious meal while they pursued Dr Tremaine's skyfleet. Aubrey divided his time between accepting morsels from Sophie and George, and popping them into Caroline's mouth as she continued her piloting of the aircraft. After they were done and cleaned up, as best they could in the confines of the cockpit, the day stretched out in the same way the countryside did below them.

Abruptly, Caroline asked Aubrey a question: 'Have you deduced why Dr Tremaine is going to Albion yet?'

'It's been much on my mind.'

'I'm sure. Any conclusions?'

'Many. None of them particularly cheerful.'

Caroline considered this for a moment. 'Why Trinovant?'

'I beg your pardon?'

'Why is he going to Trinovant? Why not Lutetia?'

Click. 'Thank you,' he said. 'That was the perfect question.'

'And you have the answer?'

'I'm getting there.' He chewed his lip, briefly. 'Bear with me here, but the overwhelming thing that distinguishes Trinovant from all other cities is its size.'

'You're being needlessly obvious again.'

It was close. He nearly had it. 'It's magical theory, Caroline. Magic is generated by the interaction of human consciousness on the universe. The more people, the greater the potential magical field.' *Gigantic click*. 'That's it.'

'Explain, Aubrey.'

The potential catastrophe made Aubrey hesitate before answering. 'Dr Tremaine wants to harness the greatest potential magical field in the world.'

'I see. That's all we need. A more powerful Dr Tremaine.'

Aubrey hardly heard. 'Remember the way I used the collective consciousnesses around no-man's-land? Imagine Dr Tremaine using all Trinovant to propel his spell. He'll be able to work the Ritual of the Way without the blood sacrifice we all assumed he needed.'

'Which is a good thing.'

'The lack of blood sacrifice is definitely a good thing. An immortal Dr Tremaine is a bad thing.'

Aubrey knew he'd have no argument from Caroline on that score. After killing her father, Dr Tremaine was irredeemable in Caroline's eyes.

'It sounds as if Dr Tremaine is desperate,' she said. 'You've upset his plans for battle for who knows how long, so he's resorting to this.'

'Perhaps.' Aubrey was unwilling to believe that Dr Tremaine was driven to anything. The more he thought about it, the more he wondered if this had been his plan all along. After all, the Ritual of the Way had never been undertaken successfully, despite the horrors some magicians had wrought in their attempts. As Aubrey had researched the dark magic, the more he'd come to suspect that several battles in ancient times had been manipulated to achieve the level of sacrifice believed necessary to perform the spell.

Aubrey suspected that Dr Tremaine had been working on this alternative method for a long time. If he were able to couple a substantial collection of magical artefacts with a Universal Language of Magic, while tapping into the magical field over Trinovant, the Ritual of the Way could be within his grasp.

The thought did little to cheer him. He wondered if he wasn't overlooking something, something that could make a difference.

He turned, looking for some common sense from George, to find that he and Sophie had managed to fall asleep.

Sleep was a stranger to Aubrey. The roar of the engine set his teeth vibrating, and the constant 'thump-swish' of the wings was jarring. Besides, he wasn't about to sleep when Caroline couldn't, but when he tried some inconsequential chat, her monosyllabic responses didn't encourage him to keep it up. She was locked on course as much as the ornithopter was.

This gave him more time to think, to prepare for a confrontation where the future of the world was at stake. His mind went to the magical connection that he shared with Dr Tremaine.

During his vigil in the cave overlooking Dr Tremaine's stronghold, Aubrey had felt the connection come and go, as was its wont. Intrigued, he'd spent time pondering the implications of the connection and its composition. He had an inkling that the Law of Entanglement and the Law of Division could shed some light on it, so while their pursuit wore on, he took out his notebook and immersed himself in a number of formulations suggested by these laws to see what light they could shed on the mysterious phenomenon.

When he became aware of the world again – some time later – the skyfleet had vanished over the horizon. With no glimpse of it, not even the thunderheads, it felt as if they were making no headway.

'Can we catch them?' he asked Caroline. He kept his voice as low as he could to avoid waking Sophie and George.

'I doubt it,' she said, 'but we're not giving up. If Tremaine's devil fleet falters, we'll have them.'

Aubrey tapped his chin. 'What if we had some assistance?'

'You have something in mind?'

'As the skyfleet was approaching the chateau, I was con-structing a spell to deflect any bombs. It occurs to me that I could rework such a spell to provide us with some impetus.'

'Providing impetus to an aircraft in motion sounds as if it might involve some level of danger.'

'I wondered about that.' Aubrey hummed a little, to himself. 'I'm thinking that I might be able to conjure a tailwind.'

'Go on.'

'If I can displace sufficient air in the right place, other air will rush in to fill the gap. Air rushing in a particular direction sounds just like wind to me.'

Caroline pursed her lips for an instant. 'You understand that ornithopters are temperamental at the best of times, don't you? And since the best of times means stable, calm conditions, your plan would suggest that we'll be flying an ornithopter in the worst of conditions.'

'Something like that.'

'Sounds like a challenge. When do we start?'

'Do you think we should wake Sophie and George first?'

Caroline rapidly ran a hand over the switches, adjusting dials and knobs. Their speed dropped noticeably. 'I've tucked the wings into a stable climbing position. The nose configuration is now well trimmed.' She glanced into the back. 'Let them sleep. They'll wake up soon enough.'

CAROLINE WAS FLUSHED AND BREATHING HEAVILY. SHE pushed back hair that Aubrey thought was wonderfully wild and free. 'Let's not do that again soon, shall we?' she said huskily.

Aubrey had to agree. The Gallian landscape was a pretty thing, but not when it was screaming toward them as it had been just a few minutes ago.

'And no more upside down, please,' Sophie added in a small voice.

'We can do without that twisty rolling, too,' George added. 'Quite lost my appetite there for a while.'

'I'll do my best in the future,' Caroline said, 'but I thought both manoeuvres were preferable to breaking up and being strewn across farmland.'

George pushed his head forward between Aubrey and Caroline. 'I say, is that the coast?'

'And I'm sure that wall of cloud ahead is actually what we're after,' Aubrey said. 'Are we still gaining?'

Caroline craned her head to catch a glimpse of the countryside they were skimming over. 'I'd say so. Not as much as when your magic wind had us in its clutches, but we should pass the skyfleet within the hour.'

'Over the straits,' Aubrey said carefully. 'Since we're doing so well, what do you all say to a slight detour?'

IN THE DYING LIGHT, DR TREMAINE'S SKYFLEET WAS SPREAD across nearly a mile in a V-shaped formation, the most gargantuan of the warships in the vanguard. It had slowed as it left Gallia behind and this had allowed the ornithopter to close on it more quickly than anticipated.

Realising this, Caroline sent the aircraft climbing, gaining altitude until the line of cloud-formed ships was stretched far beneath them, flanked by the wall of storm clouds. She had to wrestle for a moment with the starboard wing, which had developed an annoying grinding, but from this position, with the help of binoculars Sophie produced from her rucksack, Aubrey was able to study Dr Tremaine's fleet.

This was worth the time, he told himself. Gathering information about the disposition of the skyfleet might be vital in deciding how best to combat it. The Directorate, the military, needed as much intelligence as it could get.

The flagship would have been the largest battleship

in the world, if it had been on the sea. Aubrey judged it to be at least twice as long as the *Impervious*, the pride of the Albion fleet. The three turrets of twin mounted guns, fore and aft, were unheard of. Despite the fact that the ship was made of cloudstuff magically wrought to mimic the steel and iron of real battleships, it was a frightening beast. It looked as if it could destroy a city by itself.

It was accompanied by more than a dozen lesser battleships and a score of destroyers, cruisers and attendant craft. It was a terrifying fleet, correct in every detail apart from one.

'Not many crewmen,' George muttered.

Aubrey scanned the walkways and decks of all the ships but saw no-one. The gun turrets were unmanned, the catwalks were empty, the stairs were abandoned. In ships of this size, fully underway, Aubrey would have expected to see dozens of crewmen at work on the hundreds of tasks required to keep a ship steaming along happily.

Another puzzle.

He motioned Caroline to halt their advance.

Aubrey had thought, while crawling, exposed, through no-man's-land, that there had to be a Better Way. When being seen was such a life-threatening handicap, a method of avoiding notice was greatly to be desired. He knew that the Directorate, under Commander Craddock's guidance, was experimenting with approaches to disguise troops, military hardware, and even buildings, but nothing had been forthcoming.

With Sophie's talent in the area of illusion and seeming, Aubrey wondered if they might be able to approach the stormfleet and not immediately be blown out of the sky.

He looked over his shoulder. 'Sophie, how much work have you done with the Law of Familiarity?'

Sophie shrugged. 'Most disguising spells use it. When Caroline and I entered Dr Tremaine's factory in Stalsfrieden, the spell I used made the guards think that we belonged there.'

'Exactly. But have you ever used it to disguise something that wasn't human?'

'An animal?'

'What about something non-living, like a machine?'

'Ah, you want to disguise this ornithopter!'

'I say.' George leaned forward. 'Is that a good idea? I mean, shouldn't we get to Trinovant as fast as we can?'

'We won't tarry long, but anything we can find out about these ships will help in determining a strategy against them.' He rubbed the bridge of his nose. 'I want to get nearer to Dr Tremaine's flagship. I don't imagine he'll allow an Albion aircraft to come alongside, not unless he has changed considerably.'

Caroline didn't move her head. 'Sophie, I give you permission to poke Aubrey with something sharp if he starts getting pompous.'

Sophie studied Aubrey, who was still considering the implications of Caroline's thinking she could give someone permission to do something to him. 'I think he has already started,' she said.

'That's his last chance, then. Poke him if he continues.'

'Familiarity,' Aubrey said hurriedly. 'If someone looks in this direction, they need to imagine that they're seeing something that belongs.'

'Like a cloud, old man?' George offered.

'That would be useful if we remain at a distance, but I'd like to get closer than that.'

'A bird,' Sophie said suddenly. 'If someone looks across and thinks that we are a bird, it might seem unusual, but not threatening, no?'

'Perfect,' Aubrey said, 'and I think I might have something that can help here. Do you know anything about the Law of Similarity?'

Sophie shook her head.

'The Law of Similarity states that an object can be encouraged to assume the characteristics of something it resembles.'

George nodded wisely. 'That's the one you used to turn our ornithopter into a bird after we rescued Major Saltin.' He cocked his head at Sophie. 'He saved our life that way.'

'I'm thinking,' Aubrey said, doing his best to retain control of the discussion, 'that I can blend some elements from a Similarity spell into a Familiarity spell of your devising. Since this ornithopter is already bird-like, it should increase the effectiveness of your spell.'

Sophie sparkled. 'That is brilliant, Aubrey, and not pompous at all!'

'Now, get to work,' Caroline said with tilt of her head. 'This circling is stupefyingly boring.'

Sophie's increasing ability and facility with spells of seeming and appearance had been on Aubrey's mind. Her spellcasting diffidence came from lack of practice, he'd decided, and some wayward teaching when she was younger. In discussions about her training, he'd had the impression of a series of harsh, disciplinarian magic instructors who insisted on rote learning. Aubrey understood her rejection of magic, if this was the case. *He* would have struggled under such a regime, despite his love of magical learning. Sophie was sunny, clever, humorous, but she wasn't infinitely patient. Like Caroline, she wouldn't suffer fools gladly.

With a jolt, he straightened. *Then what on earth are Caroline and she doing with George and me?*

'Aubrey?' Sophie said. 'Are you all right?'

'Me? I'm perfectly well, thanks. Just thinking. And you?'

'I've nearly finished the spell. Will you look at it, please?'

Sophie's spell making was clean and precise. She'd left her workings behind before she'd written out her final version, which was useful as he could follow the thinking that lay behind what she'd crossed out and changed along the way.

He couldn't fault her logic. Even though he may have taken a different approach with the parameters for dimensionality, he accepted that her use of spatial and relative coordinates was an inspired method of ensuring that they remained disguised at all times.

He also approved of her use of Achaean. The ancient classical language was well known and relatively straight-forward to work with. For a rusty spell caster, it was a good choice.

He looked up to find her gazing at him anxiously. 'Is it sound?'

'Sophie, it's a marvel. I couldn't have done it.'

'Now you're making fun of me.'

He shook his head. 'I recognise good spellwork when I see it.'

Sophie coloured and took the notebook he gave her. 'What do we do now?'

'You cast the spell.'

'When?'

'After I've merged it with the spell to increase the birdiness of the final result. Then we should be ready.'

Thirty

SOPHIE FINISHED HER SPELL SMOOTHLY, IF A LITTLE nervously, and Aubrey immediately felt the pulse of magic about them. 'Well done, Sophie.'

George grasped her trembling hand. 'I'm always impressed by impressive women, and believe me – I'm very impressed now.'

She sighed, then smiled. 'I'm glad I could help.'

Aubrey could see how much casting the spell had affected her. Her face had blanched with the effort and her shoulders sagged.

'You've done well,' he said to her.

'Is it always like this?' She put a hand to her chest. 'I feel drained, but also as if a string had been plucked inside me.'

'Nicely put. It affects different people in different ways, but that tension and release is a common report.'

'I'm not sure if I like it.'

'Some people hate the sensation so much they give up magic altogether. Others find that they crave it.'

Sophie peered from the window. 'So now we cannot be seen?'

'Anyone who looks in this direction will see a bird. If he doesn't look for too long, he should simply go about his business. Since you've done such a fine job, he should even fail to notice the sound we're making. Most likely, he'll ignore it or assume it's coming from something else nearby.'

Caroline caught his eye. 'Are we ready?'

'Can you take us alongside the flagship?'

'Port or starboard?'

'Whatever is easier.'

'Port, I think. Hold on.'

Before Aubrey could respond, guns on the warships about them erupted, firing in the direction of the Albion shores. The ornithopter jolted and Aubrey banged his head on the bulkhead, but Caroline soon had the aircraft steady and level again.

The guns on the battleships continued to fire, flame and smoke lancing from the massive barrels. The sound was all-encompassing; the ornithopter shook as if it were possessed. Tiny metallic sounds came from all around them – rattles, pings and creaks, all of which were designed to create panic in ornithopter passengers.

'What are they firing at?' Sophie asked.

'I can't see . . .' Caroline said.

'There!' George pointed.

Some miles ahead, to the west, a hapless weathership was the target of the skyfleet's guns. Huge eruptions of spray marked where the shells had missed, but Aubrey knew it was only a matter of time. The weathership could cut its anchor and run, but with the massed barrage mustered by the skyfleet, such a course of action would be hopeless.

'Why?' Sophie asked in a tiny voice. 'It's defenceless.'

'It could send warning to Albion.' George's face was set. 'Cowardly dogs.'

Any doubts about the intention of the barrage or of the efficacy of the cloud-made weapons disappeared when the weathership erupted in twin gouts of flame. The explosion shook the ornithopter, but Caroline held it steady through the buffeting.

'Two shells struck at once,' Aubrey murmured, but he was relieved to see lifeboats pulling away. The crew must have abandoned ship, not that he blamed them.

Aubrey had no way of knowing if a message had been transmitted before the crew fled – or, indeed, if a telegraph operator was gamely tapping away when the shells finally landed. Weathership operators were tough customers – they had to be, moored far from land for months at a time, charting and recording weather patterns – and he could imagine at least one of them doing his duty.

The guns rained shells on the smoking ruins of the weathership, far beyond any need. Aubrey supposed that it was simply target practice.

'We're coming up fast.' Caroline's voice was strained.

Their circuit high above the perimeter of the flagship was an education, and a grim one at that. The flagship was immense. It was as if Dr Tremaine had taken the latest battleship plans and simply doubled everything. As they whipped past, a shadow in what was fast becoming night, Aubrey estimated that she must be at least a thousand feet long from stern to bow, and she'd displace fifty or sixty thousand tons. If she were in water, he reminded himself. Six gun turrets, three forward, three aft, with twin fifteen-inch guns in each, superfiring. If this ship were on the high seas, it would be more than a match for anything in the Albion fleet, but the amount of steel required to build something like this — not to mention the time it would take — would make such a construction impossible.

Unless it were made of cloudstuff.

Wings clattering with the effort — and with an unsettling grating noise coming from the starboard pinion — Caroline performed a feat of aviation that Aubrey would have stood and applauded, if not for the fact that he was flailing for a handhold to steady himself.

From their lofty position, she sent the ornithopter in a manic dive, slicing between the flagship and the battleship a few hundred yards away. Then she dragged the protesting craft around, under the hull of the flagship, and then up past its stern — where Aubrey was startled to see that its name was *Sylvia* — and into a rush along the vast grey flank.

Aubrey was assaulted by magic. It poured from the *Sylvia*, but as they hurtled by he was buffeted by concentrations, hard nodes of magical intensity, in specific zones, and he had the flavour in his ears that suggested the presence of the magical artefacts.

They swung alongside the massive superstructure, the towering construction amidships that housed the command deck. They sped along the flank of the giant ship, passing at the level of the bridge, far above the deck level, and Aubrey spied a lone figure on the walkway.

Instantly, every part of him wanted to cry out a warning, to seize the controls and spiral them away, to put the mass of the flagship between them and the man who was gripping the rail and slowly turning his head, scanning the skies before settling his ferocious gaze on them.

Dr Mordecai Tremaine bared his teeth, drew back, and flung a handful of nothing at them.

Thirty-one

CAROLINE'S REACTIONS WERE FASTER THAN AUBREY'S useless warning cry. She sheared and dropped the ornithopter to the port side – but it was too late.

Dr Tremaine's magic stopped them, mid-dive, as quickly as running into an aerial brick wall. Amid the cacophony of shattering glass and tortured metal, the ornithopter buckled, metal falling away from it in shreds.

Trapped in the now-useless machine, they began to fall.

Wind screamed through the ruined craft, shrieking with delight at their predicament. Caroline wrenched at the controls. 'I've lost everything!' she cried, but she didn't stop punching at switches, hammering at dials, dragging on the controls.

Far below, the sea was drawing nearer. Aubrey could see whitecaps and the tiny lifeboats, the survivors from the destruction of the weathership.

Aubrey closed his eyes and tried to ignore all distractions – especially the distraction of imminent death – and tried to remember the details of the only spell he knew that could save them. The only hope was a vastly more encompassing version of his levitation spell. It needed to include his friends and him, but also the ornithopter – it would be no use at all if their descent was arrested but they were still inside a plummeting machine. He barked the syllables, realised with a spurt of horror that he'd mangled the component for duration, backtracked and spat out a new version just in time for the ocean to rise and smash them.

AUBREY EMERGED FROM A SWIRLING CHAOS TO A NIGHTMARE of confusion. The only immediate compensation was that he could breathe. Somewhat. If he were careful.

He was in a world of water (that kept rolling over the top of him when he least expected it), darkness (that did its usual job of concealing objects long enough for them to sneak up and do various kinds of damage) and noise (which was just dashed annoying). He flailed weakly, then took another large mouthful of water – salt water – which only made things worse.

His collar was tugged. Dazed and floundering, he suspected it was another inanimate object trying to drown him when a voice came to him. 'Aubrey! This way!'

He shook his head and it cleared somewhat, only to find that he was still in what was left of the ornithopter as it wallowed in the waves, undecided about whether it was going to plunge into the depths.

Caroline was framed in the doorway. She'd lost her beret. Her hair was in disarray. She stretched out a hand. 'Hurry!'

Aubrey had a sudden, awful realisation that even though he hadn't perished, the matter wasn't over yet. He clutched his satchel of precious notes, then clawed off his seatbelt, just as the shattered windscreen let in a huge surge. The shockingly cold water dragged him over the back of his seat and scraped him against what had been the ceiling of the ornithopter, but now was more like a sieve.

The water receded. Aubrey had sense enough to sling his satchel around his neck and grab hold of a stanchion. He coughed, wiped his eyes with his other hand and found an anxious Caroline still waiting for him. He lunged for her hand and together they tumbled out through the doorway.

Moments later they were reunited with George and Sophie, shivering despite the greatcoats the seamen had surrendered after dragging them into the lifeboats. The boat rolled in the swell, while the wind had the edge that comes from driving for miles over non-tropical waters. Aubrey clutched the gunwale with one hand, Caroline's hand with the other, grateful for this little wooden refuge in the immensity of the sea.

A baby-faced commander scrambled to join them. 'You're from the Directorate,' he said, eyes widening when he took in their sodden uniforms. 'You should be able to tell us what's going on, then.' He looked more closely at Aubrey. 'I know you,' he said slowly, then he performed the difficult task of recoiling while squatting in a crowded lifeboat. 'You're the traitor!'

Immediately, Aubrey was the focus of the entire crew

of ex-weathershipmen. Minutes ago, they had been welcoming, partners in adversity and the like. Now they turned resentful eyes on him, ready to take revenge for being bombed.

He heard a click beside his ear. In other circumstances, once he recognised it he would have been extremely anxious or, given the chance, running in the other direction. This time, however, it was a comfort.

'He isn't a traitor,' Caroline said. She gestured with her revolver. 'But I'm not sure we could convince you of this, here and now. So, instead, you're going to row us to Imworth harbour and drop us off. All the time, I'll have this very powerful revolver trained on you, so do row well.'

'There's eight of us,' a voice that Aubrey noted came from the far end of the boat, at the stern, 'and that's a six-shot Symons. You can't get all of us.'

'That's a point,' Caroline said brightly, 'but if it comes to that we'll only have two of you left. I'm sure we could overpower two of you, if we have to. Besides, what does it matter if only six of you perish if you're one of the six?'

'What if you miss?' the same argumentative voice pointed out. Aubrey noticed that some of his crewmates, those closer to Caroline and her revolver, tried to shut him up, but he had the tone of someone who'd argue on his death bed.

'I don't miss,' Caroline said.

'How do we know that?'

'Oh, you're asking for a test, are you? Very well. Can I ask you to sit up straight while your crewmates lean to either side? No? Very well then. Skipper, I suggest that you get your men rowing with some vigour.'

This announcement was greeted with only a modicum

of grumbling. Aubrey guessed that Caroline's no-nonsense demeanour had convinced them more than any swaggering threats could have.

A shadow fell on them and the skipper cast an eye heavenwards with well-mastered apprehension. The sky-fleet had reformed after its circling and destruction of the weathership. It was heading away from them. 'Is Albion being invaded?'

'Invaded?' Aubrey looked up at the sky. 'No. It's far worse than that.'

THE COAST OF ALBION STUBBORNLY REFUSED TO GET ANY nearer, even after two hours of determined rowing from the disgruntled crew. With the gentle rolling of the lifeboat, added to Caroline's closeness and the rushed spell casting that had saved their lives, Aubrey was struggling to stay awake and failing when George leaned across to him, speaking low so the weathershipmen couldn't hear. 'I think I know where we are.'

With some effort, Aubrey restrained himself from attempting a quip about being at the aft end of a lifeboat, and spoke in the same hushed tones. 'Imworth is over that way, isn't it? To the north-west?'

'True, but we've a fair distance before we get there.'

'Where we'll have some explaining to do.'

'Which is why we should put in over there.'

George gestured with a single finger, shielding it with his body from the scrutiny of their enforced shipmates. A scattering of lights was showing on the cliff tops a few miles away.

Aubrey peered through the night, doing his best not to make it look obvious. The cliffs loomed over a narrow strip of beach where waves boomed, sending up spray that looked like mist at this distance.

'It doesn't look like a good landing place.'

'That's the point. Imworth is the only good harbour along this stretch of coast, but if we can land here and climb to the top of the cliffs, the train line isn't far away. We'll be far from here before the alarm can be raised.'

Aubrey yawned. His eyes watered, blearing the clifftop lights and turned them into little stars. 'If we can land, I think I can get us to the top.'

THE WEATHERSHIP SKIPPER ARGUED WHEN AUBREY ordered a landing, but Caroline's revolver-backed counterargument carried the day. As the lifeboat was buffeted by the roaring waves – and once when rocks grated heart-stoppingly along the keel – Aubrey wondered if George's plan were such a good one at all.

The skipper proved to be a decent fellow. When Aubrey and his friends stood dripping on the narrow strip of wave-hammered stones, he suggested that they surrender their firearms and he'd take them to Imworth. When they refused, he shook his head and ordered his men to push off.

The wind whipped spray in their faces. George grabbed Sophie as a brute of a wave nearly bowled her off her feet.

'Now what, Aubrey?' Caroline asked. Like all of them, she was drenched to the waist – a result of leaping out of the lifeboat into the wild surf – but she still was able to look collected and stylish.

'Hold hands. All of you.'

Aubrey was becoming polished with levitation spells. They soon left the shingle behind and drifted through the gloom, alongside the improbably white face of the cliffs and into the scrubby, stubborn bracken that faced the sea.

An hour later, after Sophie had laid a subtle disguising spell on Aubrey's features, they stumbled wearily into tiny East Stallington Station, a few miles from where they'd landed. George used the public telephone at the station to report to the Directorate, confirming the identity of the skyfleet that had broached the borders of Albion and the surmises about its intention. He'd barely hung up when the Trinovant train pulled in. Within seconds, Caroline had leaped into the cabin of the locomotive and used her pistol to commandeer it. She wanted to ensure that that the driver didn't do anything silly like adhering to a timetable and stopping all stations. Aubrey appreciated such thoughtfulness as he made himself as comfortable as possible in the warm, noisy cabin, and went to sleep with his satchel on his lap.

TRINOVANT WAS IN THE CLUTCHES OF THE SMALL HOURS of the morning by the time the train reached St Swithins. Aubrey and his friends leaped from the train as soon as it had slowed enough, and sidled through a place that was crowded despite it being a time when all good citizens should be abed.

Aubrey stopped at a grimy, red-brick pillar near a darkened workshop entrance. He yawned, then peered at the helmeted figures on the platform opposite, tall amid the anxious Trinovantans who were waiting, suitcases and valises by their sides, to leave the capital. 'I know how this will sound,' he said to his friends, 'but how do I look?'

'Not at all yourself.' Caroline stretched, reaching for the ceiling with both hands linked. 'And I assume that's just what you're after.'

'Sophie, you have a real talent for this sort of thing,' Aubrey said.

Sophie was looking about anxiously at the nervous throng. 'Are you sure? I can try another spell if you are unhappy.'

George turned away from the platform, folding his arms. 'Police.'

Aubrey straightened his jacket. 'Let us go about our business, then, as all innocent people should.'

Aubrey held his breath as he and his friends squeezed past the four police constables in greatcoats who were casting about with lanterns and checking doors. He nodded at them and received wary acknowledgement in return as the nervous young men recognised the uniforms of the Directorate. Even the remarkably attractive Caroline and Sophie failed to bring a smile to the lips of the constables, and Aubrey wondered exactly what they'd been told. Were they looking for Aubrey Fitzwilliam, traitor of Albion, or was this simply part of the general climate of mistrust that war had brought?

Once free of the crowd that was choking the station, they made their way toward the Eastride underground station. Walking through the quiet, night-time streets, Aubrey noticed how the stars were hidden by clouds, a low overcast sky hanging over the capital. Crossing at the intersection of Bennett and Garland Streets, a ghostly beckoning caught him as he was about to step from the footpath and he nearly overbalanced. Caroline caught his elbow, glanced at him and frowned as he rubbed his chest with his free hand. 'What is it?'

Aubrey couldn't help but look skywards. To the north, out over Stapledon and Allingham, a mass of clouds broke apart. The outlines of Dr Tremaine's skyfleet, black against the dark grey of the thunderheads, were unmistakable. 'He's here.'

Thirty-two

WHEN THEY REACHED DARNLEIGH HOUSE, THEY were expected – and immediately taken to the planning room to find Commander Craddock and Commander Tallis.

The heads of the two branches of the Directorate were circling around the Big Board – a huge table with a gigantic map of Albion. As if it were a child's game, operatives were moving pieces about. Most were white, indicating Albion regiments, squadrons and fleets, but an ominous cluster was black, and it was arranged directly over Trinovant.

The room itself was windowless. Noticeboards covered the walls, with dozens of desks taking up the space directly underneath. Telephones rang with muted urgency while hordes of operatives took notes, passing them to other operatives who scurried off, handing them to the brooding senior figures around the Big Board or decamping via one of the many doors to other parts of the building.

The atmosphere was of controlled, but tense, authority. Voices were hushed, movements deliberate. The scraping sound as operatives leaned over and used long-handled rakes to move pieces on the Big Board was insistent and portentous.

Craddock glanced their way as they entered, then tapped Tallis on the shoulder. Together, they left the Big Board and swept Aubrey and his friends to a corner that held a small conference of senior operatives until a word from Tallis sent them packing.

'The situation isn't good,' Craddock said immediately, 'but with your warning we're doing what we can. Our remote sensers confirm that Tremaine himself is up there, circling the capital.'

'Twenty-five thousand feet is far beyond the capabilities of any of our dirigibles,' Tallis growled. He bounced on his toes, hands behind his back, and looked as if he personally wanted to punch Dr Tremaine in the face. 'We're preparing squads of aircraft, doing what we can, ready to throw everything at him.'

'We need to, sir,' Aubrey said. 'Dr Tremaine is aiming to bypass the need for a blood sacrifice. Instead, he's aiming to work directly with the magical field generated by Trinovant itself. Nowhere else on earth is there such a concentration of people in one area, which suggests that he needs all of it.'

Tallis scowled. 'What the devil are you talking about?'

'On such a scale?' Craddock said, ignoring Tallis. 'Impossible.'

'I believe Dr Tremaine has two things that will help

him. Firstly, the potential of the accumulated magical artefacts. Secondly, he's discovered the Universal Language for Magic.'

'Ah,' Craddock rocked back. 'The abducted magical theorists.'

'We'll need a full report of your activities, but not now,' Tallis said. 'We understand that you've seen Tremaine's stronghold, and you have some observations from the Divodorum front that could be important.'

'Yes, sir,' Aubrey said and thought of the pages of notes he'd taken.

'And we had the incident in Korsur,' Caroline added. 'It may be important for the analysts to hear about that.'

'Korsur?' Craddock said vaguely, his mind clearly on Aubrey's previous revelations. 'I hope Tremaine hasn't been up to anything in Korsur.'

Now, that's ominous, Aubrey thought. 'Why not, sir?'

Craddock made an impatient gesture with a hand. His attention was on the Big Board. 'I'm sorry I brought it up. We have more important things to worry about.'

'And Dr Tremaine probably had more important things to do,' Aubrey said, 'yet he dropped everything to take possession of a large piece of Crystal Johannes from Korsur.'

Sharply, Craddock turned away from the Big Board. 'Dr Tremaine has some Crystal Johannes? For all our sakes, tell me this isn't so!'

'A large piece, sir,' Aubrey said, shocked by Commander Craddock's reaction. The head of the Magic Department rarely showed emotion, yet here anger and fear were clear on his face.

'As big as a church door,' George put in. 'That's how the villagers described it.'

'Craddock?' Tallis barked. 'What is it, man? What's special about this stuff that has you so worried?'

Craddock had his eyes closed and was rubbing his brows with the tips of his fingers. 'Long ago, when it was more common than today, Crystal Johannes was used by the magicians of the day to help their spells. Properly used, it can have a focusing effect, concentrating a latent magical field. I had thought this property forgotten since none had been found for so long, but evidently I was wrong.'

'It's the sort of thing Dr Tremaine would know,' Aubrey said softly, 'and would figure into his plans.'

Caroline looked from Craddock to Aubrey. 'So this means that Dr Tremaine's spell could be even more powerful than you'd thought?'

'Oh yes,' Craddock said. 'If he uses the Crystal Johannes he will have an untold magnification of his power.'

We really didn't need that, Aubrey thought. He caught George's eye and began to look for ways to slip out of the planning room.

An operative hurried up and thrust a slip of paper at Tallis, who read it and scowled even more volcanically. 'The blasted High Command won't authorise our deployment of aerial squadrons!'

Craddock sighed. 'Fools.'

'They say they're in the middle of preparing for a push in Gallia and need air support. They think this skyfleet is a diversion.'

'Can I help?'

Aubrey turned. A figure he hadn't noticed earlier was approaching. 'Father!'

'Aubrey.' Sir Darius extended his hand, held Aubrey's

gaze for a moment, then greeted the others. 'Caroline, George, good to see you. And Miss Delroy – a pleasure.'

It was done swiftly, but Aubrey admired the way that, even in the middle of a crisis, his father did enough to make them feel part of the enterprise.

'Prime Minister,' Craddock said, 'matters are coming to a head, but we're having trouble with the High Command. It's crucial that we move now and yet we're meeting recalcitrance instead of cooperation.'

Aubrey watched his father intently. Sir Darius didn't try to mollify Craddock, who was more agitated than Aubrey had ever known him to be. Craddock simply stood there, very still, his hands pressed together in front of him. Panic and Sir Darius were strangers, Aubrey realised. It was part of what had made him a formidable soldier. In a crisis, instead of becoming frantic he remained fixed, holding himself still until he had chosen a way ahead.

Sir Darius addressed Aubrey. 'What do you think?'

Aubrey was taken aback. His father was asking with straightforward urgency. Aubrey had seen him in this mode a hundred times – he wanted advice, and he wanted it from the best available person. Yet he'd bypassed the most senior intelligence chiefs in Albion and, instead, was asking him.

'We need to act immediately,' Aubrey said and he was glad his voice was as even and controlled as his father's was. 'Every opportunity to stop Tremaine must be used.'

'Good man.' Sir Darius turned to Craddock and Tallis and Aubrey's surroundings came back. The faint ringing of telephones, the hushed conversations, the dusty light from the electric globes overhead.

The world proceeded.

'Craddock, Tallis,' Sir Darius said. 'I'm authorising immediate deployment of your people. You'll have whatever you need. I'll take full responsibility for sending a skirmishing force in advance of the main sortie. Whatever and whenever that is.'

'Finley Moor, sir,' Tallis said. 'Can you get your staff to let them know that Directorate people will need help as well as the army forces?'

'Immediately.' Sir Darius shook a fist. 'Capital. Now to get the High Command moving.' He took two steps and then swivelled, suddenly solemn. 'Good luck.'

Aubrey watched his father stride off, charging to a battle of his own.

Caroline squeezed his arm. 'George wants you.'

George was at the Big Board, with Sophie. He was waving. Aubrey glanced at Craddock and Tallis, but they'd been besieged by half a dozen document-carrying operatives.

'Look, old man,' George said when Aubrey and Caroline joined him. 'Just in case you were thinking of nipping off to Finley Moor, I thought I'd let you know we'll have trouble.'

'Finley Moor? Why would I be thinking of going to Finley Moor?'

'I'm imagining that you might be feeling the need to find an ornithopter. I wouldn't be surprised if jolly soon we're going to be cutting corners, avoiding protocols, leapfrogging obstacles, that sort of thing.'

'And why would you imagine that?'

'Standard operating procedure with you, old man. All I'm saying is that we're ready when you are, but we won't be able to get to Finley Moor the usual way by going through Carstairs. The 12th Lancers are using Marling Road. We'd never get through.'

Aubrey was impressed by George's planning out a route to the military airfield, but then something else took his attention. Looking down on the Big Board had jolted him, so much detail presenting itself. It was easy to imagine he was in Dr Tremaine's skyfleet, looking down on the sprawling expanse of Trinovant – the city, the river, the railways, spreading over the countryside. He could see all the landmarks, the urban conglomeration stretched out for him to survey.

Something was missing. Something vital, something important wasn't there, but he couldn't put his finger on it. He swept his gaze across Newbourne, The Mire, Densmore, Ashfields Station, but he still didn't know what it was.

When he found Fielding Cross, he looked for where Maidstone would be. It was when he found the location for the Fitzwilliam family home that it struck him and he knew what was missing.

People. He couldn't see any people. The city was there, but none of the individuals who made it work and live and breathe. They weren't important enough to feature.

The 'click' that rocked Aubrey was so monumental that he had to grab the edge of the table to stop being thrown off his feet. 'Oh no,' he whispered. 'Oh no.'

Caroline pressed close. 'Aubrey?'

'It's worse than I thought.' He straightened and found that his hands were trembling. Caroline took them and they stopped. 'Dr Tremaine has found something better than the Ritual of the Way.'

'You said he was going to use the collective

consciousness of Trinovant to make his magic more powerful.'

'That's right – but I've been neglecting the sacrifice.' He put a hand to his temple. 'The Ritual of the Way needed blood, huge amounts of it. Dr Tremaine wants to make sure of achieving his goal of immortality, though, so he's going one step further.'

'What's one step further than a wholesale blood sacrifice?'

'Dr Tremaine is getting ready to snuff out the consciousness of everyone in Trinovant.'

CRADDOCK WAS STONY-FACED WHEN AUBREY SHARED his insight. Tallis swore, loudly enough to make all the people in the room look his way before hastily returning to their business. 'We have squads ready to board Tremaine's fleet and take him,' he said, 'as long as that magic whatnot is available. Craddock?'

Craddock eyed Aubrey. 'We've had magical teams at work on altitude enhancements in order to get our aircraft up to Tremaine's skyfleet. The notes you left about your levitation escapade in Lutetia last year have been helpful.'

'Ah. I may have something to add to that.'

'You'll have a chance to implement it in person, then.'

'Sir?'

'When I said that we were throwing everything at Tremaine, that's what I meant. Is your unit able to go?'

Aubrey went to speak, but first looked to his friends. They were ready: he could see it. They were steady, determined, unfazed by the possibilities that lay ahead, and he knew he was lucky to have them as friends.

Aubrey saluted. 'Sirs. Permission to depart.'

'Permission granted,' Craddock said. 'And godspeed.'

Thirty-three

THE JOURNEY TO FINLEY MOOR AIRFIELD WOULD have been impossible if not for Commander Tallis's suggestion to use motorcycles instead of a motorcar. After a side trip to the Armourer and the Magic Chandler to equip them for their mission, Aubrey and his friends raced out of the rear of Darnleigh House to find the sleek machines waiting with motors running and sidecars attached. George leaped into the saddle, tested the throttle and, with one hand, managed to strap on the helmet that the motor mechanic thrust at him. Sophie was ready in the sidecar before he was, goggles and helmet in place. She thumped the cowling with impatience.

Aubrey hesitated in front of the other motorcycle. 'Do you want to drive?'

Caroline studied the machine with interest. 'I've never ridden a motorcycle.'

'I thought it might be one of your hidden talents. A friend of your mother's hairdresser was an international motorcycle champion and taught you in a few lessons.'

'It isn't, but I'm willing to try.'

'I'm sure you are.' Aubrey took the helmet from the motor mechanic and slung his rifle on his back. 'Normally, I'd say yes, but I don't think this is the time for experimenting.'

Despite her heavy backpack, Caroline leaped easily into the sidecar. She tucked her hair up under her helmet. Her eyes shone through the goggles. 'With all speed, Aubrey, let us go.'

The roads were extremely quiet until they came to within a few miles of Finley Moor. Then it looked as if every lorry, wagon, motorcar or dog cart capable of carrying men, women or equipment was pushing toward the military airfield. Aubrey held his breath and followed George's lead as his friend swerved, wove, and roared his way through the traffic, using footpaths, verges and gutters as much as the heavily populated tarmac. Generously, George gave pedestrians a chance to show their agility as the motorcycles sped by in a manner that would, in normal circumstances, have had a dozen constables chasing them.

As their tyres shrieked in a particularly violent piece of cornering, leaving a lamp post almost unscathed, Aubrey risked a glance at Caroline. The sidecar had one wheel off the ground, but she clung on, smiling broadly.

Aubrey had time – in such moments, he could think very quickly – to imagine a future where he and Caroline could spend time careering about on motorcycles. It was a joyous enough image to make him all the more determined to bring the war to an end. If a beautiful and exhilarated sweetheart on a motorcycle wasn't worth fighting for, what was?

He twitched the handgrips to avoid striking the gutter, took another glance to see Caroline looking straight at him. She tried to look stern, failed, then jabbed a finger straight ahead, mouthing, 'Keep your eyes on the road.'

Easier said than done, he thought. *When you have the choice of Caroline Hepworth or anything else in the world to look at, the world loses out. Except* – he bared his teeth, leaned and swerved around a flat-tyred lorry that had stopped in the middle of the road – *when imminent death needs attention.*

A mile out and they abandoned the road altogether. They hurtled along the grass verge that separated the road from the chain wire fence of the airfield, dodging road signs and, once, leaping over an open drain in a feat that momentarily made Aubrey's heart lodge somewhere behind his Adam's apple.

The guards at the gatehouse had been apprised of their imminent arrival, but took care to scan their credentials before waving them through. Inside the fence, the airfield was like Trinovant in morning rush hour but, instead of top hats and umbrellas, military uniforms were the dress of the day.

The black-uniformed Directorate operatives were predominant, but other services were not uncommon, and it appeared as if the normal divisions between the various branches of the military had been suspended for the moment. Infantrymen were helping Directorate mechanics carry long – but apparently very light – metal struts. A company of sailors from the *Inimitable* were lashing poles to create a footbridge over the busiest thoroughfare through the base. Civilians were about in numbers, some wandering uncertainly, others directing serviceman with that special air of authority that comes from being in charge of a small district sub-branch of a lesser department like the Apple Quality Board.

They found the airfield headquarters. Aubrey leaped off his motorcycle and left the engine running. In minutes, breathless, he had his directions and took the lead, shouting where necessary to get people to move out of the way. Which they did, and in turn they yelled at other people to get out of *their* way, in effect creating a cascade of imprecations that worked its way backward from Aubrey's progress, leaving a spreading bow wave of disruption behind them.

Every part of the airfield was alive with workers and vehicles. Near the mooring masts and the domes of the gasholders, airships were being armed and provisioned. Aubrey was dismayed to see that none of the twelve massive craft was fully gassed up, not even the brand-new A 405. It would take nearly a day before any of them was ready – and that was only if the giant gasholders were full. If gas had to be generated, it could take days.

He grabbed the arm of a junior airman who was hurrying toward the dirigibles. 'Get some magicians onto it,' he snapped.

The young airman stared at Aubrey. 'What did you say?'

'Find some magicians, Directorate people if you can, magicians with specialties in fluid magic and compression magic. Get them draining half the airships and using the gas to inflate the others.'

The airman looked as if he didn't know whether to

call Aubrey a madman or a genius, then he glanced at the sky. 'Magicians.'

'Hurry!'

They came to the ornithopter section of the airfield. Dozens were being checked and fuelled, while some were already climbing into the air with their characteristic jerky wingsweeps. Nearby, some elderly observation balloons had been unearthed and a squad of frustrated operatives was trying to untangle tethers and holding stays.

George directed Aubrey's attention to the mechanics crawling over the ornithopters like ants on a honey sandwich. 'Pulling out all the stops, it looks like.'

Ornithopters were almost exclusively scouting and fast transport aircraft, useful where a dirigible would be too slow or too conspicuous. Armament was considered almost uncouth. The army didn't want pilots thinking they were anything like airborne cavalry, jousting in the skies. Ornithopters were much too temperamental and much too expensive for that.

However, orders about unarmed ornithopters in war zones didn't appeal to the men who actually did the piloting. Being characteristically independent of mind, the pilots tended to take matters into their own hands. Even so, the deadliest attack mounted by an ornithopter generally came if a pilot leaned out of the window and used his pistol, or flung something like an incendiary bomb without managing to catch it on a wing, which had happened more than once and hardened the army's view about arming the aircraft.

It looked as if this hardening had softened, however, and thawed quickly in the emergency. Makeshift though the arrangements were, weapons were coming to ornithopters.

No effort was being made for uniformity, something that only emphasised the extreme nature of the emergency – nothing else could explain the overcoming of the military's need for uniform fittings. That had been thrown out of the window, along with the drapes, the curtain rod and any furniture that happened to be nearby.

Teams of mechanics were working with pilots and instructors on the best way to give the aircraft some firepower. Improvised though it was, the work was proceeding with zeal, with much riveting, brazing and welding – ammunition being kept well away while heat-related work was undertaken. Machine guns were being bolted to the fuselages of a number of ornithopters, but one game mechanic was cutting a hole in the roof of one craft. A pilot watched this with an extraordinary mixture of anguish and excitement warring on his face.

Mechanics attached racks for bombs and swivel braces for rifles. Many of these adaptations were destroying the lines of the beautiful machines, but forbearance was the attitude from the pilots who were supervising. All of them, to a man and a woman, stood with hands clasped behind their backs as if it would stop them lunging forward to stop the ruining of their craft.

It was when Aubrey saw a heavy iron beam being welded to the nose of one ornithopter that the scale of this emergency was brought home with renewed force. In this case, it was the mechanic who was reluctant and the pilot who was insistent. At the end of the beam was a cage, just big enough for something explosive.

Aubrey grimaced. If ramming the enemy was considered a reasonable tactic, it was a crisis indeed. He glanced at George, who raised his eyebrows, and he understood that they were making a silent pact not to draw this modification to the attention of Caroline and Sophie.

The figure in overalls waiting for them when Aubrey brought the motorcycle to a halt wasn't a private or a corporal, despite the grease stains. His salute was smart and totally without resentment. 'Fitzwilliam. Glad you're here. I'm Captain Galloway, Army Service Corps. We're here to help.'

Aubrey started. 'You know who I am?'

'I was told to expect you.' He raised an eyebrow. 'And I was told that you aren't actually a traitor.'

Aubrey went to shake, but Galloway declined. 'You won't need greasy hands, not where you're going. Now,' he consulted a clipboard, 'you've been given one of the new specials, a T16 Merlin Scout. Faster and more responsive than anything you've flown before. No armaments, I'm afraid, but I've been told you've made your own arrangements on that front.'

'In a manner of speaking.'

Galloway slapped the fuselage. 'Good, good. The Merlin's also capable of being pressurised, as we understand you'll be flying the crate at its limits.'

'I won't be doing the piloting,' Aubrey said.

'I will,' Caroline said, taking off her motorcycle helmet and donning a leather flying helmet. 'Tell me more.'

'Right you are. Tech specs are here.' He handed the documents to Caroline. 'But I have no idea if they're worth anything any more.'

'I beg your pardon?' Aubrey had to shout as a sluggish, partly filled airship droned slowly overhead, lines dangling and effectively being towed by a lorry.

Galloway pointed to the three black-clad operatives who were clustered about the tailfins of the Merlin. 'Your magical chaps. They've been working hard, applying their mumbo-jumbo all over the place. They muttered something about altitude enhancements and controlled levitation, but it's all nonsense to me. Still, I'm in favour of anything that helps us with those johnnies.'

Galloway jabbed a pen skywards. Cruising steadily, skirting the edge of the city away to the south, was Dr Tremaine's skyfleet. The ships caught the sun, but were no less ominous for that.

In the hasty moments before they had left Darnleigh House, Aubrey had tried to encapsulate the observations they'd made of the skyfleet in their nearly fatal approach so the advice could help the other attacking units. He stressed the magical nature, and that even though the ships appeared to have no crew they were likely to be deadly, nonetheless. His advice had been to concentrate on the flagship and to be aware that the other ships would do their best to prevent the *Sylvia* from suffering damage. Ultimately, they were expendable, but Aubrey knew that Dr Tremaine's magic would ensure they'd be lethal in their protection.

'We'll do what we can,' Aubrey said to Galloway.

'Good man.'

The magical operatives were both grey with tiredness. They stumbled over their words when they tried to explain what they'd been up to, which didn't fill Aubrey with confidence.

The older of the two, a steely-eyed woman Aubrey had seen at Darnleigh House working with junior operatives, gestured at the tail assembly. 'That's the device. It's . . .' She waved a hand at a brass box, the size of her hand, attached to the underside next to an oil conduit. 'Enhancing the lift ability of the ornithopter.'

The younger operative reached out and tapped it with a finger. 'Careful, though. You'll have to work a spell to control the rate of ascent.'

The older operative squinted at the box. 'We should have tested it more, you know, but we didn't have time.'

Again, this wasn't the sort of assurance Aubrey was after – but he had little choice.

'Good luck,' the younger operative said, and immediately the two sought Captain Galloway, who consulted his clipboard and directed them toward the next ornithopter in line.

Galloway rejoined Aubrey and Caroline, who'd finished inspecting the pilot's controls. 'We're done here. You can take off as soon as that signalman gives you the yellow flag.'

Standing on the tarmac twenty yards away was an overalled mechanic with a pair of flags under his arms, goggles on his face and an impressive set of lungs in his chest. He was bellowing over the top of the devil's chorus of mechanical noise, pointing red flags at the aircraft that were on NO ACCOUNT to move yet. Yellow flags signalled which aircraft were to go and, one by one, four ornithopters gathered themselves and thrashed into the sky, sending dust, twigs and people scattering.

George and Sophie had already piled into the back of the ornithopter, so Aubrey sprinted around to his side and sprang inside, finding, after some fumbling, a place for his rifle. Caroline adjusted her helmet, acknowledged the flag holder with a nod – and was rewarded with a grin, Aubrey noted – and slipped into her seat. 'Buckle up,' she said needlessly and, before she had any further comment, they were all driven back into their seats by the violence of their take-off.

Thirty-four

HE CLAMOURING OF THE WINGS AND THE HAMMERING of the engine was always at its greatest during climbing, so Aubrey sat as mutely as his friends, and prepared himself.

All the other ornithopter crews were under the same orders: to do what they could to stop Dr Tremaine using magical and more direct means. To most of the pilots, that meant engaging in aerial combat. Some were determined to board the skyfleet ships and wreak enough havoc to destroy them. Aubrey was happy for them to attempt all this and more but, having been close to the skyfleet and seen how large each of the ships was, he wondered if they could be brought down by conventional means. Their aborted inspection of the ships suggested that they had many of the qualities of regular vessels, but he was keen to get nearer to see if assuming concrete substance had left the cloudstuff skyfleet vulnerable.

He shook his head. Dr Tremaine's goal wouldn't be thwarted by scuttling his fleet. His *magic* had to be stopped.

But if the other crews could distract Dr Tremaine and keep him occupied, it might give Aubrey and his friends time to find the rogue sorcerer. Then it was up to Aubrey and his magic bullet.

The Armourer at Darnleigh House had enough Symons rifles for Aubrey to take his pick. All of them had been well fired-in and were perfectly maintained, in much better condition than the unfortunate Oberndorf that von Stralick had purloined from that farmhouse. Aubrey had taken a handful of .303 shells and, as Caroline herded the shuddering aircraft skyward, he plucked one of them from his pocket.

It had been the rifle that had let him down at Dr Tremaine's retreat, bursting like that. He was confident that the principle – and his spellwork – was sound. Now that he had good equipment, all he needed was a decent opportunity and he could trap the master sorcerer. He'd be rendered harmless and could be brought to justice, and the people of Trinovant would be safe.

All Aubrey had to do was to concentrate amid the noise and movement of an ascending ornithopter, then cast a series of fiendishly difficult spells, and make a magic bullet.

THE RUBBERY NATURE OF TIME WAS ALWAYS BROUGHT home to Aubrey when he worked on magic. The intensity of his focus and the intellectual effort needed to shape magic meant that time either slipped past or ground to a halt. This time, when he was done and the Symons had the powerful spell in its breech, he became aware of his surroundings again just as the sound of the wings changed. Instead of all his weight being on his back, pressing him into his seat, he found himself leaning forward. They were levelling off. 'That's our ceiling,' Caroline announced. 'The Merlin won't go any higher.'

Aubrey peered out of the window. The earth was far away, Trinovant spread out in all directions from the heart of the city to the faraway outskirts blending into countryside. He could see the other ornithopters labouring upward, all trying to gain altitude.

He tilted his head. Dr Tremaine's skyfleet was still thousands of feet overhead and maintaining its steady course: a great circle taking it right around the city of Trinovant, from Lambshome in the south to Parmenter in the east, Mayfield in the north and Marbury in the west.

The skyfleet was a daunting sight, clearly visible to all the inhabitants of the city. Having already experienced bombing from dirigibles, Aubrey knew the skyfleet would be bringing dread to the population as Dr Tremaine went about his magical preparation.

The thought gave him pause, and once again he wondered at the complexity of Dr Tremaine's spellwork. Could the sense of dismay and fear that the skyfleet was imposing be useful in some way? If the consciousnesses he was harvesting were in a state of horror, could this also improve the efficacy of his bid for immortality? This could explain the outrageousness of the skyfleet, the size and the impressiveness of the assault. It was designed to daunt.

'Time to put the altitude enhancer to work.' He'd been conscious of the magical field emanated by the box to the rear of the aircraft, a node of magical brightness among many throughout the complex machine. It was quiescent, though, waiting for his spell to activate and control it.

He consulted the tech specs and tried to put aside the effects of casting his magic bullet projectile spell. It was a fourth generation carbon copy, blurry and difficult to read. Someone had scrawled out a series of suggestions but the more Aubrey looked at it, the more it looked like a list of hopeful ideas than a definitive guide to operation. The gist was that an amplification spell needed to be overlaid on the box, one that could be ratcheted up by degrees. Choice of language, duration and – apparently – chance of success was up to him.

Caroline glanced at him – a brief, flashing look that was enough to spur him on. He took out his notebook and pencil and he scrawled out a well-practised standby: a Mycenaean amplification spell he'd used many times before.

'I'm not sure exactly how this is going to work,' he said after he pencilled in a reminder to append his signature element, 'so hold on.'

'Forewarned is forearmed,' she said and her hands danced across the control panel. 'When you're ready.'

Aubrey gave the spell his best and immediately the Merlin shot upward like a rocket. Feeling somewhat like an earwig caught in a hosepipe at the worst possible moment, Aubrey craned his neck and saw, miles away to the south, Dr Tremaine's skyfleet.

'Over there!' Aubrey cried. 'The flagship!'

Caroline leaned into the controls. George groaned as the ornithopter tilted, then righted itself, and suddenly they were screaming upward at an angle. Aubrey was pressed against the door and he hoped that the mechanic in charge of door latches had been in top form when putting this one together.

'We're close, Aubrey!' Caroline cried.

The hulls of the skyfleet were growing larger and larger as they neared, flanked by the storm clouds that escorted the fleet like well-built bodyguards helping rich patrons on a night on the town. Around them, other ornithopters were shooting upward erratically, some immediately plunging back down again.

Aubrey hastened to cut off the spell before they rose too far and brought themselves into a direct line with the guns of the fleet.

Instantly, their upward surge halted. The gigantic shape of Tremaine's flagship cut off the sun and they were plunged into shadow while they bobbed like a balloon a few hundred feet below it.

Satisfied, and unwilling to trust to the altitude enhancer again, Aubrey started the other spell he'd prepared as his part in getting them close to Dr Tremaine's location without being seen, all of which made his initial plan of bringing magic suppressors to neutralise Dr Tremaine's magic impossible.

Like most of his outlandish schemes, this one had seemed reasonable when it had first come to him. He'd prepared a spell derived from the Law of Sympathy ('Like affects like') to encourage a link between the hull of the warship and the steel of the ornithopter. An attractive link wouldn't be difficult to propagate, he reasoned, since even though the hull was made of cloudstuff, it was *aspiring* to steelhood, no doubt aping the form and qualities of steel through an application of the Law of Propinquity.

The Law of Attraction provided a backbone to the spell, made all the easier by this propensity of ferrous materials to attract each other.

Awfully exposed, bobbing in the air as they were solely due to the altitude-enhancing device, Aubrey hurried out the spell. They rose, quickly, and before he had time to make any adjustments, they struck the hull with a resounding clang.

They hung there, silently looking at each other, and the whole ornithopter vibrated as if it had decided, on a whim, to become a bell. The cabin shook, the frame vibrated, every single piece of steel or iron around them hummed.

Caroline turned to him, a needless question on her lips. Aubrey wanted to slap himself on the forehead, but decided that fixing the spell would be a better use of his time. He hadn't anticipated that it would be making every iron-based component of the ornithopter want to embrace the overwhelming iron-like presence just above them. Hurriedly, before the ornithopter could shake itself apart in its eagerness, Aubrey eased back on the attraction spell. Not enough to disengage them, but enough to stop the ornithopter from disassembling itself.

When the quivering all about them diminished and then vanished, Aubrey relaxed the death grip he had on his pencil and notebook. 'There,' he said. 'Just as planned.'

Sophie tapped him on the shoulder. 'Aubrey, how are we going to get onto the ship?'

Thirty-five

'Don't worry,' Aubrey said, as reassuringly as someone could when he and his friends were hanging from the belly of an enemy battleship made from magically wrought cloudstuff. 'I have this part under control.'

He paused and waited for a chorus of disbelief at this notion, but it was a measure of the situation that a serious-looking George merely nodded, while Caroline locked eyes with him. 'Go on.'

'I think it's fair to say that you'll have to trust me here.'

A brace of Albion ornithopters swooped along what would have been the waterline of the flagship, if the craft had been afloat. One of them was buffeted by a blast before it climbed rapidly and disappeared from view.

'Aubrey,' Caroline said, 'none of us would be here if we didn't trust you. At the moment, I'm sure we'd follow even if you asked us to step outside.'

'I'm glad, because that's just what I'm looking for.'

AUBREY HAD ALWAYS APPRECIATED SILK. HE LIKED ITS texture, the sheen, the touch of the exotic about it and the way that it was the only clothing fibre made by insects – locust leather, in his opinion, not being a legitimate garment material.

So the rope with which his friends and he were tied together being silk was a lovely touch, if unnecessarily luxurious. He would have settled for good old manila hemp, but silk was lighter and easier on the hands.

Leading the way, with his rifle slung across his back, Aubrey shuffled his hands along the hull of the *Sylvia*, propelling himself forward, and grimaced as he fumbled around a rivet. He uttered a small spell adjustment to ensure that his friends and he were constantly being buoyed upward, rising strongly enough that they had to hold their hands over their heads in order to avoid painful cranial-battleship collisions.

Their progress once they'd left the relative safety of the ornithopter had been a peculiar bobbing accompanied by what could be described as an inverted walking on hands. He'd been assisted by the surprisingly thick and warm air – part of Dr Tremaine's magic, Aubrey assumed, enclosing the *Sylvia* in a bubble of comfort for whoever was on board – so moving air about was something he didn't have to organise.

The experience was disorienting, with the massive bulk of the magically created warship directly overhead while Albion streamed by far, far below. Steadfastly, Aubrey didn't look down after that initial, nervous glance, for the spiralling drop was only too easy to imagine – and imagination, in this instance, wouldn't do him any good. He kept his attention doggedly on their destination: the point at which the hull curved upward to become the sides of the *Sylvia*. To their right, in the distance, the enormous propellers rotated, churning away at the air. To their left, the bow crested the non-existent waves. Pressing against their hands were rivets, bolts and seams.

The cloudstuff hull was peculiar to the touch. At close quarters, it looked as if the surface were swirling but, to the fingers, it was as solid as the steel it was imitating. Dr Tremaine had gone to some pains to make the ship as real as possible. Aubrey could only attribute such a rigorous approach to Dr Tremaine's general spell-casting excellence. If he was going to conjure up a battleship, it was going to be a very fine battleship indeed.

Aubrey was jarred out of his contemplation by a thunderstroke that made the hull ring. Quickly, it was followed by a series of equally appalling blows. A rapid flickering flare of orange-white light to starboard threw a nearby battleship into high contrast, enough to see the storm clouds to the north.

The aerial battle had begun.

A few hundred yards away, an ornithopter plunged, dropping below the level of the skyfleet with an ominous plume of black smoke billowing from its tail section. Its wings were beating frantically and Aubrey had some hope that the pilot would bring the stricken craft safely to the ground. He wished them well.

Aubrey scanned the skies. Around them, the attack force of ornithopters was doing its best, but the pilots were having trouble with their altitude enhancers. He could clearly see a dozen or more ornithopters struggling for control. A handful were relatively stable and were firing at the battleships with machine guns, sending tracers flashing through the skies, bright streaks like wasps on fire. Some were descending, aiming to swoop under the skyfleet ships and away from their guns. This left vulnerable hulls exposed and several ornithopters were streaming along the lengths of the enemy ships, directing their weapons upward and raking the hulls with fire.

Naturally, this made their own position under the hull of the enemy flagship extremely precarious. Aubrey wasn't in favour of the prospect of coming under enemy fire and coming under friendly fire was an even less attractive option. He looked over his shoulder and urged his friends onward.

The closer they came to the upward curve, the more of the sky they were able to see. Aubrey soon had a view of half the skyfleet as it continued in its stately progress, terrifying all of Trinovant. The skyfleet's ships were firing, the unmanned guns magically aiming at the few ornithopters that had managed to control the altitude enhancers enough to climb above the plane of the vessels. Turrets rotated, barrels adjusted elevation with horrible speed, then orange and black clouds burst along the flanks of the ships as the mighty armaments let loose to bring down their attackers. Other ornithopters completed their attack on the belly of the ships and immediately came under fire as they swung out from underneath and sought to find another target. The noise was deafening, vast and painful, with the giant flagship shivering every time it let loose a broadside.

Off to the east, one of the ornithopters had a pilot more capable or more daring than most. Its wings thrashed, striving for altitude, and were having some effect. The aircraft yawed, canting sideways but still buoyed by the altitude enhancer. It flailed like a drowning man, but kept climbing slowly, and Aubrey could only think that the pilot was bringing the craft into position for an attacking dive.

Aubrey measured distances by eye. The skyfleet was steaming in a great curve to the north-west. If it kept on that heading, one of the destroyer escorts would soon cross directly underneath the struggling ornithopter, which would be in the perfect position to do some damage, if it were carrying bombs.

Without warning, the wings of the ornithopter folded back. It trembled for a moment, floating on the power of the altitude enhancer, then it plummeted.

The ornithopter struck the deck of the destroyer, just aft of the superstructure. A huge explosion rocked the enemy ship. Fire and smoke fanned outward in a huge, demented spray. The destroyer ploughed on and soon the smoke was unrolling along its sides in black waves.

Aubrey's friends had drawn up close alongside him. They stared, shocked as he was, at the destroyer. 'They couldn't have survived being shot down like that, could they?' Sophie asked, her eyes wide with horror. She had one hand over her head, holding her away from the hull of the *Sylvia*. The other was firmly in George's grasp.

'I don't think they were shot down,' George replied slowly.

'They weren't hit by anything I saw,' Aubrey agreed. 'I think they turned off their altitude enhancer.'

No-one spoke for a moment. 'They must have been desperate,' George said, finally.

The smoke from the destroyer had diminished. Aubrey could see no sign of fire from the deck. It steamed on, barely touched by the assault. 'They did their best.'

And it wasn't enough was unspoken, but hung in the air next to them, ignored but only too obvious, like an off-colour speech at a wedding.

Caroline nudged him from behind. 'We're in a position to do something,' she said. 'Let's not waste it.'

Aubrey wondered if that was what the pilot of the crushed ornithopter had thought.

Soon, the hull began to trend upward. He stopped, flexing his arms and resting his head against the hull, and waited for his friends to catch up.

Caroline was immediately behind him, followed by Sophie, with George determinedly bringing up the rear. Aubrey dangled until they came close. 'The next stage is a little tricky,' he announced.

George cast an eye back at the Merlin, forlorn and lonely in the middle of the ship's hull. 'Trickier than that little hand-over-hand jaunt?'

'A few more yards and we'll have the starboard stabiliser to get around. Then we won't have anything overhead any more,' Aubrey said.

Caroline cocked an eye at the hull. 'So, if you keep the levitation spell active, we'll simply float straight up?'

'That's it. Straight up the side of the ship. Once over the stabiliser, we'll need to find the gangway so we can enter.'

'Or we could simply drift right up to the rail. Over that, and we're on the deck,' Caroline suggested.

'In plain view of anyone on the bridge,' Aubrey said. 'Let's not go that way unless we have to.'

He paused and gazed outward. The skyfleet owned the sky. Even if Dr Tremaine had no other plan in mind, no ambition for personal immortality, this advance in warfare was a fearful thing. He had created a weapons base that could cruise, aloof and undisturbed, and then simply pulverise anything below it. Looking down from such a height, it wouldn't be like attacking people at all – people would be nothing but ants. It was a world away from the intensity of the trenches, where the enemy had a face – and a sound and a smell. Fighting hand to hand was wretched but at least it impressed on the combatants that they were engaged in battle, not unconnected from it all. Far too easy to feel no responsibility that way.

As if I needed another reason to nobble this skyfleet, Aubrey thought.

He pushed off and let his negative buoyancy drift him upward until he reached the wing-like stabiliser. He felt a tug on the cord around his waist and he looked down to see that Caroline had emerged from under the hull and was on her way to joining him. He gave her an encouraging wave, then he clambered around the stabiliser and rose again.

Overhead, the guns roared again, but soon their job was taken over by the lesser armaments, the twenty-millimetres peppering the sky. Ornithopters darted and dived, doing their best to remain below the angle of the big guns, but they were still exposed. They were fewer in numbers now, and Aubrey flinched when one exploded and tumbled away.

Aubrey had judged things so that their rate of ascent was gentle enough to get them to the gangway smoothly without leaving them exposed for too long. Soon, while the aerial battle raged around them, they were past what would have been the waterline of the great vessel and the landing platform was within reach. Aubrey held his breath and, when the platform came close, he seized the metal with both hands and closed his eyes, briefly, grateful for the solidity that was now underfoot after half an hour of having nothing beneath them except a very distant and very hard Trinovant.

One by one, his friends joined him. George untied the silk rope and looped it until he could stow it in his pack. Aubrey peered up the ladder and along the sides of the ship, looking for anyone who could be at the rails to observe the aerial battle, but the ship was free of spectators.

Despite seeing no crew on any of the flanking ships, Aubrey couldn't be sure that Dr Tremaine wouldn't have a crew of soldiers aboard the flagship.

He shared his concerns and Sophie had a suggestion. 'A change of appearance?'

'Just the thing.'

Sophie cast a light Familiarity spell. It was very delicate – Aubrey didn't want to risk bringing them to the notice of Dr Tremaine – and the casting didn't take long. Sophie frowned, but before she could wonder aloud if it had worked, Aubrey reassured her. 'I can feel the magic. Any Holmlanders will think we look like Holmlanders, once we're inside.'

The hatch at the head of the inclined ladder was open – arrogantly open – and Aubrey paused again for a moment. He tried to listen over the sound of the guns, but shook his head with frustration. With the din of the battle, he wouldn't have heard a draught horse galloping up and down the corridor.

After a deep, steadying breath, he stepped inside Dr Tremaine's flagship.

A passageway, dark apart from a crusty electric light right at the end, twenty yards away. The hatch and the bulkheads were military grey, the no-nonsense colour announcing that this ship was all about lethal guns and heavy armour, not namby-pamby things like colour schemes. Aubrey spread himself along one wall, doing his best to merge with it while a part of him marvelled at how real it was. Inside, there was nothing cloud-like about it. It had the phlegmatic solidity of a real battleship.

He shook his head. Was some level of magic involved here? Was Dr Tremaine's magic using Aubrey's own expectations of how a battleship should appear and shaping the surroundings? Wherever he looked, the details were perfect: fire hoses neatly coiled by brass outlets, raised thresholds of doors (hatches!), the smell of oil and cordite, sweat and boiled cabbage.

He beckoned. Caroline slipped through the hatch with her pistol at the ready, then Sophie, then George. The rapid thumping of the guns eased for a moment and the dominant sound became the turbines, which Aubrey now realised he'd been feeling through the soles of his boots ever since they stepped onto the landing platform.

Aubrey signalled to the others to holster their pistols. Sophie's Familiarity spell could cope with much dissonance, but the outright threat signalled by a drawn firearm would probably strain its ameliorating influence. It was far better to act as if they belonged there, strolling with confidence and speaking in Holmlandish, anything to help any Holmlanders they might find on the ship to overlook the details that set Aubrey and his friends apart.

This, of course, meant that George had to remain silent, a part that he played assiduously. He took up a position next to Sophie and behind Aubrey and Caroline. A glance over Aubrey's shoulder told him that his friend was walking with his hands behind his back – confident, at ease, in charge – as Sophie spoke. George was judging by the rhythms of her speech and the expressions on her face when to shake his head, when to nod, when to essay a disbelieving grunt.

The hands behind the back was a nice touch, Aubrey thought, but it served the double purpose of keeping George's hands near the small pistol he had secreted in the rear of his waistband under his jacket.

Since the magical connection he shared with Tremaine was currently vague and unhelpful, careful exploration was the key if they were to find Dr Tremaine. The bridge – the domain of any good commander – was atop the superstructure in the middle of the main deck, so Aubrey took the first ladder that presented itself, then kept moving through passageways and breezeways, ignoring intersections that, to judge from the noise, led to engineering sections and machinery spaces, pumps and foundries.

So intent was he on the charade, listening to Caroline's bland points about victualling and giving the Familiarity spell something to work with, that it took Aubrey some time to realise that they hadn't encountered anyone.

They'd passed crew quarters and what looked like a carpenter's shop, but they hadn't run into, passed or overtaken any Holmland sailors. In between the thumping of the guns, their feet actually echoed on the polished timber. Even when an massive explosion nearby made the *Sylvia* stagger, no curious faces presented themselves at hatches, no cries of alarm went up from the depths of the boiler room.

'A ghost ship,' he said in Holmlandish to Caroline.

She gave him a startled look and paused in the middle of her explanation of how to make pea soup for four hundred sailors. 'Not literally, I hope.'

'I was alluding to the lack of crew. We seem to be alone.'

'Or the sailors are all somewhere else,' Sophie said, but the suggestion wasn't comforting. Aubrey didn't really want to imagine a place where the entire crew of a battleship would be gathered, waiting, armed and ready for them.

Thirty-six

THEY STEPPED OUT ONTO THE MAIN DECK THROUGH a hatch near the portside rails and were once again in the middle of a raging aerial battle. A few hundred yards away one of the skyfleet's destroyers was on fire, flames rising high along its entire length. An explosion burst through its side and the stern dropped precipitously so that the whole ship was sailing at an awkward angle, bow up, stern down, more evidence that in Dr Tremaine's efforts to create a threatening skyfleet, the cloudstuff had become solid and material — to the detriment of the vessels, in this circumstance.

This moment of satisfaction was balanced by the bleak possibility of a rain of solid cloudstuff falling on Trinovant. It would be almost as destructive as bombs.

Aubrey found himself hoping that Dr Tremaine's spellwork was up to its usual standard and that the skyships would keep their structural integrity once damaged.

He'd be happy if the damaged ships drifted away from the battle, harmless, instead of falling apart and subjecting Trinovant to more death from the skies.

A hideous ratcheting nearby made Aubrey spin around to see the massive central turret of the *Sylvia* moving, with its fifteen-inch guns turning in their direction.

Caroline pulled him down behind a ventilator. He clapped his hands over his ears just as the big guns cut loose. The deck shook and air itself punched him hard enough to take the breath from his lungs. The shells screamed as they flew from the massive barrels, shrieking maniacally as if gleeful at being set free.

Aubrey squirmed around on his stomach and saw four ornithopters darting about near the crippled vessel. His heart went out to plucky pilots who'd coaxed their uncooperative machines that far.

The big guns fell silent, as if embarrassed at their inability to bring down a few flapping nuisances, and the machine guns and smaller armaments on the deck took over with sharp, emphatic chattering, a metallic chorus that mounted in intensity as round after round howled toward the Albion aircraft.

Aubrey wasn't surprised, really, that all of this aiming, firing and reloading was happening without any sign of a human hand. The machine guns swivelled and the six-inch guns tracked targets entirely by themselves. He was aware of the magic that enabled such autonomous, implacable behaviour and it efficiently made the most of mechanical processes while supplementing them with magical power. The ships may have once been as insubstantial as the clouds they were made of, but Dr Tremaine had made them as solid as anything in the Holmland navy.

One of the ornithopters was swooping over the stern of the crippled destroyer. Tracer bullets lanced from it as it tried to damage the rudder and propellers. Aubrey had no idea if the steering mechanism were of any use in sailing through the sky – he suspected not – but he applauded the ingenuity of the attack, even while he was aghast at such close manoeuvring, where a minute misjudgement could doom the ornithopter and its crew.

The ornithopter became a fireball. One moment it was banking close to the stern of the ship it was attacking, the next it erupted. It tumbled, trailing a tail of fire behind it like a comet, and Aubrey was momentarily crushed. That such bravery was rewarded with such a death. There was no poetry, no deserved outcomes, just messy and inconvenient ends.

Aubrey didn't want to ignore the deaths he'd just witnessed, nor try to forget them, but he wasn't going to allow them to stop him. They had been a reminder that there was little nobility in a conflict like this, but that didn't mean that he should give up.

George and Sophie were scrambling toward the rails on the port side of the *Sylvia*, both open-mouthed in astonishment as a dirigible rose, rapidly piercing the gap between the *Sylvia* and its companion battleship half a mile away. Its metallic surface caught the flames of the crippled destroyer and made it a shimmering presence; as it rose, it blotted out a fair portion of the skies. Amid the darting, jerky flight of the ornithopters and the ponderous motion of the warships, the dirigible was eerily graceful in the aerial battleground, moving with majestic calm.

It was the A 405 – assisted by a bank of magical altitude enhancers.

The giant airship was fully as long as the *Sylvia*, a match for it in size and, perhaps, capable of contesting it for domination of the skies. Aubrey held his breath as it ascended rapidly, the massive engines straining to push it past the lethal level where the guns of the skyfleet could be brought to bear. Tracer bullets whipped from machine guns toward the A 405, but either the aluminium cladding was sufficient to deflect the bullets or the distance was too great and the great airship was unaffected as it climbed.

Aubrey wanted to stand up and cheer the brave aviators who were crewing the A 405, but he was grateful for the protection of the ventilator when the airship returned fire – proof that the time spent in regassing and fitting the airship with altitude enhancers had also been spent on more lethal improvements. The ventilator rang when a volley of shots stitched it. Aubrey and Caroline flattened themselves to the deck. When the shooting moved on with the progress of the airship, crossing the deck and making a mess of a series of wooden covered hatchways, Aubrey risked a peek. With so many gun barrels protruding, the gondola attached to the underside of the A 405 looked like a porcupine. Flame flashed from the barrels as the machine guns chattered, filling the air with humming death.

Ornithopters were streaking about, using the distraction provided by the presence of the A 405 to pepper the warships. Explosions erupted on skyfleet vessels, the result of bombs dropped by game ornithopter crew members. For a time, the scene was reminiscent of one of the gaudier fireworks displays commemorating the late King's birthday.

A deep-throated thump came from the A 405. The airship heaved and yawed, bucking like a skittish horse, a sight remarkable in such a large craft. The bow of the battleship on the far side of the A 405 was enveloped in a gigantic fireball. The airship actually staggered, its nose pushed aside by the violence of the explosion. A few seconds later and the *Sylvia* itself was struck by the concussion. The massive flagship rolled sickeningly and Aubrey found the deck tilting away from him. Desperately, he grasped Caroline's forearm when she began to slide away from him. With his other hand he clutched the corner of a hatch cover and hung on until the ship caught itself, hesitated, then began the long roll back.

As the aerial battlefield returned to view, Aubrey lifted his head to see that the A 405 was no longer the sleek, elegant craft that had come to fight. The front third of the dirigible was rapidly losing its shape, with aluminium panels falling from it like confetti. The guns in the gondola kept firing, but their volleys were now haphazard as the airship wallowed, having lost its airworthiness.

On the other side, however, the battleship the A 405 had attacked was fully aflame. The fireball that had swallowed the bow was fiercely working its way along the length of the vessel, which was listing badly and losing its way. The ship began to curve away from the skyfleet formation, crippled and useless, its superstructure canted at forty-five degrees or more, but still buoyed by the magic of Dr Tremaine.

The A 405 began to fall. It went slowly, and Aubrey could only hope that many of the gasbags were undamaged by the assault that had torn open the bow of the massive craft. In a last effort, firing from the gondola redoubled.

Heavier calibre bullets replaced the light machine gun fire, ricocheting from the turrets and the cranes of the *Sylvia*, then small shells followed and began to do significant damage. Glass shattered, and one of the antenna arms snapped from the main array over the bridge. It crashed to the deck near the forecastle, narrowly missing George and Sophie, who were huddled behind the conning tower.

Dr Tremaine may have a magically enhanced aerial weapon platform, Aubrey decided, holding onto his beret with both hands, but someone quick-thinking in the Albion military had decided that two could play that game.

He signalled to his friends and then he ran for the nearest deckhouse – a narrow structure near the gun turret – and flung it open. He took one last look at the crazily brave A 405 and its crew firing for all they were worth and he wished them well. If it didn't take any more damage, it should be able to land safely, but it wasn't about to continue the battle, which was a pity. More ornithopters were joining the fray, however, as the pilots came to terms with the altitude enhancers. In the distance, a brace of incendiary devices struck a destroyer. It was ablaze, but still kept formation in the dogged circling of Trinovant.

Aubrey found himself in an ammunition supply shaft, something that he wasn't sanguine about. When under attack, he would have preferred not being near ordnance or anything else explosive. He climbed down the ladder hastily, to allow his friends to escape from the dangerously exposed deck. The deckhouse hatch slammed shut, George crying out that they were all safe. Aubrey descended faster, past the racks and racks of shells waiting to be fed into the hungry maws of the guns above.

At the bottom of the shaft was the generous powder and shot magazine, which not only provided the shells for the big guns, but was also one of the main stores for the ammunition for the rest of the ship's armaments. A knuckle rap confirmed that the walls were far thicker than in the rest of the ship, which was sensible even in a ship made of cloudstuff, as the munitions store was a place that any enemy would love to hit. Aubrey found time – a lingering instant or two – to admire the magically enhanced conveyance and loading apparatus, a combination of clever machinery and friction-reducing spellwork that worked entirely without human intervention. Remarkable stuff.

When Aubrey reached the bottom of the shaft, he waited anxiously for his friends to join him while the *Sylvia* rang to the battle around it. Caroline steered him out of the munitions store and onto a heavy meshed walkway. It extended out over a dark and clangorous area that shook with the hammering of pumps, so his ears had no respite from the assault they had been exposed to. Again, Aubrey wondered at Dr Tremaine's efforts at verisimilitude. The ship had no water to pump out of the hold – what was the point of operational pumps?

Gone were the narrow corridors of the upper decks. This part of the ship was more like a large factory with open walkways and exposed machinery, the ceiling far overhead, studded with electrical lights.

They reached an intersection. Boiler rooms were ahead, but a ghostly wave of magic brushed Aubrey as he tried to puzzle out the Holmlandish sign that detailed what they might find to their left and right. The industrial clamour of the bowels of the ship was overlaid with a pungent floral sensation, sound and smell being swirled together as his magical senses tried to cope with what they were experiencing.

Then Caroline asked the question which had remained unasked – but needed asking. 'Where is he?'

Aubrey touched his chest. The magical connection that linked him with Dr Tremaine was quiescent, barely there at all and giving no indication of the rogue sorcerer's location, but having come so far he wasn't about to let such a thing stop him, especially not since he'd been thinking about the challenge of finding Dr Tremaine ever since the ornithopter had left the ground.

Back in Stalsfrieden, in Baron von Grolman's factory, Aubrey had observed Dr Tremaine enhance the connection when he wanted to examine its nature – and Aubrey's curiosity made him a *very* good observer. If Dr Tremaine could augment the connector, why couldn't Aubrey do the same? He'd have to be careful, but if he could awaken it – just slightly – it could be enough to show the way.

'I need to do some magic,' he announced.

'I hope this isn't just a whim,' George said. Like the others, he was scanning their surroundings, as if expecting a horde of Holmlanders to descend on them at any minute. 'Tell me it's something useful.'

'If I'm right, it should tell me where Dr Tremaine is.'

As one, Aubrey's friends looked at each other. A brief, silent conversation ensued, with a minute nod here, a tiny shrug there, and then, without a word, his friends deployed themselves, leaving Aubrey standing in the middle of the intersection. Caroline took up a position behind a fire station, some ten yards away. George was near a ventilator shaft. Sophie stood where she could watch three ladders leading upward. All had drawn their sidearms and all were very obviously giving him time and room to do what was needed.

Aubrey shuffled his feet a little and pushed his hands together in front of him, feeling the tension in his shoulders and upper arms, and he realised that he'd spent much of his time since arriving on the *Sylvia* in the singularly useless act of clenching his fists. Even his palms were aching, so hard had he been at it. Frustration? Anger? His body reacted to what was going on around him, even when he was doing his best to remain calm.

He settled himself, then whispered a subtle intensification spell that attempted to replicate Dr Tremaine's effortless augmentation of the magical connector. Aubrey paid particular attention to the scaling of the intensification and built in a difficult metrical factor which he monitored while he cast the spell. When he felt the stirrings of the connector, he cut off the augmentation and ended the spell, conscious that he wanted a more secure link without arousing Dr Tremaine's suspicions.

He touched his chest, lightly, then pointed left. 'That way.'

Caroline was at his side in an instant. 'You're sure?'

'He's not on the bridge. He's down here. Toward the stern.'

George had his arm around Sophie's shoulders as they approached. She was rubbing her temples under George's concerned gaze. 'What is it, Sophie? The noise?'

'I don't think so. I felt something.'

'What did it feel like?'

'Pressure, like a headache, but from the outside.'

Aubrey gnawed his lip. Magic was cascading all about them. At the moment, he felt it like paisley on his palate, but how was Sophie experiencing it? Her newly awakened magical awareness was undeveloped. Not everyone gained that synaesthetic jumbling, which was as much a curse as a blessing. Aubrey heard saltiness, and he caught his lower lip with his teeth. 'You're feeling magic. Can you tell where it's coming from?'

She shook her head, distressed. The curls of hair on her brow, protruding from her beret, were damp with perspiration. 'It is all around. Everywhere.'

'That it is.' Aubrey gazed about, then he turned in a slow circle. So perfect was the construction, so realistic was it, that he had to keep reminding himself that it was all created out of cloud by the master magician. Magic was embedded in every bolt, every stanchion, every hand rail. It was a formidable display, but as Aubrey concentrated his magical senses he could tell that the magic about him was stable, holding the cloudstuff in the necessary battleship configuration – but not all the magic about was as settled. When he faced the stern of the ship – in the direction his magical link insisted that Dr Tremaine lay – it was like gazing into the open door of a furnace.

'It's going to get worse,' he said to Sophie. 'I think the magical artefacts that Dr Tremaine has been collecting are down there too.'

They set off. The pulling on his chest was faint, but it steered him sternwards, every step drawing closer to both Dr Tremaine and the intense magic that was – to his magical senses – fairly lighting up the stern of the ship.

Soon, after passing immense boilers and vast uptakes

that disappeared to the funnels above, they reached a bulkhead that blocked their way. A single hatch, dogged and toggled, waited for them. Aubrey felt the steady stream of magic that poured straight through the bulkhead and confirmed that they'd reached the magical heart of the ship.

'What is it, old man?' George said. 'Stop looking so cool and collected.'

'Me? I was admiring your calm. All of you.'

'I'm far from calm,' Caroline said. She checked her revolver again. 'My heart's beating like a clockwork toy.'

Sophie's eyes widened. 'I was thinking how brave you all were. I promised myself I would be, too.'

'Brave?' George said. 'Us? I'm a quivering jelly.' He looked down. 'Underneath, that is.'

Aubrey loved them all. 'Let's unite in abject terror, then, accepting our foibles, checking our weapons, and sallying forth.'

'And leaving our pompousness behind,' Caroline added with a quirk of her lip that Aubrey wanted to capture and hold forever.

Thirty-seven

*P*REPARED AS AUBREY WAS FOR ANYTHING — A USEFUL operating standard whenever Dr Tremaine was concerned — the sight that met them on the other side of the hatch was simply outside the realm of rational anticipation. It was like a fish trying to imagine what a dust storm would be like.

Aubrey had to remind himself that they were inside the belly of a battleship — albeit a magical one made of cloudstuff — because as soon as they stepped through the hatch they could have been in the Museum of Albion.

Silence had replaced the head-aching drone of the warship's turbines. A cathedral-like space spread in front of them, with light coming from expanses of glass, skylights in any rational building but impossibilities this deep in the heart of a warship.

It's Dr Tremaine's work, Aubrey found himself repeating. *It's Dr Tremaine's work.*

The ex-Sorcerer Royal's name was almost a spell in its own right. Using it, perversely, reassured Aubrey that he hadn't gone insane.

The museumness of the space was created not just by the hush that filled it, the air of respectful studiousness, but by the rich blue carpet, the rows of tall glass cabinets and the slightly dusty smell that is essential in every serious collection. Where the chamber ended was difficult to determine; the far wall was so distant as to be misty, but the perspective was unsettling enough to make Aubrey suspicious.

The place was so much like the Hall of Antiquities at the Museum of Albion that Aubrey's sense of déjà vu thought it was looking at itself in a mirror, backwards.

Swamping all this, Aubrey felt a swell of potent magic from all around, clashing with his ordinary senses and making him grit his teeth to maintain a grasp on his surroundings. Sophie gasped at the surge, a flood of fickle magic. It was volatile, shifting in nature, but blazing with immense power. Aubrey had encountered something like this last year, but the magical blaze that Dr Tremaine had summoned beneath the streets of Trinovant was a much diminished version of what he was experiencing now. That magic inferno had been a torrent of chaotic, unformed magic still being shaped by Dr Tremaine's will. What he was now sensing had some of the same flavour, but the presence of Dr Tremaine – although bright and central to this outpouring of magic – wasn't the sole shaping consciousness involved. Aubrey had the impression of dozens of others working with the magic, and he vaulted over uneasiness and moved directly to being distinctly alarmed.

'Can you tolerate it, Sophie?' he asked.

'I am well,' she said with more determination than conviction. 'I was taken by surprise, but it's easing now.'

Aubrey told himself to keep an eye out, to make sure that the chaotic sensory impressions didn't overwhelm her.

He studied the nearest cabinet, then the others. They stood well away from each other, a hundred feet or more separating each one. The arrangement struck him as odd, so isolated were the cabinets. Either some arcane configuration was satisfied by the array, or having them nearer each other was a bad idea – and this notion only served to heighten the disquiet that had been a permanent inner lodger, ever since he'd set foot on the *Sylvia*.

He approached the nearest cabinet, then stopped, suddenly, and counted.

Nine rows of three. Twenty-seven. The number of magical artefacts that the remote sensers detected at Fremont, just before Aubrey's great spell caused them to scatter.

Except he could feel no magic coming from these cabinets.

Caroline pointed, unwilling to disturb the silence, at the wrist-thick cable that entered the top of each cabinet. They each snaked away to join a bundle of cables that ran along the ceiling – *another* clue that this wasn't an ordinary museum. Magical power throbbed in the nearest cable, pulsing until it joined the bundles overhead, which were thick with magical potency.

George came close, scanning the heights, shading his eyes. 'We could have a hundred snipers up there.'

'This doesn't seem like the sort of place to have snipers,' Sophie said quietly. She touched her forehead with a finger, lightly, and winced.

'Can you feel any illusions here, Sophie?' Aubrey asked.

'I cannot tell. This place . . . I am drowning in magic.'

George put a hand on her shoulder. He had his revolver in the other and while he comforted Sophie, his gaze didn't stop roaming about.

On closer inspection of the cabinets, Aubrey decided that the place was less like a Museum of Antiquities than a Collection of Curiosities. The first displays would have been at home in any respectable institution – a bronze platter the size of hat, a small golden brooch, a carved totem – but mingled with these were peculiar items that any serious curator would have laughed at: a cracked glass marble, a stuffed gerenuk, a battered tin bath with a hole in the side.

The cabinets themselves were intriguing. While they had the four stubby legs and the solid, dark wood frames that would have seen them at home in any well-endowed collection, the glass was embedded with fine silver wires, creating a meshwork, each square the size of Aubrey's thumb tip.

He stood back for a moment. What were the properties of silver? Apart from being valuable, it had some useful physical attributes that he had trouble, for the moment, recalling. All that came to mind was how dentists used silver for fillings in teeth.

He narrowed his eyes. Craddock's cryptic query about thefts from dentists – had this been an indication that Dr Tremaine had been accumulating silver on such a scale as to need thievery from the guardians of oral hygiene?

He let his mind work while he bent and peered into the nearest cabinet. Despite his being unable to find any light source, the cabinet glowed, displaying its contents to fullest effects: a vase of some classical origin or other. The next cabinet had a leather shield embossed with a faded green horse, rearing.

Carefully, inspecting the carpet before each step, Caroline had eased her way around to the back of the cabinet. Aubrey joined her to find that she was studying the cable arrangement that emerged from the top of the display.

The cable was as thick as Aubrey's wrist and sheathed in black rubber. He stood on tiptoe. 'It's attached to the silver mesh,' he said after careful scrutiny, shifting his rifle from one shoulder to the other so he could reach for the junction. 'And I'd suggest that if we sawed through the covering, the cable would be silver all the way through.'

'To what purpose?' Caroline said. She ran a finger along the wooden frame and then, to Aubrey's alarm, she tapped on the glass with a fingernail.

'I'm considering propounding a number of new laws. Not laws of magic, but Laws that Could Prove Useful in Staying Alive. The First Law of Dealing with Dr Tremaine would go something like this: "With Dr Mordecai Tremaine, anything, no matter how disconnected and outlandish, is likely to be part of a scheme of his."'

'Very droll, Aubrey. I take it that silver cables fit into this?'

'Remember the loss of the Gallian silver plate? And the dentists?'

'Aubrey, I know that your brain is probably fizzing at the moment, but slow down. The dentists aren't lost.'

'I know that.' Aubrey rubbed his hands together. Things were falling into place. 'Do you recall how Dr Tremaine has used copper in some of his magic?'

'The thing that attacked you in that Holmlander café, its body was made of copper wire.'

'All the better to mesh with the copper wire of the telephone line.'

'And the golems in the Stalsfrieden factory, they had copper components.'

'Again, a combination of magic and electricity – with some biological elements in this case.' Aubrey chewed his lip for a moment and a hum started to rise in his throat. He clamped down on it. 'Copper is a wonderful metal if you want to work with electricity, but it has its limitations. Dr Tremaine needs more.'

'More?'

'More of everything. In order to achieve his goal, he needs more power, more effort, more magic. He's making each component of this magic as efficient as possible, to maximise its chances of success.' Aubrey looked towards the stern of the battleship. 'Silver is a better electrical conductor than copper, and I'll wager that Dr Tremaine has found a way to use this to increase the channelling of magical power.'

Aubrey paced a few steps, grappling with the obser-vations, theories and deductions he'd been juggling for weeks. 'These are the twenty-seven magical artefacts that were at Fremont. Dr Tremaine has brought them here to help power his magic.' He put both hands on the cabinet frame and leaned close. The vase was tall and black, with antique figures incised on its sides, caught for millennia in their chariot race. 'I can't feel any magic coming from the displays because the silver mesh catches it, then conducts it up and into the cables overhead. The mesh is a shield.'

THEY FOUND SOPHIE AND GEORGE PEERING AT A RUSTY spear. With reverential tones, Sophie said, 'I think this could be the Spear of Salange.' She winced and rubbed her forehead. 'Salange was a great hero who died defending the king of Gallia against a thousand warriors. He was fearless and loyal, but his spear was lost hundreds of years ago.'

'Dr Tremaine has managed to find it,' George said. He gestured with his head. 'Your Rashid Stone is over there, old man.'

'I thought it would be here somewhere.' Aubrey hesitated. He would have liked to investigate the Rashid Stone but he was conscious of the time they had already spent in their cautious advance. 'Caroline, what's the best way to organise our approach?'

'The manual says it's a matter of using the available cover.'

'What does it say about the element of surprise?'

'"In an offensive manoeuvre, surprise effectively doubles the numbers of your force."'

'Much like the Scholar Tan: *With surprise, one becomes two*.'

'You obviously have a plan, Aubrey – why don't you share it? This is hardly the time or place for guessing games.'

'The cables. What if I levitate us and we can haul ourselves along to wherever they're going? That way, we should have the element of surprise on our side. No-one will be looking up.'

Caroline tapped her foot while she stared at the floor. Then she looked up. 'It's a good plan.'

'Won't we be exposed, floating about like that?' George asked.

'It depends on how fast you can pull yourself along,' Aubrey said. 'I'll make sure that I can get us down quickly, if your hundred snipers happen to appear.'

George grimaced. 'I have a feeling that I'd much rather be facing a hundred snipers than what's waiting for us down there, but we can't have everything, can we?'

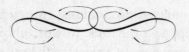

Thirty-eight

Despite Aubrey's objections, Caroline insisted on organising the order of their advance. She ticked off his objections one by one until he even tried 'I'm in command', fully knowing how feeble it sounded.

She smiled tolerantly. 'And a fine commander you are, too. Now, I'll lead off. George, you take the rear.'

Aubrey contented himself with staying very close behind Caroline as they swarmed along the festoons of cables that were strung along the barrel-vaulted ceiling. He found time, in between rehearsing an extremely localised heat spell and a dazzling light spell, to admire her litheness as she made the awkward hand-over-hand grappling look like flying. He knew it may have been improper or poorly timed or inappropriate, heading as they were to a confrontation that could mean the end of everything, but it was hard not to notice some things.

More than once, his Symons rifle was nearly his undoing. It slipped from side to side, unbalancing him and once dangling directly underneath him. His shoulders were in constant motion, and his rifle strap worked its way around his body in the most incommoding way. Finally, he worked out that it sat best if he thrust his head through the strap, crossing it over his chest. It was more secure, but it also meant that he'd be unable to access the rifle quickly.

They followed the main bunching of cables that ran along the centre of the ceiling. Lesser cables and wires joined from either side of the hall, gradually making the ceiling look as if a fishing net were suspended there.

As they pulled themselves forward, Aubrey's fingers began to tingle, as if he were receiving a low-level electrical shock. He looked back to see that Sophie was frowning and he guessed she was feeling the same.

The end of the hall gradually resolved itself from what had appeared a misty distance. At first, Aubrey doubted his eyes but, when they came to within a stone's throw, he gave up and accepted that they were, indeed, facing the entrance to a classical temple.

At the end of the Collection of Curiosities, giant pillars stood on either side of a gap. They supported what Aubrey thought was an arch, but he realised it was essentially a continuation of the barrel-vaulted ceiling they'd been following.

Caroline led off and they floated ahead, then they clustered together, hanging, using their closeness to cope with the scale of what they were entering.

The arch opened onto an immense circular area surmounted by a dome that was dizzying in its circumference and its height. Numbed by the profound majesty of the place, Aubrey wouldn't have been surprised to see clouds forming in the faraway loftiness. More giant pillars marched around the perimeter, reinforcing the impression of a classical temple – but one inflated many, many times. Right in the centre of the floor was a round window a few yards across, admitting light from the world below. A spicy hint drifted through the air, reminding Aubrey of incense. At first he'd thought it silent inside the dome, but when he listened more carefully, at the edge of perception was a faint, constant hum.

Aubrey didn't need any confirmation of Dr Tremaine's powers, but this unlikely edifice inside a magically conjured battleship was evidence of his mastery of magic. The dome was a feat that would be impossible without prodigious magic. No natural material – stone, metal, timber – could support its own weight over such an expanse, a hundred yards across. As well, its diameter was easily larger than the beam width of the *Sylvia*, a casual twisting of the Law of Dimensionality – but to what end?

After the initial, overwhelming impact, Aubrey was puzzled by the gaudiness of the whole thing. It was loud, bombastic, vainglorious. Dr Tremaine enjoyed theatricality, but the magnitude of this display was unlike him.

Aubrey had never thought that the ex-Sorcerer Royal was prey to the overweening pride that affected so many of those who achieved power, even though his power was far beyond the measuring of most mortals. His ambitions, although extraordinary, were entirely self-centred. Extending his life was an entirely natural decision, making the most of an excellent state of affairs where he was who he was. Power, riches, control were only important in that they enabled Dr Tremaine to be Dr Tremaine forever. No need for godhood or anything like that. Tremaine Eternal was all that anyone could wish, after all.

Which is why this display upset Aubrey. It was too grand. Who was he showing off for? When he had nearly succeeded in destroying Albion from beneath, his base of operations had been a noisy, clanking monstrosity of pipes and cables: ultimate functionality. Here, though, was a statement of pride that Aubrey would have thought Dr Tremaine completely indifferent to.

Just inside the arch, Caroline leaned back against the curved inner surface of the dome, just above the pediment, and pointed. He narrowed his eyes, blinked, and peered again.

Each pillar stood on a large block of white marble. On top of many of these blocks, before the fluted lines of the pillar began, was a lifelike human statue.

'Caryatids,' Caroline said softly.

Aubrey nodded, but he wondered at how tall the caryatids were, the size of the dome making it difficult to gain a real sense of perspective.

The air of careful precision created by the silent space was only ruined by countless cracks in the surface of the floor, spidery fractures that spread in all directions, marring its surface right from the raised walkway just inside the circle of pillars to the very edge of the central pool of light. Aubrey shaded his eyes, blocking off the central shaft of light, and the cracks sparkled in a way that was startlingly familiar.

'Silver?' Sophie murmured.

Aubrey thought so. The floor wasn't cracked. It was

covered with a silver tracery that was almost vegetative, as if it had grown across the floor and overrun it in its abundance.

Sophie tapped him on the shoulder, then extended her arm. He followed her gesture and saw how the festooned cables entered the dome and left the black sheathing behind. Shining silver, they spread all over its sides like a tenacious jungle creeper, achieving the same encompassing effect as on the floor. The silver tracery crept down the sides of the pillars that didn't have caryatids, joining the floor and the ceilings and making the whole place a mesh of exquisitely conducting silver.

This was more silver than could be provided for by melting down a few silver platters — this was the output of entire silver mines. Aubrey knew that Holmland, once upon a time, had silver mines in the south, near Augsbruck, but they had run dry two centuries ago. Most of its silver these days came from across the sea, from the Andean countries, but Holmland had no access to them. Thanks to the Albion navy, Holmland shipments from this part of the world — including the guano Holmland had needed before inventing the synthetic ammonia process — had been blockaded.

Dr Tremaine must have had access to another source of silver.

Aubrey almost reeled backward as a half-remembered sliver of information slapped into his brain, as if it had been extended for miles on a very large elastic band and had just snapped back.

His mother. Caroline. The near disaster of the arctic voyage. The assassination attempt near St Ivan's in the far north of Muscovia, which had been almost certainly the work of Holmlanders. St Ivan's was the last stopping-off point for polar expeditions – but also the site of undeveloped lead and silver mines.

When the attempt on his mother's life had occurred, it had perplexed him. Why were Holmland agents positioned in that area? On the off chance that Lady Rose, wife of the Albion PM, would show up there sooner or later, given her penchant for Arctic seabirds? Did that mean that Holmland also had some lonely agents – ones who had offended someone higher up – perched on whatever that island was called in the middle of the great ocean, the one with all the iguanas and giant tortoises and finches with interchangeable beaks that proved that finches were very adaptable and would have taken over the world if not for being trapped on the very same island that these forlorn agents spent most of their time regretting that they'd ever heard of?

Or were the agents in St Ivan's on another mission, one so secret that any possibility of a whisper making its way back to Albion must be dealt with immediately by assassination? Commandeering a silver mine or two, for instance?

Dr Tremaine's plans ran very deep and were laid a long time ago. He was like a chess master, one who saw dozens of moves ahead while playing a score of simultaneous games, blindfolded, with a secret rule book only he knew about.

Aubrey shivered and then started, a combination of physical reactions not to be recommended, like sneezing and yawning at the same time. He had a horrible thought that perhaps their very presence was part of one of Dr Tremaine's plans. Perhaps they were being manipulated to appear at this very time and this very place for reasons which would only become apparent when Dr Tremaine had them trapped and their life was ebbing away.

Aubrey shook his head. He couldn't afford to think like that. If he did, giving up was the only sensible thing to do, since Dr Tremaine knew everything, controlled everything. That would be intolerable. Aubrey Fitzwilliam wasn't one to give up. He wasn't about to let Dr Tremaine have his way. He was tired of the great manipulator turning the whole world into a machine designed to bring about full and utter realisation of his plans.

No. Like the Gallian peasants who'd found another interesting use for a sturdy wooden shoe, Aubrey was about to throw something into Dr Tremaine's works.

The cables spreading into the domed temple left them with nothing to drag themselves by, but Aubrey wasn't concerned. He gently pushed himself off and drifted, like a soap bubble, up and along the inner surface of the dome. When he came close to the silver webbing, he carefully bumped himself away and continued to rise, higher and higher, toward the central shaft of light.

Caroline, Sophie and George followed his course.

As Aubrey came closer to the very top of the dome he slowed his progress by placing a palm on the silver webbing, then he grimaced as he felt the magic trickling through it, a bizarre sensation like numbers hurrying along his skin.

Peering down hundreds of feet, Aubrey found that he was looking through the window in the floor to Trinovant far below. It was almost as if he were standing above a pool of water and seeing the rocky floor beneath the water. The roads and buildings of Newbourne rolled past, then the wool stores and carpet factories of Shoreham Road.

Caroline came close and whispered into his ear. 'Sophie is hurting.'

Sophie was waiting, but she had shied away from the central shaft of light. She doubled over and clutched at her head. George was at her side, and shot Aubrey an imploring look.

Aubrey motioned. His friends gathered and they put their heads together. 'The magic is affecting you, Sophie. I think you'll be less uncomfortable once we get down.'

She nodded miserably. 'I didn't know it would be like this.'

'I'll let us down slowly. As we go, let's separate and spread ourselves around the dome. I'll move to twelve o'clock.' Momentary puzzlement, then nods all around. 'Caroline, take six o'clock, George nine o'clock, Sophie three o'clock. He's nearby, so let's see if we can flush him out.'

Aubrey spoke the cancellation spell quietly and he felt the flip-flop in his stomach that announced that his buoyancy had changed. Instead of being lighter than air he was now very slightly heavier. He kept that state constant while they each worked their way, palms against the meshwork, to their positions around the perimeter of the dome. When they reached the pediment level, Aubrey accelerated their rate of descent, until his friends and he were descending at something like walking pace.

Aubrey kept his back to the pillar and worked to drag his rifle from his shoulders. If Dr Tremaine presented himself, he wanted to be ready.

His feet told him that they'd reached the base of the pillar and he held the rifle at the ready. George landed, arms spread, knees bent, alert. Sophie waved. Aubrey couldn't see Caroline, as the central shaft of light blocked his view in that direction.

He flexed his knees and cast the spell that returned their last remaining weight to them. He grimaced as his joints creaked, adjusting to their load-bearing responsibilities again. He swallowed hard and he tracked across the monumental space with his rifle, his finger on the trigger, ready to fire as soon as he saw the man who had created this improbable place.

George, to his right, crouched, one hand on the marble in front of him. Aubrey did the same as he watched for movement. Dr Tremaine was nearby, but he couldn't tell in what direction, or how far away he was. The magic all around him was playing havoc with his perceptions.

Aubrey went to climb down from the base of the pillar but froze, mid-clamber, when he glanced over his shoulder.

The bottom of the pillar wasn't a caryatid, it was a clear tube. Ten feet of crystal separated the pillar from its base, and inside this tube was a gaunt, haunted-looking man dressed in tweeds. Enclosing his head was one of the cages from Dr Tremaine's stronghold. A long silver tendril snaked up from the top of the helmet and vanished up into the middle of the pillar.

Professor Bromhead. The erstwhile Trismegistus chair of magic at Greythorn University. One of Dr Tremaine's captives.

Wildly, Aubrey looked around Dr Tremaine's creation. Many of the pillars had a similar figure at the base.

Without a thought as to who could be watching, solely responding to the plight of the dead-eyed magical theoretician, Aubrey scrambled until he was face to face with the unfortunate Bromhead. He spread his hands on the crystal that separated them. It was tough, not giving at all, even when he hammered on it with a fist and then the butt of his rifle, sending booming echoes around the stillness.

The only sign that Professor Bromhead was alive was the slight movement of his throat. His knees were bent, his shoulders hunched, his chin drooping almost to his chest. He didn't react to Aubrey's fearsome pounding.

'He cannot hear you. None of them can.'

Aubrey's nerves were so taut that when he spun on one foot he nearly fell off the base of the pillar.

Leaning against the base of the next column was Sylvia Tremaine, Dr Tremaine's younger sister.

Thirty-nine

SYLVIA TREMAINE WAS SO MUCH MORE ALIVE THAN the last time Aubrey had encountered her, which, since she had been at death's door, made reasonable sense. Her eyes were bright, her skin was tight and supple, her black hair lustrous, but it was the mobility of her face, the smooth confidence with which she leaned, arms crossed, against the marble, and even the canary yellow dress and gloves she wore that signalled that she was whole and integrated, far from the poor splinter of a soul that Aubrey had encountered inside the Tremaine Pearl.

'I'm glad you finally appeared.' She smothered a yawn. 'It's getting so boring here.'

'Boring?' Aubrey groped for the right response. They were in the middle of a war that had already cost the lives of thousands and displaced many more. Her brother was on the cusp of reaping the consciousness of a million or more in a stroke. While all of this was going on, Sylvia Tremaine was bored?

Without taking his eyes from her, Aubrey eased himself to the edge of the pillar base and dropped to the floor. 'Where's your brother?' he asked. It came out brusquely.

'He's back there somewhere, making his arrangements.' She tossed her head, gesturing between the pillars. Aubrey risked a glance, but couldn't see anything. A few paces away, greyness swallowed everything.

'I see. You're looking well.'

'I am well. Thanks to you, Mordecai finally found a way to revive and restore me.'

'Thanks to me?'

'Something about your shattered soul, binding and a magical connection, if I remember correctly.'

Aubrey didn't like the way she was looking at him. It reminded him too much of an animal with an eye on something small and tasty. 'Unfortunately it interrupted his great work, but it couldn't be helped.'

Aubrey realised that it was extremely difficult to look casual while holding a military rifle in both hands, but he summoned all the experience he had had on the stage to take the part of the juvenile lead – feckless and well-meaning in every way. He ambled, taking his time, doing his best to look aimless but working his way towards the central column of light. He gazed about the rotundity, giving his best shot at nonchalance. When he couldn't see any of his friends he forced himself to be calm. *They've hidden themselves*, he thought. *They're doing exactly what they should.* 'This doesn't look like your brother's work.'

Sylvia followed him and laughed. It echoed from the pillars and the dome overhead. 'Mordecai has an erratic sense of the dramatic, I'm afraid. He didn't think it important, for instance, to set the stage for the greatest feat of magic of all time.'

'I see. This is *your* conception of an appropriate stage, then?'

'Given what I had to work with, it's good enough. The concentrating lens that you're marching toward, for instance, is hard to fit into any sort of design. And that's not to mention that awful fountain of light and the magician array.'

'Magician array?'

She swept a hand around the great circle of pillars. 'These magicians that Mordecai has gathered, harnessed in series or parallel or whatever it is. Essential though Mordecai says they are, they were the very devil to work into something harmonious. I'm rather glad of my solution.'

'Every column holds a person.'

'More or less. More or less a person, I mean.'

'How many?'

'One hundred and twenty-eight. It's a number with some significance apparently. I'll let Mordecai explain that when he gets here.'

'Which will be soon?'

'He has some things to complete. Until then, I have to stop you from spoiling things.'

'Spoiling things? That rather depends on your point of view, doesn't it?'

'It's my point of view that counts, at the moment, because I have this.'

He jerked around. Sylvia held a pistol that she didn't have a few moments ago. 'I think I was supposed to shoot you with it as soon as you arrived.'

'He was expecting me?'

'Oh yes. He said you were near.'

Aubrey took out his juvenile lead smile. 'You don't want to shoot me.'

'Yes I do. You're trying to stop us becoming immortal.'

'And what's wrong with that?' *Now would be a good time for Caroline to lunge at her*, he thought, making sure to keep Sylvia's gaze locked on his. *Or George to knock her over. Or Sophie to hit her with something.*

'Now, that rather depends on your point of view, doesn't it?' She mocked him with a laugh, and Aubrey knew that he was in more trouble than he'd thought. He'd mistaken her chat for humanity and thought that he'd seen a chink of light there, but he'd been deluding himself. She was a Tremaine, as self-centred as her brother. 'Stopping our plans is wrong, according to us. That's all you need to know.'

'Why haven't you shot me, then?'

'I'm bored, remember? I've been waiting for ages for Mordecai to finalise things. When I'm bored, I like things to play with.'

Aubrey had a brief moment of regret about his rifle not being loaded with conventional rounds, dismissed it, and began sizing up distances. How far could he run? How fast? To the columns or to the shaft of light? 'I think I left a pack of cards just outside. Let me get them for you.'

'Mordecai doesn't like to gloat, you know.' She paused, and tapped the barrel of the revolver against her cheek. 'No, that's not it. It's not that he doesn't like it, he just doesn't see the point. Whereas I understand that gloating is fun. Grovelling can be quite diverting, you know.'

'You want me to grovel while you gloat.'

'If you would, I'd appreciate it.' She pouted. 'If you won't, of course, I'll shoot you.'

'You do know that people who talk most about shooting do least of it, don't you?'

'Really? Oh, I do so like giving the lie to things.'

With that, from a distance of only twenty yards, Sylvia Tremaine shot him.

The dome echoed with the boom of the pistol. Sylvia stared at her firearm with dismay while Aubrey stared at his unmarked, unharmed self and heard a waft of hot aridity that could only be magic.

'I hate it when I miss,' Sylvia said, then she actually stamped her foot on the floor.

'Don't do that, Sylvia. It makes you look petulant.'

Aubrey had seen it before, but he was still impressed. It was as if the whole chamber, bigger than any arena, had suddenly become smaller when Mordecai Tremaine entered it, striding out from between two pillars.

Without thinking, Aubrey raised the rifle, sighted – and then it disappeared from his grip. He blinked and staggered a few steps, thrown off balance by the sudden lack of weight in his hands.

Dr Tremaine had the rifle. He grunted and brought it up to his face, to inspect.

Normally a sartorialist's dream, the rogue sorcerer had no top coat, his sleeves were rolled up and his white shirt – smeared with grease and unidentifiable stains – was missing a collar and open at the neck. His trousers were held up with black braces. His boots were scuffed and stained.

He shook his head in either disappointment or disgust, then took the rifle by the muzzle. He swung it in a great circle at the full extent of his arm, then let go.

Aubrey gaped. The rifle sailed in a great arc, tumbling end over end, traversing the hundreds of feet to the column of light. It struck and disappeared, with only the tiniest flare to show its demise.

Dr Tremaine's gaze fell on Aubrey. He pulled a greasy rag from his back pocket and wiped his hands. 'Fitzwilliam. I felt you nearby.'

Aubrey straightened, touching his chest where the magical link had jumped at Dr Tremaine's entrance. He shrugged, hiding his dismay at how easily Dr Tremaine had disposed of his careful plan. 'I wouldn't want to miss the show.'

Dr Tremaine finished with the rag and shoved it in the pocket of his trousers. He glanced at his sister with a combination of affection and exasperation. 'There'd be no show if not for her. I would have just gone ahead.'

'Ah, Mordecai.' She linked arms with him. 'How many times do I have to tell you? Never miss a chance for a gesture that is both extravagant and grandiose!'

He snorted. 'Whatever for? We're the only ones here.'

'If we don't do it for ourselves, who else matters?'

Dr Tremaine gave that some thought, then shrugged. 'Why haven't you removed him?'

'A moment's entertainment,' she said, 'but now you're here.' She raised the pistol again. Aubrey shuffled to the left, then the right. 'Stand still,' she ordered.

'I think not.'

'Very well then. A moving target is the sort of challenge I enjoy.'

Aubrey was prepared to admit that beauty came in many forms. A well-proportioned building, for instance, was beautiful, as was the countryside on a spring day.

A flower could be beautiful, if it were the right sort. Caroline Hepworth was undoubtedly beautiful, in any circumstances.

He'd never considered an act of mayhem beautiful, but when George Doyle swung down from the heights on the end of a silk rope, bowling both Sylvia and Dr Tremaine from their feet, it was beauty of such an exalted kind that he wanted to weep, or cheer, or both.

Sylvia was thrown up against the base of a pillar, her pistol spinning along the marble floor. She lay motionless. Dr Tremaine rolled and was on his feet in an instant, just in time to encounter a second act of beauty, one that transcended the first in the same way that an angel transcends the lowest pig in the sty.

George Doyle was ready for the rogue sorcerer. With every sinew and every muscle working perfectly, George delivered an uppercut that began somewhere around ankle level and accelerated until it struck Dr Tremaine on the point of the chin with enough force to lift the rogue sorcerer's feet off the ground. His eyes rolled and he fell backward, toppling to the floor like a tree. He, too, didn't move.

Aubrey had never seen Dr Tremaine even inconvenienced by their attempts to assault him but the unexpectedness and the perfection of George's assault had slipped under his guard. Aubrey went to applaud. George grimaced and shoved his hand under his armpit. 'What are you waiting for, old man? Do something magical!'

The booming of a shot made both Aubrey and George duck. Aubrey whirled to see Sylvia staring at her pistol again before Caroline sprang on her from behind the column. Caroline wrenched the pistol from Sylvia's hand

and flung her aside with a blinding shift of weight and a flurry of arms. 'Hurry, Aubrey!' she cried.

Hunching his shoulders, and calling himself craven for running away from helping his friends, he ran for the pillars. Another report echoed, from Caroline's pistol this time as she spared a moment from grappling with Sylvia to snap off a shot. All Dr Tremaine did, as he shook his head and climbed to his feet after George's magnificent blow, was to irritably slap the bullet out of the air. It struck the base of the nearby column hard enough to take a sizeable chunk out of it, but Dr Tremaine showed no signs of hurt.

So much for the magical projectile, Aubrey thought. *It's time for the other plan.*

Aubrey liked to think he was no fool. For too long, he'd seen Dr Tremaine's mode of operation. Plots within plots, parallel schemes running alongside fallback plans, feints masking important subsidiary operations, all the complex weavings of a master strategist. Along with these observations, he'd had the words of the Scholar Tan to guide him: *Plans are like birthdays. One is good, many is better.*

Aubrey had learned.

While he'd had great hopes for his magical projectile, he'd been careful to have a number of alternative plans in case of failure. With the renewed vigour of the magical connection, one of his alternatives had leaped up and insisted on being used.

He dived, sliding on his stomach between two columns. He skidded a few feet past the bases and came up against a grey wall of nothingness.

Aubrey lifted his head, tilting it back and staring at the featureless barrier. His ordinary senses told him that it was smooth to the touch, almost slick. It had a sheen that shifted subtly. His magical senses told him that it was alive with unshaped magical potential.

He'd seen it before. It was the same material that underlay the refuge that had kept the unwell Sylvia Tremaine safe, the prison inside the Tremaine Pearl. This was the stuff Dr Tremaine bent to his will to create mazes, sanctuaries, and this impossible construction inside a battleship. It was magic, waiting to be shaped.

He shot to his feet. As much as he'd like to investigate this material further, he had more important work to do. If he wanted to help his friends, he had to do it quickly.

A hand fell on his shoulder and he did his best to convert the yell of fright into a battle cry. He did, however, seize the arm attached to the hand and wrench it around, but when he did so, he realised that Sophie must have been taking some lessons from Caroline, for with three quick movements, she jabbed him in the armpit, causing him to gasp with pain, twisted his elbow, causing him to loosen his grip, and bent his wrist, causing him to repeat his initial gasp with an extra layer of agony.

Sophie let go and put both hands to her mouth. 'Oh, Aubrey.' Her Gallian accent was stronger in her distress; Aubrey would normally have found it charming, but pain interfered with his appreciation.

'Sophie,' he said through gritted teeth. 'Are you all right?'

'I cast a spell,' Sophie said. 'We seem to be not where we are.'

'I beg your pardon?'

She waved a hand, distressed, groping for the words. 'Displaced. We are displaced. A few feet. They miss when they aim at us.'

'Splendid.' Aubrey now understood why Sylvia had failed to shoot him. 'You have your pistol? Watch over me while I do some magic, will you?'

She smiled bravely. 'I shall,' she said, then her mouth formed a O and her eyes went wide. Immediately, she had her pistol in both hands and fired three shots in rapid succession, carefully bringing the revolver back into position after each round.

Aubrey whirled, and cried out at what he saw.

Sylvia had backed away to the perimeter and was leaning against one of the great marble bases. Blood trickled from the corner of her mouth. She glared at George and Caroline, who were standing, shoulder to shoulder, pistols in hand, but instead of firing at Dr Tremaine – who was fifty feet away, ignoring them and stalking toward the window in the middle of the floor – all their attention was on the target of Sophie's well-aimed shots.

A towering mechanical figure had clanked out from the greyness behind the pillars. It stood close to Sylvia, towering over her protectively, red eyes glowing, balefully taking in the scene. She glanced up at it and pointed at George and Caroline. The gesture was curt and dismissive, the way someone would ask a servant to get rid of an unappetising dish left on a sideboard.

Even though Aubrey knew that assumptions were dangerous where Dr Tremaine was concerned, he'd thought that his spells had ruined all of the ghastly mechanical golem hybrids. If Sylvia Tremaine were in need of a bodyguard, however, she couldn't ask for better.

This creature was slightly larger than those he'd seen at Baron von Grolman's factory in Stalsfrieden. It was fully twenty feet tall and it moved with well-oiled grace.

The open armature on its limbs showed the extraordinary blending of clay and metal that marked Dr Tremaine's hideous innovation, and Aubrey wasn't surprised that in this giant prince of golem hybrids the copper wire had been replaced by shining silver.

Red eyes fastened on Aubrey's friends. The short chimney stack over its left shoulder blasted a jet of black smoke and it bounded toward them.

Sophie fired her last shot, reloaded, then sent all five rounds hammering into the golem's back. Six rounds from both Caroline and George chased the echoes of Sophie's shots around the dome but the golem wasn't inconvenienced at all. It advanced on George and Caroline, who had wisely separated as they shot. Footfalls booming on the marble, it took a huge swipe at George, who ducked and rolled away, but he needn't have bothered. Thanks to Sophie's displacement spell, the creature's massive fist missed by a good few yards, leaving George unharmed and decidedly perplexed. He lay on his stomach and sought for a vulnerable spot, then gave up and simply blasted away at the creature.

Sophie ran out into the open space, pushing cartridges into her pistol as she went. Caroline fired her pistol twice, darted away, then fired twice more. The right knee of the creature shuddered – but it didn't fall. Whirring, it swung an arm at her just as Sophie sent a volley of shots at its head.

Dr Tremaine was ignoring the bedlam. He stood with a hand on his chin, gazing down at the round window. Then he reached into a pocket and took out something so mundane, so ordinary that Aubrey had trouble understanding what the rogue magician brandished in his hand.

A spanner. A large but perfectly commonplace spanner. Dr Tremaine hefted it for a second or two, then raised it over his head. With a grunt that could be heard over the clamour of the fighting, he flung it at the window at his feet.

The window shattered. Immediately the atmosphere in the cavernous place changed, becoming less taut, less strained as the air from the outside world rushed in. Aubrey saw how Caroline, George and Sophie were taken aback for an instant until they found the source of the change. It was only Sophie's quick action in dragging on George's arm that prevented him from being swatted by the mechanical golem while he gaped.

Dr Tremaine glanced down and nodded. Then, with one finger, he pointed up at the highest point of the dome directly overhead. Instantly, a large crystal disc detached itself. It drifted down, sedately, and settled precisely into the gap.

Instantly, a column of light shot up, forcing Dr Tremaine to stagger back a step or two, cursing, and the atmosphere in the chamber changed again. The shaft of light splashed against the dome and the entire place *tightened*, as if every constituent part, every particle, were being squeezed. It became charged with potential, thick with magic, and Aubrey knew that the Crystal Johannes was doing its job.

His magical senses told him raw magic was boiling through the lens and shooting upward like a geyser. A fantastic conglomeration of sensations sprayed from it, spinning off in whorls – a flash of apricot, a greasy noise, a heavy taste, a touch of harsh, discordant sound – then they shifted and a whole new panoply of sensations replaced them.

Aubrey was awe-struck, both excited and dismayed at what he was perceiving. The column of light was the physical manifestation of the magic that came from the people of Trinovant, concentrated by Dr Tremaine into an almost solid shaft, which struck the dome and was fed by the silver tracery all over the arena.

We're inside a machine, Aubrey thought, still trying to come to terms with what he saw. *A machine dedicated to gathering and channelling magic.*

Dr Tremaine stood facing the dazzling column of light with his arms outstretched, as if he were about to embrace it, and he began to chant.

Aubrey felt a profound shift about him, as if the entire universe had been lifted for an instant and then dropped back into place. He blinked, saw random motes of queasiness in his vision, and realised that Dr Tremaine had begun the most terrible magical spell in ten thousand years.

George let out an angry bellow and, immediately after, a cry of distress came from Sophie. More shots and Sylvia Tremaine's laughter, cold and hard, joined the echoes of Dr Tremaine's voice rolling about the dome.

Aubrey closed his eyes. Magic surrounded him, sparkling along the silver tracery embedded in the dome, the pillars, the floor, boiling in the shaft of light streaming up through the lens. On top of his already awesome power, Dr Tremaine had summoned an unheard-of concentration of magic ready to shape to his will. If he succeeded, not only would he become immortal – he would use up the consciousnesses of those trapped in the pillars about them, and of the populace of Trinovant below.

Aubrey had to do what he could. As much as he wanted to come to the aid of his friends, he couldn't waste a moment. He was torn and, not entirely sure he was making the right decision, he wished his friends luck and went to work.

His task? As it had ever been: to stop Dr Tremaine.

Forty

THE LAW OF DIVISION AND THE LAW OF ENTANGLEMENT had been much on Aubrey's mind. Whenever he had a moment to spare – in between coping with ghostly cavalry raids, summoning the Holmland war leaders and making sure he and his friends weren't killed in an ornithopter crash – he'd grappled with them. He probed them, he analysed them, he tried to recall everything he'd ever heard or read about them.

The Law of Division was a useful principle used to derive spells where objects were divided into parts, but where the parts had to retain the characteristics of the original. The Law of Entanglement described a peculiar, awkward and little-used phenomenon where magic could be used to unite two objects that could be separated by a distance, but would continue to mirror each other's state.

It wasn't their traditional applications that he was interested in. He wanted to use the 'dividing' part of a

Division spell, and combine it with an inverted form of an Entanglement spell to create something to sever the magical connection Dr Tremaine and he shared.

Aubrey was aware that this was not without its risks. Messing about with magical connectors was fraught with danger, something that he knew more than most, having spent more than a year in a state of near death thanks to a spell that had severed the connection between his body and his soul. The experience, however, had taught him a great deal. He'd learned much about preservation while in a precarious state and he had invented many magical applications to strengthen and promote his essential integrity. Complete restoration had proved beyond him – only a freak accident had reunited his body and soul again – but he did have an almost unparalleled appreciation of the effects of magical connectors.

He was hoping that if he were successful with his spells and was able to sever the connector, both Dr Tremaine and he would be affected by the shock. To what extent and how seriously, he had no idea. The connector had, at times, been a conduit for memories, feelings, impressions, and at times it was almost like an organic link, something that belonged to both of them. Slicing it in two would inevitably debilitate them. He was wagering everything, hoping that his experiences in the past would stand him in good stead.

Firstly, he concentrated on the connector, bringing his magical senses to bear on it. He groped for where it merged with his chest, then he sought for its blend of Tremaineness and Fitzwilliamness. He brought up a version of the spell he'd used earlier to rouse the link. He cast it softly, increasing the intensity factor. The connector became more tangible and he was rewarded with a startled noise from Dr Tremaine, clear even over the sounds of mayhem.

Aubrey was pleased to see a cord as thick as his thumb, snaking and curling from his chest along the floor until it reached the rogue sorcerer – who was still facing the column of magic.

Aubrey lifted the cord to eye level and, for a moment, allowed it to undulate there. It was a strange phenomenon, one that had only been hinted at in a handful of medieval texts he'd found. It bore further study. Who knew how it could be useful, between doctor and troubled patient, for instance?

Plenty of time for regrets later, he thought, *as usual*.

He began his disconnection spell, starting with the elements plucked from applications he'd constructed using the Law of Division. He favoured the clear, blunt language of Achaean for this and he spoke each term, each operator with as much calmness as he could summon, moving into the elements derived from the Law of Entanglement, inverting each one so that they would work to disentangle rather than keep together.

The spell was monolithic. It felt as if he were a slave of one of the ancient Aigyptian kings, attempting to move great blocks of stone into place. He had to strain, to summon his strength to keep the elements moving, slotting them into their positions one by one. Sweat ran from his forehead and he heard a worrying waver in his voice – but he was nearly there. An element of directionality, one of a particular dimensionality – tricky – then his signature element and he was done.

A glowing knife appeared in his hand. Aubrey's spell

hadn't prescribed the form it would take. He assumed that it had been plucked from his unconscious, for it was the very model of a cutting implement, an almost perfect representation of sharpness. The handle was golden and the blade curved slightly from hilt to tip, as subtle as a dancer.

Aubrey swayed a little, sapped by the effort of casting the spell, but he gathered himself. He twisted the cord. He manoeuvred the magic knife, inserted it in the loop he'd formed, and he cut.

CLUTCHING THE SHREDS OF HIS CONSCIOUSNESS, AUBREY was lashed with indifference. The connector had recoiled, bringing a wave of Dr Tremaine's emotions, and the overwhelming impression was of disinterest. It was humbling to realise how unimportant he was to the rogue sorcerer. Dr Tremaine's preoccupations were far loftier than worrying about Aubrey Fitzwilliam.

Staggering, bent over double, Aubrey was bombarded with a tumble of impressions, of nations, governments and magical advances. In all of them he was stunned to see how few people actually featured. His father, briefly, and Chancellor Neumann, but even they were almost featureless, more important for their positions than for their person. The only fully formed, fully realised person that emerged from this welter of memories and recollections was Dr Tremaine's sister, Sylvia. She burned with a fire that was only matched by Dr Tremaine's appreciation of himself. They were the only ones who were alive, who were vital, who were important.

Aubrey didn't feature. His interruptions to Dr Tremaine's plans did, but only as irritations to be overcome. The frustration of the foiled assassination plot against King William, the rescuing of the Gallian Heart of Gold, the ruination of the twin plot to animate Trinovant and to destroy the currency of Albion, all were inconveniences when measured against the vast canvas that Dr Tremaine was working with.

This attitude pervaded all of the feelings and thoughts that battered Aubrey as his head spun. It wasn't even contempt. It was as if people were an alien species with which Dr Tremaine – and his sister – had little in common. They simply didn't matter.

Aubrey struggled, sickened almost to the point of vomiting, but he was determined to prove Dr Tremaine wrong. People did matter.

Dr Tremaine's world roared over the top of Aubrey, and swept him away.

Even though it seemed as if an age had trudged past, when Aubrey was next able to frame coherent thought, he was dimly aware that he was lying on the marble floor. He was unable to do much about it as his limbs had apparently turned to jelly. He could lift his head, a little, to see that Dr Tremaine was lying on the floor as well, yards away from the column of magic. A stone's throw away, George was crumpled, unmoving, and Sophie was running to him. Behind them, Caroline had managed to trip the steaming golem hybrid with the silken rope, and to tangle a sword-wielding Sylvia in it as well.

Aubrey really wanted to remain there for a while and recover, but he knew that he couldn't afford that luxury.

Personal hurts, and wants, and dreams, could wait. He had to complete his plan.

Climbing to his feet was one of the harder things he'd had to do in his life. His chest felt as if it were one single, great bruise. The rest of his body wasn't much better, but it was functioning, more or less, in the same way that the Gallian police functioned, more or less. His head thrummed and thumped whenever he moved, which was unfortunate because he had no prospect of holding still because Dr Tremaine, too, was climbing to his feet.

'Fitzwilliam,' the rogue sorcerer called and Aubrey was remarkably heartened to hear that his usually powerful voice had been reduced to a croak. 'Why do you think you're different?'

Aubrey's heavy, aching head dropped. His eyes widened, slightly, painfully, when he saw, still attached to his chest, the ghostly remains of the magical cord that had once connected him to Dr Tremaine. He followed it with his magical senses and realised that his spell had been successful – it was the short length that remained on his side of the cut. Wearily, he sought for the other part and saw it was still connected to Dr Tremaine's chest.

'What do you mean?' Aubrey said and his mind, sluggish though it was, began to arrange magical elements and string them together.

Dr Tremaine was dragging his left leg as he worked his way around the column of magic. 'This thing. This connection. Gave me a glimpse at you. Your thoughts. You.' Dr Tremaine glanced upward. He changed direction and shuffled toward the light. 'You think you're different from all the others, but you're not. You're all alike.'

'We are.' Aubrey squinted. He could make out the remnants of Dr Tremaine's end of the connector more clearly, stretched limply on the floor. 'We are all alike and we are different.'

'Ah. The uniqueness argument. Tedious and meaningless.' Dr Tremaine grunted as he reached the column of power. It roared, rich with magic culled from all the consciousnesses in Trinovant. 'To me. Meaningless to me, which is all that matters. You are all alike. I can manipulate you all, move you all around, to suit my ends. None of you matters.'

Aubrey took a step in the direction of the rogue sorcerer. 'And that's going to be your downfall. If you thought more about how we are different, and the different ways we can all contribute to bringing you down, then you might have had a better chance.'

Dr Tremaine laughed. It was a weary laugh, but it held no doubt. 'A better chance? I need no chances. My plan is a certainty.'

With that, he spoke a sharp series of syllables and plunged both hands into the pillar of light. For an instant, he jerked backward, his spine arching, his teeth bared. Then a sigh came from his lips and when he turned to Aubrey his eyes were shining. All trace of pain and exhaustion had disappeared. 'Such power,' he whispered. 'Such power you'll never know.'

Aubrey hardly heard. He was still stunned at the spell Dr Tremaine had spoken. The economical, clipped, syllables bore no resemblance to any language Aubrey had ever heard. The sounds, the rhythms, the patterns were almost inhuman in their brutality. Aubrey doubted that his mouth could cope with such a thing, so awful was it – but its effect was undeniable. Was this the Universal Language for Magic?

Aubrey started to run. 'I'm glad. If it makes people like you, I don't want a part of it.'

Dr Tremaine barked a hard laugh. He withdrew one hand from the pillar of light. In it, he held a blinding mass, a lump of raw magic that changed as the rogue sorcerer worked his fingers, shaping it like clay. Small bolts of false lightning darted from it and he chuckled. 'Goodbye, Fitzwilliam.'

With a careless, backhand action, the sorcerer flipped the magical missile at Aubrey. Shedding light and magic, it hurtled at him.

Aubrey didn't stop running. He snapped out a few syllables, the elements he'd used to deflect the worst of his Transference spell onto the soldiers on either side of no-man's-land, and raised an elbow. The boiling magical missile glanced off, veered away wildly and burst harmlessly.

Aubrey didn't stop. He spat out a tiny spell that was concentrated on the specific area between the soles of his boots and the marble floor, decreasing the coefficient of friction a few thousand per cent so that it was nearly zero. He went into a long, braced slide at a speed that took his breath away.

It was like wet ice on wet ice and Aubrey's sudden transformation from a galloping nuisance to a lightning bolt surprised Dr Tremaine enough for Aubrey to throw himself forward in a long, shallow dive. He thumped onto his chest and stomach, adding to the indignities that his poor body had experienced, and slid, just missing Dr Tremaine's feet, but close enough to grab the remains of the magical connector still embedded in the sorcerer's chest.

Lying on his back, only a few feet away from the torrent of magic, Aubrey shielded his eyes and flung the loose end of the connector into it.

Dr Tremaine shouted, a huge wordless cry that filled the chamber. It roared like a storm, reverberating until it was elemental in its rage. His limbs were flung wide, starlike, his mouth jerked open and he hung, spread against the magic pillar like an insect in a museum.

His eyes were on fire. They filled with blinding light, consumed by the raw power channelled by the connector, which had swelled and grown, three or four times its previous diameter, jerking and throbbing with crude potency.

Aubrey lay on the floor, panting, horrified and triumphant at once. Dr Tremaine was caught in the grip of a magic that was beyond his control. The combined power of the magical artefacts, the captive magicians and a million Trinovantans was too much even for him when it was pumped into his very being via a magical connector. The control he wielded as a master magician was no use here, as the connector bypassed his intellect. Magic poured into him unchecked.

Aubrey had deduced that it was only Dr Tremaine's intellect and talent that allowed him to work such stuff. The connector was more primitive and more direct than that. Now the rogue sorcerer was helpless.

'Mordecai!'

Before Aubrey could move, Sylvia Tremaine ran from the shelter of a pillar base. She halted, aghast at the sight of her brother being consumed, the back of her hand to her mouth.

Then, to Aubrey's amazement, Dr Tremaine resisted.

Wracked by untold magical power, he shuddered. Slowly, his eyes closed with the ponderousness of stone. When he opened them, they were his again. He had expelled – or controlled? – the magic.

Still pinned against the column of light, the rogue sorcerer threw back his head and howled, the tendons in his neck standing out like hawsers. 'Sylvia!' he cried. He strained to release his limbs but they were held fast against the light. 'Sylvia!'

Without hesitation, Sylvia flung herself at her brother, clasping him around his neck. She cried out, he howled again, and then they started to change.

Aghast, Aubrey couldn't take his gaze away as first Dr Tremaine, then his sister, were pulled upward, losing their substance as they were drawn like oil over glass. Their wordless cries rose in pitch as, together, they smeared across the column of unrelenting, uncaring magic. Dr Tremaine struggled, but his efforts were useless. Thinner and thinner they became as they were drawn out. Light began to shine through them as their mass was stripped away. Finally, they started to shred, reducing quickly to tatters.

In a burst of light, with a last howl that was both agonised and defiant, they were gone.

Aubrey climbed to his feet, feeling a thousand years old. Caroline was at his side. He reached out and touched a nasty bruise on her cheek. 'The golem,' she said. 'Don't worry yourself about it.'

'Caroline,' he said. 'I've decided to give up worrying. It hardly seems worth the effort.'

Forty-one

AUBREY HAD NEVER BEEN TO THE PALACE AT BELVILLE, even though it was only half an hour from Lutetia. He had, however, always been intrigued by its reputation for unrivalled opulence. It had been the home of the Gallian kings for two hundred and fifty years, up until the commoners of Gallia decided they'd had enough of being oppressed by rich layabouts and decided they wanted to be oppressed by poor layabouts instead. The palace had survived rather better than the aristocrats who used to swarm about its extensive gardens, its numerous courtyards and its swooningly lavish rooms. Aubrey had heard that one court official had had the responsibility of walking about the place checking for anything that might be considered drab. If he found something, he had a stupefyingly large budget to gild it, extend it, or get a famous painter or two to daub a forest scene over it.

The Gallery of Glass was the most astonishing part of the palace and, while waiting for the formalities of treaty-signing, Aubrey had much time to admire the impressive windows spaced along one long wall of the gallery, perfectly arranged to throw light on the dozens of crystal chandeliers and make rainbows on the richly panelled far wall.

In his full Directorate uniform, adorned with the embarrassingly ornate medal that King Albert had pinned on his chest, Aubrey stood at ease next to Sophie – who also sported the same medal, one of only four in existence – in their entirely superfluous job as aides to Commander Craddock. Not far away, the bemedalled Caroline and George were filling the same role for Commander Tallis, the two commanders being the representatives of the Albion Security Intelligence Directorate at the signing.

Two months had flown by since the battle in the skies over Trinovant. Without Dr Tremaine's plans and advice, the Holmland war effort had collapsed and the new government, installed after a popular uprising, had quickly sued for peace.

Aubrey and his friends had spent much of that time in Darnleigh House, compiling accounts of the events leading up to the Battle of Trinovant and being called in to offer opinions on sightings and observations after the collapse of the Holmland government. Aubrey was intensely interested to see, for instance, a report about Manfred the Great conducting prestidigitation lessons for the king of one of the smaller islands in the Pacific. A documented rumour about one Elspeth Mattingly opening a fencing academy in remote Muscovia specialising in the sabre was harder to believe, especially once Caroline expressed doubts about Elspeth's abilities in that area, pointing out that she was sure she could thrash the spy without much effort at all.

Dr Tremaine's crippled skyfleet had begun evaporating soon after the rogue magician's demise. Every eye in Trinovant was turned skyward for two days as an urgent effort was made to ferry the magicians and the artefacts to the ground before the magical craft lost their solidity entirely. Caroline and Aubrey piloted separate ornithopters in the ultimately successful undertaking, so short-handed was aerial service since the sky battle.

Aubrey hadn't known that signing a treaty document would take three days – with the promise of more to come – but he was learning that everything in international diplomacy moved at a pace that would make a glacier look positively frisky. He patted his pocket, which reassured him – and then filled him with doubts – but he took the confusion as a good sign that life was resuming normality.

Aubrey's father was at the head of the extraordinarily long table that had been placed in the Gallery of Glass. He was with the Gallian Prime Minister, Giraud, while in between them was the new Chancellor of Holmland, Ilse Brandt.

Aubrey had difficulty remaining solemn whenever he looked at Chancellor Brandt. The sheer novelty of a woman rising to such a position told Aubrey that if the world was resuming normality, it was a delightfully new kind of normality that promised much.

Part of the reason for the delay in the final signing had been the traditional negotiating over the fine points in the treaty. In the weeks leading up to the ceremony, Sir Darius and his Foreign Office had ironed out the major issues, but Sir Darius had confided to Aubrey that he'd deliberately left some minor points vague. He understood that it would be important for Holmland to win some concessions in the negotiation.

Sir Darius had been adamant about this, even in the face of resistance from his own party. Many in Albion and Gallia wanted to punish Holmland for the war. Some wanted to go further and humiliate the country for its aggression. Suggestions were made to strip Holmland of some of its territory, while enormous sums of money were touted as appropriate reparation for the damage Holmland had done.

Sir Darius refused. He could see the dangers of such vengeful actions. He offered to resign if his party didn't support him. He pointed out that since the uprising, Holmland was a different country, and as such it needed assistance, not punishment. The Chancellor and his warmongering cronies were on trial for their crimes, with some damning evidence coming from the file that von Stralick had provided to Aubrey. Crushing Holmland would only create resentment – and a breeding ground for a dangerous future.

Not without some grumbling from backbenchers, Sir Darius won the day.

Aubrey glanced at George, which was a mistake. Days ago, his friend had decided to liven up the interminable occasion by constantly trying to make Aubrey laugh and this time, the face he pulled nearly succeeded. It was only by adding to the bite marks already on the inside of his cheeks that Aubrey maintained the demeanour expected in such a dignified setting.

A few more speeches interrupted proceedings and

Aubrey found himself wondering if he were under a misapprehension and the speeches were, in fact, the proceedings and the signing an interruption.

When the observations from the Veltranian delegate concluded, Aubrey decided it was a sign of the times that a former rebel leader could become a respected figure in an international setting. He caught Rodolfo's eye as the Veltranian shuffled his papers at the lectern, then he saluted. He was rewarded with a smile, which was a triumph, coming as it did from the notoriously doleful Rodolfo.

An end to the day was called, with no sign of a conclusion to the conference. Aubrey stifled a sigh, waited for Commander Craddock to leave, then he slipped outside. Fresh air and a lack of stuffiness — atmospheric and personal — beckoned.

Lady Rose was on the terrace, gazing out over the gardens. She wore a large hat to shade her face. Her dress was a pale yellow. 'Are they anywhere near a conclusion yet?'

'Hardly, Mother.' Aubrey pecked her on the cheek. 'It's only been three days. I'd say they're just warming up.'

'I knew there was a good reason I never accompanied your father on these diplomatic jaunts.'

Aubrey had been surprised when his mother had volunteered to come along to the Belville signing, but he knew that she had a sense of history and a sense of occasion. This collection of the high and mighty was bound to be remembered for years and it was good to be a part of it.

'I hope you know that your father is immensely proud of you,' she said suddenly, turning away from her contemplation of the flower beds that stretched into the distance.

'I do,' Aubrey said. 'He told me.'

It had been a shock when Sir Darius had taken Aubrey aside just before the first gathering in the Gallery of Glass and explained how impressed he was with Aubrey's conduct and achievements. It was the term 'heroic' and the firmness of the handshake that left Aubrey lost for words.

'I'm glad,' Lady Rose said. 'I insisted that he did, but I wasn't sure he'd work up enough courage.'

'Courage?'

'Everybody has their areas of diffidence, Aubrey. He's never been confident where you're concerned.'

Aubrey took this as well as he'd take a blow to the head. He snatched at the first thing that came to mind. 'I'm proud of him, too.'

'And so you should be.' She patted him absently on the shoulder. 'And I'm proud of both of you.'

For a time, Aubrey stood in a daze next to his mother, thinking about how endlessly surprising people were, until Lady Rose tapped him on the shoulder. 'Caroline Hepworth is a fine young woman.'

Aubrey straightened. 'I've come to that conclusion.'

Lady Rose smiled at him and picked a speck of lint from his epaulette. 'You've changed, Aubrey.'

'For the better, I hope.'

'Decidedly.' She stood back and inspected him. 'Splendid. Now, go and enjoy the rest of the day.'

Musing, Aubrey left the terrace, wandered around the corner of the sprawling mansion and reached the gardens, his glorious solitude made all the more certain when he reached the hedge maze.

The hedge maze wasn't a serious challenge, as Aubrey

had found out on the first day at Belville, but its ten-feet-high walls guaranteed that dozens of people could be within its confines without seeing each other, which made it a useful place to gain some respite from court intrigue. The builders of the maze had anticipated this, and had placed benches in niches to allow wanderers a place to sit and contemplate whatever needed contemplating.

The sun was well on its way toward setting when Aubrey chose one of these benches, leaned back, hands behind his head, and enjoyed the inaction. It felt good to be away from the drone of international diplomacy. Being even a minor public figure – fully rehabilitated in the eyes of the public since the Acting Head of the Holmland Intelligence Services, a Mr Hugo von Stralick, had confirmed that the damning photos of Aubrey had been taken under duress – meant that solitude was a rare thing. Since his welcoming back as a true son of Albion, rumours had circulated about his role in the events that had brought an end to the war. People sought him out. Most simply wanted to hear his story, but others were looking for a more commercial insight. None of them should have taken the trouble; Aubrey never spoke of his doings to anyone other than his parents and his close comrades.

He closed his eyes, breathed in the rich cypress smell of the maze walls, and did his best to empty his mind of everything.

Naturally, it was only a few minutes before he began to fidget. He opened his eyes and admired the way the light of setting sun caught the few clouds in the sky. Then he examined the bench and became fascinated by the patches of lichen growing on the stone. He wondered how old the bench was and whether he could find the records of the purchase of the garden furniture somewhere in the palace, but before he could make a note about this he was distracted by the clever topiary that had carved out the arched recess in the hedge opposite for a bust of a classical emperor – then he became intrigued by the technique of hedge cutting that allowed such a neat alcove to be made.

When George Doyle came into view – hands jammed in pockets, beaming at the sky – Aubrey had scrawled two pages of notes and ideas that had spiralled off into some thoughts about the Law of Harmony before side-stepping into a possible new application exploring the power of collective human consciousness in magic making, something that Commander Craddock, Lanka Ravi and Professor Bromhead had been working on ever since the magical theoreticians had been released from hospital.

'Still working, old man?' George took a small cake from his pocket, one of the shell-shaped, almond-flavoured delicacies he'd come to favour while at the conference. He took a bite, then blinked. 'I was going to say something then, but now I've completely forgotten.'

'It can't be important, then. Where's Sophie?'

George waved a hand. 'She should be along any minute.'

George sat next to Aubrey and finished his cake. He dusted his hands of crumbs. 'Well, what's next, old man, after all this winds up? Back to Greythorn?'

Nearby, two birds joined in a brief song that dwindled to a series of chuckles. Aubrey waited for them to start again. When they didn't, he decided they'd settled for the night. 'Next term. I want to finish my degree, of course. And you?'

'I'm not one to leave something incomplete. I'll be there.'

'Good.' Aubrey hesitated for a moment and then went on. 'And after that?'

'That's a very good question.' George groped in his pocket and looked disappointed at not finding another cake. His actions made Aubrey's hand go to his own pocket. 'I could always go farming,' George continued. 'Father would like that.'

'Would you?'

'It has its attractions, the country life and all that.' George glanced at Aubrey. 'You know, old man, I understand now why my old dad doesn't talk much about the war. Do you feel like blabbing on about it?'

'Not in the slightest.'

'Writing, though,' George said. 'That's different. I wouldn't mind having a bash at a novel.'

'A novel?'

'About the war. I think I could knock a few silly ideas out of a few heads that way.'

'I'm sure you could.' Aubrey took off his cap and scratched his head. He turned the cap over in his hands and stared at it. 'What about Sophie?'

'Sophie? The light of my life?' George looked at Aubrey, his face solemn. 'You understand, old man, that everything I've said about the future is dependent on my working out some way to keep her with me.'

'I never thought any differently. This will involve talking to her, I take it?'

'And listening, old man, don't forget listening.'

'Excellent. Here's your chance.'

Aubrey stood. George blinked, looked around, saw

Sophie and Caroline approaching along the long green corridor. He punched Aubrey on the shoulder, gently. 'See you in the palace, old friend?'

Aubrey reached out and gripped his friend's hand. 'Of course you will, old friend.'

They shook. George grinned and ran to meet Sophie. He swung her off her feet and, arm in arm, they vanished into the maze.

Caroline laughed and came to Aubrey's side. She was trim in her full Directorate field uniform – black jacket over long black skirt, black cap, gloves – which set off her green eyes beautifully. 'What on earth have you two been talking about?'

'What most people have been talking about since the armistice – the future.'

Caroline looked toward where Sophie and George had disappeared. 'Ah.'

Aubrey had tested both his courage and his nerve many times over the last few months but, even so, he wasn't sure they were prepared for what he was about to say. 'Perhaps we should, as well.'

Caroline smiled. Aubrey judged it a tiny smile, one that could have been called shy, if shy wasn't such an inappropriate word to describe Caroline Hepworth.

She took his arm and steered him in the opposite direction from the one Sophie and George had taken. 'Planning for the future is a perfectly sensible thing to do,' she said after they'd ambled along in silence for a few minutes, past two stone busts and a sundial. 'I have a university degree to resume, for instance. I need to decide what aspects of scientific classification I'm going to pursue.'

Aubrey found that as well as linking arms, they were

delightfully clasping hands. It was an entirely appropriate state of affairs, to his way of thinking. 'I'd come to the same conclusion. Not about classification – about magical studies.'

'We have a few years ahead of us, then.'

They reached one of the exits to the maze. The stairs opened out onto the long, western slope of the gardens. From their position, they could see the exquisite arrangement of fountains, paths and ponds that led to the forest in the distance. They stood for a moment, enjoying the formality.

'And after you've taken your degree?' Aubrey asked eventually.

Caroline glanced at him. The smile was now tending toward a grin. 'I'll implement my plan to take your father's job.'

Aubrey was proud of himself. All he said was: 'A female prime minister would be a splendid idea.'

Caroline squeezed his hand. He felt a jolt nearly as profound as the one that once signalled his body and soul were parting. 'It's the next logical step, now that your father has procured votes for women.'

'You may have to wait, though.'

One eyebrow rose. 'Wait?'

'I'm after his job as well, you know.'

Caroline tsked. 'Aubrey, if we can't work out who's going to be prime minister first, how can we be expected to work out anything else about our future?'

'Our future?' Aubrey touched his pocket. *Now?* 'Do you mean you and me?'

Caroline didn't answer his question. She inclined her head toward his jacket. 'For three days, Aubrey, you've been fascinated by whatever it is you have in your pocket. I've restrained myself from asking, but it's apparently important enough to interrupt your thinking about something very important.'

His heart thumping, Aubrey took out a small black velvet case. He opened it. 'It belonged to my grandmother. She insisted that I bring it along to the conference. For you.'

Caroline didn't take the ring. She put her hand to her mouth, her eyes wide. 'Aubrey, don't say anything.'

'?'

'Good. I take it that this is a family heirloom?'

He nodded.

'And that it has a certain significance? To do with commitment, promises, that kind of thing?'

He nodded again.

Caroline lifted her chin and looked into the west, where the sun was hovering before its last plunge below the horizon. The softness of the light warmed her face and Aubrey thought that – no matter what she said next – he was the most fortunate person in the world.

'Aubrey,' she said, with a disarming and endearing catch in her throat, 'we're still young.' She glanced at him. 'You can talk now.'

'Thank goodness. That we're still young, I mean.'

'We have no need to rush. Not with all the things we want to do.'

'As long as we can do them together, I'm happy.'

'This ring, then. It's a sign that we understand each other?'

Aubrey hesitated. 'I wouldn't be arrogant enough to claim I understood you, Caroline. That implies a level of insight that I'm not sure I have. In fact, can a person really understand another? I mean, on a fundamental –'

'Hush. Now isn't the time to babble.'

'You know, that suggests that there is a good time to babble.'

'Aubrey, what I meant was that we are a pair.'

Aubrey considered this. 'Simple and forthright. I like the sound of that.'

Caroline took the ring and slipped it onto her finger. The gold band looked as if it belonged there. 'Excellent.'

Caroline kissed him. Aubrey kissed her back. It was magnificent.

Caroline, a little flushed, took Aubrey's arm again. They started down the stairs toward the gardens.

Caroline nodded to the west. 'I take it that this is the sunset we're supposed to be walking off into?'

Aubrey studied it for a moment, then shrugged. 'As long as it's arm in arm.'

'Oh, it's bound to be that. And it's bound to be full of adventures.'

'I can't wait.'

MICHAEL PRYOR HAS PUBLISHED MORE THAN TWENTY fantasy books and over forty short stories, from literary fiction to science fiction to slapstick humour. Michael has been shortlisted six times for the Aurealis Awards (including for *Blaze of Glory* and *Heart of Gold*), has been nominated for a Ditmar award and longlisted for the Gold Inky award, and five of his books have been Children's Book Council of Australia Notable Books (including *Word of Honour* and *Time of Trial*). He is now writing the first book in a new series.

For more information about Michael and his books, please visit www.michaelpryor.com.au.